Pest Control

D0062397

Books by Bill Fitzhugh

The Adventures of Slim and Howdy
Highway 61 Resurfaced
Radio Activity
Heart Seizure
Fender Benders
Cross Dressing
The Organ Grinders

The Assassin Bug Thrillers
Pest Control
The Exterminators

Pest Control

An Assassin Bug Thriller

Bill Fitzhugh

Poisoned Pen Press

Poisoned Pen Press
6962 E. First Ave., Ste. 103
Scottsdale, AZ 85251
www.poisonedpenpress.com
info@poisonedpenpress.com

Printed in the United States of America

To Kendall, Eleanor, and Granny.
Thanks for all your love.
And to Jimmy Vines for believing from the start.

Assassins

Originally a sect of Moslem fanatics founded in Persia, about 1090, by Hassan ben Sabbah, their terrorism was mainly directed against the Seljuk authority.

—*Brewer's Dictionary of Phrase & Fable*

Assassin Bugs

This large family of predaceous bugs includes some blood-sucking species that attack man and other animals. They are medium to large in size, with long, narrow head, long four- or five-segmented antennae, the last segment filiform. The beak is stout, three-segmented, the tip held in a groove in the prosternum when at reas; this groove contains stridulating organs with which they make squeaking noises.

—Lester A. Swan and Charles S. Papp,
The Common Insects of North America

New York City

This muck heaves and palpitates. It is multidirectional and has a mayor.

—Donald Barthelme

It's Baghdad-on-the-subway.
—O. Henry

Chapter One

His eyes were metallic blue jewel beetles peering out at the world from underneath a pair of furry black caterpillars. He was in good shape for thirty-five, with broad shoulders and nicely muscled arms. Topping off his six-foot frame was a swarm of dark, wavy hair and a gentle smile that lent him an affable aspect, a chewy niceness. Just looking at him you'd never guess he was a professional killer.

He lived in New York City, a place where, on average, someone was hit by gunfire every eighty-eight minutes. This annoyed him greatly because it was so hard to get noticed in a place like that. And if he was going to succeed as a paid killer, he was going to need a reputation. So right now he was out to make a name for himself—a name other than the one he had.

When he was born in March of 1963, his parents—Curtis and Edna Dillon of Newark, New Jersey—were thoroughly unaware that one year earlier, Robert Allen Zimmerman of Duluth, Minnesota had released his first album under the pseudonym Bob Dylan. So, looking back, it was purely a case of bad timing when Curtis and Edna named their son Bob.

Bob Dillon.

Sure, it was spelled differently, but it sounded the same, and that was all that mattered. As a consequence Bob Dillon endured a humiliating childhood, all too frequently being forced by neighborhood bullies to sing the Dylan classic, "Rainy Day Women #12 & 35."

Bob hated doing this, not only because he couldn't sing and because he knew his off-key rendition would inevitably result in taunting and laughter, but also because he hated the song and couldn't understand why it was titled as it was since there was never any mention of women, rainy day or otherwise, much less those numbered twelve and thirty-five.

Neither could he ever understand how the song reached number two on the pop charts in 1966. To Bob it was just an endless succession of unimaginative variations on "They'll stone you when you're driving in your car…" This carried on interminably until it reached its obtuse chorus of, "Everybody must get stoned!"

Bob always imagined his childhood wouldn't have been so bad had he been forced to sing "Like a Rolling Stone" or "Mr. Tambourine Man"—songs he actually enjoyed. Fortunately, Bob possessed a resilient and compassionate character, so he never blamed his parents for the abuse he suffered at the hands of neighborhood bullies. In fact, except for the murderous profession he eventually undertook, Bob never showed even the slightest ill effect resulting from his name.

So, yeah, Bob planned on making a name for himself alright, but right now he had a contract to fulfill.

He opened the door and found himself standing at the top of a flight of stairs leading down into darkness. He hit the light switch, illuminating his khaki jump suit and the case he carried. It was dented and scuffed, evidence of a lot of jobs. A lot of killing.

Bob crept cautiously down the creaking wooden stairs, dodging spider webs as he descended into the dank basement. He crossed to a corner of the room where he set his case on the damp concrete floor. He flipped the rusting brass latches and threw it open.

As he reached into the case he glanced at his wrist and the solid-plastic Casio timepiece: 2:00 p.m. "Right on time," he muttered to a cockroach that scurried past.

With a practiced, almost mechanical, skill Bob picked up a long, slender tube and screwed it into an exotic-looking curved wooden handle. He attached a valve gate to the apparatus then connected one end of a hose to the tube and the other end to a small compression tank. Those tasks completed, he carefully opened a valve and pumped the plunger on the tank and then flipped the valve gate, watching as the cylinder pressure gauge jumped to three hundred pounds of attention. He smiled.

"I am here to deal death," Bob mused out loud. He chuckled to himself.

Next, he pulled a two-inch hole-drilling attachment from his case and attached it to the business end of a battery-powered Black and Decker drill. Then he tested it, whrrrrrrzzzzzzz.

Satisfied with his tool, Bob knelt and bored a hole near the baseboard. He pulled a penlight from his pocket, peered into the hole and saw what he was there to kill: *Periplaneta Americana*, a.k.a. the American cockroach. Dozens of them.

"If I had my way," Bob said wistfully, "your deaths would be much more dignified."

This wasn't idle chatter.

Not at all.

For Bob dreamed of a day when things would be different. Bob Dillon, Brooklyn exterminator, had invented an all-natural pest-control method that wouldn't poison the environment like conventional methods. In a best-case scenario, it was a method that just might make Bob rich.

His idea revolved around members of the *Reduviidae* family, insects commonly known as Assassin Bugs. These murderous invertebrates occupied a specific place in the overall scheme of things. Diagrammed, it looked just like this:

```
KINGDOM–Animal
-----PHYLUM–Arthropoda
-----------CLASS–Insecta
------------------ORDER–Hemiptera
------------------------FAMILY–Reduviidae
------------------------------------GENERA–(several)
------------------------------------------------SPECIES–(several)
```

These menacing insects hunted and killed others in their Class with gruesome efficiency, using their rigid and powerful piercing mouthparts to puncture the outer layer of their prey and pump in a paralyzing saliva. The Assassins injected their quarry with amylase and pectinase, enzymes which pre-digested and liquefied their victim's internal tissues, which the Assassins then sucked up through their rostrum like a buggy milkshake.

Bob was working with eight species of these insects. He planned to cross-breed these species in hopes of creating the consummate Assassin Bug—a robust, hybrid strain of predacious insect exhibiting the most desirable combination of hunting and killing traits. One species of Assassin with which Bob was working with was the Wheel Bug (*Arilus cristatus*), a voracious predator known to attack without hesitation and fearlessly suck dry insects twice its size, including even the largest species of cockroach.

The Wheel Bug was a stout grayish-black brute whose pro-thorax fanned upwards into a half-wheel of menacing coglike teeth along its midline, hence its common name. It's distinctive abdomen was characterized by what looked like tail-fins from a 1959 Cadillac. These dark dorsal ridges lay on its back at 45 degree angles and accentuated the bug's aura of menace.

Bob was also working with Masked Hunters (*Reduvius personatus*). These were relentless stalkers which brazenly entered human dwellings to secure meals of bed bugs, termites, and other insects. Stealthy and powerful, these rust-brown bugs had an intimidating and enlarged muscular thorax, as if augmented by doses of steroids and a weight program. Masked Hunters were known to pursue their quarry with an unforgiving single-mindedness that was both admirable and terrifying.

Bob imagined that the successful cross-breeding of these insects would result in a revolutionary new approach to pest management, not to mention a steady income. However, until he perfected his process of hybridization, Bob was forced to work for a franchised pest control outfit that flooded the environment with noxious poisons and required its employees to wear personality-robbing, soul-killing uniforms.

Over the left breast-pocket of Bob's uniform was a patch featuring a smiling, cartoonish insect underscored with the name: "BUG-OFF." Below, a smaller patch announced that this employee's name was "BOB." Bob found it all quite distasteful, but he had a family to feed and he took that responsibility very seriously. So every day he swallowed his pride, donned the uniform, and went to work. And today his work had brought him to the basement of a home at 536 8th Street in the Park Slope section of Brooklyn.

Bob withdrew from the wall long enough to seize his killing device. He inserted the far end of the tube into the hole, then, almost shamefully, he pulled a white, air-filtering mask over his nose and mouth and moved his trembling index finger toward the trigger. The digit tensed as if to pull, but before engaging his weapon he stopped and relaxed his grip.

Just then another man approached, a man whose patches said "RICK" and "SUPERVISOR." The man spoke as supervisors often do, "Goddammit Dillon, now what's the friggin' problem?" His accent was unmistakably New Joisy.

Bob pulled down his mask.

"Can't do it, Rick," Bob replied. "I can't triple-up on the parathion anymore; it's unsafe. It gets into the food-chain."

"Yo, fuck you and the food-chain, Mr. Greenpeace, you got a goddamn job to do!"

And that did it. Bob reached the end of his rope with Rick, and, for that matter, with Bug-Off. Family or no family, Bob decided it was time to take the plunge with his own idea. His long-time dream would finally be tested on a practical basis. But first he had to get something out of his system.

Bob started by focusing intensely on Rick.

"Hey, yo! What are you starin' at, numbnuts? Get back to work." Rick tried to turn and walk away, but the unusual menace in Bob's eyes mesmerized him, and he stood helplessly as Bob raised his spray wand and inserted it into Rick's nose.

Bob pressed forward with the wand, lifting Rick's fleshy nostril while backing him toward the wall, his trigger finger twitching. Rick's nostrils flared back in fear. He knew what a triple dose of parathion would do, even to a fat-ass, son-of-a-bitch like him.

"You know Rick, you're right," Bob said. "I do have a job to do. First I've got to write a detailed letter to the EPA, with copies to the FDA, Labor Department, Consumer Product Safety Commission, and, what the hell, maybe even the Justice Department. I think they'll be quite interested in some of the more esoteric violations you encourage us to commit every day."

With the tube in his nose, Rick spoke with a funny accent, "Hey, Vov, if dis is avout a waise, all you have to do is full the vand out of my dose and we cad dalk."

"It's too late for talking, Rick. The gig's up," Bob said.

Rick didn't like the sounds of that, so he squinched up his eyes anticipating his imminent extermination. But, in a notable demonstration of restraint, Bob dropped the spray wand and ripped the grinning-bug patch from his jumpsuit.

"I quit," he said.

As Bob walked away, Rick regained his swagger. He retrieved Bob's spray wand and waved it in the air, yelling, "That's it! I've had it with your shit, Dillon! Your ass is fired!"

Bob waved goodbye with the middle finger of his right hand and headed up 8th Avenue to Union Street, then over to 4th to catch the Broadway Express, or even the Local. It would be the longer way home, but at least he wouldn't have to make any transfers. And the thing Bob needed most before he faced Mary with the good news was some uninterrupted time to think.

Chapter Two

The parade was coming, so the excited black children in their colorful native outfits paid no attention to the white man as he moved deliberately down the neglected sidewalk with his small suitcase. If they gave him any thought at all, they probably assumed he was just a businessman—and in a sense he was. But Klaus wasn't just another exporter who dealt in the minerals and hand-crafted goods of their country; he was in the business of death. Klaus was a professional killer. He helped export souls.

Though they deny it for propriety's sake, every national government worth a damn has at least one branch employing in-house assassins. The former Soviet Union had the KGB and the lesser known MVD and GRU. Great Britain has MI5, Israel has Shin Bet and the Mossad. In the United States, the CIA, NSC, FBI, and the Justice Department all have their own "cleanup men" on staff.

In lesser-developed countries small, unofficial police squads do the work; as do, for example, the Tonston Macoutes in Haiti. But most of those killers are relatively crude mercenaries compared to the outside professionals who are available for hire.

Klaus was considered, by those who knew about such things, to be the world's best assassin. There were others, of course, and among those who kept track there was general agreement on who the top five or six were at any time.

At this particular time, holding down the number two spot was an inordinately tall Nigerian whose name was unknown.

The Far East boasted the world's number three killer in a man called Ch'ing. From the European community, coming in at four and five respectively, were the stunning and deadly Chantalle and the British cross-dressing dwarf, Reginald. The U.S. had a relative newcomer on the list—up eight spots with a bullet since the last survey—at number six. He was from Oklahoma and was known only as the Cowboy.

These people worked for governments and, occasionally, for absurdly wealthy members of the private sector. They lived in a small world and were keenly aware of their rankings on the charts, not unlike professional tennis players. One's fees was often negotiated based on one's current standings.

Klaus had been ranked number one for many years, handling even the most difficult assignments with aplomb. He had killed in twenty-seven countries, in both hemispheres, bypassing with minimal effort even the most elaborate security precautions. But Klaus was by no means a mercenary in the pure sense of the word. He did not accept every job he was offered; he was choosy, and he rigorously applied the same criterion to each offer. No amount of money could sway him from this.

Klaus' features leaned toward the Mediterranean. He was GQ handsome and somewhere in his fifties. His dove-grey eyes were warm and sad, not at all what people normally thought of as killer's eyes. His dark hair was sifted with grey and neatly styled.

Klaus' current job had brought him to one of those volatile African nations that confounded cartographers by changing names several times every few years. He was about to execute another contract.

The towering Nigerian had not been consulted on this matter for two reasons. One, assassins typically did not like to kill on the same continent on which they lived. The second, and more utilitarian reason was that the employers in this matter simply did not want to screw around with second best.

Klaus passed unnoticed through a doorway into a tall build-ing on a street just off the parade route. Once inside, he slipped unseen through another door which led to some stairs. He quickly climbed the steps of the cool, dark stairwell still carrying in his right hand the small well-worn suitcase covered in a nondescript brown fabric. At the top of the stairwell, sunlight outlined a doorway which opened onto a roof. Klaus stopped at the door's sunlit perimeter, pulled a silenced handgun from his waistband, checked it, then calmly opened the door and eased into the damaging ultraviolet rays.

He scanned the roof and spotted a lone member of the military police positioned near the roof's edge smoking a cigarette, an old Soviet-made rifle slung uselessly on his shoulder. Troublesome, Klaus thought, but no problem. He slipped behind a bulky imported Eastern-Bloc air-conditioning duct, intentionally banging his suitcase on the dull metal to get the guard's attention.

The guard turned toward the sound and half-heartedly readied his old Soviet weapon. He figured some children had come onto the roof for a better view of the parade below. Just the same, he went to check it out.

He rounded the corner to Klaus' hiding place—Fwump! Fwump! Two silenced shots entered him from behind—one in the head, the other just right-of-center between the shoulder blades. Kill shots. Extremely professional.

The guard wobbled for a moment, a look of "Shit, I should have looked behind me" in his eyes. As he wobbled, Klaus snatched the maroon beret from the guard's head, then stepped aside as the guard crumpled limp to the ground, the burning cigarette still stuck to his dead lips.

"Sorry," Klaus said, and he meant it. Klaus didn't like to kill anyone who did not, in his estimation, deserve to die. But in matters of self-preservation, he was willing to make exceptions. That's the kind of guy Klaus was. "Besides," he reasoned aloud, "the cigarettes would have killed you anyway."

Klaus adjusted the purloined beret on his head, then checked the solid gold Piaget on his wrist. "Three minutes," he remarked to the demised guard. "At least the parades run on time."

He went to where the guard had been stationed and crouched behind the short wall at the roof's edge. He opened the small brown suitcase revealing the disassembled components of a Steyr AUG .223, fitted snugly into the black foam rubber which had been tailored for the job.

With practiced, almost mechanical, movements Klaus slipped the slender barrel into the action of the exotic rifle, then screwed a silencer onto the barrel and attached an Aimpoint telescopic laser sight on top. Next he snapped on the stock and slammed home an ammo clip.

Then, without any warning, the depression hit again. These bouts of despair had been plaguing him more and more frequently, and lately Klaus had even considered turning the gun on himself. And why not? His life had become little more than an endless loop of bad *Mission Impossible* episodes, one hackneyed assassination scene following another. He half expected to come home one day to find Peter Graves waiting for him in the kitchen with one of those self-destructing mini-cassette tapes, Martin Landau in the bathroom putting on a silly disguise. Words failed to describe how much Klaus hated what his life had become.

He closed his eyes and cursed. Sometimes he wished he had simply gone into law or accounting.

Then, just like other such moments before, the moment passed as quickly as it had come. Klaus sighed and resumed his task.

In the streets below, thousands of natives lined the parade route chanting in Bantu while waving photos of their despotic leader alongside placards painted with catchy Bantu phrases produced by the despot's P.R. department.

His name was Ooganda Namidii and it was rumored that he was suffering from a deluxe case of tertiary syphilis—once considered the Rolls Royce of venereal diseases. The infection was gnawing away at his brain stem and frequently led to bouts of irritability. Recently, for example, Namidii had enacted an ethnic cleansing policy that was particularly undiscriminating—most likely because he didn't really know what ethnic cleansing meant. He had heard the phrase on a CNN story about the Bosnian Serbs and thought it sounded like a good idea. The next day, in a fit of pique caused by a searing pain in his urinary tract, Namidii had executed several hundred of his wretched countrymen.

The majority of the population lived in abject poverty due to Namidii's fiscal policies, which in the 1980's had consisted primarily of looting the treasury and investing with American financial wizards like Michael Milken and Charles Keating. Most of those who had gathered for this parade earned the equivalent of about 63 U.S. dollars each year, and that didn't go far in a country whose annual rate of inflation had recently reached 82 percent. The citizens had been reduced to eating grasshoppers, beetle grubs, and termites in order to maintain adequate protein levels in their diets.

An uninformed observer might have asked why these people were lined up four deep to cheer for this corrupt madman. The answer was simple. They were here because although they despised this tyrant, by god, he was their tyrant and he was the only thing they could call their own.

That, plus they were giving away falafel.

But all that was about to come to an abrupt end. While Namidii sat comfortably in the back seat of the shiny black Lincoln Continental convertible, waving like a fat high-school homecoming queen, he was also sitting squarely in Klaus' crosshairs, about to become another bloody splotch in history. There was no doubt in Klaus' mind that this avaricious psychopath deserved to die. That was Klaus' only criterion—that his victim deserved to die.

His finger tensed on the trigger, waiting for the perfect moment. The red dot from the laser sight found a home on Namidii's ear. And then, cloaked by the noise of the zealous crowd, the gun fired and the tyrant's reign ended amid blood and confusion.

Chapter Three

As he waited on the Union Street platform, Bob's mood alternated between euphoria and dread. On the one hand, he felt an exhilarating rush now that he had begun to pursue his dream. On the other hand, he had started to worry about how Mary would take the news, especially in light of their fiscal situation.

The grimy silver train slouched into the station and threw open its doors like a giant drooling idiot, spilling chewed-up New Yorkers onto the platform. Bob climbed aboard and plopped into the open seat at the front of the car.

He glanced up at the various advertisements overhead which seemed invariably aimed at the city's less fortunate. The ad for a Multi-Cultural Torn Earlobe Repair Clinic immediately seized his attention. But just as a grim image of what that waiting room must look like began to form in his mind, the train lurched into the darkness that lay ahead and jolted Bob's mind back to his current predicament.

Mary had recently lost her job as a senior loan officer after the Savings and Loan where she worked for three years was found belly-up on the fouled shores of the Hudson River. The current job market being what it was, Mary had been reduced to waiting tables in a coffee shop. Understandably, she was not always in a good mood these days. The fact that they were falling behind on rent and a few of the utilities didn't help matters. Given that, Bob was going to need every minute of the long train ride home to figure out to how he was going to make Mary see that the timing was just right for him to make his move.

At Court Street, transfers from the 3, 5, and M trains clambered into the car for the ride over to Manhattan. Among the crowd were five identical dark suits, obviously headed for a fun-filled afternoon of arbitrage and self-actualization in the happy streets of the financial district.

Then there was the young woman who sat down directly across from Bob and buried her pierced nose in a biology textbook. He imagined she was headed for NYU.

Except for the pierced nose, the tattoo, and the perky breasts, the young student reminded Bob of himself and his days at Brooklyn College where he met Mary.

Bob was majoring in entomology and was still trying to find a hair style that worked for him. Mary was working on a business degree with a hopeful eye on a career in finance. Her long auburn hair framed the round-cheeked face of the former high school cheerleader and Sophomore Maid of Honor runner-up that she was.

On the day they met, Bob had attended a lecture by Bernice Lifton on the History of Pesticides. The way Ms. Lifton told it, modern pesticide use began in 1867 when a mixture of copper and arsenic was used to halt the Colorado Potato Beetle's (*Leptinotarsa decemlineata*) destruction of the U.S. potato crop.

Bob hung on every word as Ms. Lifton noted with no small hint of dread that as early as 1912, scientists had begun seeing insect resistance to chemical pesticides. Bob nodded in solemn recognition of a fact he already knew, a fact that eventually was to form one of the cornerstones of his idea.

As Bob saw it, the remainder of Ms. Lifton's oration was a brilliantly organized argument chronicling the truth, and the truth was that since 1912 mankind had been hurtling pell-mell downhill toward its own gruesome, inorganic death in a vain attempt to control insects chemically.

After the lecture, Bob had been crossing the quad when he heard the screams.

"Cortlandt Street!" The train's disembodied voice again intruded into Bob's reverie. He looked around and noticed the five suits had been replaced with SoHo and Village types migrating up Broadway as they did each day at this time.

As the train pitched forward, Bob returned to that moment many years ago when he was crossing campus, unaware that he was about to meet his future wife.

At about the same time Bob had left Ms. Lifton's lecture, Mary had left the Business Administration Building. She was wearing a conservative, navy blue business suit, attempting, as many women did in the 1980's, to look more manly.

Mary had just finished making a presentation to her marketing class and her arms were loaded with the materials she had used—graphs, charts, and a mock-up point-of-purchase display for the laxative she had been assigned as her product.

She was hurrying to catch the Lexington Avenue Express when several *Apis mellifera* apparently mistook her perfume for a sex attractant pheromone and began to swarm. Her arms loaded with cargo she felt was too precious to drop, Mary began to run in a panicked and irregular circle.

Seeing the woman in distress, Bob dashed to the rescue and swatted two bees out of mid-air where they quickly died under his feet. The others fled the scene. Unstung and grateful, Mary accepted his invitation for coffee.

She was married when they first met, soon to be divorced, or so she said as she sipped her espresso. None of that was true though, it was just something Mary told guys to keep them in line while they hit on her. At the same time it made her unavailable, which, paradoxically, made her more attractive to would-be suitors. Bob would later compare this odd principle of human courtship to some of the more bizarre insect mating rituals.

From the moment Bob saw Mary, he was smitten—perhaps her perfume had worked on him as it had on the bees. Regardless, Bob believed it was more than mere coincidence that he was at the right place at the right time to deliver this beautiful woman from the evil stinging insects. And although he didn't put any stock in predestination, Bob felt this beautiful woman was destined to be his wife. Or at least destined to go to bed with him.

He pursued Mary rigorously for months. Asking her out, phoning regularly, and sometimes writing lengthy letters, full of longing, professing his love. He even wrote her the occasional poem—poems which were what really helped cinch Mary's heart.

Mary could still remember the first poem Bob sent her. He had written it on the back of an exam from a class he was taking on moths (*Heterocera* 101). Bob, with his 3.8 GPA, had aced the test, missing only one question, hence the poem:

> It was just a test, a test was all it was,
>   I studied so hard to prepare.
> But 'twas not about beetles or bees that go buzz,
>   Thus, not so well did I fare.
> I confused a small moth with one pair of wings
>   with another small moth which has two.
> I'm not always sure about these things,
>   but I am sure I love you.

Bob later admitted to borrowing some of the structure from a verse about camels written by his favorite poet, Ogden Nash.

Mary had kept every letter and poem Bob wrote her; they were locked in a trunk in the attic of her mother's house upstate.

During all of their subsequent dates, Bob would somehow turn the conversation to insects. He spoke with great enthusiasm and conviction about his plan to create a new, environmentally sensitive way to control pests. Mary was charmed by this guy with the nutty-professor hairdo and the matching dream, even if he did plagiarize his poem structure. They dated through their remaining year in college before getting married. A year later they had Katy.

At Canal Street, transfers from the Four, Six, and J trains squeezed onto Bob's car. Several Chinese immigrants cast wary eyes at a pair of turbaned Pakistani businessmen while an Iranian couple reluctantly shared their stretch of bench with a black man, his white girlfriend, and a young Vietnamese boy. With the

United Nations thusly seated, the train plunged forward carrying Bob up Broadway and down memory lane simultaneously.

In the decade after Katy was born, Mary began working her way up the ladder toward the glass ceiling while Bob toiled off and on as a high school biology teacher as well as for various pest control outfits, all the while pursuing his dream of creating an all-natural pest control method.

As for Mary, the closest thing she had to a dream was a desire to maintain a good credit rating. That wasn't to say she didn't appreciate the beauty and intensity of Bob's aspirations, but she was practical.

At Eighth Street the NYU student bounded off the train and was replaced by a bearded lunatic wearing a fatigue jacket. It was an unkept secret that this guy was twisted as a door knob.

The man fixed Bob with a stare and shouted, "Don't ya tell Henry! I'm going to Acapulco!" He then dashed into the next car. The madman's frightening glare had unsettled Bob, so he kept a vigilant eye on the door as the train wormed its way toward midtown, past Union Square, Twenty-Third, Twenty-Eighth, and Thirty-Fourth Streets. Bob was relieved when the lunatic finally got off at Times Square and begin menacing someone on the platform.

Only five more stops to figure out how to convince Mary that, despite appearances to the contrary, this was the perfect time to start his business. Perhaps telling her about his newly acquired batch of Thread-Legged Bugs (*Emesa brevicoxa*) would do the trick.

The Thread-Legged Bugs had a body-type unlike all the other Assassin Bugs that were part of Bob's experiment. They had long slender bodies with a prothorax that was not distinctly separated from their mesothorax. To the untrained eye they looked exactly like harmless stick insects, but in fact they were just as deadly as anything Bob was working with.

The Thread-legged Bug crept along like the Grim Reaper, its long, bony, but surprisingly strong legs extracted cringing victims from the crevices where they hid, thereby collecting, as

Laurence Sterne put it, the tribute due unto nature. With its greatly elongated coxa and macabre spined femur, the Thread-Legged Bug fearlessly assaulted and consumed other insects in addition to several species of spiders.

Bob hoped this would impress Mary. But even if it did, it seemed unlikely she would see it as the critical piece of evidence needed to convince her the time was right for Bob to start his All-Natural Pest Control business. But what could he tell her that she didn't already know?

"Lexington Avenue!"

She knew Bob's idea had tremendous potential. This made the score one-to-nothing in Bob's favor.

But Mary knew Bob hadn't perfected his method, so that mitigated against. Score tied at one.

"Queensboro Plaza, transfer to the Seven!"

Still, she had sworn eternal support, for better or worse, richer or poorer, 'til death do you part, and all that. Two-to-one, Bob's favor.

"Beebe Avenue!"

But Bob knew it was easier to support an abstract notion than to get behind the thing when it came time to implement it. That tied things up at two.

"Broadway!"

Bob feared Mary would focus on the financial impact of unemployment rather than the fact that he was now free to pursue his dream. Three-to-two, Mary's favor.

"Thirtieth Avenue!"

"Screw it," he thought. "I'll just tell her the truth and hope she understands."

"Astoria Boulevard!" Bob's stop.

All he could do was try. So he gathered himself and stepped into the afternoon sun, unemployed, but inspired.

Chapter Four

In a luxurious office suite on the *Champs Elysees* not far from the *Arc de Triomphe de l'Etoile*, a large man, somehow managing to look cryptic, sat on a soft Italian leather sofa wearing a five-thousand-dollar charcoal-grey suit and an expensive tie which insinuated that fools could be parted from their money in France as easily as anywhere else.

His name was Marcel, and there was no getting around the fact that he was fond of cream sauces. He was a large man in an old-fashioned sort of way, more pear-shaped Sydney Greenstreet than barrel-chested John Goodman.

Marcel was a middleman, a go-between for people who needed a crime committed and the people with the skills necessary to grant their wishes.

Marcel's young assistant, Jean, stood silently next to Monet's Terrace at *Le Havre*, which adorned the far wall. Jean looked impressionable in a single-breasted lambs wool-blend classic Shetland sports coat with flap pockets. The smooth lines of the coat were disrupted only slightly by the delicate bulge caused by his small handgun.

The remaining walls of the office were decorated with Manets and Jerry Lewis posters. The Eiffel Tower, hard and erect, made for a nice view out the window.

Marcel shifted his considerable weight forward and laid a large briefcase on the glass-and-chrome coffee table in front of his guest, Klaus, who had just flown in from a certain chaotic

African nation. Klaus opened the briefcase and took in the sight of row after row of bundled American hundred-dollar bills.

"From the grateful people of the newly formed African Democratic Republic," Marcel said.

Klaus snapped the case shut.

"Aren't you going to count it?" Marcel asked.

"That would only serve to insult you," Klaus answered.

"Not at all. I wouldn't be offended in the least."

"You should, as it would imply that I thought you were stupid enough to try to shortchange me."

Jean cocked an eyebrow and smoothed the pleats in his trousers, noting the slightly fuller silhouette resulting from the straight cut of the legs.

Marcel smirked. "Of course, you are right. It is all there." He leaned back into the depths of the sofa.

"Then we are through." Klaus stood abruptly and moved for the door. He had a charter waiting to fly him to Monte Carlo.

"Wait," Marcel said. "Before you go, I have another job to tell you about."

Klaus paused at the door, then turned, unaware that Jean approved of his tailor.

Marcel tossed a folder onto the table. After a moment's reflection, Klaus crossed to the table and picked up the folder, prompting a self-satisfied smile from Marcel.

The folder contained detailed biographical information and a photograph of a tanned, silver-haired man in his fifties.

"Hans Huweiler," Marcel explained. "He is the owner of Amaron Laboratories, Limited. His loving family would like to see him... 'retire,' thus giving them control of the company and its five hundred million dollars in assets."

Without looking any further, Klaus tossed the folder back onto the table.

"I pass," he said flatly.

"Monsieur," Marcel countered as he stuffed the papers back into the file, "the $250,000 fee would go far in settling your considerable gambling debts."

"Find someone else. A greedy family is no reason to kill," Klaus said.

Jean squinted as he toyed with the idea of pulling on the loose thread he noticed on his silk shirt, but he decided to wait until he had some scissors.

Klaus took his briefcase of cash and walked to the door. He turned back to Marcel and chilled him with an icy stare. "And you, my rotund friend, you will live much longer if you keep in mind that my debts are of no concern to you."

Marcel held his hands up, palms out, as if deflecting the stare. Klaus turned and left.

After a moment, Marcel spoke. "Well, that is just great. Now we have only two weeks to find someone for this job."

Agitated, Marcel stuffed the spilled contents back into the folder. "How do these people expect us to find anyone on such short notice? Jean, I am telling you, sometimes I wish I had simply inherited money instead of having to work so hard for it."

"Shall I call Chantalle?" Jean asked, trying to imagine what she might wear to a meeting.

Marcel crossed to the window. "I suppose you should."

Chapter Five

Bob and Mary and their daughter, Katy, lived at 2439 Thirtieth Street in the Astoria section of Queens. Their narrow two-story red-brick house had a shallow front porch which was overwhelmed by several hastily applied layers of dark green paint.

This stretch of Thirtieth Street, just off Astoria Boulevard, was located in a weary-looking but generally safe neighborhood near the end of the RR line, which ran on elevated tracks above Thirty-First Street.

It was a quiet neighborhood populated by decent lower-middle-class people who had to work for a living. People who'd have to win the lottery before they could own their homes.

The interior of 2439 Thirtieth Street was comfortable and never gave you that awful feeling you were about to run into a snotty photographer from *Architectural Digest*. A sort of inadvertent minimalism was at work in the living room, the family photo on the mantel serving as the apparent focus.

The photo featured Bob with his arms around Mary and Katy, everyone smiling deliriously. They were one dog and half a child away from being a paradigm of American family units.

The cramped kitchen emphasized a tired, olive-green electric range and a matching refrigerator which shuddered noticeably every time the compressor needed to rest.

The remaining rooms in the house were equally uninteresting, save one. With Mary's permission and assistance, Bob had transformed the downstairs bedroom into his workshop. This room was dedicated to the study of several species of invertebrate animals belonging to the class *Insecta*. This was Bob's Bug Room.

The small space was cramped with grey steel shelving units, several garage sale tables, a work desk with an ancient word processor, and a rickety swivel chair on casters.

Several plastic insects—Christmas gifts from Katy—perched on the front lip of the computer next to a couple of mummified insect carcasses. The carcasses came from the backyard, and Bob had adopted them as his mascots; there was a Mole Cricket (*Gryllotalpa hexadactyla*), a European Ground Beetle (*Carabus nemoralis*), and a Northern Walkingstick (*Diapheromera femorata*). Katy named the cricket Jiminy, after the world's only two-legged insect who carried an umbrella. The beetle and the walkingstick were named Ringo and Slim, respectively.

The room also housed dozens of terrariums, each populated with a different species of creature with chitinous exoskeleton and tri-segmented body. The "bugquariums," as Bob called them, were topped with fine mesh screens and equipped with special bluish-purple lights which gave the room an eerie, scientific glow that seemed somehow to comfort the bugs.

In addition to the eight species of Assassin Bugs that were part of Bob's experiment, the room housed other insects he had collected over the years.

Lodged like an air-conditioning unit in the room's only window was a large white box, the closed half protruding into the room, the other half exposed and open to the outside world. The box hummed electrically but was actually powered by what the Portuguese called "*Abelhas assassinas*." The American media preferred the term "killer bees."

Bob had acquired these for a college experiment on honey production and had kept them around for the honey after receiving a B+ on his project. They were generally placid, hardworking insects which didn't bother you if you didn't bother them.

In order to keep the queen from leaving to start a new colony (what beekeepers called "absconding"), Bob installed a "queen excluder," a narrow doorway which kept the queen (who was larger than the other bees) from leaving.

Meanwhile, the drones droned and the workers spent the days gathering pollen, drinking nectar, and feeding royal jelly to the queen and larvae.

Whenever Bob harvested their honey (which the bees did consider a bother), he used his homemade bee smoker—a device which delivered burned burlap smoke to calm the hive. Always budget conscious, Bob had made his own smoker instead of buying one. He had fashioned his out of some galvanized steel scraps.

On the opposite side of the room, as far as possible from the source of Bob's honey, were the Bee Assassins (*Apiomerus crassipes*). The intervening feet prevented the insects from taunting one another.

An important part of Bob's experiments, the Bee Assassins were cat-quick and resourceful killers which fed on any insect guileless enough to happen within range. Ruby-red with handsome black markings, the Bee Assassin waited patiently until a victim came near. Then, with alarming quickness, it pounced on its prey, thrusting its piercing mouthpart into the victim's back before injecting a paralyzing salivic fluid.

Then, with both simple and compound eyes staring coldly into space, the Bee Assassin slowly sucked the body juices from its prey, leaving behind nothing more than a withered corpse.

Bob hoped to cross-breed the Bee Assassin's quickness into one of his cockroach killing hybrids.

Next to them were the Jagged Ambush Bugs (*Phymata erosa*), savage kill-crazy insects which slaughtered other bugs even when they weren't feeding. They simply liked to kill.

Pale greenish-yellow with clubbed antennae, the Jagged Ambush Bug was so-called because of the ragged spines which lined the sides of its prothorax. Its forelegs were swollen with muscle and perfectly adapted to seizing and holding prey as it fed. It would rip a silverfish in half for the sole purpose of amusing itself. It's orange eyes had large, black pupil-like spots on them and the eyes rotated sickeningly like a chameleon's, resulting in an unsettling, murderous stare.

Recently, Bob had made progress with his scheme for cross-breeding the various Assassins to create the souped-up hybrid he wanted. But that progress had not come easily. At first, Bob had hoped cross-breeding them would be as simple as cross-breeding dogs appeared to be. Naturally, it turned out to be more difficult than that. Bob started his futile attempts at cross-breeding simply by putting males and females of different species together in the bugquariums. However, he had a hard time coaxing certain species to copulate with one another and so, in frustration, he once put a mayonnaise jar lid filled with apricot wine in the bugquarium and dimmed the lights. While this resulted in some entertaining drunken insect behavior, it didn't solve his problem.

Bob eventually enlisted the help of one of his former college professors who showed him how to cross-fertilize the eggs to achieve the desired hybrid life forms. The relative ease of the breeding process was due to the fact that the insects were genetically close enough to cross-breed directly.

Three of the remaining bugquariums were reserved for beetles, termites, and cockroaches—toothsome delights for the predacious insects.

Bob kept one of the terrariums populated with standard House Crickets (*Acheta domestica*) because he loved the sound they made with the stridulating organs on the dorsal surface of the tegmina. There were few things in life Bob enjoyed more than the noise crickets made when they rubbed their files against their scrapers. The sound reminded him of camping trips with his dad.

Every summer Bob's father took him to Big Moose Lake in the Adirondacks. There they fished and hiked all day and at night they sat by the campfire, roasting weenies and marshmallows, the heat of the orange and blue flames arresting Bob's eyes so he stared at the fire, hypnotized, until his father would suddenly shout, "Fireflies!" snapping Bob from his sleepy-eyed stare and sending him chasing the winged light through the darkness.

Fireflies, Bob now knew, were *Lampyrid Beetles* which used the enzyme luciferase and something called luciferin to create their flashing light.

Bob remembered these trips fondly, and they were one of the reasons he wanted to leave New York City. He wanted to live in a place where man-made lights didn't drown out the twinkle of the stars, a place where you could fish and chase fireflies.

But for now, all Bob could do was keep a few crickets around as noisy reminders of this goal.

Occasionally late at night, as Bob researched some aspect of insect genetics, he found himself mesmerized by the sounds the bugs made in concert.

For reasons Bob never understood, the Bug Room would suddenly go quiet. Then a sort of low-level white noise would begin—the aggregate sound caused by the waving of maxillary palpi and proboscides, plus the brattling of roaches—the stiff, hair-like spurs on their legs lightly scraping metal as they scuttled across the fine mesh screens atop the bugquariums.

The clacking of smacking mandibles offered a lively percussive element, and the slurping and sucking of labial palpi smoothed the rough harmonic edges.

Then, from their white box, the bees would join in, the humming of their wings vibrating cello-like from the string section of this insect symphony. Finally, all of this was underscored by the soothing tone of the crickets' chirping.

If he were in a playful and manipulative mood, Bob would vary the temperature in the crickets' terrarium, thereby altering the rate of their chirping. Then, with a pencil, he would tap on the bees' container, aggravating them and thereby changing their hum from a hopeful major to a foreboding minor key.

Thus, with his number two baton in hand, Bob gleefully conducted the stridulating organ opus in bee minor.

In addition to the sounds, the room had a smell all its own.

Individually, Assassin Bugs didn't seem to have a fragrance, but when grouped together (and possibly fearing they were part of some hideous experiment) they secreted an aroma that was sweet but not unpleasant.

The bee hive's soft odor came from the pheromones which they secreted.

The roaches and termites were a different story. Their offensive redolence was magnified significantly when such large numbers lived in confined quarters. Fortunately, their stink was mitigated by the other smells in the room. The sundry bug scents co-mingled with one another, resulting in what Bob liked to think of as his own brand of jitterbug perfume. Bob enjoyed the buggy bouquet.

The grey steel shelving units held an impressive library of reference books on Bob's segmented-bodied friends, including some of the classics, like *Know Your Parts—Head, Thorax, and Abdomen: The ABC's of General Insect Anatomy; Sexual Attractants and Reproductive Practices of the Order of Hymenoptera; and Diptera—True Order or Just Another Sub-Class?*

Several shelves were reserved for volumes on the chemical agents used to kill and control insects, including *Death in a Can—a History of Chlorinated Hydrocarbons; D.D.T. and the E.P.A. Abbreviations for Ruin; and Meditations on Pyrethrins with Technical Piperonyl Butoxide.*

Of course, Bob had everything ever published by the late Pedro W. Wygodzinsky, the one-time curator of entomology at the American Museum of Natural History and acknowledged expert on Assassin Bugs. Bob also enjoyed the nonfiction of Sue Hubbell, especially her works *A Book of Bees* and *Broadsides from the Other Orders—a Book of Bugs.*

But the books that held the most interest for Bob—the books that were going to serve as the blueprints to his dream—were *Biological Control Agents and Effective Use of Predator Insects.* What these volumes and others like them advocated were natural, nontoxic means of managing the insects that so outnumbered mankind.

This, Bob's instinct told him, was his destiny: to control the world of pests naturally. And the only thing standing between Bob and his destiny was an overworked waitress with an unused business degree.

Chapter Six

"I am so sorry, Marcel," she said, "but I am booked through the end of the year. I have business in Haiti next week. I'm in Rwanda after that, then I'm doing some consulting in Mogadishu."

The woman was so beautiful that it had been said she could kill with her looks, though she usually employed a custom-made sniper's rifle and explosive, teflon-jacketed bullets. Her name was Chantalle and she was in Marcel's office discussing employment opportunities.

"I understand," Marcel said with a hint of disappointment. "It is a last-minute job. I do not know how these people expect me to work on such short notice." He sighed. "I tried Reginald, but he is in Singapore and won't be available until next month. My clients want this matter taken care of before that."

Jean was sitting on the sofa next to Chantalle, but was not paying particular attention to the conversation. He was lost somewhere in the softness of Chantalle's angora sweater.

"What about Ch'ing?" Chantalle asked.

"He has custody of his kids for the rest of the month and he just won't give that up for a contract this size. Who would have guessed he would turn out to be such a doting father?"

"And I suppose our friend Klaus is too scrupulous to handle your Mr. Huweiler?" Chantalle spat out the question with contempt.

"Ohhhhh, but of course. 'A greedy family is no reason to kill,' he says. Really! What do such things matter?"

Chantalle shook her head, embarrassed by Klaus' ethics.

"Well," Marcel wheezed as he stood to show Chantalle out, "I shall not waste any more of your time. This is my problem, and I will just have to deal with it."

"Well, good luck, *mon ami*. Keep me in mind for the future." She kissed Marcel's cheeks and with a "*Ciao!*" she was gone.

"What about that new American, the Cowboy?" Jean asked from the sofa. He imagined a rugged, tan roughneck in faded denim and handsewn, oil-tanned premium leather boots.

"No. From what I have heard, his approach lacks the refinement we need. And I will thank you not to mention the Nigerian. Seven feet tall and black as coal, I somehow think he would stand out in Switzerland. No, I am afraid we are going to have to solicit some offers." His tone betrayed his distaste for advertising.

"I don't know why you sound so appalled," Jean said. "It worked perfectly well the last time." Jean gently fingered the inseam of his breezy-cool linen/cotton-blend slacks before crossing the room to a large filing cabinet.

"I don't like it," Marcel said irritably. "People come to me for my network of contacts, not because I know how to use the want ads."

"Still, it works," Jean said. He pulled open a drawer stuffed with files. "Where shall we place it? *The Daily Mail*? We could go to London and—"

"No," Marcel interrupted, "the *New York Times* has a much better cost per thousand, especially the Sunday edition."

Jean flipped through the files until he found the folder he wanted. He pulled it and began reading. "So, which one shall we use? 'Seeking Experienced General Contractor'?"

"No. Never use the same ad twice in a row." Marcel waddled across the room.

"How about the one for a mechanic?"

"No, with our luck Jan Michael Vincent would respond." "Very well," Jean said, flipping to the next page in the folder. "How about the one for a grave digger?"

"I don't like that one," Marcel said with a shudder. "It's too ghoulish."

"Funeral director?"

"No."

"Undertaker?"

"No. I don't like any of these." Marcel looked as if he might pout, "I am afraid we will have to write a new one."

They stood in silence for a moment, thinking. Marcel frowned and crossed to the window looking out over gay Paree.

Jean's mind wandered to a solid seersucker blazer he had seen in a catalogue that morning. Two-button front and single-vent back with patch flap pockets and natural shoulders.

Suddenly Marcel felt quite clever. He turned to Jean and smugly announced, "I have it!"

Chapter Seven

Bob's confidence waned dramatically as he entered the house that afternoon, so he headed to his Bug Room for some inspiration.

Hanging on a nail just inside the room was Bob's custom-made baseball cap, a gift from Mary on his last birthday. The bulk of the cap was ink-black, but the stitching was dark red. Emblazoned across the front in bold, dark-red stitching was the word "EXTERMINATOR." Bob snugged the cap onto his head and scooted toward his desk.

He picked up his magnifying glass and crossed to the bugquarium containing the Eastern Bloodsucking Conenose (*Triatoma sanguisuga*), sometimes called the Mexican Bedbug. He bent over and, with the magnifying glass, looked closely at one of the bugs resting next to the glass wall.

The Bloodsucking Conenose was shaped like a miniature tennis racket with eyes, legs, and tiny antennae on the tip of a tapered grip. It had an oblong abdomen which was brown with orange stripes extending to the sides. The thorax was sturdy and had a slight ridge bridging the sides horizontally. Its head was slender and ended with a menacing, tapered beak, unlike the typically curved beak found in the other *Reduvius* members. It was as elegant a killing device as existed in the insect world, unforgiving and final in its application.

Bob laid the magnifying glass on table and prepared to meet with Mary.

He expected to find her getting ready for another night at the coffee shop. This wasn't going to be an easy sell.

He entered the bedroom and announced with a flourish, "Honey, I've got great news!"

"AHHHH!" Mary screamed. She wasn't expecting Bob home this early, so his sudden materialization and enthusiastic decree caused her to topple over onto the bed as she struggled into a pair of panty hose with a smutty run in the thigh.

Bob bounded onto the bed and began kissing Mary's neck. "What are you doing here? I thought you were in Brooklyn."

"Like I said, I've got great news!"

"You got a raise?" Mary asked between kisses.

"Better," Bob said.

"They made you supervisor?"

"Better," he replied.

"So give already." Mary was not in the mood for guessing games, but Bob's playful nature always made her smile.

"I got fired!"

Mary's smile vanished. She pushed Bob onto the floor. This wasn't exactly what had come to mind when Bob had announced he had great news.

"You what?" she asked.

"Well, actually, I quit, but a second later Rick fired me, so it depends on how you look at it. I sort of doubt I'll qualify for unemployment since I jammed my spray wand up his nose, but he asked for it. He was giving me the usual shit and told me to triple my parathion again. So I—"

"Bob, I don't care if he told you to eat the damn bugs! You know we can't afford this."

Mary's uncharacteristic use of profanity underscored her anxiety, Bob thought.

"C'mon, don't be so negative. This is great! Think about it. This couldn't be better if we had planned it. The timing's perfect," Bob said, putting more than a little spin on the truth.

"Bob, no, we can't do this," Mary said. "We absolutely cannot afford it right now, so don't even start."

The Dillon's financial situation was the same as many Americans'. Even when Mary had worked at the Savings and Loan and Bob was full-time at Bug-Off, their combined income allowed them only to cover the monthly nut and to save enough to cover the next major car repair or the occasional weekend vacation on the New Jersey coast.

At its peak, their savings had reached $1,689.58, but then Katy had needed some minor surgery. Since the plan with the $2,000 deductible was the only way they could afford complete medical coverage and since Congress had decided there really wasn't a health care crisis after all, well, the savings were long gone. And since Mary was down to earning tips and Bob's paychecks were meager at best, they had fallen behind on their bills quickly. In fact, they were just a few months from being homeless—or trying to squeeze friends and relatives for cash.

"C'mon, honey, think about it," Bob said, "everybody's concerned about the environment, right? And nobody likes roaches and termites. Put those facts together and what pops into your head?"

"Visions of bankruptcy," Mary said.

"No, silly, Bob's All-Natural Pest Control!"

"Oh no, not again."

"I'm telling you, sweetheart, there's no better time than now to start it up."

"With what?!" Mary wanted to know. "Have you seen our bank statement lately? It looks like Cory Pavin's score card after nine holes on a good day."

Cory Pavin? Bob never realized Mary was so fluent in golf. "What's your point?" he asked.

"You can't start a business without money," Mary said, "and if you take a good look around, Mr. Venture Capital, you'll notice that we not only don't have any actual money, but we don't even have anything left to sell to generate any."

To demonstrate her point, Mary picked up a piece of gold jewelry from her dresser and thrust it toward Bob.

"In fact, your grandmother's locket is the only thing of any value we've got left, and you'll have to pry it out of my dead fingers before you sell it to fund this venture of yours! If I've got anything to do with it, Katy is going to give this to her daughter one day…"

Bob interrupted, wielding his optimism like a blunt object. "Honey, think about it this way, if I don't do something to stop people from spraying triple doses of parathion, Katy's uterus is gonna shrivel up like a prune and she won't even be able to have a daughter."

Alright, Mary thought, Bob's got a point. But, still.

"Pratt's been over here twice today looking for the rest of the rent," Mary said in an attempt to derail the dream express. "What are we going to do about that?" She stepped into her tacky and stained polyester waitresses' outfit, turning around for Bob to zip her up.

"Did you know you had what looks like ketchup on the back here?" Bob asked.

"Don't change the subject," Mary said, "It's strawberry syrup."

"What do we owe Pratt?" Bob asked.

"Three hundred twenty bucks." Mary turned around and stuck a finger in Bob's face. "I don't want this to mess up my credit rating. We've got to pay the rent!"

Bob kissed the tip of Mary's finger. "You are such a worrier," he said. "I'll come up with something, or who knows, you might get a few big tippers in tonight. Anyway, being a little low on operating capital doesn't hurt us a bit."

"And how is that, Mr. Rockefeller?" Mary asked.

"Because," Bob said, "one of the advantages of an all-natural pest control business is low start-up costs."

Mary calmed at the thought of low-cost anything and, as always, Bob's determination to make his dream come true appealed to her.

"How low?" she asked, bending.

"Hard to say, really. I need a few hundred more Wheel Bugs for the cross-breeding, then with a willing property owner with some infested buildings and…Oh! That reminds me, a friend of a friend mentioned my idea to Sy Silverstein."

"Sy 'I-own-most-of-Midtown' Silverstein? The developer? That Sy Silverstein?" Mary was impressed.

"The very same," Bob said. "He's stuck with lots of see-through, so I'm trying to get a meeting with him. If he'll let me use a few of his buildings, all I need is a couple of weeks to try out the different hybrids and then we're in business."

"Assuming the bugs work," Mary said.

"Yeah, well, there is that," Bob admitted. "But that's what makes this whole thing so exciting, don't you think?"

"I'll get excited when your first check clears."

By now, Mary was outfitted for another night in the hash house trenches. She grabbed her purse and migrated downstairs. Bob followed, hoping to close the sale.

They reached the kitchen where Katy, their ten-year-old daughter, sat at the table. Her attention bounced between a bowl of sugary cereal, a professional wrestling magazine, and an old RCA showing MTV's *Videos That Don't Suck*.

Katy's nickname was "Doodlebug," which was the common name for the larval stage of a predacious insect called the Antlion (*Hesperoleon abdominalis*).

In their "doodlebug" stage Antlions have oval, plump abdomens and oversized heads with long spiny jaws, short legs, and bristles all over their bodies. And while the plump abdomen and the oversized head parts described Katy during her own larval stage, that is not why Bob gave her that nickname. Katy earned the name because, like the voracious Antlion larvae, she ate so much when she was little.

Katy was now vaguely bow-legged and had finally grown into her head. Her once plump and oval abdomen was now stretched over a frame that was a bit tall for her age.

Katy was a prime candidate for one of those studies which struggled to show a correlation between televised mayhem and violence committed by TV viewers against their fellow man.

Raised in New York, Katy had heard about, read about, or actually witnessed the innumerable atrocities that the citizens of that city committed against one another. And since getting cable and CNN, she had been able to view videotaped footage of similar behavior practiced around the world.

Katy loved *Beavis and Butthead*, the MTV cartoon paean to asinine teenage savagery and idiocy where the characters spent their free time playing fungo with frogs. She had seen every Schwarzenegger movie ever made, and whenever she and her friends had a spare moment and a king-size bed they practiced some of the more hazardous professional wrestling moves they had seen on the many World Wrestling Federation extravaganzas they watched.

Katy was grateful for the new network television warning labels. As far as she was concerned they simply made it easier to find the types of programs she wasn't supposed to watch.

According to the brain trusts at organizations like Americans for Responsible Television, Katy should already have killed both of her parents, several of the neighbors, and some neighborhood pets as a result of the egregious violence she had witnessed via the media. But, in truth, the most violent thing Katy had ever been involved with directly was a spanking she once got while spending the night with Ann, a chubby friend from her Girl Scout troop.

Ann's mother, Lillian—even by politically correct standards— was an overprotective tub of lard who was frequently seen at school board meetings wearing a faded floral muumuu while trying to have *Catcher in the Rye* removed from the library.

On the night in question, Lillian rented two of her favorite movies for the girls to watch: *Jerrico, the Wonder Clown*, a typically dismal Dean Martin/Jerry Lewis schlock-fest featuring Zsa Zsa Gabor, and *Polly of the Circus,* an ill-conceived vehicle for Marion Davies as a libidinous trapeze artist and Clark Gable as the minister after whom she libidoed.

Once home, Lillian handed out red foam-rubber down noses and sacks of peanuts to the girls and they settled in for their under-the-big-top double feature. As Lillian guffawed at all the awful shtick of the former and gushed at the appalling melodrama of the latter, Katy and Ann inserted index fingers into their mouths, the international gesture for "gag me with a tent pole."

When Lillian left the room for her fifth sack of peanuts, Katy convinced Ann to flip on *Cops* in defiance of Lillian's warning to the contrary.

When Lillian returned, her sensibilities were shocked almost beyond repair as she witnessed the arrest of a man on charges of assault. The last thing the accused said before Lillian flipped back to the libidinous trapeze artist was, "Ain't nobody beats my sister unless he marries her."

Lillian spanked both Ann and Katy and sent them straight to bed. The irony of that message was lost on all but Katy.

At any rate, if you believed the experts on the effects of media-portrayed violence, Katy was a time bomb waiting to go off, but right now, she was simply slurping up another spoonful of cereal and listening to her parents' lively conversation.

Mary, in constant motion as she prepared to leave for work, had a few questions before she was willing to give Bob what he wanted.

"How long do you think it will take?"

"Six months?" Bob bargained.

"I'll give you two," Mary counteroffered.

Katy perked up at all this talk of lunar periods. "Wow, are you pregnant?"

"What? Uh, no, just eat," Mary said.

Bob felt he was getting through. "Fair enough. The hybrids are almost ready, and I've got a good feeling about this deal with Mr. Silverstein. All I need is one job. Word-of-mouth will take care of the rest."

"Okay, two months, but it's gotta be part-time. In the meanwhile you've gotta bring in some money or we're S.O.L."

Katy looked to her father for his interpretation of the cryptic abbreviation.

"Loosely interpreted it means, uh, sort of lousy," he lied.

"Do we have a deal?" Mary needed his word.

Bob held up his hand. "Resumes go out tomorrow."

"And if you get a job offer?" Mary said open-endedly.

"I'll take any job that's offered. You've got my word."

"Alright. Two months. That's it. But, Bob, listen to me." Bob knew by the brevity of her sentences that Mary was serious. "You have a degree in entomology. Use it. See if you can find a teaching position, something with a steady paycheck. Katy and I are tired of living hand-to-mouth."

"We are?" Katy asked.

Elated, Bob hugged his wife.

"You won't regret this." Bob could smell his dream coming true. "I love you."

"You better," Mary said as she looked deep into Bob's eyes. The poor but happy couple kissed. When they broke their embrace Mary grabbed her purse and headed to the door.

"I'll be late tonight," Mary said. "I'm going to try to get a double shift."

She kissed Katy and, in one practiced motion, scooped the wrestling magazine into the trash, flipped the TV to *Sesame Street*, and disappeared out the back door.

"What's going on, Dad?" Katy asked as she shoveled another spoonful of cereal into her mouth.

"We're starting our own business."

"Can I help?" Katy asked.

"Well, I can't pay much."

"That's alright, I won't work much."

Bob smiled. He put his EXTERMINATOR cap on Katy's head. Katy spun it around so the bill faced backwards, gangsta-style. Bob put his arm around Katy. "You know, Doodlebug, I've had this dream for a long time. And with you and your mom helping, I just know we're going to make it come true."

Katy looked at her dad, milk wandering down her chin. "I hope so," she said, "otherwise we're shit outta luck, huh?"

As Bob considered the disciplinary options available to him, the doorbell rang.

He went to answer the door and Katy flipped back to MTV.

Given what Mary had told him, Bob had a good idea of who might be ringing the doorbell at this time of day. He peered through the distortion of the peephole and, sure enough, there was the convex head of Dick Pratt. He was a stumpy little ogre with a malignant disposition and advanced male pattern baldness. Indicative of his level of ingenuity, Pratt had conceived what he considered an innovative solution to the latter problem. He had cultivated a sheath of extraordinarily long, ropy hairs on the right side of his head which he then slicked with pomade and flopped completely over his scalp, the result of which was to give the impression that he was fooling no one except himself. Through the fish-eye lens of the peephole, Bob could see a smoldering Parodi sticking out of Pratt's convex face.

Bob took one last breath of clean air before he opened the door and stepped out onto the front stoop.

"Hi, Dick," Bob said. "How ya doin'?"

Pratt sucked on his cigar and said nothing.

"Listen," Bob continued, "I was going to call—"

"Hey, Mr. Goddamn Tambourine man," Pratt shrieked. "Play a song for me…a little somethin' to the tune of 300 'n' 20 bucks!"

Some spit landed on Bob when Pratt said "bucks!"

Bob closed the door behind him. "Listen, Dick…"

"Yo'.l You're past due, scumbag!" Pratt said in his angular Bronx accent. "And let me tell you what the deal's gonna be if you don't come up with some money real fast."

As Pratt continued his abusive screed, Bob noticed a Con Ed truck pulling to a stop in front of his house.

The driver, a competent-looking woman with long brown hair tumbling out from underneath her hard hat, stepped down from the truck's cab and checked her clipboard to see that this was the correct address. She headed up the walkway to where Pratt was still railing at Bob.

"Hey, yo, scumbag!" Pratt yelled, unaware of the Con Ed woman standing directly behind him. "Are you listening to me or what? I said I want my friggin' money!"

"Can you give me a few more days? I just lost my job."

"Like I give a rat's ass," Pratt said. "Pay your rent or find yourself a Fridgidaire box for three. You get my drift?"

"Excuse me," the woman said, startling Pratt so that he spit his stubby cigar onto the walkway.

"Yo! Who the hell are you?" Pratt asked, his lecherous gaze lingering around the darted portion of her official jumpsuit.

"I'm from Con Ed," she said as she looked down on Pratt. "I'm looking for a Mr. Bob Dillon."

"Yeah, well it ain't me, babe," Pratt said as he leaned over to retrieve his filthy little Parodi. "He's the lame-o, but I ain't through with him yet, so you'll just have to keep your little panties and your hard hat on till I'm done."

The woman's head popped backwards and she snapped, "So who the hell are you?"

Pratt postured back, squinting his eyes, and said, "Yo, I'm his friggin' landlord, that's who." He turned back to Bob.

The woman looked askance at Pratt's hair, and addressed Bob. "Is your name really Bob Dillon?"

"Afraid so," Bob said.

She smiled. "Boy, I bet that made for a fun childhood."

"Yo! Who asked you?" Pratt blurted.

No one noticed as the door behind Bob opened slightly. Katy peered out through the crack and listened.

"Hey, what's your problem, stumpy?" the woman asked. "I'm just making a little friendly conversation with Mr. Dillon here."

"Hey, yo, this ain't no friggin' coffee klatch," Pratt said. "I wanna know what you're doing on my goddamn property."

"Well, not that it's any of your damn business, but your tenant has fallen a little behind on his electric bill and I'm here to turn off the juice."

"Oops," Bob said.

Katy was embarrassed when she heard this.

"Hey, yo, ain't that just grand?" Pratt said. "Well get in line toots, 'cause Mr. Limp Dick here owes me some rent money and you're not gonna see dime one till I'm paid. Ya got it?"

Just then, Katy smelled something besides Pratt's cigar. It was essence of opportunity wafting up her tiny little nostrils, so she opened the door and stepped onto the porch.

"Hey, Mr. Pratt," Katy said. "Wanna buy some Girl Scout cookies?"

"Piss off, kid," he snarled. "I'm trying to squeeze some dough outta your deadbeat dad here."

"Hey, watch your language," the Con Ed woman said. "That's no way to talk in front of the kid."

"That's alright," Katy said. "I don't mind."

"Look, Dick," Bob said, "I just need a little time."

"Listen you freeloadin' asswipe…" Pratt continued.

"Hey," Bob said, "there's no need for that language."

"Yeah, what did I just tell you about that?" the Con Ed woman added.

"Yo, sorry, I didn't know you were all so sensitive," Pratt said. "Let me put it to ya this way…pay up or I'll throw you the hell out. I'll be back tomorrow."

Pratt turned and huffed back to his house, which, unfortunately for Bob, was directly across the street.

"How about you, lady? You wanna buy some Girl Scout cookies?" Katy smiled up toward the hard hat and the hair.

"Sure, why not?" the hard hat said with a smile of her own. "How about a box of those mint ones?"

"Alright!" Katy disappeared to retrieve the cookies.

"Thanks, that was nice," Bob said. "Listen, I know I'm behind, but…"

"Hey, don't worry about it," the woman said. "I got a little latitude now that I got some seniority. I don't wanna turn your power off."

"I appreciate that."

"I tell you what you need to do, though," she said as she wrote on her clipboard. "Just drop by the payment center and pay whatever you can. We won't turn you off if you show a little good faith."

"Great. Thanks," Bob said. "I'll do that."

Katy returned with a box of mint cookies and thrust them at the woman from Con Ed. "That'll be five bucks, please."

"Five?" the woman asked. "They're two-fifty over at the Waldbaum store."

"Yeah," Katy said, gesturing gently toward her father, "but I got more overhead to cover than they do."

Chapter Eight

Bob stared vacantly out the window of the storefront copy shop, illuminated by the warm rolling light that escaped from the Cannon TR-2000 Commercial Copier every time it cloned his flyer.

Instead of the traditional résumé Mary almost certainly had in mind, Bob had created a flyer about his all-natural pest-control idea. Such a flyer was guaranteed to keep him from being bothered by real job offers, and, Bob thought, there was always the chance it could generate an inquiry from someone interested in his concept. After all, at various times Americans had believed polyester, Cheese Whiz, and Richard Nixon were all great ideas. Why shouldn't they go for something with real substance?

The first version of Bob's flyer had been burdened with an abundance of scientific terminology, but he decided it was too factual and didn't have enough of what advertisers called "sizzle." So he redesigned it, opting for short, punchy copy and an arresting visual to grab the reader's attention. To that end, the flyer was fashioned like a pirate's flag—a white skull-and-crossbones on a black background. The copy, which was typed over the skull, went like this:

Professional exterminator—Bonded!
Fifteen years field experience!
Proficient with poisons, traps, e-guns, etc!
Gone private with lethal new concept!

No pest left alive! Leaves no traces!
No nerve damage! Act now!

Satisfied with his new design, Bob waited patiently for the machine to give him fifty copies for his limited direct-mail campaign. As the machine whirred on, Bob stared out the window thinking about his future.

Despite his Rotarian optimism, Bob was realistic enough to know his goal wouldn't be easy to attain. Mary told him something like 70 percent of new businesses failed within the first six months. Another 20 percent went tits-up within the year. That left the other ten percent to succeed on hard work, a bit of luck, and choosing the right Yellow Pages. The worst part was, Bob couldn't even qualify for this grim race unless he could crossbreed the perfect assassin bug in the first place.

Even if Bob came up with a Frankenstein bug that worked, he still needed two things: infested buildings and a cooperative building owner. The former would be easy enough to find in this city; the latter, well, he was working on it. If he could just get that meeting with Mr. Silverstein.

There were a lot of "ifs" between here and Bob's dream, like potholes on West Fifty-Fourth Street.

Bob was so mesmerized by the hum and rhythm of the copy machine that he didn't notice the guy in the "BUG-OFF" baseball cap who crossed Bedford Avenue and was standing on the sidewalk waving at Bob. After a moment, the man rapped on the window, snapping Bob back to reality. Bob acknowledged him with a smile.

His name was Johnny Meehl, a blue-collar Brooklyn guy who had worked with Bob. Johnny lumbered into the copy shop. "Yo, Bobby-boy. Whatsup? Ya lookin' kinda dazed and confused there."

"Hey Johnny, just copyin' the ole résumé."

"Whatsup with that?" Johnny asked. "I thought since you told Rick to piss off, you was startin' your own business."

"Yeah, I'm workin' on it. These things take time, ya know."

"I heard that," Johnny said as he read one of the flyers. "Listen, you almost through there? How 'bout we go to Freddie's for a cold one?"

"I'd love to, Johnny, but I'm flat-assed broke."

"Hey, I don't want to hear no no's. I'm buyin'."

Bob thought a free beer was just the thing he needed, so he smiled and stacked the warm copies of his flyer along with some envelopes and stamps and headed out the door with Johnny.

Adjacent to the copy shop was Freddie's Tavern, not a fern bar by anyone's definition. The clientele was guys deep in denial; no wives, girlfriends, or other enablers here. Co-dependency was the unused secret password and cheap draft was the only thing that ever empowered anyone here. No light beer in the cooler, and "Feelings" had never been near the jukebox.

Freddie's decor was standard fare, posters of Maris, Ewing, Namath, and other New York sports heroes. There were the usual neon beer signs and electric beer promotional paraphernalia. And posted behind the bar were hundreds of Polaroid snapshots of patrons in various stages of inebriation.

Sitting at the bar, Bob and Johnny hunkered down behind two empty pitchers while working on a third. Johnny picked up the pitcher and sucked noisily from it. A moment later he let fly with a monster AAARRRRRRRRRRRUP!

"He shoots, he scores!" Bob said.

This was pure hilarity to the pest controllers, and they laughed and slapped each other on the back, carrying on like men in bars like Freddie's are wont to do.

When a small roach scurried down the bar, a beery business proposition popped into Bob's head. He turned to the barkeep. "Yo, Freddie, you got roaches. You oughta hire me. I'm gonna start my own business."

"Hey, it's atmosphere," Freddie explained. "I don't mess with it. You guys want another?"

At that moment, it occurred to Bob that life was good. He had a beautiful wife and child, a friend who was buying the beer, and most importantly, he had a dream. Of course, after three pitchers of Budweiser, life tends to seem good, regardless of how things really are. That's the point of beer.

Around the midpoint of pitcher number five, Bob and Johnny began considering the philosophical implications of the pitcher that sat in front of them.

Johnny, who lacked a degree in philosophy, nonetheless offered his analysis. "Issall empty…"

Bob, who had once taken a class in existentialism and was, therefore, more qualified than Johnny to address such weighty concepts countered with, "Issall full…"

The debate raged on.

"You're jus' a opmotis…a otpomis…a op…you always look on the good sida things."

"The optimist," Bob slurred, "sees the bagel and the donut sees the…wait a second, that's not right." Bob paused to gather his thoughts. "The optimist sees the donut and the pessimist sees the hole. I don't know where I got 'bagel' from."

"I know where you can get great bagels!" Johnny said.

"No, no, no, bagels don't have nothing to do with it. What were we talking about?" Bob asked. "Oh yeah, I remember… Lemme ask you a question, Johnny whaddya want from life?"

This was the sort of question Johnny never bothered with, so he stopped to give it some serious thought. After several seconds, the answer became apparent to him.

"I dunno, the stuff I got, I guess. Job, a family, cable. A satellite dish would be nice, some good hockey tickets now and then. How 'bout you?"

"All I want outta life is my own truck with one of those big fiberglass bugs on the top. Ya know what I mean?"

Johnny nodded in agreement. "I know eggsactly whatcha mean, boy that would be nice. But how the hell ya plan on gettin' it?" Johnny slurred. "They don't just give 'em away, ya know."

"I already told you, I'm startin' my own business. It's a brand-new idea, Bob's All-Natural Pest Control. Killin' bugs without chemicals."

Johnny, who had worked for a dozen different pest control outfits in the past ten years, pointed out that wasn't exactly a new idea.

"There's a lot of competition out there for that sort of thing," Johnny said.

They spent the next twenty minutes discussing the merits of other, non-chemical methods for killing household insects.

There was an old electronic apparatus which emitted an ultrasonic frequency designed to send household pests fleeing. However, after mice were found nesting in the devices, the attorney general put the manufacturer out of business.

There were other, more technologically sound methods of pest control, including microwaves, super-heated air, liquid nitrogen, and electric shock. But Bob knew their drawbacks.

The problems were revealed in a study at U.C. Berkeley. The study showed microwaving left eight percent of termites still alive and wooden framework severely burned. The electro-gun, a device delivering substantial currents of electricity, left 20 percent of the termites alive.

Some pest controllers worked with extremes in heat and cold to eradicate insects from buildings. Liquid nitrogen worked by freezing the pests to a numbing 290 degrees below zero; however, you had to drill holes throughout your house to apply it, and it tended to warp drywall. Superheated air raised the internal temperature of structural wood to nearly 190 degrees. This killed the insects near the heat source, but others survived. There was also the problem with structural wood warping.

The problem was that these methods were primarily termite-specific and some of them left enough bugs alive to reproduce and start all over again. Another problem—and to Bob, the more important one—was that someone else had already invented them.

Bob struggled to explain his idea to his friend, but Johnny's limited knowledge of insects was troublesome.

"What the hell kind of bugs did you say?" Johnny asked.

"Assassin Bugs," Bob said. "They're from the *Reduviidae* family."

"Never heard of 'em." Johnny confessed. "You sure you're not just making this up? I mean, I work with bugs, you'd think I'd have heard of these things."

"If you don't believe me," Bob said, "you oughta come see my workshop, it's filled with 'em. You oughta see these suckers, they're mean as hell!"

"And you're cross-breeding 'em? Whew! Better be careful, you're screwing around with Mother Nature." Johnny warned.

"Hey, it's natural," Bob said. "Well, okay, I admit I gotta create a bug that doesn't already exist, but otherwise it's natural. No chlorinated hydrocarbons or organic phosphates to poison the water supply or screw up your nervous system."

"Hey!" Johnny said. "The hell you got against chlorinated hydrocarbons?" Johnny pointed at the constantly twitching muscles around his right eye. "You making fun of this?"

"Uh course not!" Bob said. "It's hardly noticeable."

"Yeah, well I'll tell you a thing or two, buddy. This twitch put two kids through public school!" Johnny said. "And it'd put two more through there if I could still have kids." Johnny paused, almost making the connection. "What the hell are you anyway, one of those crackpot environmentalists?"

"No way. I'm just trying to get a business going, that's all. It's a damn good idea and you know what? If it works I'll be rich." Bob sipped his beer. "It's about money, I spose. Like you said, they ain't exactly givin' away those trucks with the big bugs on 'em."

"So," Johnny said. "I guess the question is, where're you gonna get enough money to get you a truck?"

"I guess I need to get a job," Bob said.

"You had a job."

"No, I need a job that pays better." Bob looked to Freddie, who was at the end of the bar reading the paper. "Hey, Freddie, izzat a Sunday paper? Let me see the classifieds."

Freddie slid the thick section of want ads down the bar, upsetting a bowl of beer nuts on the way.

Johnny opened the paper randomly and focused his eyes well enough to read. Soon Johnny acted as if he'd struck gold.

"Hey!" he shouted. "How's 650 a week working part-time sound?"

"Pretty damn good," Bob said. "What's the job?"

"Uhhh, it's uhhh, oh. Never mind, that's for lap dancing."

"Hey," Bob said, "I wonder if Bug-Off's trying to find someone to replace me." Bob took the want ads and turned to the P's. He scanned the columns.

"Let's see," Bob said, "uhh...Paralegal, Payroll Clerk, PBX Supervisor, Personnel Administrator—"

Bob stopped reading and his eyes grew wide. "Judas H. Jones! Look at this!" Bob poked a finger at the paper, nearly tearing the page in half. He started spinning around gleefully on his bar stool.

Johnny tried to see where Bob was pointing, but the circular motion made it difficult. "Stop spinning and let me see!"

Bob stopped and read aloud, "'Professional Exterminator needed ASAP. $50K in a weekend! Major pest difficulty. Send resumes to: 251 Kavkastrasse, Zurich 2VA-6P2. Pros only.'"

"Fifty thousand dollars?" Johnny said. "That's gotta be a misprint! Lemme see." He reached for the paper, but Bob spun around again, causing Johnny to crash headfirst onto the bar.

Bam! "Owwww."

Bob's mind reeled, not only from the beer and from spinning around on his stool, but from the thought of how far $50,000 would go toward making his dream come true. With that much money, he could have two bugs on his truck.

Bob wobbled for a moment. "I think I'm gonna vomit."

Johnny snatched the paper so he could see the ad for himself. "$50,000! What kinna job do you think it is? Rats? It's gotta be rats, don't ya think?"

"Those gotta be some mighty damn big rats for that kinda money," Bob said.

"Zurich..." Johnny said. "That's in Sweden, isn't it?"

"No, jughead, it's Switzerland."

"Whoever woudda thought Switzerland had a big rat problem?"

"It's probably all that Swiss cheese," Bob said. "There's probably tons of it just lying around and the rats eat it and that's probably how they get so damn big."

"I bet you're right. Damn! A bunch of giant Swiss-cheese-eating rats. No wonder they're paying so much. But how come you think they're advertising here?"

"Well, where else they going to find somebody experienced with rats like that, huh? Nowhere but New York, baby!" Bob was so excited he sounded like Dick Vitale. "And who's sittin' here with a big stack of résumés?"

"Fuckinay!" Johnny waved his right hand at Freddie and his left hand at the Polaroid. "Yo Freddie, gimme the camera."

Freddie slid the camera down the bar, blowing the bowl of beer nuts over the side.

"It's a good idea to send a photo along with your résumé," Johnny reasoned as he took aim with the Polaroid. "They like to see who they're dealing with."

"Yeah, that's a good idea," Bob said as he wobbled on his stool and adjusted his red-and-black EXTERMINATOR cap.

"Uncross your eyes," Johnny suggested.

Bob straightened out his peepers.

Click! Flash! Whirr…The camera spit out a developing photo of Bob, his besotted eyes narrowed to menacing slits as he tried to focus. He looked either very drunk or very dangerous, depending on how you interpreted it.

Then, despite Johnny's assistance, Bob inserted the photo and one of his flyers into an envelope. He dipped his tongue into his beer, then he licked the envelope and sealed it. "There. That 50 K's as good as mine."

Bob's eyes then rolled back into his head and he fell off his stool, dead drunk and dreaming of a big fiberglass bug perched triumphantly on his own truck.

Chapter Nine

Louis, the fawning casino host at Monte Carlo and alleged distant cousin of Francois Blanc, the casino's founder, greeted Klaus with a sweeping bow. A tuxedoed waiter arrived with a Bombay martini, up with a twist, balanced on a silver tray.

Klaus sipped the chilled offering. "Perfect, as always. Thank you, Louis."

Klaus carried a shiny new briefcase which Louis knew meant Klaus had been paid recently and was there "to relax." This was good news for the casino, and Louis saw to it that Klaus was treated royally. Klaus handed over the briefcase and Louis headed for the cashier's office.

Klaus hadn't always gambled. But in recent years, as the bouts of depression recurred more often, he had discovered something that soothed his sickness. As long as he was gambling he couldn't brood about what he was beginning to see as his complete failure in life.

Once Klaus made that connection, he began spending more and more time at the famous casinos of the world. Depending on where his work took him, he might be seen playing roulette in San Remo, keno in Havana, or craps in Nassau or Rio, but usually he played baccarat and chemin de fer in Monte Carlo. He said it relaxed him and the money he lost did not matter.

At first he won more than he lost, but he began playing more recklessly and losses soon surpassed winnings. He also began wagering on sporting events; always betting the underdog, the longshot, the one sure to lose. Tampa Bay in the Super Bowl, Vietnam in the World Cup, white heavyweights, that sort of thing.

Among those who knew Klaus and who speculated on the reasons for his gambling, there were several theories. The first was rather pedestrian and muddled and went like this: because Klaus' work was so dangerous and stimulating he had become desensitized to normal recreational excitement and wagering large sums of money was the only way to get a thrill. An ancillary to this theory was because Klaus could not afford to take risks at his job he had to find another way to satisfy that need.

The second theory, held by his more Freudian-leaning friends, was that the destructive aspect of his id had overwhelmed the constructive drives, resulting in a palpable death wish.

He had no wife or family. He had nothing that resembled a hobby and he hated his job. In short, he had little reason to live.

Others speculated that Klaus was starting to feel guilty about all those he had killed and death was the only way to atone. Thus, the theory went, Klaus subconsciously hoped to lose so much money that someday he would not be able to pay those he owed and they would finally come and put him out of his misery.

For his part, Klaus dismissed these theories and others with the customary, "sometimes a cigar is just a cigar" response.

Whatever his reasons, Klaus simply sipped his martini and headed for the baccarat table.

Chapter Ten

The woman from *Time* magazine was duly impressed by Bob's fantastic collection of insects and his library on entomology. The photographer recorded the Bug Room for posterity and possibly for a best-selling coffee table book. There was even the chance that Bob, with his heretofore unimagined natural pest-control concept, would be chosen as *Time*'s Man of the Year. At least that's how it went in this particular fantasy.

Bob was in his Bug Room, tinkering with his hybrids and dreaming about the interview with the woman from *Time*. Surely she'd ask how he became interested in bugs in the first place.

Bob would explain that, like most boys, he was fascinated with spiders, snakes, scorpions, and the other menacing creatures of the animal kingdom. He loved those stories—the urban legends boys repeat endlessly and which never lose the ability to terrify. Like the one about the woman with the beehive hairdo who constantly applied hair spray to her 'do instead of washing it. As that story went, it was only when the woman dropped dead one day for no apparent reason that the coroner looked inside her hair. Inside was a nest of black widow spiders.

Bob also recalled the earwig legend—which probably involved the European Earwig (*Forficula auricularia*), as it was more common on the East Coast than the ring-legged variety (*Euborellia annulipes*). This story began late one night, when a female earwig crawled into some luckless man's ear while he slept. With her demonically curved pincerlike cerci, the earwig mucked through the bitter orange earwax and nibbled her way around the eardrum, past the semicircular canals and the cochlea, and eventually into the brain where she deposited her thirty eggs. On her way out she became mired in the morass of ear wax and died.

The next day the man went to a physician—presumably ear, nose, and throat—to complain about a pain in his ear. The doctor peered inside, located the offending insect, and removed it. He prescribed something to cut down on the waxy build-up and pronounced that everything would be fine.

Fourteen days later, however, the eggs inside his brain hatched and the thirty offspring began eating their way through the man's hypothalamus. Screaming in horror and agony he died, blood and bits of brain matter oozing from his ears.

Of course there was no truth to this legend. There was nothing in the literature about earwigs burrowing into the human brain to lay their eggs, but it made for a good story.

Bob's scientific, interest in bugs began in eighth grade when he was in the library ostensibly doing a book report on Jack London's *The Call Of The Wild* as punishment for smart-mouthing his English Lit teacher. However, instead of reading London's primitivistic canine parable, Bob was flipping through *The Common Insects of North America* looking at pictures of wasps. It was there that the so-called Tarantula Hawk Wasp (*Pepsis mildei*) caught his eye.

Bob imagined a great spider, the size of a wharf rat with a wingspan of four–to–six feet, all covered with mangy feathers and hair. To Bob's dismay, he learned the Tarantula Hawk Wasp grew no larger than 1.2 inches. Nevertheless, the drawing showed a savage looking blue-black beast with red wings and antennae and a long curved stinger. The book also described in lurid detail how the female Tarantula Hawk Wasp slowly approached a much larger spider. Somehow the Tarantula Hawk Wasp hypnotized its prey until the malevolent insect buried its stinger deep in the spellbound arachnid and pumped it full of poison. The paralyzed spider was then dragged to a burrow and implanted with an egg. It served as food for the developing wasp larva, eaten from the inside out.

Wow, young Bob thought, this was better than the earwig story! He never dreamed bugs could be this exciting.

Bob stayed at the library late that day, eventually completing a fascinating, if partially fictionalized, report on the Tarantula Hawk Wasp of northern Mexico. He received an A+ and such praise from his teacher that he began his life-long devotion to things *Insecta*.

This dedication eventually led to a degree in entomology, and for a while Bob entertained the notion of getting his doctorate and becoming a college professor or a researcher investigating the insects' role as vectors of viral, bacterial, and protozoal diseases. But somewhere along the line he cooled on that idea.

Then one day after reading (though not thoroughly comprehending) William Borroughs' *Naked Lunch*, Bob got his idea.

The idea led to his dream and his dream eventually led to his Bug Room where he now sat wiggling in his dilapidated swivel chair, munching a bowl of Lucky Charms while scrutinizing something on the table in front of him. Bob was comfortable, wearing a stained undershirt, his black-and-red EXTERMINATOR cap, and a pair of boxers decorated with red and black ants which Mary had given him last Christmas.

On the table was a cardboard box with tiny, screen-covered air holes punched in a circle on the top. In bright red letters, the box boldly announced: *"ARILUS CRISTATUS (Reduviidae)."* It was a batch of Wheel Bugs. They bred well with other *Reduviidae*, and their trait as voracious predators always passed on to the ensuing generation of hybrids.

Bob had also liked the fact that Wheel Bugs looked as if they were designed by the same Northrop engineers who created the stealth fighter; its exoskeleton hard and angular with overlapping plates of some sort of exotic radar-absorbing carbon fiber material. This was a serious-looking bug.

Between each spoon of marshmallowed cereal Bob glanced alternately at the bugs and an open textbook.

Not far from Bob's house, a Mercedes limousine with blacked-out windows cruised up Forty-Eighth Street, past New Calvary Cemetery. Marcel and Jean, who had recently arrived from Paris, were in the back of the limousine. Marcel was wearing another extra-large $5,000 suit and a questionable tie. Jean, his fashionable assistant, was less expensively dressed, but at least his tie picked up some of the color from his shirt.

The Mercedes wheeled to the curb and the men looked through the tinted window at Bob's house. Marcel took in the *mise-en-scène*. "This is it. A safe house undoubtedly."

"What else could it be?" Jean asked disdainfully.

Marcel opened the door to get out.

"Be careful," Jean said as he brushed at some lint that stuck to Marcel's dark taupe worsted wool slacks. "Remember, we know nothing of this man. For all we know he is one of those psychotic Vietnam veterans."

Bob was tilting the bowl of spongy cereal toward his mouth when the doorbell rang. The unexpected noise caused him to spill milk down his cheeks. Assuming it was Pratt dropping by to squeeze the blood from his turnip, Bob's annoyance level doubled. But Bob wasn't one to duck the landlord, so with a mouth full of green clovers and yellow moons, he went to answer the door.

Marcel shifted nervously as he stood by the door, the wood creaking under his substantial heft. He was startled when the door opened and revealed Bob, still chewing cereal. Bob somehow looked menacing wearing only his boxers, his EXTERMINATOR cap, a milk mustache, and a pink heart-shaped marshmallow on his cheek.

Marcel stepped back, frightened. A standoff ensued as they eyed one another.

In the Mercedes, Jean recoiled in horror at the poly-cotton blend of Bob's boxers.

Finally, Marcel's trembling hand pulled something from the manila folder he held. He looked at Bob. "Robert Dillon?" he inquired, Frenchly.

Bob squinted at the bright sunlight, producing a Clint Eastwood effect. He spoke warily. "Uh, yeah." He burped a milky white burp.

"The professional…exterminator?"

"That's right." Bob wiped the milk on the back of his hand.

"May I come in?" Marcel asked. He was apprehensive and slightly disgusted.

Bob looked at the fat man in the shiny suit. "Uh, you a bill collector?"

Marcel shifted on his feet while glancing about. "No, we recently received your, uh, how shall I say…your resume?" Bob saw that the stranger was clutching the skull-and-crossbones flyer he had designed.

"Huh?" Bob was confused. He had mailed his flyer to several real estate outfits hoping to interest one of them in his idea. He also wanted to fulfill his promise to Mary that he would seek work. But all those companies had told him to piss off with his idiotic bug idea, or words to that effect. But still, here was someone on his front stoop waving a copy of the flyer.

"So, uh, you're interested in my new method?" Bob asked.

Marcel looked around nervously. "Yes, that's right. May I come in?"

"Yes, please." Bob stepped aside and gestured Marcel in. As he closed the door, Bob noticed the large Mercedes parked at the curb. It was an unusual sight. The only other German car Bob had ever seen in his neighborhood was a beat-up 1969 Volkswagen Bug.

Bob joined Marcel in the living room. "I'm sorry, I didn't get your name."

"Call me Marcel." He scanned the living room. The interior looked to him the way he imagined a lower-middle-class American home should look, and he felt a professional urge to comment.

"This is a very thorough cover," he said as he gestured toward the room.

Bob had no idea what Marcel meant, but not wanting to get off on the wrong foot with a potential client, he thanked him and offered him a seat. Someone had actually responded to his flyer! Talk about complete surprise. This was fantastic! If things like this kept dropping out of the clear blue sky, Bob would have that truck with the bug on top of it in no time.

Marcel settled deep into the sofa and poked around at the dog-eared magazines on the coffee table as he spoke. "Obviously, we received your response to our advertisement in the paper." Marcel paused to see if Bob would pick up the ball and run with it. This was an extremely touchy situation, Marcel having no idea what sort of killer Bob might be.

As Marcel worried, Bob wondered why Europeans stressed the second syllable in the word, pronouncing it ad-VERT-isment instead of ad-ver-TISE-ment. He also wondered what adVERT-is-ment Marcel was talking about.

Then it came to him. That drunken night at Freddie's and the ad in the New York Times.

"Oh!" Bob blurted. "You must be the Swiss guy with the rat problem!"

"The rat problem?" Marcel said.

"No? Oh, that's right, I just assumed it was rats. It could just as easily be roaches, couldn't it? Pests in general, doesn't matter, I can handle it."

"Yes," Marcel said, "it is indeed a pest I need your assistance with."

"Yeah, it's funny. You know, I don't even remember why I assumed it was rats in the first place. Truth is, I don't remember much from that night, but that doesn't matter. Anyway, now I remember your ad. I guess the French accent threw me off, but I suppose it makes sense that you've got one, I mean France is pretty close to Switzerland, isn't it?"

Marcel had expected Bob to be cautious. After all, Bob was a professional killer and had to be sure he wasn't dealing with the authorities. So he was speaking cryptically.

"Yes, the countries border one another," Marcel said slyly.

"Well, you've come to the right place. My method is thoroughly researched," Bob lied. "I think you'll be very impressed. In fact, let me show you something."

Bob jumped up and ran to the Bug Room. He rooted through the documents piled on his work desk before grabbing a single sheet of paper. He returned to the living room and handed the paper to Marcel.

"This is the only one I could find to show you, it's kind of a mess back there, but it'll give you an idea of what I'm talking about," Bob said.

Marcel read:

> The Spined Assassin Bug (*Sinea diadema*). One of the most ruthless and cunning thugs in the insect world. Its glistening black exoskeleton is covered with eight rigid, needle-sharp spines, each of which has a bright yellow ring at its base. Originally a defensive mechanism, over time the Spined Assassin has evolved to use the spines as weapons, trapping prey against solid objects, then driving ahead like an unmanned bulldozer until its quarry is run through like a pin-cushion. The Spined Assassin feeds on the fluids of various large insects.

This cinched it for Marcel. The word "assassin" was right there on the page, yet it was couched in such a way that it could not implicate Bob as a killer for hire.

"Yes, this is brilliant," Marcel said as he put the sheet of paper on the coffee table. "But let me ask you a question, now that we are on the same page, so to speak."

"No, go ahead. Believe me, I understand. I imagine you're going to need some things explained."

"Yes, uh, exactly." Marcel moved to the front edge of the sofa and leaned toward Bob. "After receiving your…inquiry, my associates and I wondered why we had not heard of you before."

"Well, for the past few years I've worked exclusively for this company…"

Marcel understood. "Ahhh. The Company. Very good. That would explain it." Marcel was thrilled to be getting someone with CIA training. "And you left the Company because…"

"We had a policy disagreement. So I'm on my own now."

"Out in the cold, as they say."

"Uh, I guess you could say that. So what can I do for you?"

Marcel handed Bob a folder. "Well, as you might imagine, we need something taken care of."

Bob opened the folder, expecting to find blueprints or photographs of the building Marcel was hiring him to disinfest. Instead, he found a photograph and some biographical information on a man named Hans Huweiler. He also found the Polaroid of himself taken that beery night at Freddie's. Something was wrong, Bob thought, but at the moment he couldn't figure out what.

Marcel cleared his throat. "I must say, of all the inquiries we received, we were most amused by your, what would you call it, your handbill?"

"Oh, my flyer? You liked that, huh?"

"Quite." Marcel chuckled nervously. "Natural Pest Control. That was, how would you say it? Quite inventive. We especially enjoyed the skull-and-crossbones. A nice touch."

"Thanks, I designed it myself." Bob nodded at the folder and the picture of Mr. Hans Huweiler. "Uh, what's this? Is this the guy with the pest problem?"

"Uh, no. He is the problem," Marcel said.

Bob thought he had missed something during the course of the conversation. "I don't understand what you're saying."

"Mr. Huweiler is your…uh, your pest."

Bob hesitated before speaking. "The pest who needs to be exterminated?"

"*C'est ça!*" Marcel smiled.

Bob stared at Marcel as he tried to figure out what the hell was going on. He reviewed all the evidence: the Mercedes limo, a man with an extremely expensive suit, the oblique questions and comments, and the ad in the New York Times offering $50,000 for a weekend exterminator job.

It suddenly occurred to Bob that someone with a French accent was making a big mistake. And Bob was beginning to get a rough idea of what that mistake was. This man wanted someone dead. And he wanted Bob to make him that way.

Bob quickly closed the folder and thrust it back at Marcel, who interpreted the sudden, violent movement as one of aggression.

Bob was genuinely frightened.

Marcel was thoroughly terrified.

"Will you take the job?" Marcel asked nervously.

"What?! Uh, no, no thanks, I don't think so," Bob said nervously as he got up. Marcel stood also.

"The pay is 50,000 American," Marcel offered, fearing for his own life.

Some papers slipped from the folder and fluttered toward the floor. Bob made an astoundingly quick move to catch them.

Marcel jumped back, hoping he was not going to be killed where he stood.

Bob had to nip this in the bud. "No, you don't understand. I am not interested in this. This is not my line of work."

Marcel was confused momentarily until he realized Bob was negotiating. "Ahhh. I see," Marcel said. "Very well. I am authorized to go as high as one hundred thousand. But it must appear accidental."

Bob moved abruptly toward the front hall. Marcel followed, assuming the negotiations were coming to a close.

"Look, if it can't be killed with Malathion, Diazinon, or Combat, I don't kill it."

"I understand," Marcel said with a wave of the hand. "Whatever method you choose is fine as long as it appears accidental."

"No. Listen to what I'm saying, I just kill bugs," Bob insisted. "I'm not interested in this. Do you understand?"

"Of course, bugs. And this is not the sort of thing we would ever ask you to do. Very good." Marcel was getting the hang of it.

"No, you're not listening to me. Come here." Bob took Marcel by the arm and led him down the hallway to the Bug Room. Marcel's eyes fixed immediately on the bookshelves where he saw copies of *Organic Death* and *The Art of Poison*. He also noticed Bob's gleaming steel homemade bee smoker which he imagined was an efficient and deadly weapon rarely seen by nonprofessionals.

Marcel pulled away from Bob, convinced he had the right man for the job. He made his way back to the front door, then paused, offering the folder to Bob. "Will you need this?"

"No, really. I think you should leave now." Bob opened the door.

Of course, Marcel thought, a photographic memory.

"I am not interested, alright? And I'm sorry if I caused you any inconvenience."

"Yes, of course, at your convenience. That will be fine. But sooner is better than later if it fits your schedule."

Bob urged Marcel out the door and shut it. Marcel quickly retreated to the Mercedes and slipped in the back.

"You are white as a ghost," Jean whispered urgently as he looked out at Bob's house. "Did he accept?"

Marcel nodded. "Yes, but he forced the higher price."

"Are you sure about him?"

Marcel dabbed the sweat from his brow and looked at Jean with death in his eyes. "I am lucky to be alive." He pulled Bob's photo from the folder and looked at it. "He is even more dangerous than he looks."

Chapter Eleven

The white Ferrari Testarossa exploded out of the St. Gotthard tunnel on its way to Chamonix. The man at the wheel of this beautiful, sleek machine had an appointment for some fun with someone who was not his wife's age.

It was a good day for driving, and Mr. Hans Huweiler was howling along a winding road through the Swiss Alps at about 140 KPH, exceedingly fast, even by metric standards.

Between shifts, Hans drank from a bottle of Remy Martin while conducting Mozart's "*Eine kleine Nachtmusik*" as it blasted from the expensive stereo.

As Hans was coaxing the cellos into a more emotive mood, the Testarossa squealed into a nasty and not particularly well engineered curve in the road, forcing him to drop his bottle and take the wheel with both hands momentarily.

Just before the apex of the curve, Hans reached down for the glugging decanter. A split second later, Hans and his Ferrari parted company with the road in a white blur and, in perfect time with Herr Mozart, cartwheeled beautifully down the side of the mountain, an awful waste of machinery and cognac.

Chapter Twelve

Marcel and Jean were in the Lear jet cruising through German airspace at 37,000 feet when the fax machine began to whir.

Jean, looking elegant yet casual in a juniper-green Mongolian cashmere with polo collar, retrieved the copy of the newspaper article that was being transmitted to them.

The headline read: "HUWEILER DIES IN ALPS CRASH." He handed it, with a smile, to Marcel.

After absorbing the details of the lead paragraph, Marcel put the article aside. "*Tres bon.*" He smiled as he pulled a pen from his coat pocket. "Our 'pest problem' is *finis*. Bring me the package."

As Jean retrieved a large envelope from a compartment in the rear of the jet, Marcel wrote a note on the back of a calling card: "*Merci, Messr.* Exterminator."

Jean handed the envelope to Marcel, who opened it, revealing $100,000 in American currency. Marcel put the calling card in the envelope, then sealed it. "See that our friend receives this."

Chapter Thirteen

The cupboard was bare, save for a couple of packages of Top Ramen, a can of generic tomato sauce, and the rapidly diminishing box of Lucky Charms. Not wanting to deprive his family of a potential pseudo-spaghetti dinner, Bob opted for the cereal.

He turned the box upside down and shook out the last few morsels. A dead cockroach toppled into the half-full bowl of cereal.

Bob fished the roach out from among the clover-and moon-shaped marshmallows. It had probably died from an overdose of preservatives. Bob considered the reddish-brown bug. Abundant in the Paleozoic era, its species had not changed noticeably in 400 million years. Their fossil remains were so plentiful in one strata of geologic time that some referred to it as the Age of Cockroaches. Today there were about 55 known species in the United States, most of which lived outdoors. Only five species commonly lived indoors. And although Bob knew they weren't the cleanest insects around, cockroaches had never bothered him, certainly not the way the Common Housefly (*Musca domestica*) did. After all, contrary to popular belief, cockroaches didn't spread human diseases.

The housefly, on the other hand, mucked about on moist shit before landing on human food and regurgitating fecal matter, thereby transmitting typhoid, dysentery, diarrhea, pinworms, hookworms, and tapeworms. The housefly disgusted Bob.

One Saturday afternoon Mary watched in amazement as Bob, wearing heavy-duty rubber gloves, pursued a fly through the house for 45 minutes until finally smashing it against a wall.

But the occasional cockroach Bob could live with. He removed the brittle winged creature from his cereal and carried it by its antennae to the trash can.

In the fridge, the milk carton was almost empty, maybe six tablespoons left. Bob went to the sink and added some tap water. Point zero, zero, two percent milk, Bob thought. Less fat and no flavor. He poured the thin white liquid onto his cereal.

Bob sat, staring at his forlorn meal, trying for the moment not to let his situation get him down. He sighed.

As he brought the spoon to his mouth, Bob noticed his watch. "Oh shit!" he blurted, blowing a green clover marshmallow across the room in a thin mist of point zero, zero two percent milk. Bob had almost forgotten. He was scheduled to meet with the owner of Maison Henri, a French bistro on the Upper West Side currently enjoying a vogue and a bit of a roach problem.

Bob would be pitching his natural pest-control method to Henri, the big enchilada or, rather, the big crepe himself. If Henri bought the idea, it would give Bob the opportunity to test the first of his hybrids—"Strain Zero" as he called it—on a scale larger than his bugquariums.

Bob had started his numbering system with zero instead of one because, like "Ground Zero" of a nuclear blast and "Patient Zero" of the AIDS epidemic, "Strain Zero" sounded ominous and hinted at death and destruction, which is exactly what he was hoping for in his hybrid bugs.

Bob sloshed the bowl of cereal into the fridge so it wouldn't go to waste. He dashed out the back door and headed for his car, a deteriorating Ford Pinto with the infamous rear-mounted gas tank. The car Bob really wanted was an AMC Hornet, but, pathetically, it was beyond his means and so he had settled for the aged and potentially explosive Ford.

He mounted the old Pinto, which backfired and sputtered to life. Then, as fast as he could make it go, Bob wheeled the tired machine out of the alley and onto the street, smoking down the road on his way to the appointment he almost forgot.

About three seconds later the doorbell rang.

Standing patiently on the thick green paint of the front stoop of Bob's house at 2439 Thirtieth Street was a friendly UPS delivery guy holding the thick package of cash which Marcel had sent as payment for the Huweiler job.

As the UPS guy knocked vigorously, one of the house numbers, the nine, fell to the ground. He stooped to pick it up and a voice came from behind, "Hey, yo! You got something for that douche bag Dillon?"

The friendly UPS guy turned to find a nasty little man chewing on a small cheap cigar.

The UPS guy looked at the package. "Uh, Dillon, yeah, that's right. Who're you?" he asked politely.

"Yo, I'm his friggin' landlord, pal. I'll take it."

Pratt snatched the friendly UPS guy's Etch-A-Sketch-like clipboard and signed for the package.

"Landlord, huh?" the friendly UPS guy said as he handed Pratt the fallen house number. "Well, you oughta fix that. Gotta have house numbers, ya know, it's the law."

A look halfway between incredulity and indignity crossed Pratt's face. "Yo, who're you, the goddamn Housin' Authority?" Pratt tossed the nine onto Bob's welcome mat, then snatched the package and stormed off back to his house across the street.

Inside his front hall, Pratt tossed the package into the corner by a pair of dirty work boots, planning to hold it hostage until he got his $320 from Bob.

Chapter Fourteen

The Muzak eased a soothing version of Johnny Rivers' "Secret Agent Man" into the New York City field office of the Central Intelligence Agency. In a corner office, two men in dark suits, one older, one younger—both the men and the suits—stood at a fax machine as it received a transmission.

Parker was a rookie agent. He was tall and his jet-black hair was thick with styling gel and plowed through with a wide-toothed comb which left furrows wide enough to plant anything but an idea. He smelled like a men's fashion magazine stuffed with too many scented cologne ads; his fellow agents joked that a subscription card might drop from inside his coat at any minute.

After reading *Will* during his senior year in high school, Parker realized he wanted to be like G. Gordon Liddy when he grew up, so he went to Ohio State and earned an advanced degree in criminal justice, interning with the Agency during the summers. Upon graduation he applied for a job. He took (and rather enjoyed) the mandatory urinalysis drug screening test, and was accepted.

He liked it there, he fit in, he would go far.

As with all rookies, Parker was teamed with an older, more experienced partner—in this case, a man named Mike Wolfe. Wolfe had a head brimming with big, white, Peter Graves hair; it was his best feature and kept others from noticing how much his gut pooched out below. Wolfe was a Brylcreem man who preferred the bracing fragrance of Old Spice. Wolfe had never read *Will*, but he had once tried to out-drink Liddy. He found out the hard way he wasn't in the same league and ended up in an emergency room with an acute case of alcoholic gastritis.

Wolfe was old school. He joined the intelligence community in 1945 when he was hired by the Office of Strategic Services. In 1947, when the OSS was succeeded by the CIA, the National Security Agency, and other bureaus, Wolfe went with the Agency.

He was nearing retirement, and not a moment too soon as far as he was concerned. Things had become far too complicated in the espionage business, unnecessarily so, in Wolfe's mind. Things were simpler in the old days and Wolfe preferred them that way. He had no desire to learn the dozens of computer programs the younger agents were fluent with or how to interpret infrared satellite photography or any of the new technology that was essential for the dangerous games they played.

Wolfe hated techno-spying. He was, as Edmund Fuller had put it, the leftover progressive of an earlier generation. He preferred simple phone bugs and intercepting cables, long-range telephoto lenses, and following hunches and gut instincts.

That the Cold War had ended when it did was still a sore spot for Wolfe. He had given up several dozen good rounds of golf during the summer of '91 to learn enough Russian to go on a mission there before his retirement. He had hoped to do this so he could claim, however speciously, that he had a hand in the downfall of what he—a lifelong Barry Goldwater supporter—considered the Evil Empire.

This, Wolfe thought, would be his denouement, the perfect end to a long and otherwise undistinguished career that would land him some sort of profitable post-retirement consulting position to supplement his modest federal pension. And perhaps, additionally, he would do like that guy Gene Hackman played in *The French Connection* had done…that New York cop, what was his name, Popeye Doyle?

He would write a book that would become a best-seller and Hollywood would come calling. He might even end up on the cover of *People* magazine. All of this, he hoped, would make up for the fact that he had not built up much of a nest egg. And, he figured, if all that failed, maybe he'd get a little something extra in his envelope come Christmas-time.

And though Wolfe did not like all the data-based espionage, he did like breaking in new agents. It gave him the opportunity to tell his yawning tales to a willing, or at least captive, audience and to denigrate the new ways of sleuthing.

"Goddam faxes, I hate these things," Wolfe announced. "All this technology is worthless, gives you a false sense of security. How do you know what those satellite pictures are supposed to be? I mean, I want somebody to tell me what's wrong with good old-fashioned sneaking onto missile sites to confirm information, that's what I want to know."

The Muzak segued ironically to a stringy sweet version of "The Times They Are a-Changin'."

"Well, sir, this isn't the Korean missile information you were expecting," Parker explained. "This is data on that guy who killed Huweiler. Field Intelligence turned him up."

"The Huweiler assassination, huh?" Wolfe perked up at this, sensing this might be the case he'd been looking for. If this new assassin turned out to be as good as rumors indicated and Wolfe could bring him into the Company, that would be his ticket. A story like this could nudge Le Carre and Clancy and Grisham right off the best-seller list.

"That was some top-notch work from what I hear," Wolfe said. "What's this guy's background; who the hell is he?"

"Don't know yet, sir, he just crawled out of the woodwork." Parker glanced at the fax, then handed it to Wolfe. "His name's Bob Dillon."

Wolfe looked surprised. "Bob Dylan? Like the singer?"

"It's spelled different," Parker said.

The fax in question was the photograph of Bob, looking dangerous in his EXTERMINATOR cap while seated at Freddie's bar. The portrait was now a bit blurred, being a third-generation fax transmission of the picture. (One might imagine that Marcel's fashionable assistant, Jean, had sent this in exchange for a little clothes money.) Wolfe looked at the picture, then pointed something out for the less-experienced agent. "Look at the eyes. They always give away a killer."

"He looks drunk to me," replied the greenhorn.

Wolfe shook his head disdainfully, then returned his gaze to the fax. "That's because you're a rookie and you've come to rely on all that damn technology. No, once you've been in this business as long as I have, you learn to spot a killer." Wolfe thumped the fax with his index finger. "And this guy's a killer." He headed for his office to make some calls. "Get me everything you can on this guy. I want the entire Dillon catalogue on my desk this afternoon. And I want hard copies of everything, none of this E-mail shit," he said technophobically.

"Yes, sir."

"I'm thinking that Huweiler job looked a lot like that unclaimed kill in Istanbul last month. We might just have to add this Dillon character to the top ten list."

Chapter Fifteen

Stress washed Mary's face as she scrubbed the dishes. The rent was still overdue and several other bills were outstanding. The "reminder" notices were quickly becoming outright threatening; promising to deny her family the basic utilities—phone, gas, electricity, and cable.

Mary had long prided herself in maintaining a perfect credit rating, and the fear that her record would be defiled gnawed at her relentlessly. If her degree in business administration had taught Mary nothing else, it taught her that people were judged not by their character but by their credit ratings.

While Mary fretted about financial problems, Katy sat at the table in her Girl Scout uniform counting money from a piggy bank. "I got twenty-four dollars from selling cookies," Katy said thoughtfully. "Would that help Daddy start his business?"

Touched, Mary turned and looked at Katy. "Sweetie, that money's for your troop, it's not yours to spend, but thanks. Your dad will find a way to start his business."

"Okay, but don't say I didn't offer."

As it turned out, Bob was on the other side of the kitchen door listening. He had been on his way to tell Mary some good news when he saw the five-segmented maxillary palpi of a Silverfish (*Lepisma saccharina*) disappear under the edge of the rug. It was an unusual sighting for daytime and especially disturbing to Bob because silverfish tended to eat the bindings of his bug books.

He applied the sum of his weight onto the spot of the rug where he expected the little bristletail was hiding. While he did this, he listened with both pride and guilt as his daughter offered her hard-earned money to help him.

Here he was, he thought, a perfectly capable man with a family to support, yet he wasn't providing. He was suddenly face-to-face with the fact that his daughter, a second-year Girl Scout, was considering embezzlement in order to help him get his business started. It had come to this.

Snap out of it, Bob thought. There was no need to feel sorry for himself. Things were looking up! He had good news and that's what he was going to tell Mary.

Satisfied that he had squashed the glistening silverfish, Bob gathered himself and quietly entered the kitchen, shushing Katy, who immediately became a willing conspirator. He crept up behind Mary and put his arms around her waist, causing her to scream and throw a plate into the air. Inevitably, it crashed to the floor, which Katy thought was pretty cool.

"Jesus, Bob, you scared the crap out of me!"

"Sorry, hon. Why so tense?" Bob asked, sounding like a bad television commercial for decaffeinated coffee.

"Why shouldn't I be tense?" Mary snapped. "My husband's out of work, I make three bucks an hour plus tips in a city of six percent tippers, our daughter has more money than the two of us combined, and we owe the landlord 320 bucks."

"Oh, that," Bob said with a sly smile. "Well, would it help you to know I got a job?"

"You got a what?"

"Well, you know Mr. Silverstein? The guy with all the buildings? I finally got him on the phone."

"You got the job?"

"Well, not yet, but it's a great lead. He wants a demonstration. So I'm going to start working on that tomorrow."

Mary deflated for a moment before Bob continued, toying dangerously with her emotions. "But remember the French restaurant? *Maison Henri?*"

"You got that? Please tell me you got that!"

Bob swaggered a bit to convey his affirmative response. Mary hugged him vigorously before asking the critical question. "How much?"

Bob held out a check for her inspection. Mary's eyes nearly popped out of her head, which Katy also would have thought was pretty cool.

"Five hundred dollars!?" Mary could hardly believe it. Katy was impressed too. "Wow! Can we get a color TV?"

Mary hugged Bob again. "Honey, this is wonderful! Oh, I can hardly believe this. Let's celebrate! Let's go crazy, do something completely extravagant."

Bob pushed the deflate button again. He folded the check and put it into his pocket. "We can't spend this just yet, sweetheart. I gotta be sure I can get rid of the bugs."

Mary surprised Bob when she grabbed him firmly by the lapels and pulled him close like a testy loan shark. "Promise me one thing," Mary said forcefully. "Promise you won't even think about trying your natural method. You haven't got those bugs figured out yet, Bob. For now, use poison. Strychnine, arsenic, parathion, use enough to drop a charging wildebeest! Kill the bugs, Bob. We need that money!"

Bob was dismayed by Mary's lust for money and freewheeling prescription of organo-chlorines and organophosphates. "Yeah, sure, okay, honey," Bob said. "I promise."

He hoped only that he could keep his promise, for this was a perfect opportunity to test one of the hybrid Assassin Bugs. And, obviously, the more strains he eliminated, the closer he would be to perfecting his all-natural method and, therefore, the closer he would be to getting his family out of New York and starting a better life for all of them.

Perhaps there was a loophole somewhere in his promise. He made a mental note to look.

Chapter Sixteen

Pratt was on his tenth beer. When he saw the globule of brown spittle and tobacco floating in the small moat circling the top of the can, he lifted it to his lips and slurped it up. He peeled back the stained aquamarine curtains of his living room and looked across the street to Bob's house.

"I'm tellin' ya, Doris," Pratt yelled to the interior of his house, "that scumbag Dillon has pushed me far enough with this late rent routine! That maggot is got a goddamn room full of friggin' bugs over there! What the hell's up with that? Doris? You listenin' to me? You better be listenin', 'cause you know what happens when you don't listen." Pratt balled up a little fist and shook it in the air. "I'm not kiddin'. I don't care if you like that deadbeat's wife or not, I'm gonna take the bum to court on these friggin' bugs, I swear on my mother's grave!"

He tilted the can upright, drained it, then licked at the moat for the remaining brown juice.

"Goddammit, Doris, get off your lazy fat ass, and bring me another beer before I have to come in there and smack you again."

Chapter Seventeen

Mary urged the exhausted Pinto along Central Park South through the tolerable Sunday morning traffic, as it belched enough smoke to kill the inhabitants of a large African termite mound. The magnetic sign on the car door read "Bob's All-Natural Pest Control." Mary wheeled the advertisement through Columbus Circle and headed up Central Park West the few blocks to Sixty-Fourth. At the green awning of *Maison Henri*, she pulled to the curb.

Bob, wearing tan coveralls and his EXTERMINATOR cap, removed himself from the passenger side and unloaded a cache of deadly-looking extermination equipment from the back, arranging it carefully on the sidewalk.

"Thanks, hon. I'll get the train home," he said. "Probably be back by six."

"Remember," Mary reminded Bob over her shoulder, "use poison. Lots and lots of poison."

Bob smiled agreeably into the rearview mirror as he shut the hatch. He knew what she really meant was, above all else, he had to be sure to kill the bugs; no matter how he did it.

As Bob leaned in the passenger window to kiss Mary goodbye, a crusty-looking panhandler approached and spoke in a hoarse voice. "Hey, Romeo, got any spare change?"

Startled, Bob turned, feeling at his pockets. "Uh, no, sorry."

Bob could smell the guy from several yards away, and he wondered if the stench would function as an insect repellent.

The pungent panhandler kept approaching and, in violation of all non-aggressive panhandling laws, violently shoved Bob aside. The man leaned in the window toward Mary.

"How 'bout you, sweetmeat? Whaddya got for a hungry and homeless veteran?" He reached across Mary and grabbed her purse. She tried to take it back, but the panhandler's scent wasn't the only thing that was strong. He ripped it from Mary's grip and began rifling through the purse, right there on the hood of the car.

Bob scrambled to his feet. "Hey! Gimme that!"

The panhandler whirled and punched Bob smack in the face, sprawling him onto the sidewalk. In a twinkling, the man produced a sharpened screwdriver and pounced on Bob. He held the sharpened edge flat against Bob's terrified face, just under his eye, pushing skin against bone and threatening to slice through with the next increase in pressure. "Want me to cut you a new asshole, asshole?" the man asked.

The natives passing by acted as if they didn't see what was happening. Kitty Genovese lived, so to speak.

Before Bob could answer the panhandler's presumably rhetorical question, the Pinto's door blew open and dented the side of the panhandler's smelly head. WHACK! The screwdriver rolled into a sewer grate.

Mary leapt from the car, grabbed her purse, and pounced on the now-senseless beggar. She punctuated her words by pounding his head against the sidewalk, "I…don't…have…a…dollar… to…my…name…you…son…of…a…bitch!"

Bob struggled to his feet and pulled Mary off the stunned man, who sat up, wide-eyed. "Jesus, lady, you gotta problem!"

"Damn right I do! You wanna fight about it?"

Bob held Mary like a rabid dog pulling hard on her leash. He threatened the beggar. "Better leave before I let her go."

Confident they wouldn't actually have to intervene or otherwise get involved, passersby gathered to watch. Someone from the crowd yelled, "Let her go!" Another voice put 20 bucks on the woman to win. There were no takers.

The panhandler gathered himself and rose from the sidewalk. "She's an animal! I feel sorry for you mister!"

"Don't. She eats less than a Rottweiler," Bob said.

The panhandler stumbled away. The crowd, disappointed they didn't get to see some sidewalk justice, dispersed.

Mary was a jangle of nerves.

"Are you okay, honey?" Bob asked as he smoothed her hair.

"Yeah, I guess. How about you?"

"Yeah, I'm alright." he said as he rubbed his head.

Bob and Mary looked at each other, shook their heads, and simultaneously repeated what had become their mantra, "God, I hate this city."

Down the street, the panhandler looked back toward Bob and Mary mumbling, "Man, I hate this town."

Chapter Eighteen

Katy had the television on in the Bug Room and was watching a gratuitously violent program involving a desperate and horrible struggle between a shotgun-wielding dimwit with a speech impediment, and a burrowing, old-world mammal of the hare family. "I've had it with you, you siwwy wabbit!" the deranged hunter screeched before leveling a twelve-gauge at his victim.

Katy was taking a break from a school project while Bob and Mary were out.

The siwwy wabbit anthropomorphically stuck his finger into the end of the shotgun as the demented sportsman squeezed the trigger. BAM! Katy laughed at the blackened face of Mr. Fudd.

Two days earlier, Katy's teacher had assigned a different animal to each student and asked for a report on Monday. As soon as *Looney Tunes* were over, Katy would get right back to work on it.

As her teacher meted out the animals, Katy hoped for something dangerous like an alligator or a shark. At first she was disappointed when her teacher assigned her the Honeybee (*Apis mellifera*), but then she remembered the hive of *"Abelhas assassinas"* that lived in the white box in the window of the Bug Room. They were not only honeybees, but KILLER honeybees!

Katy became even more excited about the assignment when she found a book called *The Killer Bees* by Anthony Potter.

The book was about the African Honeybees (*Apis mellifera adansonnii*) Dr. Warwick Kerr transported to Brazil in 1956.

Katy's telling of the story involved a greedy old scientist who brought these really mean African bees to Brazil because they made more honey than Brazilian bees, and more honey meant more money. One day, somebody who had to be a real bonehead let the African queen bees out of the hives and they spread all over South America and killed everyone in sight.

Katy thought it was very cool, in a gross kind of way, that the killer bees attacked in huge swarms, and when the victims screamed the bees flew into their mouths and during autopsies on the victims they found dozens of bees in their stomachs! Wow!

She also thought it was pretty neat that African bee venom was twice as potent as American bee venom and that it had a neurotoxin that boring old American bee venom didn't have. The worst American bees could do was mess up your respiratory system, which was easily treated with antihistamines and adrenaline. But nerve damages. Wow! That's cool!

African bee venom was so powerful the U.S. Army experimented with the stuff at their Chemical-Biological Warfare Center at Edgewood Arsenal, even though they denied it. They had even isolated one component of the venom, something called Phospholipase A, which was also found in cobra, coral snake, and rattlesnake venom—so you knew it had to be good.

Katy's informative, if partially fictionalized, research paper would end with a somewhat overstated conclusion that soon millions of Americans would be found dead and bloated in the Southwest desert from thousands of bee stings with lots of bees still buzzing in their stomachs.

As the teacher would be expecting Katy's report to focus more on honey production and the use of bees as crop pollinators, she would doubtless send Katy to the school psychologist, who, after the usual battery of tests, would pronounce that Katy was okay, but desensitized from watching too much televised violence. "You siwwy psykawagist!" BAM! Ha, ha, ha.

During a commercial break, Katy looked into the bugquarium with the Western Corsairs (*Rasahus thoracicus*), another species of Assassin Bug that was part of Bob's experiment.

The Western Corsair was a remorseless killer with an uncanny instinct for ferreting out concealed quarry. Its head elongated past the eyes and sported two curious beaded antennae. When not in use, its curved rostrum was tucked neatly underneath in a cross-ridged groove between the forelegs; at killing time, the rostrum flicked into action like an angry, sucking switchblade.

Its amber-colored thorax was powerful and squatty; at the abdomen it widened slightly and darkened to a rich golden brown, rounding nicely at its bristly cercus. The Western Corsair was important to Bob's research because it attacked not only adult pests but also savored eggs and larvae of various destructive insects. Bob hoped to cross-breed this trait to a roach killer.

Katy tapped on the bugquarium, just to stir the Corsairs up. She enjoyed getting them agitated because she thought the way they scurried around poking at each other was pretty funny.

She was tapping at the glass again when the doorbell rang.

She opened the door to find the cheap cigar on the front stoop—in the mouth of the always foul Dick Pratt.

"Hi, Mr. Pratt," Katy said. "Did you decide to buy some cookies after all?"

Pratt scowled. "Blow me, kid. Where's the deadbeat?"

"He's not a deadbeat," Katy said in defense of her father. "He went to work on a job. So don't worry, he's gonna pay you."

"Yo, ya damn right he's gonna pay me!" Pratt said as he jabbed a stubby finger at Katy. "'Cause if he don't, yer gonna find yer little pink ass out on the sidewalk!"

For a moment Pratt considered smacking Katy across the face, just to let her know he was in charge, but he decided he wanted a beer more than that so he turned and stormed off.

Katy thought for a moment before speaking.

"Wait. Mr. Pratt? I've got some money."

Pratt froze. He turned slowly.

"Yeah?"

It was an ugly sight; a grown man on his knees, counting the coins that lay among the shards of a Girl Scout's broken piggy bank. As the smoke from his cheap cigar curled into his eyes, Pratt looked unhappy. He turned to Katy. "This all you got?"

Chapter Nineteen

The pile of extermination equipment Bob had stacked near the side entrance of *Maison Henri* included several large metal canisters covered with skull-and-crossbones and Mr. Yuck stickers, indicating the canisters were filled with noxious toxins.

Bob had brought these for Mary's benefit. His real arsenal was hidden among his myriad tools of chemical extermination—several shoe-box sized containers with a blood-red "ASSASSINS, STRAIN ZERO" stenciled on the sides.

Strain Zero was a cross between the Western Corsair and the Thread-legged Bug; these hybrids had inherited their elongated coxa and spined femur from their mother. They had the most unusual body type of all the strains—a powerful and squatty thorax of amber perched on dark, thin, but surprisingly strong limbs, sort of like Danny DiVito's trunk perched on Manute Bol's legs.

Bob knocked on the back door and was let into the kitchen by Henri himself.

"*Bon jour,*" said Henri. "You have brought your murderous insects, I trust?"

He bent over and tapped at the side of the box. The Thread-Legged Corsairs made an angry squeaking noise. Henri jumped back and brushed his hands.

"I wouldn't get too close if I were you," Bob warned. "These guys are pissed about being in these boxes and they're hungry enough to eat the ass end out of a dead skunk, if you know what I mean."

"*Ma foi*," Henri uttered as if the image had somehow violated him. He peeked again at the squeaking insects, then eyed Bob suspiciously before disappearing through the back door, leaving Bob to do his work.

Bob went into the main dining room and set his bug boxes on a table for four. He dropped his tool kit onto the floor. From the tool kit he removed a drill, a three-foot length of three-quarter-inch clear plastic tubing, and a container of putty. Then, with his industrial-strength neoprene knee pads hitched tightly around his knees cutting off the circulation and making his feet all tingly, Bob spent the day introducing his Strain Zero hybrids to the wall spaces of *Maison Henri* while dreaming of his future.

Chapter Twenty

The Pinto belched gun-blue cracked-ring smoke as it hauled Mary back across the Queensboro Bridge. She was somewhere above the West Channel of the East River, dreaming a dream of her own about how far the money from the *Maison Henri* job would go toward maintaining her excellent credit rating and some new panty hose. Yet something nagged at her.

Despite Bob's promise to use poison, she wondered if she should have stayed and supervised…just to make sure.

Midway across the span, high above Roosevelt Island, Mary glanced to her right at Goldwater Memorial Hospital, knowing that's where Bob would end up if he ignored her edict to use copious amounts of poison at *Maison Henri*.

Chapter Twenty-one

The lunchtime crowd at the trendy bistro was well-heeled and hungry. The polite clank of silver on china barely covered the sounds of mastication as diners devoured *bisque de homard* and *selle de veau*.

Strain Zero had been on the job for ten days. Bob, wearing a snappy khaki jumpsuit, and Henri, in his traditional chef's whites, toured the chic eatery to see if the Assassin Bugs had been equal to the task.

They first inspected the private dining room, unused at lunchtime. It was immaculate. Henri watched as Bob probed and peered into some dark places where roaches would be hiding. Not a bug in sight. For that matter, there were no hybrids in evidence either, but that didn't matter to Henri. They passed through the busy main room, giving it only a cursory glance on their way toward the kitchen.

"Well, Henry," Bob said confidently. "It looks like we got the little buggers, doesn't it?"

A fleshy dowager, her mouth stuffed with *Souffle Rothschild*, looked up when she heard the khaki jumpsuit speak to the chef's whites. Her concerned look said she was paying for something more authentic than "Henry."

"Ez I hiv tuld yu, ma neme is Ahn-ree," Henri said with a curled lip and an accent thicker than pate. "Ahn-ree, Monsieur bug-person. I am from *Anjou*."

Ahn-ree leaned down to the stocky doyen and whispered in an exaggerated tone, *"Mauvais quart d'heure,"* as if to say this was an uncomfortable moment which would be over quickly.

She nodded knowingly, though she had no idea what the Frenchman had said.

As Henri spun and headed toward the kitchen to continue the inspection, Bob, much to his dismay, spotted a particularly large Brown-Banded Tropical cockroach (*Supella supellectillium*) doing the achy-breaky across an otherwise unoccupied table. Bob quickly scooped the offending specimen into his pocket and whacked his thigh with an open palm.

CRUNCH!

Bob whiffed the odor from the pulverized roach and fanned the air in the hopes that Ahn-ree would not get wind of his failure.

Henri entered the kitchen and was inspecting the prep area when Bob saw another pair of large, mottled wings, their reddish-brown hue indicating a female. With practiced precision, Bob scooped, pocketed, and whacked her stinging his thigh with the force of his slap. CRUNCH! Henri quickly turned to see what the commotion was about.

Bob, who was again fanning the air, acted as if he were trying to keep cool. "Awfully hot in here, Ahn-ree. What do have those ovens set at, five hundred degrees?"

Ahn-ree paused as he smelled something rotten, but dismissed it as bleu cheese.

Soon his inspection was complete and the Frenchman was satisfied. "Well, it seems your *methode du naturel* has rid me of my problem. Come to ze office and I will pey you ze balance of your fee."

Bob smiled, thinking he was home free. He began visualizing his truck with the big fiberglass bug on top until, suddenly, with heartbreaking shrillness, one of the cooks screamed and recoiled in horror, shattering Bob's reverie.

Bob and Henri rushed over to a pot of vichyssoise, which, to Bob's chagrin, now served as an Olympic-sized swimming pool for roaches. Several of the 55 known species were represented in the pool, and it appeared the Australian Cockroach (*Periplaneta australasiae*) was winning with a nice crawl stroke.

Henri, not a sports fan, reacted. "*Merdel Mon dieul Ami de court Un tour de cochon!*" Bob knew very little French, but could tell by Henri's tone that he was not happy with the soup recipe. Desperate, he turned the flame on under the pot.

"Ah ha! Die, you little bastards!" Bob yelled as he turned to Henri. "This is the last step of my method, Ahn-ree. My Assassins have chased them from their hiding places and herded them into one large container so we can ..." His speech fizzled out. The entire kitchen staff stared, gape-jawed. Bob knew he was French toast, but he wasn't ready to quit just yet.

"You know," Bob said as he fished one of the roaches out of the pot, "these things are great with snails."

Henri was not amused. Bob finally gave it up.

The math was quite simple; that was the good news. Bob totaled his checkbook balance:

$$\$512.47$$
$$\underline{-500.00}$$
$$12.47$$

When the subtraction was complete, Bob handed the $500 check to an impatient and perturbed Henri. "There," Bob said weakly. "Your deposit."

Henri ceremoniously slapped Bob on both cheeks with the check, then turned and huffed away.

Bob stood there, crestfallen. Notwithstanding the two insects he had stuffed into his pocket, he had really thought he'd done it. He'd really believed he'd created a strain of Assassin that had completely debugged a commercial building—and a restaurant of all places! He should have known better than to be so encouraged by a daytime inspection. In fact, for roaches to appear during the day at all, they had to be forced out by a population explosion. What were his Assassin Bugs doing? Bob envisioned his hybrids conducting seminars on reproduction in the wall spaces.

Bob was leaving the kitchen when a waiter approached, nose in the air, carrying two large, leafy salads on his tray. Bob couldn't resist. He reached into his pocket and tossed his two multi-legged "croutons" into the salads.

As he stood on the sidewalk, the screams from inside told him someone had been disappointed with the *barbe-de-capucin*. He smiled guiltily as he headed for the subway, trying to figure out what went wrong and how the hell he would explain things to Mary.

Chapter Twenty-two

After three double shifts in five days, Mary was in a defeated and foul mood. The house looked like the Gaza Strip and she was determined to clean it up. As she vacuumed with her right hand, she lifted a cheap end table with her left. Clunk! A leg fell off. Exasperated, Mary stared at her new tripod, tempted to chew the other three legs off. She was frustrated, tired, and hungry. Low blood sugar was making her especially edgy.

Unfortunately for Bob, he walked in the front door just at this moment. "Great news, sweetheart!" he announced.

Mary couldn't help herself, she was still a sucker for Bob and his positive attitude. She turned off the vacuum.

"You did it? You got paid? Oh honey, that's wonderful! I'll call Mr. Pratt and we can…"

"Well, slow down," Bob said. "I didn't exactly get paid." Mary hoped she heard wrong. Maybe Bob said he wanted to get laid.

"But what a fantastic learning experience!" Bob said as he put his arm around Mary's shoulder. "I think that's the best way for us to look at this."

Mary was floored. Her Gibraltar-like support of Bob, weakened by the eroding effects of his failures, was about to collapse like a muddy hillside in Southern California.

"Bob, I told you to use the poison," Mary said.

"I know, but think about it like this, sweetheart, we've eliminated one of the strains. Don't underestimate how important that is! Though to be frank, I really thought this strain would work. It tested great in the lab."

Mary hoisted the broken table leg in blunt object fashion.

"Now, honey, let's not do anything rash," Bob pleaded as he backed toward the wall. "Let's look at the positive side…"

"Are you out of your goddamn mind? There is no goddamn positive side," Mary screeched, using more profanity in two sentences than she normally used in two months. "You promised me you'd use poison!"

"I know, but…"

Mary stopped, the table leg dangling limply from her hand. She felt like Bob had cheated on her. "You lied to me," she said.

The table leg dropped to the floor with a muffled thump, crushing a small Black Carpet Beetle (*Attagenus megatoma*) between the rug and the padding.

"Honey, I had a reason," Bob said. "If I eliminated—"

"No." Mary interrupted. "It's very simple. You lied."

Mary calmly headed upstairs. Too calmly. Zenlike. She called out for Katy to pack a suitcase. Bob followed her to the bedroom, where Mary hurled a suitcase onto the bed and began stuffing it with clothes.

"C'mon, honey, I know what you're thinking," Bob pleaded. "We've been through this before. Right now the only thing you can see is our checking account balance."

"Ahhh," Mary said, "the checking account balance." She stopped packing and fixed Bob with a stare. "What is it now, $12.47? Perhaps it's time we buy that cottage in the Hamptons we've had our eye on for so long."

Mary closed the suitcase and yelled down the hall, "Katy, come downstairs as soon as you're packed!"

Bob trailed Mary as she huffed downstairs with her suitcase. "I swear I thought it would work. Even if it didn't, I thought he'd give me a chance to try again with poison."

At the bottom of the stairs Mary put her suitcase down. "You lied to me," she said.

"I know, honey, and I'm sorry," Bob said. "Really, I am."

"Follow me," Mary said. She turned and stalked to the Bug Room, Bob close behind. She went to the computer and grabbed Jiminy, Ringo, and Slim—Bob's dried insect mascots.

"Don't worry, I'm not going to hurt them," Mary said just before dropping them on the floor and crushing them into dust.

"Oh, I lied," Mary said. "Sorry about that, honey. Really, I am." She looked down at the pulverized invertebrates and reacted with mock surprise. "Looks like that apology didn't change a thing."

Mary turned and stormed out of the room. Bob followed.

Thump. Thump. Thump. Katy dragged her suitcase down the stairs. Katy was determined to make her parents stop fighting. "Guess what?" Katy said. "I got an A-plus on my killer bee report!"

"That's nice," said Mary. "Now wait outside."

"Don't you want to know what I learned about bees?"

"Not right now, sweetheart," Bob said. "Maybe later."

But Katy didn't want to wait until later. "You know how they have new bees?"

"Katy, wait outside," Mary said.

She refused. "A queen and a drone mate in midair, then they fall to the ground," Katy continued. "And to free herself, the queen has to pull the male gen-a-tail-ya from his body. I bet that hurts, don't you?"

Bob and Mary were struck speechless by the image of midair copulation.

Katy had theorized that her parents would stop fighting if they had to discipline her, so she set about earning her punishment by continuing about the genitalia.

"So the queen has this icky guy thing stuck in her, right? So what's she supposed to do? I mean, she can't fly around with one of those things, 'cause then she'd be the king instead of the queen, so she gets the workers to help her pull it out. Then she has some babies or eggs or larva or something."

"Where did you get that?" Mary snapped at her.

"It was in one of Daddy's books," Katy said.

"It's true," Bob said. "That's how they mate."

"Katy! Outside! Now!" Mary barked.

Katy knew one-word sentences meant it was time to comply. She reluctantly went out the door.

"We've been over this, Bob," Mary said. "You have to accept your responsibilities! There's no time for dreaming anymore. Have you forgotten that we're behind on our rent?"

Bob's look said, "I wish you wouldn't rub it in."

"If we can't even pay rent," Mary continued, "how do you expect to save money for Katy's college education, huh? How?"

"That's why I'm doing this," Bob said. "I could work for Bug-Off for the rest of my life and we'd still never have the money for Katy to go to college. You have to be a doctor or a lawyer or a plumber to get ahead these days. Dickheads working for other dickheads live paycheck-to-paycheck, treading water. You have to be your own boss to make enough money."

Mary's business degree and knowledge of rising tuition costs told her Bob was right. But treading water was better than drowning.

Mary opened the door and Katy fell into the front hall, her little ear having been pressed to the door. She smiled innocently.

"Besides, Mary, you promised to give me two months."

"And you promised you'd use the poison."

Bob didn't have a snappy comeback to that.

"At least Katy will get fed at Mother's," Mary said, her voice dripping with sarcasm as she prepared to leave.

"I'm not hungry," Katy said, siding with her dad.

"Yes you are," Mary informed her.

"Mary, I'm doing this because I love you and I don't want to end up retiring thirty years from now with nothing more than a brass rat trap and a pat on the back. Would Katy be proud of that? Would you?"

"No way," Katy said. "I'd be totally embarrassed."

"This isn't about down the road, Bob," Mary said. "This is about now."

A cab pulled to the curb and Mary hefted the suitcases. "You know Mom's number."

"Honey, please. Don't leave."

Mary put down the suitcases and hugged her husband.

"Bob, you know Katy and I love you more than anything, but you've got to stop gambling with our future. I'm through living hand-to-mouth. You've got to pull yourself together and look at the big picture."

"Mary, I need your help if I'm going to make this work. Please don't go. Please."

Mary took Katy's hand and led her toward the cab.

Katy was near tears. "Bye, Daddy. I love you." She broke free from her mother's hand and ran to Bob, who hugged her.

"I love you too, Doodlebug. And don't worry, it'll be alright."

Mary fought back her own tears. She didn't want to do this, but it was the only way she could get through to Bob. She went to Katy and took her hand again. It was a terrible moment as Mary led her daughter down the walkway to the cab.

Bob followed a few steps, trembling the way he did whenever he got pulled over by the police for speeding. The doors slammed and the cab pulled away heading for Astoria Boulevard. The last thing Bob saw as the cab faded away was Katy waving good-bye and wiping a tear from her sad, little face. Bob waved back weakly and then they were gone, the cab heading north under the pall of approaching storm clouds.

It had come to this, Bob thought. Mary leaving him because he wanted to pursue his dream.

No, that wasn't fair. It wasn't his dream that made her leave. She was stressed because they had no money and Bob had lied to her.

But wasn't there a bright side to all this? Sure, she was mad at him now, she had every right to be, but that would pass. Besides, Mary could use some time off and Katy always liked visiting her grandma. With them gone, Bob would be free to work on his experiments and maybe make this thing happen. Then Mary would come back and things would be alright. Hell, when he thought about it, this was a blessing in disguise.

But his optimism rang hollow, even in his own head. Bob had lied to the one person who believed in him; he drove her out and now he was trying to rationalize the results.

Whenever Bob had to mull things over he went to his Bug Room and sat in the beat up old swivel chair. He took as much comfort in the eerie blue lights as his bugs did. As he listened to the pitter and chirp of the crickets, he realized they were somewhere in the baseboards. The crickets must have escaped and taken up residence in the wall space.

He checked the crickets bugquarium, but there were no signs of an escape. Perhaps the ones in the baseboard had come to free the others. Screw it, he thought, he'd worry about that later. Right now he had bigger problems.

Bob wondered if he would have to abandon his dream in order to get Mary back. He wondered if Katy would be emotionally scarred for life by this little melodrama. And, as the crickets in the baseboard continued chirping, he wondered if they were communicating with their colleagues in the bugquariums. If so, what was the message?

As Bob contemplated these questions, he fingered Mary's gold locket. Maybe he'd mail it to her with a letter begging her forgiveness. In the letter he would include a renewed promise to use heptachlor or chlordane the next time he got a job. After all, what was a little exposure to carcinogens when compared to his marriage? His experiments could wait.

Bob was beginning to sort things out for himself when the doorbell rang. Bob reluctantly got up and answered it.

"So you think I'm jokin' about this rent money or what?"

"Listen, Dick," Bob said with an edge in his voice. "Since I lost my job, things have gotten pretty tough."

"Tough? Yeah, I bet. Especially with your wife packin' up and leavin'…and who can blame her? Who'd wanna be stuck with a limp-dick like you?"

"Look, that's none of your goddamn business."

Pratt stepped close to Bob and began poking him in the chest with his index finger as he lectured. "Hey, I ain't here for shits and grins, pal. I got a UPS package at my house with your name on it and you ain't gettin' it till I see some goddamn green! You still owe me three-twenty, you useless douche bag!"

Bob was tired of Pratt's verbal abuse and, since he wasn't expecting anything from UPS, he spoke with some extra bravado. "Keep the goddamn package," Bob said. "It's probably my Publishers Clearinghouse money."

"Funny guy. You know, you're a real scumbag, Dillon. You can't keep a pissant job more than a couple of months at a time, so you got your own kid out there sellin' cookies to pay your rent. Whatta friggin' loser."

Bob had no idea what Pratt meant by that and he was afraid to ask.

Pratt turned to leave, then he stopped and turned back to Bob. "Oh, yeah," he said, "that 24 bucks your kid gave me… consider it interest on what you owe."

Now Bob understood. He stood at the front door, paralyzed with shame, his doleful expression not unlike that of Burt Hooten after Reggie Jackson hit that first home run in the bottom of the fourth in game six of the '77 World Series. Even the Bug Room wouldn't console him now. Finally he roused himself to go for a walk.

The storm clouds were moving in and Bob could smell the impending rain. As he shuffled down Twenty-First Street looking like a dejected member of the Dodger's pitching staff, he saw a Birch Skeletonizer (*Bucculatrix canadensisella*), bright brown, its wings crossed with silvery white bars. Perched on the oak tree, it munched contentedly. Bob felt a large, warm drop of liquid land on his head. When he heard the rolling thunder and saw the black clouds he knew a hard rain was going to fall.

The swollen drop tickled Bob's scalp as it rolled toward his neck. He thought about turning around and going home instead of skulking down the streets in a downpour, but he decided the latter tableau would suit his dampened mood, so he resolved to get wet.

More thunder in the distance coincided with a ravenous growl from Bob's stomach. He had been so preoccupied with Mary and Katy leaving and the visit from Pratt that he hadn't eaten all day. Now he was hungry.

Ahead, an unpleasant-looking hot dog vendor worked the corner. Bob approached just as the surly weenie merchant decided to call it a day. The man was eager to close shop before the flood, so he waited impatiently, tapping his tongs peevishly against the relish container as Bob groped around in his pockets for some change. When Bob came up with nothing but rabbit ears, the vendor plopped Bob's pink weenie back into the water and hurried away for cover. Bob's stomach growled like an angry little shih tzu.

The downpour began in earnest. Buckets of rain indulged Bob's desire for a scene *pathetique*, so he walked on, trying to decide whether to abandon his dream to get back the women he loved.

That's when he noticed the sign just ahead:

THE BEEBE AVENUE MISSION
LEAVE YOUR TROUBLES AT THE DOOR
ALL WELCOME FOR SOUP AND SERVICES

Not one for religious services, Bob stood on the sidewalk considering the offer of soup. But before he made up his mind, the door opened and a sturdy black woman with an odd scar above her left eye, near the bridge of her nose, looked out at Bob.

She shook her head like a disapproving mother and smiled a big friendly smile. "Child, you better get in out of that rain before you catch your death."

"Huh?" Bob hadn't heard what she said.

"Come in," she said. "I'll give you shelter from this here storm."

Bob accepted the offer and stepped into the mission, where it was warm and dry and clean and the soup smelled good.

"I've never been in one of these," he said self-consciously.

"Nothing to be 'shamed about. Lotsa proud folks in here eatin' my soup; enjoyin' it too."

"It sure smells good," Bob said.

"Yes it does," Gertrude said, looking Bob over. He appeared hungry and defeated like most of the men and women she helped. "Looks like you been waiting for that trickle-down money them Republicans promised a while back. Mos' folks come in here, only trickle-down they know is they jus' got peed on." Gertrude laughed and got a smile out of Bob. "There you go. I knowed they was a smile in there somewhere."

Gertrude continued her political analysis. "'Course, now we got that Democrat in the office. That nice Mr. Clinton and all those promises he made...I expect I'll be outta bidness any minute now the way he say he's gonna fix everything up, so you better hurry and help me get rid of some of this soup."

She wiped her hand on her apron, then held it out to Bob. "My name's Gertrude, what's yours?"

"I'm Bob," he said, stepping out of the puddle that had formed at his feet.

"Come on and have some soup, Bob."

Bob hesitated; he felt awkward.

"What's wrong?" Gertrude asked.

"I don't have any money."

Gertrude reacted in mock horror. "Whoo, mercy! That is a problem. Yo ain't gcttin' no window table then!" She laughed at her own theatrics.

"No, really," Bob said, "I'd feel bad eating your soup since I can't pay for it."

Gertrude sized him up before seizing on a way around this problem. "Okay, that's fair enough. I'll let you work it off, but I wanna gets my money's worth outta you, so you're gonna have to eat first, otherwise you be too weak to work."

Gertrude served Bob a bowl of soup and a large piece of sweet corn bread cooked in a cast-iron skillet. They chatted as Bob fed the shih tzu in his belly. Gertrude, it turned out, was originally from Yazoo City, Mississippi, but had moved to New York soon after the good people of that state elected a governor named Clay Scaggs, whom she described as a dirt-farming, tobacco-chewing, white-trash peckerheaded redneck cracker with less mental horsepower than a broke-down mule.

She moved to New York to get away from all the South stood for and because she had friends there. The scar above her left eye was from her childhood. She was hit by a rock thrown during what was supposed to be a dirt-clod fight. When she got home, her mother sewed up the resulting gash with a needle and thread. The result was a funny cockeyed look that made Bob wonder whether her left eye ever closed completely.

After mollifying the noisy mutt in his stomach, Gertrude took Bob to the kitchen, which was filled with massive stockpots and battered old skillets that needed washing. While they cleaned, Bob told Gertrude all his problems. He explained why he quit his last job, and how he had this idea to kill insects with other insects, and how he wanted to get his own truck with a fiber-glass bug on top.

He also told her about the woman from Con Ed coming by to turn off their electricity. "So what was I supposed to do?" Bob asked rhetorically. "We pretty much have to have electricity, right?"

"That's right," Gertrude said.

"So I sold some records at one of those used record stores."

"Ain't that a shame," Gertrude said.

"I sold my 'Superfly' soundtrack plus my entire 'Iron Butterfly' collection, including the 'Metamorphosis' album, just to get enough to make the minimum payment. But at least they didn't cut off the power."

"You did the right thing, child," Gertrude said.

Bob told Gertrude about how upset Mary was when she found out he lied about using the poison at *Maison Henri*, and how she took Katy and left that morning and Katy was crying. And he was ashamed when he learned that Katy had given Pratt her twenty-four dollars in Girl Scout cookie money. As Bob blathered, Gertrude listened patiently, occasionally interjecting "uh huh" and "I know what choo mean" and "I heard that."

Bob picked up a large pot and started scrubbing. Gertrude stood next to him, drying a pan.

"Sounds like she jus' worried 'bout Katy, that's all," Gertrude said. "I think she loves you a lot."

"You really think so?" Bob asked.

They stopped working for a minute as Gertrude spoke.

"Honey, I know so. I can tell. You a good man. You jus' gotta get this bug thing workin' and start payin' the bills and she'll be back jus' like that!" Gertrude snapped her fingers.

"I hope so," Bob said.

Gertrude put her big pink-palmed hand on Bob's shoulder. "Listen to me. You got somethin' burnin' in you that I try to git lit agin in everybody that comes in here. And that's a dream. Without your dream, you got nothin'. Lord knows this city's as bad to dreamers as the South is to a nigger. It tries to kick the dream out of everybody what's got one, but don't you let it die. You gotta make it happen. And you can do that."

They turned back to the pots and pans.

Bob was curious. "What's your dream?" he asked.

Gertrude laughed. She spoke without looking up. "To fix all them broken dreams out there." Gertrude turned to Bob, a twinkle in her cocked eye. She winked the one that would close.

By the time the kitchen was clean, Bob had decided to take Gertrude's advice and go home and spend some time in the Bug Room, trying to get his bug thing workin'.

Gertrude helped him with his jacket.

"Thanks for the soup, Gertrude. I—"

Gertrude cut him off. "You jus' get out there and do what you gotta do. That's my thanks. Don't you worry, it'll all work out. I know about these things."

Bob paused for a moment, smiled, then gave Gertrude a hug before heading back up the street toward home.

Chapter Twenty-three

Wolfe rifled through the large pile of documents stacked on his desk. Parker stood by, listening attentively to his mentor.

"Birth certificate, high school transcripts, tax returns, marriage license...this is the best goddamn cover I've ever seen," Wolfe said.

He gestured across the hall with his head. "Those chuckle-heads over in witness protection don't get nearly this detailed. Of course, that's why most of those people end up dead. We've got to get this Dillon guy on the payroll. And look at this," Wolfe said conclusively as he stabbed at Bob's file with a meaty index finger, "absolutely no travel records. He doesn't even have a passport, for chrissake! Makes it look like he's never even left the city. This guy is very, very good. And you know what I like best about him?"

"No sir," Parker said obligingly.

"I'll tell you. He's a traditionalist, none of that high-tech crap for this guy, no sir." He jabbed at another document in the file. "See this? He works with poisons. I like a man who works with poison. By God, I'd be willing to bet he doesn't use one of those pussy laser sights when he does a shoot. I bet he just lines 'em up in the old crosshairs and...Pop!" Wolfe smacked his hands together and smiled at the thought of a good, old-fashioned killer.

"What about the Madari and Pescadores assassinations?" Parker asked. "Do you think this guy did them?"

"That's where the good money is," Wolfe said as he leaned back in his chair. "Look, no one else has taken credit for them and they were both every bit as clean as the Huweiler hit. I think it's safe to say they were 'exterminated' and, if that's true, then this guy is making a serious assault on the top ten hit man parade. In fact, it's starting to look like our old friend Klaus may soon find himself replaced as king of the hill."

A young, low-level security clearance employee, possibly an intern or maybe a Junior Achievement placement, entered the office carrying a batch of albums and cassette tapes.

"Excuse me, sir, someone said you wanted these Dylan records?"

Wolfe stared at the intern and worried that he represented the future of intelligence gathering. Oh, what the hell, he thought, it really wouldn't be any worse than what they'd had in the past. He gestured for the kid to put the stuff on his credenza.

Chapter Twenty-four

As the cab hurtled northward on the Bronx River Parkway, the driver cursed under his breath in a Punjabi dialect at the White Admiral Butterflies (*Limenitis arthemis*) splattered on his windshield. The profanities grew louder as he tried to wash them off with the windshield wipers, causing them to smear messily on the glass. He groused at the thought of having to dislodge the winged beasts from the grill of his cab. As the driver swore at the smashed *Lepidopteras*—unaware that the name came from Greek words meaning "scale" and "wing"—a large, unidentified bug smacked into the windshield with a frightful slap, startling him and prompting more obscenities. Allah's name was eventually taken in vain.

Katy had regained her perspective on her parents' argument, and the bugs on the windshield reminded her of a joke.

"Mom, do you know what's the last thing that goes through a bug's head when it hits a windshield?"

"No, honey, I don't," Mary replied, only halfway paying attention.

"His butt." Katy laughed. "Get it? His butt?"

"Yes, I get it." Mary rolled her eyes and smiled. "Thank you for sharing that with me, honey."

Mary stared out the window and thought about Bob. Yes, he had lied to her, but his intentions were good. He wasn't pursuing this for his own gain; he wanted to provide for them and accomplish something they could be proud of. She also knew he couldn't, with a clear conscience, keep poisoning the planet with parathion and disulfoton and methamidophos. Who could?

Was one lie the limit of Mary's love for her dreamer? No, that wasn't it. It was the money. If they weren't so far behind on rent, she simply would have torn a strip off him for lying. But she had no idea how far Bob was from completing his experiments. And the farther away he was, the farther behind they'd get in rent payments.

Mary knew the importance of money. That's why she studied finance in college. College. Those were the days—when being poor wasn't a problem; it was an art form.

She remembered her second date with Bob. Like most college students, he didn't have the resources for fancy restaurants, so he took Mary to the IHOP that night, followed by a folk entomology lecture sponsored by his department.

The lecturer pointed out that with the exception of bats (the only true flying mammal) only two types of animals shared the gift of flight—birds and insects. But whereas the bird's ability to fly had elevated it to godlike status in cultures around the world (the Phoenix, for example); insects were not so well treated by the myth makers. The obvious exception was the Scarab Beetle (*Scarabaeus sacer*) of ancient Egypt, which was associated with the sun god Ra.

The lecturer's theory was that since insects were more despised than deified, they were more likely to be the source of superstitions rather than the stuff of mythology. He explained that Pliny (the Elder), the famed Roman encyclopedist, was the most frequently cited source of superstitions involving insects.

As Mary listened to the catalogue of old wives' tales, Bob turned to her occasionally with exaggerated expressions of horror, surprise, or disgust. He liked to make Mary laugh and he usually succeeded.

Mary recalled fondly that she let Bob kiss her good-night after that date, and kiss her he did, long and hard. She might even have let him cop a feel.

Suddenly, another unidentified bug slapped the windshield with a frightening smack bringing Mary back to the cab as it hurtled northward toward Tarrytown. She had let Bob kiss her many times in the intervening years and she didn't have a body part he hadn't touched. But now he had lied to her, and now she had left him. And now she hoped only that she was doing the right thing.

Chapter Twenty-five

According to Greek mythology, the goddess Gaea sprang from Chaos and became the mother of all things including Uranus, who became the first ruler of the universe.

In a twisted union that would make Jerry Lee Lewis blush, Gaea later married Uranus and bore him 12 children, who became known collectively as the Titans.

Cronus was the youngest Titan, who castrated and dethroned his father Uranus, whose blood fell onto earth, and produced the vengeful Furies.

Cronus then took over running the universe.

In keeping with family tradition (and the "unbroken cycle" phenomenon that happens in so many dysfunctional families), Cronus married his sister Rhea and had more (by this point, one would imagine, hideously inbred) children; among them, Zeus and Hera.

Zeus eventually became the leader of a consortium of gods who ruled the universe from Mt. Olympus, hence their name, the Olympians.

In an epic battle known as the Titanomachy, Zeus led the Olympians against the Titans and won, leaving Zeus to succeed Cronus as the supreme god and free to carry on family tradition. So he married his sister Hera.

So how is it imaginable that someone with such a polluted gene pool could become the supreme god of the universe? That's where this gets interesting.

According to legend, Rhea gave birth to Zeus in a cave belonging to sacred bees. The bees became the nursemaids of Zeus and he was raised on their divine honey, which had miraculous purifying powers. Nourished, and presumably cleansed by this sacred, magical honey, Zeus eventually became the symbol of power, rule, and law; the rewarder of good and punisher of evil.

The sacred cave of Zeus' birth was on the island of Crete, which lay in the Eastern Mediterranean marking the southern limit of the Aegean Sea. Roughly half a million people lived on Crete these days, among those was an assassin named Klaus.

The spirits of the ancient Greek gods haunted the isle of Crete. As a place to live, it was an unusual choice for someone whose favorite pastime required frequent trips to the great casinos of Europe. But Klaus had lived here as a child and it still felt like home. Perhaps the spirit of Zeus comforted the souls of killers. Then again, perhaps Klaus just liked a fancy place with a nice ocean view.

As the sun set on a docked fishing boat, a group of men with lined, leathery faces tied knots in thick ropes and wrapped their fishing nets. Klaus, with several fish slung over his shoulder, stepped off the vessel, bid the others goodbye and headed up an ancient cobblestone road, exchanging pleasantries with those he passed on the way.

Everyone knew what Klaus did for a living, but they also knew his philosophy and, on balance, they felt he was a good man whose odd calling was a necessary evil in a world overstocked with immorality. In Klaus' mind, and in the minds of his fellow Cretans, the egregious violators of human rights surrendered their own right to life and thus deserved to die.

Like the ancient Greek gods at Olympus, the powerful people who hired professionals like Klaus felt compelled or obligated to look after the lives of those they perceived as powerless. These people held a bloody moral standard that accepted the killing of one corrupt soul to save many innocent ones. The likes of Idi Amin, Pol Pot, and Pinochet were fair game, but assassins who would kill a Gandhi, a Kennedy, or a Mandella were themselves to be hunted down and killed.

Klaus killed with professional detachment, never with malevolence. He didn't hate those he killed, he just believed they deserved to die, otherwise he wouldn't kill them.

His melancholy aspect implied that he didn't enjoy what he did, that he felt somehow trapped by his fate. He was a tragic figure, if not beloved, then at least pitied.

Klaus had thought a lot lately about retiring. But every time he finished a job another was presented, and Klaus would allow himself to think that this might be the one to make a difference.

So he killed again, collected his fee, and started the cycle anew. On average Klaus executed two contracts per year, all while maintaining his standard of excellence. But rumors were beginning to spread that Klaus was losing his edge and a newcomer was gunning for the number-one spot on the list.

In a way it was true—Klaus was losing his edge. He was growing increasingly tired of his pointless life. Ridding the world of scum once held a semblance of satisfaction for Klaus, but now it was merely an unfulfilling part-time job that allowed him to gamble. Gambling was the only form of self-destruction he could manage. He liked to drink, but not enough to kill himself. And true suicide, well, Klaus had considered it, but he lacked the courage. "Thus conscience doth make cowards of us all," rang in his head.

Ahead in the fading light Klaus saw his beautiful villa on the hilltop and something made him smile. He suddenly remembered a line from Scripture, specifically Romans 6:23. "The wages of sin is death," it said. Klaus thought that if the wages of sin was death, then apparently the wages of death was a nice place in the Greek islands. He chuckled at his joke as he continued up the hill.

Klaus entered his home, the fish dangling from the string still slung over his shoulder. He hesitated as something struck him as wrong, but he couldn't put his finger on what it was.

Had he left a burner going on the stove? Was the iron on? Or was someone there to kill him? It was possible. Like gunslingers from the American West of old, assassins were sometimes the targets of upstarts who wanted to make a name for themselves by proving they were the fastest gun.

Klaus wasn't sure if he had bad company or if it was just the paranoia that seemed to be growing worse with each passing day. He continued to the kitchen and set the fish in the sink.

And again the uneasy feeling that something was amiss made him look around. He caught a glimpse of movement out of the corner of his eye and he dropped to the floor just as a spray of machine gun fire ripped away at the cupboards above his head. Someone was there alright, but not to kill him, otherwise he would already be dead. No, this was apparently just a courtesy call.

When the shooting stopped, Klaus listened for a moment, then carefully poked his head around the corner. A man sitting on the sofa in the shadows of the living room spoke. "Good evening, Klaus. Are we having fish for dinner?"

Klaus stood. He recognized the voice. The man in the shadows was flanked by several thugs.

Klaus counted the sidekicks. "Well, I have some leftover *souvlaki*, but I don't think there's enough for six."

The Shadow Man spoke again. "I am curious about your payment. It's not like you to be late."

"I have your money."

"It does me no good if you have the money," the Shadow Man said peevishly.

Klaus crossed to a hidden safe and removed the briefcase of cash he had recently received from Marcel. He tossed the case to one of the thugs. "This is half of what I owe you. Things have been slow."

"Slow?" the Shadow Man asked skeptically. "It was my understanding that you passed on the Huweiler assignment."

"That is none of your concern," Klaus said.

"It concerns me greatly when someone who owes so much regularly passes on such lucrative work. I fear if you pass on any more, this new man—the Exterminator I believe he is called—he will get all of your business, and that would deprive you of the income to which I have grown accustomed."

"That is my problem," Klaus said.

"It is until it affects your ability to pay your debts, then it becomes my problem. I will return in one week. If you do not have what you owe me, that visit will not be as pleasant as this."

The Shadow Man stood and led his entourage toward the door.

"Wait!" Klaus said urgently.

The Shadow Man stopped suddenly. The members of his entourage bumped comically into one another from behind.

Klaus spoke. "I suppose this means you won't be staying for dinner?"

Chapter Twenty-six

After Mary and Katy left, Bob's life changed dramatically. Time normally shared with them was now spent in his Bug Room preparing for his big presentation to Sy Silverstein. If he was going to fail, it wouldn't be due to lack of preparation. Some days he spent as many as 18 hours with the bugs and the blue lights. He believed deeply this presentation to Mr. Silverstein would be a defining moment in his life, and so he worked relentlessly and with vengeance.

Finally, the day arrived.

They met in the Queens, New York office of Silverstein, a successful old real estate developer. It was an impressive room dominated by the largest oak desk Bob had ever seen, seven feet across and four feet deep. You could slaughter farm animals on this thing. There was a wet bar on one side of the office and a bathroom behind a door on the other. Dozens of real estate awards adorned the far wall and the expansive window behind the desk offered a stunning view of Manhattan.

Bob had an easel with charts and graphs set up in front of Sy's desk and a card table he'd brought was placed by Sy's wall of escrow tributes. Sitting on top of the table was a bugquarium, which, oddly enough, contained a dollhouse.

Bob and Sy pressed their faces to the glass of the bugquarium, looking intently into the dollhouse kitchen, which was complete with a tiny table and a Barbie doll frying rubber eggs over a bogus burner. Provoking no reaction in the plastic cook, one of the cupboard doors suddenly wiggled, threatening to burst open. A thin brown antennae emerged from under the door, then quickly withdrew. A moment later the cupboard door wiggled again, then popped open.

A large brown American cockroach emerged. Bob narrated the scene with great urgency.

"There it is!" he blurted. "Now watch!"

The roach scurried under Barbie's feet, probing rudely about her perfect thighs with its antennae. Another cupboard suddenly burst open and a large, pernicious-looking mutant insect stepped out. It was a cross between the Masked Hunter and the Wheel Bug. It appeared to have an armored coat and a palpable musculature not normally seen in the insect world.

The cockroach literally shit when it saw this killer hybrid, no doubt recognizing the stout three-segmented beak as the instrument of his impending doom.

The roach dodged desperately behind a chair, then a table leg, then tried to crawl back into the cupboard, but to no avail. The Assassin seized the roach with its powerful front legs and, in a lightning-quick movement, flipped him over. He jammed his pointy beak into the roach's soft belly and pumped him full of digesting enzymes.

The roach's legs twitched spastically, then fell still, relaxing limp to the side. It was a hideous spectacle. But it was also nature's ballet, choreographed by Bob Dillon.

Bob straightened up proudly, leaving an oily nose print on the terrarium glass. "Mr. Silverstein, meet the Assassin Bug."

Sy, short and in his seventies, stood back, obviously impressed. He nodded thoughtfully as he lit an enormous cigar without saying a word, a silent George Burns impression. He pulled once or twice on his big cheroot to get it going, then spoke. "Alright, so what you're sayin' is you're gonna turn more bugs loose in my buildings than I already got?" The years of cigar smoke made his voice sound like a wood rasp on Formica.

"More or less," Bob confessed. He knew it sounded weird.

"I like you, kid," said Sy. "You got balls comin' to me with a meshuggahna scheme like this. Balls I like."

Sy draped a withered arm over Bob's shoulder and inadvertently blew cigar smoke in Bob's face as they walked across the stately office toward Sy's magnificent desk.

Bob coughed politely as he crossed to the easel where the graphs and charts awaited their turn. Sy stopped, narrowed his eyes, and looked at Bob. "You didn't go to some goddamn business school, did you?"

"Uh, no sir," Bob said.

"Good. These punks with the fancy-schmancy MBA's don't know shit from kreplach. I'll tell ya, kid," Sy continued, "my grandkids got me recycling years ago. When I realized how much crap I'd been throwing out every week, I invested in a recycling company. Made my money back in two years. So what I'm saying is, I like this safe environment angle you got. Just run it by me one more time."

Sy took his seat behind his enormous oak desk. He looked like a wrinkled child peering over the edge of a dinner table.

"Okay," Bob began, "in 1970 there were 224 species of pesticide-resistant insects. By 1990 that number had doubled."

Bob pointed at his first graph to illustrate his point.

"The more resistant insects become," he said, "the more toxic we make the pesticides, and the more toxic we make pesticides, the more we poison the planet."

"So you're saying pesticides are eventually gonna become either useless or too dangerous to use?" Sy asked.

"Exactly," Bob said. "In fact, the makers of one popular pesticide have revised its formula 34 times in the last 29 years. See, roaches pass on pesticide resistance within just a few generations, and since they breed so fast and in such large numbers, it's hard for pesticide manufacturers to keep up."

"Riiiight," Sy mused.

"Okay, a female cockroach might lay two thousand eggs in her life, which lasts about a year. Now, if half those eggs result in females and they lay two thousand eggs each, you got two million roaches. Even if only half survive, you got a million roaches within four months. And that's from a single fertilized female."

"Oy!" Sy exclaimed. "You know, I read something about a blanket of flies in one of those books you sent me."

"The offspring of two houseflies mating in January would cover the earth by May with a blanket 50 feet thick?"

"That's it," Sy said. "That's a lot of flies."

"Of course," Bob said, "that assumed they all survived, which they don't."

Bob felt he was getting his point across, so he intensified his pitch. He slapped the back of his right hand into the palm of his left as he hurled numbers at the rumpled real estate developer.

"There are 200,000 insects for each human on the planet, that's 300 pounds of bug for each pound of person! We are so hopelessly outnumbered that the best we can hope for is peaceful coexistence."

Sy nodded and waved his cigar excitedly. "Alright, already, I'm sold. Tell me about your bugs again."

Bob went to the easel and flipped to some colorful renderings of the eight insects he was working with. "Assassin Bugs are predaceous insects. I've cross-bred eight different species in an attempt to create the perfect insect-killing machine. I tried to breed a strain that feeds exclusively on the types of insects found in urban buildings."

Sy seemed to be taking all this in, so Bob continued.

"The plan is to release these hybrids into the wall spaces of buildings where they'll kill the roaches, silverfish, and termites. They're bred so they won't bother vertebrates and they don't eat human food products. They just live in the wall-spaces eating other bugs. You never see 'em."

"Riiiight," Sy said again, not completely understanding.

Bob moved to the front of Sy's desk and leaned across toward the small grey head peering up at him.

"Now, I've got four strains of hybrids," Bob said, "but I don't know which strain will kill roaches or the others on a scale larger than these terrariums. So what I need is…"

"Buildings." This was the part Sy understood. "Buildings, I got. C'mere."

Sy pushed away from his desk and led Bob to the windows of the corner office which offered a sweeping view of Manhattan.

"Look at that, kid," Sy said with a sweeping gesturing. "I bought my first building in '36. I was 21. It was a rattrap in the Bronx. Everybody laughed." After a dramatic pause and a cloud of smoke, Sy continued. "Two hundred and seven buildings later, they ain't laughin'."

"I just need four buildings, Mr. Silverstein," Bob said with all his hopeful heart. "That's all."

"And you expect me to give you four of mine just because you got a good idea?" Sy laughed.

Bob's heart suddenly sank. Things had been going so well up to this point.

"If I had a dollar for every good idea that flopped..." Sy said without finishing his thought. "Listen, kid, a good idea's only half the battle. I'm telling you, I've seen some terrific ideas go spinning right down the crapper because that's all they were, good ideas. Let's assume for a minute you can make this crazy idea work. The bugs killing other bugs and all that." Sy returned to his chair. "The next question is, how the hell are you going to market it?"

Bob's confidence returned. "I'm glad you asked," he said as he returned to the easel and the next chart. "The first thing we have to do is change the way consumers view household pest control. Research by pesticide manufacturers shows that Americans view metaphorically as a battle of Good versus Evil."

"You don't say?" Sy sent a smoke signal from behind the desk indicating he was intrigued.

"The advertisers of household pesticides found American consumers have what they call a frontier, or cowboy, mentality." Bob sounded like a prosecutor in the midst of a passionate closing argument. "Think of the names the ad agencies created for the products—Raid!, Combat, Hot Shot, Bug Bombs, Black Flag. Research shows that images of warfare still appeal to the American military-industrial mind-set."

Sy studied the chart on the easel.

"The research also shows Americans tend to look at the world in a simple black-and-white perspective," Bob said as he turned to the next chart. "This makes things easy to categorize and makes difficult questions easier to answer. See, Americans don't like grey areas. They like Good Guys versus Bad Guys, Cops versus Robbers, Jets versus the Colts. Americans want to see themselves as the Good Guys in the struggle against the evil roaches. See, the way the advertisers sell it, the American family is clean and virtuous and the cockroach is dirty and vile. The can of Raid! is the six-shooter of the Old West or the handgun used to defend one's home against the invasion of the filthy hordes."

Bob paced like an evangelist working a tent full of faithful.

"Americans believe they have the God-given right to rid their homes of any and all living things they don't want sharing their bounty. And when Americans shoot the Bad Guy, do they want to see him crawl away? No sir!"

Bob spun quickly to face Sy, his fingers mimicking a gun. "Bang!" he said. "They want to see him die then and there, right in front of them."

Sy shook his head. "You're killing yourself, kid," he said. "What you're saying is this all-natural idea ain't gonna fly in a market that likes quick-fix aerosol answers."

Bob slapped his hand down on the desk. "Mr. Silverstein," he nearly yelled, "what was the population of the United States in 1950?"

"Why the hell are you asking me?" Sy asked. "I'm a real estate developer, not a goddamn census taker."

"There were approximately one hundred and fifty million people in the United States at that time," Bob said. "And what was America like then? Diverse? Multicultural? No sir. The 1950s was white bread and conformity. You either got in line and stayed there or you had a date with the House UnAmerican Activities Committee."

"I was there, I know what it was like," Sy said.

"In a marketplace like the United States in the 1950s," said Bob, "it was relatively easy to get rich. For example, if you sold hot dogs, all you had to do was sell all those like-minded people one kind of hot dog and you could become a weenie czar."

"Weenies schmeenies," Sy barked, "just get to your point!"

Buoyed by Sy's enthusiasm, Bob leaned across the huge oak desk toward his tiny audience.

"Today there are 260 million people in this country and conformity has lost its appeal. Choice is now the name of the game. Translated to our hot dog example that means you can make a fortune today by selling hickory-smoked turkey dogs, or Gaza Strip Kosher dogs, or low-salt fat-free diet dogs, or Long Dong Silver Foot Long dogs. It's a simple numbers game, Sy. If you can get one buck from just 20 percent of the population you'll make 50 million dollars!"

Sy could see the picture Bob was painting. "I like it," Sy said, urging Bob on to his inevitable conclusion.

"In other words," Bob continued, "the only thing necessary today is to appeal to a small percentage of the large number of consumers, and that is our strategy. Niche marketing!"

Sy stared in wonder as Bob clambered onto his desk, now towering ten feet tall on top of the huge piece of furniture. The mad prophet of pesticidal doom began shouting.

"The future belongs to those who can smell it coming, Mr. Silverstein! Our niche is environmentalism! My all-natural method will not only reduce the damage to the environment, but with the current swing toward eco-thoughtfulness and some luck, we'll make millions!"

After this extraordinary performance, Bob panted for air. He wiped the sweat from his forehead and, with a great deal of embarrassment, suddenly realized he was standing on Sy's desk.

Sy was flabbergasted by Bob's exhibition. Bob didn't know what else to say. He eased himself off the front of the desk and tried to smooth the wrinkled lease agreements he had been standing on.

Sy was as embarrassed as Bob by the events that had just transpired. They were like cousins who had unexpectedly and spontaneously made love behind a tree during a family reunion picnic. They knew it was unseemly, but they enjoyed it nonetheless, and there was an unspoken agreement that they would both pretend it hadn't happened.

Sy crossed the office to the bathroom. He spoke loudly as he washed his hands. "Listen, kid, you sold me. I got some places with so many bugs if they were payin' rent, I'd have tax problems. You can try your killer bug routine on them."

"That's perfect! That's all I need."

"Okay. Now, if it doesn't work, we're square. Right? Won't cost me a thing?" Sy emerged from the bathroom drying his hands.

"Right," Bob said.

"On the other hand, if it works, you let me franchise the thing and I'll set you up in business anywhere you want. Deal?"

"Deal," Bob said, holding out his hand.

As they shook hands, Sy continued fumigating the room with cigar smoke.

"You won't regret this, Mr. Silverstein."

Sy crossed to his computer and with a few deft keystrokes quickly printed out a contract and the terms of their agreement. Bob would conduct his Assassin Bug experiments on four of Sy's buildings: (1) an abandoned sixteen-story department store near Madison Square Garden (2) a dilapidated apartment building on the Lower Bast Side (3) a former restaurant in SoHo and (4) an old warehouse in Queens.

If it worked as planned, Bob thought, they would both fare well. If it didn't, well, Bob decided not to think about that.

Chapter Twenty-seven

There was a spring in Bob's step as he returned home from his presentation. He bounded onto the front porch and noticed one of his house numbers, the nine, lying on the doormat where Pratt had tossed it earlier. Bob picked it up, found the tiny nail that held it in place, and tried to reaffix it to the wall. Without a hammer Bob was unable to get the nail in far enough to secure the nine tightly. The top-heavy digit spun around, resulting in a six and a new address for the Dillon's.

Bob removed his shoe so he could nail the sucker in. Then he noticed a large brown sedan with black-wall tires pulling up. The irony of unmarked cars was that they stood out so. Bob wondered why the government bought them. Were they cheaper?

Parker, the young CIA agent, got out of the sedan. He approached Bob's house, warily eyeing the man with the shoe in his hand from behind his dark sunglasses.

Bob wondered if this guy might be from the Department of Fair Housing. "If you're looking for that slumlord Pratt, he lives across the street," Bob said, gesturing with his footwear.

"Mr. Dillon?" Parker queried. "Would you come with me, please?"

Bob tried to imagine what sort of mistake the Ray-Banned government employee might be making. "If you're here about those Traveling Wilburys, you've got the wrong Dylan."

"Let's go, Mr. Dillon," Parker said matter-of-factly.

Bob wasn't the kind to get into cars with strangers, so he stood his ground. "Who the hell are you? What's this about?"

Parker pulled one side of his jacket back, displaying his gun. "Please," he said firmly. "We're with the government."

The part about being with the government didn't make much difference to Bob and the "please" was completely unnecessary. All that really mattered was the large handgun in the man's shoulder holster.

"Let's go, Mr. Dillon."

Bob looked at the upside-down nine before limping warily down the walkway toward the car. He got in the back of the sedan where Mike Wolfe waited.

The sedan pulled away from the curb, the passengers riding in silence for a moment. Finally, Wolfe spoke. "So, you're the freewheelin' Bob Dillon."

"That's right," Bob replied, having heard that one before. "Who the hell are you?"

Wolfe extended his hand. "Mike Wolfe, CIA," he said.

Bob shook Wolfe's hand and nodded. "CIA," Bob replied suspiciously. He looked at Parker and gestured with the shoe in his hand. "Those sunglasses, are they government issue?" Parker stared at Bob, stone-faced.

"Listen," Bob said, "leaving aside for a moment the obvious question of what the hell the CIA might want with me...How the hell do I know you two are really with them?"

"I'm afraid we're not allowed to give out that sort of information," Parker said.

Bob looked at Wolfe, who smiled as he spoke. "He's right; that's policy. You'll just have to take our word. We could show you ID, but then you'd just ask how you're supposed to know they aren't forgeries, right?"

"Right," Bob replied. "Besides, anyone who'd try to pass that off as logic must work for the government." Bob slipped his shoe back on. The three men rode silently into Jackson Heights as Bob tried to figure out which of his friends could afford to stage such an expensive and unusual practical joke.

"That's quite a cover you've got," Parker said, finally breaking the silence.

"It is?" Bob asked. A fleeting sense of déjà vu flirted with his confusion.

Another awkward moment passed before Wolfe spoke again. "'Pest Control,' I really love that." Wolfe winked at Bob.

"Thanks," Bob replied skeptically. "You got to make a living somehow."

"Ain't it the truth," Wolfe said as the sedan turned on 103rd Street. After a moment Wolfe continued, "Listen, first of all I want to tell you how impressed we were with how you handled the Huweiler job."

Bob wondered who the hell this Huweiler was. The name sounded familiar. Was he that guy with the deli in Brooklyn? Bob had sprayed for roaches there, but he didn't recall the owner's name. "Huweiler?" he asked. "I don't think I know any Huweiler."

"Of course not," Wolfe said defensively. "Did I say Huweiler? Forget I mentioned it." Wolfe knew a pro wouldn't admit to an assassination. He turned in his seat to face Bob more directly. "Listen, let me be candid. We need a favor."

Bob chuckled. "The CIA wants a favor? From me?" Wolfe nodded sincerely.

"You gotta be kiddin'."

"We're the CIA, Mr. Dillon. We don't do a lot of kidding," Parker said.

Wolfe gave Parker a look that said, "Let me do the talking." "Okay, it's more a job than a favor," he said.

There was only one way this could make any sense at all.

"Ohhhhhh, wait a second," Bob said. "Did you guys get ahold of one of my flyers? You know, I always figured there was some fixed-bidding kickback process to get contracts for federal jobs. But listen, if you want me to handle some sort of an infestation down at your headquarters, that's no sweat. I can do that."

Parker reacted, wide-eyed. If he understood correctly, Bob was under the impression that they wanted him to kill someone within the Agency and, what's more, he was ready, willing, and able to do so. Parker's look conveyed this to Wolfe.

"I love it," said Wolfe with a chuckle. "We've known him for three minutes and he's already offering to arrange for our promotions." Wolfe laughed before continuing. "No, nothing that extreme. We just need some…pest control, if you know what I mean." Wolfe winked at Bob again. Bob eyed him as if he had just escaped from the Bellevue Giggling Academy.

Wolfe opened a folder and handed Bob a photograph of a tough-looking Latin gentleman. "Ronaldo DeJesus-Riviera," Wolfe said. "As I suppose you know, he controls the world's largest cocaine cartel."

"I'll take your word for it," Bob replied.

"Good. Recently, Ronaldo stopped making payments to, uh, certain worthy parties, and now he needs to be 'handled.'" Wolfe winked a third time as he continued. "And since you don't have any idea about who handled the Huweiler matter so professionally, we've come to you."

It hit Bob like the end of a date with Mike Tyson. Bam! That night at Freddie's when he responded to that ad in the *Times*. That goofy Frenchman, what was his name, Marcel? That's where he had heard the name Huweiler. Apparently some improbable sequence of events had come to pass that led these nitwits to believe he was a hit man. And now they were trying to hire him to kill a drug lord who wasn't making his payments to the CIA on time. These two were serious, Bob thought. Extremely stupid, but serious.

"Listen, fellas," Bob said. "I'm not exactly sure what happened here, but, uh, somehow you guys got the idea that I'm a hired killer."

Wolfe and Parker exchanged a curious glance as Bob continued. Most of the contract killers they dealt with didn't talk this much.

"The truth is," Bob continued, "I've never killed anybody in my life."

"That's understood," Wolfe said quickly and with authority. Parker nodded agreement.

"No, really. I only kill bugs."

"Absolutely," Wolfe said, understanding the game perfectly.

"Listen," Bob said finally, "I'm going to tell you the same thing I told that Marcel guy. I am not interested in whatever it is you're offering."

Parker looked to Wolfe for the true meaning of Bob's statement. To Wolfe it meant two things—one, Bob had in fact dealt with Marcel, the man assumed to have arranged for Huweiler's death, and two, that Bob was indeed saying the exact opposite of what he meant. Wolfe nodded knowingly.

"If it's good enough for Marcel, it's good enough for me. The fee is $500,000."

"Guys, I'm speakin' English here." Bob's voice had an urgency to it. "I'm not whoever or whatever you think I am. I'm strictly a bug squisher. Look, the closest I ever came to killing anyone was—and you gotta swear not to let this out, 'cause I could get in real trouble for this, alright?"

Wolfe and Parker indicated their fealty as Bob leaned in to confide with them.

"Alright. The closest I ever came to killing anyone was myself when I used some yellow phosphorus on a really tough rat job in Brooklyn. I know the stuff's illegal—hell, it oughtta be, that stuff'll kill a man if he steps on it barefooted. But I know this guy with a cousin in Paraguay who sends it in the mail and these were some really big rats …" Bob trailed off as he remembered the rats.

Parker again looked to Wolfe as he decoded Bob's statement. Wolfe knew Bob was negotiating.

"Ahhh, I understand, Riviera *es muy mucho rata*. Yes, he will be difficult." Wolfe considered his words carefully. "Alright. Seven hundred fifty thousand."

Bob laughed. "You're not listening, are you? Let me try this again. I'm just a regular guy who lives in Queens with a wife and kid and no interest in your *muy mucho ratas*."

"Yes, and as my young colleague noted earlier, it is an exquisite cover," Wolfe complimented him. "Okay, a million, but that's as high as I'm allowed to go."

Sensing he was not getting through, Bob stared at Wolfe for a moment before he finally gave up.

"Jesus, why don't you just drop me here?" Bob said.

Assuming this meant they had come to terms, Wolfe indicated to the driver to pull over.

"Excellent," Wolfe said.

The driver pulled over and let Bob out of the car.

As Bob walked away, the window rolled down and Wolfe leaned out. "Of course, should anything go awry, we will disavow all knowledge."

"Natch," Bob replied. "I'd expect nothing less."

The window rolled up and the car pulled away from the curb.

Inside the sedan, Parker's brow furrowed above his sunglasses. He turned to his mentor, unsure what had transpired. "Sir, I think he's really an exterminator."

"Of course he's an exterminator, you biscuit head. Where've you been for the last five minutes?" Then with an admiring tone, Wolfe continued, "The Exterminator. I love it."

Wolfe sat back to enjoy the moment. He had just secured his future by bringing a hot new "mechanic" into the fold. His retirement years had just taken a turn for the comfortable.

Chapter Twenty-eight

Most butterflies fly five–to–eight feet above the ground during migration, but some, like the stout members of the genus *Lymanopoda*, can cruise at altitudes above 14,000 feet.

At the moment, several sturdy members of that genus, their venation distinguished by the connecting cross-vein of the sub-costa and radius at the midpoint of the discal cell, were crossing the Andes in Bolivia.

For thousands of years the Andes provided the economic base for those who lived in and around them. They were mined for gold, silver, copper, and emeralds; the foothills coerced into surrendering oil and natural gas. Over the centuries various crops have been cultivated for export from this region, among them bananas, tobacco, and of course coffee, which contains the celebrated alkaloid caffeine.

But roughly 25 years ago, Juan Valdez and his caffeine beans were forcibly relocated to Colombia.

These days the real money maker around there was the coca plant, from which another, somewhat more potent, alkaloid is derived.

About halfway between La Paz and Nevado Illimani, at around 12,500 feet, a magnificent estate had recently been carved into the Andean mountainside. And when they were migrating, one could watch butterflies from the expansive veranda of this Bolivian palace while sipping a cup of yerba mate. The estate was the home of Ronaldo DeJesus-Riviera and his brother, Miguel DeJesus-Riviera, controllers of a ruthless and wildly successful cocaine cartel.

Ronaldo, the older of the two, spent most of his time more coked up than a blast furnace. He liked what he did and he did what he liked, a big ego, and a bad attitude. He was a major asshole and he could afford to be one, with a net worth in the neighborhood of $475 million.

Ronaldo and Miguel were having a sales and marketing meeting one afternoon in one of the rooms of their palace. A large map of the United States, broken down into sales regions, was hanging on one of the walls.

Ronaldo turned from the map and went to a nearby table where he snorted a big line of his product off an antique mirror before rubbing some on his gums. He prodded at his cheekbones, hoping to open his swollen sinus cavities. When that failed, he dipped his fingers in a glass of tequila, then put them to his nose and sniffed. He gagged a bit when the tequila, cocaine, and mucus mixture reached the back of his throat.

Miguel, his conscientious younger brother, stood by the fax machine as it received a transmission.

Ronaldo fidgeted as he spoke urgently from across the room. "That must be the junior high school marketing survey information I asked for. Bring it here now before someone else gets it!"

"Relax," Miguel said. "It's just something from our Interpol contact." Miguel waited patiently as the machine slowly spun the document out to his waiting hand. The fax was a fourth-generation copy of the photograph of Bob wearing his EXTERMINATOR cap. The second page was printed information which Miguel read. He began to laugh.

Ronaldo, who didn't like to be left out of anything, was annoyed at his brother's chortling. "What is so damn funny, little brother?"

"See for yourself," Miguel said as he handed over the papers. "It seems Uncle Sam is a bit peeved that you have stopped making your payments. Your friends at the CIA have taken out another contract on you. This time they've got somebody who calls himself 'The Exterminator.'"

Ronaldo got a laugh out of that too...until he saw the fax. His face went white. "Jesus, Mary, and Joseph! I see death in this man's eyes."

"Relax," Miguel said as he gestured at the antique mirror. "You're doing so much of that shit you're getting paranoid."

"Paranoid?" Ronaldo screamed suspiciously. "I am not paranoid!" Ronaldo pulled his gun and jammed it in Miguel's face. "I am just being safe."

Furious, Miguel grabbed the gun and stuck it back in his brother's face. "You idiot! You keep puttin' that shit up your nose and you'll piss away everything we've worked for!"

The fury passed quickly and Miguel realized what he was doing. Disgusted at his own behavior, he threw the gun across the room. It skidded nicely on the expensive tile floor.

"Goddamit," he muttered as he walked away from his troublesome older brother. "So what if some *pendejo* cowboy comes down here? He'll never get past the front gate. What you need to worry about is getting yourself straight."

Ronaldo was still pissed. And loaded. He killed the glass of tequila. "Don't you ever touch me again, little brother! This is my organization and don't you forget it!"

Chapter Twenty-nine

In the living room of Klaus' lavish, airy villa, there were various photos of Klaus with various international public figures. Among the people with whom Klaus had posed was a younger George Bush, circa 1977. In the background of the photo, small colored tiles inlaid in the floor served as evidence that the photo was taken at CIA headquarters when George was in charge.

Next to that was one of Klaus with Nikolai Bulganin, Nikita Khrushchev, and Viktor M. Chebrikov, onetime head of the KGB. The eight-by-ten glossy appeared to have been taken at a performance of *Giselle* by the Bolshoi.

Outside on the large terrace overlooking the village and the azure Mediterranean, Klaus and his hungry friend Basil sat at a table. Basil was eating a baked chicken with his hands. Grease and rosemary clung to his fingers; he was a messy eater.

Klaus was on the phone, simultaneously consulting the sports page of a Greek newspaper. On the table were copies of *Sports Illustrated, Sporting News,* and other sports publications. A Baretta 8000 9-mm was also within reach. Klaus looked a bit irritated as he strained to hear over Basil's noisy masticating.

"No," Klaus yelled into the phone. "Maradona's a has-been, give me Italy for, uh, ten thousand." He listened for a moment before continuing. "No, I want longer odds. Yes, perfect. New Orleans in the Super Bowl. Good." Klaus hung up.

Basil paused from his chicken long enough to hand Klaus a sheet of paper.

"This was in your fax machine," Basil said. "I believe he is the one all the fuss is about." Basil's fingers left a greasy stain on the paper.

Klaus looked at the fax. It was the now internationally circulated photograph of Bob. Whoever had sent this to Klaus had also written in "The Exterminator, AKA Robert Dillon, NYC."

"This is the famous Exterminator?" Klaus asked. "He looks like he is straight from a comic book." Klaus paused a moment, looking first at the fax, then at Basil. "You know, I am really beginning to hate this business." He crumpled the fax angrily.

"Klaus, please. You've never liked it."

"Well, I like it even less now," Klaus said as he turned an unfocused gaze toward the horizon.

"I am tired, Basil. Tired of the whole thing."

"You're not tired," Basil said. "You're annoyed that the CIA is paying an unknown a million dollars for a hit."

Klaus quickly cooled. "They want him to kill Riviera? Fine. No one with a gram of intelligence would accept such a job. It is an impossible hit."

"Not for Klaus," Basil chided.

"I did not want it."

"They did not offer it to you."

"I think it is time for me to quit."

Basil pondered this for a moment, then proceeded delicately. "And do what? You have an expensive hobby, Klaus. And if you do not honor the debts it creates, you will be, how shall I say, forcibly retired."

"Perhaps that is what I want," Klaus said glumly. "After all, they say every man must fall."

Basil set the drumstick down and wiped his fingers. "Klaus, listen to me," he said. "You are the best at what you do, but you must be willing to accept whatever jobs are offered if you wish to continue indulging your extravagant little diversion. If you insist on clinging to your lofty standards, this Exterminator may take everything away from you. You don't want that, and I certainly don't. You know how much I enjoy house-sitting for you."

Klaus wasn't worried about losing everything. His material possessions meant little to him and any feelings of self-worth were dwindling fast.

"Goddammit, who is this American son of a bitch?"

"Perhaps you should find out." Basil stripped the drumstick of its remaining flesh.

Klaus picked the Beretta up off the table, looked at it. "Perhaps I should."

Quick as a striking viper, Klaus pointed and fired at a scrubby tree in the backyard.

BAM! An olive dropped intact from its branch.

BAM! He plugged the olive before it hit the ground.

Chapter Thirty

Mr. Silverstein's abandoned 16-story building occupied half a city block not far from the Empire State Building. The deserted structure had entrances on both Broadway and Sixth Avenue, though the lobby was built in such a way that you couldn't see straight through from one sidewalk to the other.

Thanks to Broadway's diagonal path through Manhattan this building was not one of the many bleak rectangles that marred the skyline. Instead, it was trapezoidal with two parallel sides on Thirty-First and Thirty-Second Streets. It was the sort of building where a Damon Runyon character might have gone in an attempt to shake Big Nig or Daffy Jack, assuming any of them ever wandered that far south of Times Square.

Such a character could duck into the building on the Broadway side and sneak out on Sixth. And just like that he'd be on his way to win some big money at Harry the Horse's floating crap game or to smile a nice smile to a doll what's got a nice smile of her own, and who's not afraid of sharing it one bit.

At any rate, Bob entered what was now a deserted department store from the Sixth Avenue side, skirting the messy sidewalk construction which obscured the door on Broadway. He headed to the third floor, carrying his tool kit and several boxes marked "ASSASSINS, STRAIN ONE." There he dropped his load by one of the sales counters and continued to wander, sizing up his job. He lifted a discarded gift-wrap box and watched several earwigs scurry for cover. They reminded him of that old story and he unconsciously put a finger in one ear and scratched.

The place was ideal for testing Strain One of his hybrids. If the other buildings were this perfect, he would surely succeed. Nothing could stop him now, not even his own gross miscalculations, like the mistake with Strain Zero.

After the *Maison Henri* debacle, Bob had gone back to his notes to try to determine what had gone wrong with Strain Zero. After a lot of thought, he'd concluded that he'd failed to account for reproduction time. It was a simple numbers game. His killer bugs had to reproduce as fast or faster than the bugs they were after or they would simply loose the battle—for the same reason George Custer had lost to the Sioux and the Cheyenne.

However, Bob's notes indicated Strain Zero had reproduced quickly in the comfort of the bugquariums. So, the question was, why had they failed to reproduce in the wilds of *Maison Henri*?

To answer that question, Bob would have had to return to the restaurant. Because of the "roach crouton" incident, however, Bob was considered exterminator non-grata by Henri. Consequently, Bob had bribed a *sous* chef to let him in after closing one night so he could inspect the premises and obtain samples of his hybrids. What Bob discovered was that the residual pesticides left from previous attempts to control roaches had rendered Strain Zero utterly sterile, barren, and impotent. They couldn't get their teeny little John Thomases to stand up and salute even if they'd had 'em, which of course they didn't.

Temporarily discouraged by the irony, Bob found himself still stuck in New York with the all-natural pest-control blues. But he had learned a lesson and made some important adjustments in the selection of pesticide-resistance traits in his cross-breedings.

He looked around the failed department store and ambled around a structural column, coming face-to-face with one of the orphaned mannequins, a naked male type.

Bob politely shook one of its hands, which came off. He introduced himself.

"How are ya? Bob Dillon, Bob's Natural Pest Control. Maybe you've heard of me." He pretended to listen to what the mannequin had to say. "Oh yeah? Not impressed, huh?" Bob pointed at the mannequin's lack of genitalia. "Well, I wouldn't be talking if I were you."

A phone on one of the sales desks rang, so Bob excused himself and gave the poor naked fellow his hand back.

He grabbed the phone. "Hello?" He listened. "Yes, Mr. Silverstein, I found it, no problem." He paused again. "Yes, sir, I'm about to install the first batch of bugs right now." He listened for another moment. "Yes sir, next Thursday. I'll meet you here then and we'll see how they're doing. Yes, sir, we should be able to tell by then. Terrific. Thanks again."

Bob hung up, then went to work.

He took his drill and a container of putty from the toolbox, then grabbed one of the boxes marked "ASSASSINS, STRAIN ONE." This was the Masked Hunter/Wheel Bug hybrid which had resulted in a robust savage; mulish in its tenacious pursuit of prey and comfortable operating within the dark confines of wall spaces. Bob had high expectations for this particular strain.

He set the putty on the floor next to the bugs as he drilled a hole two inches in diameter just above the baseboard of one wall. He set the drill aside, picked up his box of hybrids, and peered inside to give the bugs a pep talk.

"Okay, guys, this is your big chance to get into the pest-control Hall of Fame. Make your phylum proud."

Bob jammed a length of clear plastic tubing into the perforated circle at the bottom of the bug box, like a straw into a boxed fruit juice. He put the other end of the tubing into the hole in the wall and watched with fatherly pride as his Assassin Bugs scurried into the wall space. After a minute, he tapped at the bottom of the container to make sure all the bugs were out, then he sealed the hole with the putty, nice and neat.

As Bob repeated this procedure again and again, he thought about what success would mean to him and his family. First, and foremost, it would bring them back together.

Secondly, they could leave New York, a longtime goal. Leave the bigotry, violence, intolerance. Leave the distrust. People in New York had made such a science of ignoring one another that they never made eye contact with people on the street. Bob and Mary also hated the practiced superiority of many New Yorkers. It seemed that when you lived in a place as filthy and overcrowded and violent as New York, you had to convince yourself that the place was an exciting cultural and intellectual mecca, and that you were a key player in the madness.

Bob and Mary didn't want to raise Katy that way. They wanted to go somewhere you could pass others on the street, catch their eye, and say, "Hi. Good morning. How are you today?" Somewhere like Idaho, Oregon, or Iowa. Almost any state beginning with a vowel would be good, except maybe the "A" states. Alabama, Arkansas, Alaska. Bob had heard stories about huge flying cockroaches in the Deep South that repulsed him. And the mosquitoes of Alaskan summers were of mythic proportions. Arizona might be alright…

Finally, success would mean Bob could have a nice new truck of his own, one with a big fiberglass bug on the top. That's when an exterminator knows he's made it, when he's at the wheel of a sleek new truck topped with a big…a big what?

Now that he thought about it, he wasn't sure what type of bug one topped one's truck with. Were there only a few big fiberglass bugs on the market? Or did you have them custom made?

Hmmm, what would it be? A massive Toad Bug (*Gelastocoris oculatus*) would be nice, or perhaps a Giant Stag Beetle (*Lucanus elaphus*).

Bob finally patched the last hole. There were two dozen more patch marks along the baseboards. Bob stood and proudly surveyed his work. As he scanned the room, his eye came to rest on a phone and he decided to make a call to see if he could answer a nagging question.

He flipped through the blue pages of a phone book where the city, county, and federal governments list their departments, bureaus, divisions, and agencies. He found the number he was looking for and dialed.

A voice came on the other line. "Hello? Who are you trying to reach?"

Bob hesitated, thinking he had the wrong number. "Is this the CIA?"

"I'm not allowed to say, sir. Who were you calling?"

Bob figured that was as close to a yes as he was going to get.

"Listen, I know this is going to sound weird, but my name's Bob Dillon. A couple of guys recently came by my house and identified themselves as CIA and I think they were trying to hire me to kill someone, and I was just wondering if you could confirm that these guys really work there. I mean, I understand you can't say if you're the CIA, but, well, anyway, I think their names were Wolfe and Parker."

"Sorry, sir," said the voice at the other end, "I'm not allowed to divulge that information. And even if Agents Wolfe and Parker worked here, I'd have to deny it."

"Well," Bob said, "could you tell me if they don't work there?"

"No sir," the voice replied. "I can't do that."

"I see," Bob said. "Is there an assassination department you could connect me to?"

"I'm sorry, sir. I can't help you with that either."

"Well, thanks, you've been a truckload of help." Bob hung up. What the hell, he thought, at least he'd tried.

He started walking away, ready to get back to work on another floor of the building, then he stopped. He turned back and stared at the phone, thinking about Mary. Maybe he should reach out and touch her.

Chapter Thirty-one

"Okay, I love you too, Doodlebug. Can you put Mommy back on?"

Mary came on the line.

"Hi. Uh, listen, sweetheart…" Bob reached into his pocket and pulled out Mary's gold locket. "Why don't you guys come on home?" he asked. "Yeah, I remember what you said, but when I saw you left the locket, I knew you hadn't gone for good. So what I—" Bob paused as Mary interrupted to make a long-distance point.

But for every question Mary had, Bob had an answer. He explained that he got the Silverstein job and was calling from one of the buildings. Mary wasn't impressed; she wanted to know if he'd been paid.

Bob explained that if he pulled this off, Silverstein would set him up in business and they would get a vested interest in the syndication and franchising of his idea. If it worked, they could get out of New York, move wherever they wanted, and when the time came, they could afford to send Katy to college.

"Isn't that just as good as a check?" Bob asked hopefully.

Mary answered without a word. Click, dial tone, good-bye.

"Hello? Honey? Are you there?" Bob had his answer.

Chapter Thirty-two

Mary's hand slid slowly off the receiver, already having second thoughts about hanging up on Bob.

"I miss Daddy," Katy said, looking at her sadly from across the room. Although Katy had an impressive range of manipulative expressions, this was genuine emotion.

"I know, sweetie," Mary said. "I miss him too."

Katy looked away and skulked out the back door as if her mother had betrayed her. Mary opened her mouth, but nothing came out. She didn't know what to say, so she watched Katy wander sadly through the backyard to the small patch of concrete that served as the barbecue area.

My god, Mary thought, what was going on? Was this how her marriage was going to end? Crashing and burning like so many late-night talk shows or poorly maintained traffic helicopters?

Or was it Mary's fault because she wasn't willing to support him while he pursued his dream? And what about Katy? What was all this doing to her?

Mary had to talk to Katy, explain what was going on. She went out and sat down on the concrete next to her daughter, who was staring intently at the ground.

"What are you doing?" Mary asked.

"Watching the ants," Katy replied.

A column of Pavement Ants (*Tetramorium caespitum*) marched along the concrete, each carrying a disproportionately large load.

Katy thought ants were pretty cool, especially after her dad had told her about the vicious Legionary Ants (*Labidus coecus*), sometimes called Army Ants. These ferocious pests routinely devoured other insects as well as small vertebrate animals like chickens. Intrigued and motivated by that gruesome tidbit, Katy had done a little research on her own, borrowing some of her dad's insect books, and had discovered that some ants actually enslaved ants from other species. Wow! Imagine that! Ant slaves! They were probably forced to make their masters' beds and clean up their rooms and take out the garbage and stuff like that.

Katy also read that another kind of ant actually secreted formic acid from its anal glands. Ouch! she thought, but still, pretty cool.

Mary watched as Katy picked up a twig and laid it in the ants' path, being careful not to crush any of the workers. The ants hesitated briefly, while a flurry of antennae communicated that their minions should walk over the obstacle and carry on their job—complaints would not be entertained.

"Honey," Mary said softly, "I'm sorry I took you away from your dad. Can I try and explain?"

Katy didn't look up as she spoke to her mother. "'Member the last time Daddy tried to start the business and he got real sad when it wasn't working and you told him you believed in him and you'd support him and stuff and said he should keep at it as long as it was what he wanted to do? 'Member?"

Mary smiled wryly and nodded; she was afraid she knew where her precocious little doodlebug was going.

"Why are things different now?" Katy asked, hitting below the belt with a perceptive point.

"Well, honey, sometimes, especially when you get older, things don't turn out to be as simple as you thought they were."

Mary picked up a small rock and put it in the ants' path. They walked around it and continued their work.

"Do you still love Daddy?"

"Of course I do. It's just that he didn't keep his word to me and I got upset and I thought he might need time to think about what he did."

"You didn't keep your word either. 'Cause you said you'd do whatever you had to so he could work with the bugs until he got it right."

Katy was determined to nail her on this.

"Well…you're right, honey. I guess your dad and I both need time to think about it."

Mary blocked the ants' path with a large leaf and watched as about fifty of them assembled and pulled the leaf out of the way. It seemed that no matter what obstacle she put in front of them, they would overcome it.

As Mary continued testing the ants, she discovered how remarkably strong and resolute they were. They reminded her of Bob. Except, of course, for their geniculated antennae.

Chapter Thirty-three

The security force around the Bolivian fortress of Miguel and Ronaldo DeJesus Rivieria was as impressive as it was expensive—fifty well-armed soldiers patrolled the grounds; sentries with full night-vision goggles watched from a dozen twenty foot tall towers; heat and motion sensors dotted the hillside and connected to a central security computer, and attack dogs patrolled both inside and outside the twelve foot high wall that surrounded the compound. Every member of the force also had state-of-the-art communications equipment and all were well trained in how to deal with intruders.

The only person ever to attempt an assassination here had been tracked from 2,000 yards outside the wall by a sophisticated tracking device installed in the flora surrounding the compound. The guards had known in advance, however, that the killer was coming. And as any security consultant will tell you, information, especially inside information, beats electronics any day of the week.

That last attempt had come when a high-ranking member of the Medellin cartel's security force had betrayed his employer and sold Miguel information regarding an assassination attempt. He even supplied Miguel with the day of the hit.

After consulting with the head of security, Ronaldo and Miguel decided to let the killer get inside so he would have nowhere to run when they descended on him.

The day came and so did the killer. All along the watchtowers, the sentries kept a view while Miguel and Ronaldo watched from inside on video monitors. The killer must have felt proud and invisible after bypassing the electric perimeter, scaling the wall, and getting halfway to the palace without the slightest hitch. It would have been a short-lived euphoria, however. After the gunfire stopped, the bullet-riddled gunman was stripped to the bone by the vicious and hungry dogs.

As Ronaldo stood over the mangled corpse, he turned to his brother and said, "Pride, my young brother, goeth before the fall."

Miguel, as it turned out, knew his Proverbs better than Ronaldo. He recited, "Pride goeth before destruction, and an haughty spirit before a fall.'"

What followed as they headed back inside was a pedant's debate on quotation and paraphrasing.

But that was almost a year ago. Since then, there had been no breaches of security and the latest CIA contract on Ronaldo seemed no cause for alarm. Or so they thought.

It was after midnight when the ski-masked man dressed entirely in black stood on Ronaldo's balcony looking down. Oddly, he pulled out a grappling hook, attached it to the railing and tossed the rope to the ground below.

The masked man then tried the door leading inside. Damn! It was locked. He then tried a nearby window. It was open, so the man climbed in.

A moment later and the man in black was in the bedroom, standing ominously at the foot of Ronaldo's bed. Ronaldo, who never slept well due to his appetite for alkaloids, sensed something and woke, fumbling around for the light. When he finally turned the switch, illuminating the room with a harsh 75 watts, he saw the man in black raise his gun.

"*Madre de dios*! No!" Ronaldo pleaded to no avail.

FWUMP! FWUMP! Two silenced shots, one dead drug lord.

The man in black peeked out the doorway then calmly exited through the door to the hall. He slipped down and into Miguel's room.

Once inside, he flipped on the lights and peeled off his ski-mask. It was, perhaps, the only man capable of circumventing the security forces. It was Miguel, Ronaldo's next-of-kin.

He quickly stripped to his briefs and put on a bathrobe. He then mussed his hair and hit the alarm button before bursting back into the hallway screaming, "Seal the compound! There is an assassin! Someone has shot my brother! Get the doctor!"

Mayhem ensued. Within seconds twenty soldiers appeared, all with guns drawn. They searched for the killer as Miguel stayed at Ronaldo's side feigning grief.

Outside the dogs barked in a blood-hunting frenzy. Shots occasionally fired into the dark Bolivian night.

Several soldiers poked around in closets and behind the furniture while Miguel laid the grief on pretty thick. Suddenly, and much to Miguel's surprise, Ronaldo lurched, his chest heaving for air.

Was that a gasp for breath?! Did anyone see it?! Miguel wondered.

In an exaggerated show of anguish, Miguel began wailing. He embraced Ronaldo's head, smothering his nose and mouth to snuff out whatever life might have been left. The gurgling noises muffled into Miguel's sour armpit and Ronaldo finally kicked the bucket—or, as Ronaldo's uncle from Nicaragua might have said, he peeled the garlic. Then again, if Ronaldo himself had been given his choice of idiom for the occasion, he might have chosen what they said in El Salvador…he tied up his bundle.

Ronaldo always loved the idioms of Central and South America. He felt they were more colorful than their English counterparts. For example, whereas a Bolivian in New York would be a fish out of water, a New Yorker in Bolivia would be a cockroach at a chicken dance. But of course none of that mattered anymore because Ronaldo was dead as a dodo.

A soldier checked the locked balcony doors, another looked in the lavatory. "He came in through the bathroom window!" the soldier yelled.

"Well, what are you waiting for?" Miguel barked. "Find him! Kill him! No, bring him to me! I will kill him with my bare hands!" Miguel was quite the thespian. "And you!" he said as he grabbed a passing soldier. "Alert the press! Tell them my brother has been killed by an American assassin and that I have a statement for them!"

The security forces and the hounds combed the compound and the surrounding mountainside until daybreak, but no killer was ever found. The grappling hook and rope were the only clues left behind.

Miguel eventually called off the search and gathered the entire security force into the large flagstone courtyard. The men were relieved to hear that Miguel wasn't angry the assassin had escaped. However, there was a nasty rumor going around that someone was going to have to pay for letting the assassin into the palace in the first place. And they soon realized that a large flagstone courtyard in the center of the palace was a great spot for a grieving relative with an automatic weapon to exact revenge.

But in the end, Miguel did little more than shove a few of the men around and call them 'fraidy cats, weenie-boys, and pussies before heading off to take over the business.

He swept into Ronaldo's office and, over the next several days, redecorated. There was a garish $4,000 Caucasus Mountains kilim for the south wall displayed far too close to the $3,200 Peruvian corner cabinet. The $1,500 Bernard Colin hand-forged coffee table clashed with the $9,500-a-pair Spanish Colonial Revival bronze floor lamps. The $10,000 monumental Art Deco floor vase threatened to scuffle with the $3,800 1910s Duffner & Kimberley stained glass lamp, while the $5,800 English pine case clock revolted against the $1,600 Orkney Islands chair with the rush back.

In the midst of the impending furniture skirmish, a soldier entered.

"Are the reporters here?" Miguel asked.

The soldier nodded.

"Show them in."

The soldier ushered three dozen reporters into the office. Miguel was blinded by the exploding xenon flashes that fired repeatedly from the still cameras and the brutal beams of electric blue light that sprayed from the video units. Miguel winced and shielded his eyes as the reporters peppered him with questions about his brother's death. Miguel raised a hand to silence them.

"Please, I have a statement to read. I will not entertain your questions." He produced a piece of paper and read from it: "Awhile ago we learned that America's Central Intelligence Agency had put out a contract on my brother. Several days ago," Miguel said, pausing, "it appears they succeeded."

Miguel took a moment to feign gathering himself. He wanted to display machismo in the face of grief. "On his death bed, Ronaldo said three things to me. First, he said I was to take control of all Riviera business interests. Second, he said I was to avenge his death. Third, and finally, he said '*capullo de rosa.*'"

As members of the press glanced curiously at one another murmuring "Rosebud," Miguel pressed a button on his desk. The office door swung open and the scribes gasped in unison when they saw the man called Ramon.

His features were disfigured and menacing. The scarring on the right side of his face was the result of a blow torch savagely applied by pro-Sandinista forces during Ramon's days as an optimistic political science major in his native Nicaragua. Ramon had hoped one day to run for office to unite his people and bring peace and prosperity to his country. Unfortunately one of his term papers, a poorly written biography of Augusto Cesar Sandino, fell into the wrong hands and was thoroughly misinterpreted. What resulted was best described as a very bad mark.

In a cruel, if simple, twist of fate, two months after the blow torch incident, the left side of Ramon's face was splashed with hydrochloric acid by U.S.-backed Contra rebels who read and also misinterpreted his Sandino paper.

Souring on the political process in his native land, Ramon—now an angry, mean-spirited man—packed his bags and moved to Bolivia. There he joined Riviera's private army where he became an expert in the use of high explosives as a means of influencing elected officials and members of the judiciary.

Miguel gestured at Ramon. "I am sending my best soldier to avenge my brother's death." Miguel hammered his fist on the podium as he spoke with increasing intensity. "I will not rest until this American assassin, this Exterminator, is cold in his grave with bugs feasting on his rotting flesh!"

Chapter Thirty-four

Mike Wolfe looked at Ronaldo Riviera's file and smiled. He opened his top drawer and removed a rubber stamp. He moistened the stamp with red ink and stamped the file—"INACTIVE." He closed the file and handed it to Parker. "Well, I think our Mr. Dillon may have just cracked the top ten list. Pay the man."

Parker dutifully went to his computer. He moused around on the pad, rolling and clicking and electronically sending the necessary information to the accounting department, where it was promptly processed.

Two stories down in accounts payable, the paper platen spooled a blank check into the check printer. The account name on the check was Consolidated International Associates, Inc. At "Pay to the order of," a laser-sharp stream of black ink neatly spit the name "Bob Dylan" onto the check. The machine then paused, as if sensing its mistake. Efficiently reversing itself, it erased n-a-l-y-D. A second later, correcting the error, it spelled out D-i-1-1-o-n. Then, under "Amount," "One Million dollars and no/100."

Chapter Thirty-five

The Lexington Avenue local was crowded for the early morning commute—greedy lawyers and investment bankers heading downtown buried their heads ostrich-like in the sand of their *Wall Street Journals*, secretaries stared vacantly into their bleak futures, and frightened elderly couples clung desperately to one another hoping they wouldn't be killed before lunch.

Standing among the huddled masses yearning to be free was Bob with his tool kit and several more boxes of bugs marked "Assassins, Strain Two."

Unlike the others, Bob was looking forward to the day. He was on his way to the Lower East Side, where he would move his second strain of hybrids into a dilapidated apartment building. This, he hoped, would bring him one day closer to perfecting his method and one day closer to a reunion with Mary and Katy.

Doing his best to avoid threatening anyone with eye contact, Bob read the overhead advertisement for the Gay and Lesbian Lover Psychological Abuse Hotline that was next to an ad promising Clear Beautiful Skin via some sort of chemical peel.

Directly beneath that ad was an elderly woman standing in the aisle, struggling to hold on to her purse and the stanchion at the same time. Seated in front of the teetering old woman was a man wearing a fatigue jacket and a bushy blond beard that looked like an electrocuted cat.

Suddenly the man screamed, "She's a big girl now and she belongs to me!" He looked around to see if anyone wanted to argue the point. There were no takers.

Bob remembered the man from the day he quit his job with Bug-Off. The man's suspiciously darting eyes complimented nicely the facial tic that danced on the left side of his face. You didn't need a Rorschach to see this guy was nuttier than pecan pie—an amalgam of Norman Bates, Bernard Goetz, and Colin Ferguson from the paranoid school of schizophrenia. He was the sort who was prone to scratch where it didn't itch.

Still, certifiable or not, it was rude to make the grandmotherly woman stand, so Bob broke one of the many unwritten rules of the city and spoke up.

"Hey, pal, why don't you let the lady sit down?" he said.

Before the words were out of his mouth, Bob knew he had screwed up.

The man's face twisted tight, threatening to pinch off his nose. He reached aggressively into his jacket.

"Uh, listen," Bob said nervously. "If you'd rather not, it's okay. I know how sometimes you just have to sit. Right now, for instance. No problem, forget I mentioned it."

But it appeared to be too late, the damage had been done. The man looked like a human thermonuclear device rapidly approaching critical mass.

Suddenly, six passengers leapt to their feet and forced the disinclined elderly woman to sit.

"I said fuckitallgoddammit!" the lunatic screamed again. "You ain't gonna keep me down on Maggie's farm no more! No sir!" Then, as if he had settled his inner dispute, the man calmed noticeably, snatched a section of newspaper from the floor, and began reading.

The elderly woman closed her eyes and prayed.

Bob and his bugs remained standing until he transferred to the Sixth Avenue local at Washington Square.

Bob emerged from the subway on Delancey Street and began his trek through the Lower East Side, looking for a run-down apartment building with a Silverstein Enterprises sign in the window.

At Bowery he passed a woman wearing a leopard-skin, pillbox hat, bell bottoms, platform shoes, and blue-tinted granny glasses. He watched as the woman crossed Delancey and disappeared into the Planet Waves Beauty Salon.

This used to be Little Italy, but the neighborhood had lately been subsumed by an ever expanding Chinatown. Tough-looking Asian kids with Elvis hairdos played handball and hoops where Pacino types had once ruled. All that was left of Little Italy seemed centered on Mulberry, Hester, and Grand Streets a couple of blocks southwest of there.

Bob continued down Bowery before crossing over to Chrystie Street, where he found the apartment building he was looking for. It was white with key-lime-green trim and a matching fire escape. He fished a large ring of keys from his pocket, unlocked the door, and entered the neglected structure. This would be the new home for Bob's second strain of hybrids.

Strain Two was the Ambush Bug/Spined Assassin mix, a bug with an intelligent killing pattern. Several of these hybrids would work together to pile small amounts of food in an opening and then hide, waiting for a victim to ambush. Bach morning after snacking on duped vermin all night these hybrids would eat their pile of bait food like so much dessert before calling it quits.

A totally unexpected characteristic that appeared in this hybrid was its mating drive. This was the randiest of the mutant insects, attempting copulation with everything it encountered, including inanimate objects. Naturally, Bob was enthusiastic about these little buggerers.

After getting a feel for the floor plan of the building, Bob determined where he would begin. He went into a large, windowed apartment halfway down the hall on the second floor and drilled a hole near the baseboard of one of the load-bearing walls. He pulled a length of three-quarter-inch clear plastic tubing from his tool kit and secured it into the hole in the wall.

He carefully opened the top of one of the boxes marked "ASSASSINS, STRAIN TWO" and took one of his modified Assassin Bugs out. It made a squeaking noise with its stridulating organs as Bob quickly closed the box to prevent a mass escape.

Bob looked the killer bug squarely in the segmented antennae. "Go get 'em, tiger," he said earnestly.

He jammed the length of clear plastic tubing into the side of the box and fed the remaining bugs into the hole in the wall. He patched the hole and then repeated the procedure throughout the building until 500 Strain Two Assassins were belligerently patrolling the wall spaces in search of sustenance.

Chapter Thirty-six

Gate 47 at JFK's international terminal was bustling. Passengers poured off the rampway and past the reader board indicating the arrival of Flight 354 from La Paz, Bolivia. Among the crowd was a man with a horribly scarred face.

As it happened, the seat belt sign had just been turned off on the TWA flight at Gate 34, just in from Athens.

Ramon retrieved his luggage from the spastically rotating conveyor which dispensed Samsonite bags like a giant staggering Pez dispenser.

Three carousels away, Klaus gathered his hanging bag and his small brown suitcase.

The fight for cabs was furious by American standards, but for those from large European and South American cities, it was a cakewalk. Klaus found one quickly but as he approached the door Ramon stepped up, thinking it was his. Klaus, ever the diplomat, did not express revulsion at the sight of Ramon's grotesquely disfigured face.

"I am sorry," Klaus said, "I think this one is mine."

"No, I believe I was first," Ramon replied.

Klaus graciously waved a hand. "My mistake. Please take it, there will be others."

"Hey, yo! Is one of ya getting in the goddamn cab or what?" the native cabdriver asked. "I ain't got all goddamn day."

Ramon eyed Klaus up for a moment, decided the handsome European was okay, then mentioned he was going to the West Side.

"I am going to Midtown," said Klaus.

"Would you consider sharing the cab?" Ramon agreed. So they tossed their bags into the trunk and slid into the back seat.

"Yo! It's about goddamn time," the cabbie said.

Klaus and Ramon rode in silence for a while. But Klaus felt awkward sitting so close to someone without acknowledging his presence.

"Were you on the flight from Athens?" Klaus asked.

"No, I have come from Bolivia."

"A beautiful country. I especially love the Andes. Have you come on business or pleasure?"

"You might say both," Ramon said. "I enjoy my work. I am in...plastics. And you?"

"Strictly business, I'm afraid," Klaus explained to the disfigured Bolivian face. "I no longer enjoy what I do."

The gnarled face nodded and the two assassins rode in silence for the remainder of the trip.

They arrived at Klaus' hotel first, the Rihga Royal, an elegant yet relaxed hotel located midway between Central Park and the Theater District. Klaus liked the first-class service and the excellent water pressure in the showers. Thanking Ramon, he got out and disappeared through the gold revolving door as the cab screeched back onto the streets.

Safely ensconced in his suite, Klaus opened his suitcase and checked the contents. Inside were several exotic handguns as well as components for an explosive device. So much for international airport security.

Klaus closed the case and slipped it under the bed.

He grabbed the remote control and flipped on the television tuning to ESPN to catch some scores. Klaus always had several wagers going in whatever sports were in season, so he liked to keep abreast of his situation. Midway through the NBA Eastern Conference scores someone knocked on Klaus' door.

Klaus was calm, as if expecting a visitor. He opened the door to find a sloe-eyed man in a dark suit carrying a briefcase. They exchanged almost imperceptible nods and Klaus let him in.

"Do you have what I requested?" Klaus asked the dark suit.

The man produced a file from the briefcase and waited as Klaus flipped through the contents: photos of Bob taken under surveillance, a birth certificate, a wedding license, a TRW report, and federal tax returns. Klaus looked at the 1040s and saw that Bob listed his occupation as "Professional Exterminator." He certainly was a cheeky bastard.

Satisfied, Klaus closed the folder and handed the man an envelope. "Two thousand?"

The man nodded, slipped the envelope into his suit pocket, and left without ever saying a word. Klaus locked the door.

As private investigators go, this guy was among the best and he was reasonably priced to boot. He supplied Klaus with all there was to know about one Robert Dillon of Queens, New York. It turned out that every source of public information had a file on him. The sheer volume of information would indicate that Bob Dillon was John Q. Public. But Klaus wasn't so sure.

Klaus sat at the small table by the window and poured over the contents of the file. In killing, just as in gambling, information could give you an edge. It saved time, was fairly cheap, and could prevent big mistakes. It didn't guarantee success, but it was a good way to hedge your bet.

Klaus read through the file twice. He looked at detailed street maps of the five boroughs and marked with a red felt pen all the locations where the sloe-eyed man indicated he had followed Bob. The red marks corresponded with the locations of the four Silverstein buildings where Bob's experiments were ongoing, though the investigator indicated he was unable to determine exactly what Bob had been doing in the buildings.

The investigator had also compiled a chronology of Bob's movements to help ferret out any patterns. After four hours poring over the material, Klaus still wasn't sure whether Bob Dillon was a threat to his life or just a schmuck who didn't qualify for a Visa Card. Tomorrow he would do some investigating of his own.

It was one a.m. when Klaus closed the folder and returned to ESPN hoping to catch the final scores of the West Coast games.

Chapter Thirty-seven

The big brown UPS truck came up Bob's street in the morning sunshine and parked in front of his house as it had before.

After attempting his delivery at Bob's, the UPS guy left one of his friendly yellow notes explaining the fate of the package, crossed to Pratt's house, and rang the bell.

"Whaddya want?" Pratt yelled through the door.

The UPS guy yelled back, "Another package for Mr. Dillon. He's not home, can I leave it with you again?"

Pratt threw open his door. "What am I, a friggin' post office box?" He grabbed the package. "Givitame."

The UPS guy thanked Pratt without the slightest bit of sarcasm and bounded back to his big brown truck.

Inside, Pratt tossed the new package down next to the first one. Now the clever landlord had two hostages to hold against his 320 dollars in back rent.

You had to get up pretty early in the morning to fool old Dick Pratt.

Chapter Thirty-eight

The UPS guy was right, Bob wasn't home right then. In fact, at that moment, he was walking down Sixth Avenue preoccupied with an unusual thought.

Minutes earlier, coming through Times Square, he had been propositioned by two leather-clad women of the domination persuasion who were standing outside a retail bondage emporium called Street Legal B & D.

"Hey sugar," one of them said. "I'll be your baby tonight." She snapped her whip.

Not being the overly submissive type, Bob had declined her offer as tempting, but financially impossible at the moment. The woman told him to come back if he ever got a better job.

Ever since encountering the two disciplinarians, Bob had been trying to figure out the plural for dominatrix. Dominatri? Dominatrixes? Maybe he'd write to William Safire who seemed to know about these things.

As Bob contemplated a potential draft of his letter to the language maven, he was totally unaware that Klaus was watching him through binoculars from a covered position on the third floor maintenance roof of the Atlantic Bank of New York.

The information Klaus had purchased proved to be good; Bob appeared to be headed again for the abandoned 16-story building. Klaus wondered what went on in there.

As he watched, Klaus noticed someone following Bob, and it wasn't the sloe-eyed man in the dark suit. It was someone else;

someone Klaus had seen before, someone he wouldn't forget. It was Ramon, the man with the hideous face with whom he had shared the cab ride from the airport.

"Plastics, huh?" Klaus chuckled; he knew the truth. And the truth, which had suddenly dawned on him, was that the "plastics" man was another hired killer.

Klaus knew that Miguel Riviera had sent a hit man to New York to ice the Exterminator, who, Riviera alleged, had killed his brother Ronaldo in fulfillment of a CIA contract. Klaus' CIA contacts denied any involvement in the matter. As a matter of policy Klaus took that denial as a confirmation. Finally, why else would this repugnant man from Bolivia be following Bob, the man so many people believed to be the Exterminator? He had to be Riviera's hit man.

Klaus had to make some decisions. First, he had to decide whether Bob was really an assassin. If he decided Bob was a professional killer, then he had to choose whether to wait for Ramon to do the job or whether he should do it himself. Klaus was inclined toward the latter. He disliked uncertainty—he was something of a control freak that way—and the best way for him to know when the Exterminator was going to be exterminated was to do the deed himself.

However, since (A) Klaus wasn't sure about Bob (B) there was no money in this for Klaus and (C) the disfigured Bolivian was already on the case, Klaus decided to hold off for a moment. No need to get dirty if someone else is willing to do it, and Klaus reasoned, anyone as ugly as Ramon had to be good.

Besides, while Klaus' philosophy prevented him from killing anyone he didn't think deserved to die, it didn't require him to intervene if someone else was about to commit murder.

Being a consummate professional, Klaus believed it was good to watch a colleague at work. You never knew what you might learn. He watched Bob disappear into the abandoned building and saw Ramon walk slowly past, then stop. Ramon checked his watch, then made an entry in a notebook.

Inside, Bob wandered around examining his handiwork and checking for any developing problems. He found a few dehydrated roach carcasses—which was an encouraging sign—but he wasn't about to celebrate just yet.

Ramon waited patiently on the sidewalk on Sixth Avenue. Klaus spent the day peering into the building with his binoculars, trying to figure out what Bob was up to. Since Bob was crawling along the baseboard most of the time, Klaus didn't see much.

What on earth did an assassin do all day in a vacant 16-story building? Perhaps he stored weapons there and perhaps the basement had been turned into a firing range for target practice. Regardless, if this was all the Exterminator was going to do Klaus could not confirm the rumors that brought him here in the first place. And if he could not confirm those rumors, Klaus would not be able to kill the man.

Late that afternoon, as Bob locked up the building on his way out, Ramon checked his watch and made another notation in his notebook. He was compiling the information Klaus already had.

When Bob was safely down the street, Ramon went to the door, picked the lock, and disappeared into the building.

Klaus searched the windows until Ramon appeared on the second floor. Ramon placed his briefcase on a table and opened it, revealing several blocks of what Klaus recognized as everyone's favorite plastic explosive, C-4.

"Ahh, plastics…very cute," Klaus said to himself. Ramon was going to blow Bob to kingdom come.

Klaus preferred his high-powered rifle to other methods, but a good killer went with his strength, and Ramon's was apparently explosives.

Ramon removed six blocks of the putty from his briefcase and attached detonators. Klaus, who was handy with a wide variety of explosives, thought that six was overkill, but then again it was better to be safe than sorry, especially when trying to kill a killer…if that's what Bob really was.

Next Ramon removed six small, bowl-shaped objects and stuffed explosives into each of them. When he turned them over,

Klaus saw they looked like wall-mounted thermostats. Klaus silently approved of the masquerade. Ramon then attached the thermostat-bombs to six structural columns in the building before going to his briefcase and flipping a switch on a digital transmitting device. An LED readout lit up.

Finally Ramon flipped one more switch and closed the briefcase. Moments later, Klaus watched as Ramon left the building and headed up Sixth Avenue toward Greeley Square.

Because Klaus already knew Bob's schedule and since he understood Ramon's strategy, he knew when to return—there was no need to follow either Bob or Ramon around that night. Klaus decided to go to the Knicks-Pacers game at the Garden— an early season match-up. Surely the odds would be heavy against Indiana and Klaus could get some good action.

Chapter Thirty-nine

Mary stood in the hallway halfheartedly trying to talk herself out of it. But after all this time away from Bob and all the soul-searching she couldn't really help herself; she had to do it. She reached up and took a hold of the dangling rope and pulled hard, testing its strength. Then, resolved to her task, she doubled her purchase on the rope and pulled it toward her head and past her neck until the staircase came down from the ceiling. She climbed into the spooky attic where the trunk of her memories sat covered with dust and anchoring cobwebs.

The combination was easy to remember because it was Bob's birthday, March 12. She wrestled the rusted tumblers to 3-1-2 and creaked the old trunk open. The smell of memories rushed into her nose, causing her to sneeze. There were embarrassing old photographs, high school yearbooks, and knickknacks whose significance had long been forgotten. What, for example, was the meaning of the mismatched jigsaw puzzle pieces? She couldn't remember, but she couldn't throw them out either. She dug deep into the trunk, a curator poking through a back room, and there among the artifacts of her little museum, were the collected letters and poems of one Bob Dillon. Had they belonged to the other Bob Dylan, these missives would have been worth a small fortune. As it was, their value was incalculable.

She savored the old addresses and old stamps and Bob's familiar handwriting on the occasional "P.S." scrawled on the envelope after the fact. She smiled as she flipped through the funky postcards. Finally she opened one of the letters and read it:

My dear, beautiful, sweet Mary—

I was in the middle of writing a paper for my comparative entomology class (a critical look at Stanbrick's classic, *Sowbugs and Pillbugs—Is Carbazole the Answer?*) But I couldn't stop thinking about you, so I had to stop and write lest my affections creep into my paper. I don't want to come off as a passionate pro-carbazole knucklehead.

Remember last week at the bar when you asked who my favorite band was? If you recall, before I could answer, that fight broke out at the jukebox.

The answer is—big surprise—the Beatles.

And if you were to ask me to name my favorite Beatle, I would have to say—*Dynastes tityus*.

See, Rhinoceros Beetles are among the largest of the *Coleopterans* (from the Greek, meaning sheath-winged) and, for reasons I can't explain, I think they are also the most romantic. They're massive bugs that reach nearly seven inches in length in the tropics.

To me, they're the V-8 engines of the insect world with 454 cubic inches of buggy power—and at the same time, I see them as big lugs, awkward and sentimental, just trying to impress their sweethearts. You just have to love them the way I love you.

Now, not that you would ever ask—but if you did, I would have to say my second favorite beetle is the Bombardier Beetle (*Brachinus americanus*). These guys are dark metallic blue and dangerous, just like your eyes. When attacked they discharge a spray of blazing hot quinic acid which will cause blisters on human skin and, needless to say, will scare the shit out of frogs and ants.

This beetle produces the acid by mixing hydroquinone and hydrogen peroxide which, until needed, are kept neatly stored in separate glands in their cuticle-lined abdominal chamber. The constituent chemicals are discharged on demand into a separate sac, where they react with the enzyme peroxidase. The reaction results in quinones and a significant amount of heat. The introduction of oxygen allows the quinones to be expelled with great force and an audible "pop" from a nozzle at the tip of the beetles' abdomen (something John, Paul, George and Ringo could never do). The heat converts the acid to a gaseous cloud which looks like a puff of smoke. And, as if that weren't enough, their aim is fantastic!

Like me, a Bombardier Beetle in love will not let anyone or anything get between him and his beloved without a fight to the death. And just as they are pugnacious and protective, I like to imagine they are sensitive and tender when it comes to romance. I can't help but think these beetles are flowers, candlelight, and soft music kinds of bugs ("If I fell in love with you, would you promise to be true, and help meeeeeeeee understand?")

At any rate, I've strayed from whatever point I may have intended to make when I began this letter, and now I must return to my paper, and I'm sure you have more important things to do too.

Love, Bob.

P.S. I hope this letter isn't overly romantic and mushy because I know that can sometimes be a turn-off this early in a relationship. I can't wait to see you again.

As Mary folded the letter back into the envelope, she smiled and remembered fondly the early days of being in love with her funny little bug man. As she put the envelope back into the trunk, she also remembered why she fell in love and why she swore to be at his side forever.

Then, as she closed the trunk and locked it, she wondered why she wasn't there.

Chapter Forty

Klaus woke in a good mood. The night before, Reggie Miller had gone off for 46 points and the Pacers had beaten the Knicks. Having bet heavily on the underdogs from the Hoosier State, Klaus won a substantial sum for the first time in a long while.

After breakfast Klaus headed for West Thirty-First Street and Sixth Avenue and his perch on the third-floor maintenance roof of the Atlantic Bank of New York. There he would wait.

Bob arrived exactly when the investigator had said he would. He was wearing a faded New York Yankees cap and jacket. Klaus looked at his watch. "You won't live long being this predictable, my friend," he said.

Through the binoculars Klaus glanced casually about the streets below looking for Ramon, his South American colleague. Ramon was there, parked in a loading zone on Thirty-Second Street, conducting surveillance from an obviously rented Dodge Spirit.

After Bob entered the old department store building, Klaus watched Ramon remove a length of heavy chain from the trunk of his car. He crossed Sixth Avenue to Bob's building and chained the doors shut before crossing the street again and entering the Sixth Avenue Coffee Shop, almost directly beneath Klaus' position. He took a booth by the window.

Bob wandered around the building waiting for Sy, who was supposed to meet him to see what had been done so far. "Mr. Silverstein? You here?" he yelled.

Klaus watched and wondered why Ramon hadn't detonated the charges. "What are you waiting for? Just do it," he thought.

And had it been up to him, Ramon would, indeed, have just done it. However, at that moment, inside the coffee shop, Ramon had been set upon by a particularly crusty old waitress.

"So what'll it be, Pepe?" she snarled xenophobically. "The *huevos rancheros* or what? I ain't got all day, ya know!"

Ramon gave her a stony look.

"Don't look at me that way, Pedro! You hungry or not? This ain't no place for a *siesta*! Whaddya want? Fish or cut bait!"

Outside on Thirty-Second Street, an efficient member of New York's Parking Enforcement Bureau was interpreting the signs by Ramon's Dodge Spirit. The car was clearly in violation, so she wrote a ticket and slipped it under the wiper before radioing the tow truck dispatcher.

Klaus, meanwhile, had reached the conclusion that either Ramon's triggering device had failed or he had been mugged before he could activate the thing. It just went to show how hard it was to get good help these days. He watched Bob take off his Yankees jacket and cap and put them on a naked mannequin, then reach for the phone.

The phone on the sales desk rang twice before Bob got to it. "Hello?" Bob answered. "Yes, Mr. Silverstein. Yeah, I'm ready. Are you on your way?"

Sy was on his cell phone, calling from his booth at the deli across the street on the Broadway side of the building. "Listen, kid, it can wait a minute. I'm at the Broadway Deli having a sandwich. Why don't you meet me over here?"

Meanwhile the surly waitress in the Sixth Avenue Coffee Shop forced a menu on Ramon. "C'mon, I ain't got all day, Jose," she snapped.

The sidewalk construction on the Broadway side of the old department store had resulted in some elaborate scaffolding and a covered walkway which completely obscured the door on that side of the building. Thus neither Klaus nor Ramon was aware the door even existed, much less that Bob had used it to exit the building and was now crossing the Great White Way.

Bob joined Sy at the Broadway Deli and watched as he stuffed the last bits of a tasty pastry down his gullet. After paying the tab, they headed back out to the street.

At the Sixth Avenue Coffee Shop, Ramon pointed randomly at the menu. The waitress said, "What're you pointing at, for God's sake? The Spanish omelet? I shoulda guessed." She snatched the menu. "It's about damn time," she muttered as she huffed away.

Unable to see what Ramon was doing, Klaus surveyed the 16-story building as he waited for Bob to return to view. All he could see was the mannequin dressed like a baseball player.

Bob and Sy, meanwhile, were waiting for a break in traffic before crossing Broadway. With Sy, you needed a big break.

Finally free of the pesky waitress, Ramon hurriedly focused his binoculars on the department store windows looking for Bob. When he saw the back of the Yankee cap and jacket he smiled. "Damn Yanquis," he muttered.

He surreptitiously placed his briefcase on the seat beside him, close to the window. He opened the case, turned on his signal transmitter, and flipped the switch.

The readout flashed "ARMED" and beeped.

A moment later he gently depressed the detonate button.

As they waited for a break in traffic, Bob spoke to Sy, "Mr. Silverstein, I've got a really good feeling about this."

About that time, a low rumbling noise began. Bob and Sy paused when they heard the odd sound, but before either could comment, the entire 16-story building imploded and gracefully caved in on itself as neatly as if a professional demolition company had done the job.

Bob stared in disbelief. Sy's look was one of composed fascination. Klaus watched impassively and wondered what had taken so long.

Stunned, Bob watched as his dream rode the wild dust cloud mushrooming skyward. Sy took a long, thoughtful pull on his cigar and exhaled a small cloud of his own.

After a moment, Bob began stammering, "I...uh...this isn't... I didn't..."

Sy waved his big belvedere philosophically. "Listen, kid, I don't doubt the effectiveness of your method, but I was under the impression the building would remain standing."

Unable to manage subject, verb, and direct object, Bob just sputtered, "But...I...it..."

Sy tried to encourage Bob. "Alright, so look, maybe it was termites. I still think you're onto something with this idea. And don't worry, it's insured." Sy looked at his watch. "Listen, I gotta go."

"But... it... I..."

Few of the diners in the Sixth Avenue Coffee Shop seemed to notice that the 16-story building across the street had just collapsed; the city had been decaying all around them for years. Ramon closed his briefcase just as the waitress threw his omelet and tab down in front of him.

"Enjoy, Gomez," she said.

As Sy's limo disappeared up Broadway, Bob stood on the sidewalk staring across the street as if his life were being projected onto a giant screen. It was turning out to be a reel of bloopers.

Finally he managed to summon the motor skills to cross the street, oblivious to the screeching tires and cursing hacks. Spellbound, he weaved his way slowly toward the massive pile of rubble that had been a 16-story building moments earlier. He stopped and gawked at the debris. An arm from one of the homeless mannequins reached out for help. With his right foot, Bob poked forlornly at the rubble and was distressed to see several cockroaches scurry for cover.

So much for Strain Two, he thought. The presence of so many roaches indicated his assassin bugs had failed, but why? He lifted a few more bricks, attempting to find some of his hybrids, hoping to find a clue. But with each stone turned, he found only more roaches. His hybrids were nowhere to be seen, and without them he would never know what had gone wrong.

Bob tried to think it through: Strain Two was the Masked Hunter/Wheel Bug hybrid, which, in hindsight, Bob admitted was never his favorite. It was a stubborn little son of a bitch, a trait he initially hoped would make it a tenacious hunter but on reflection could just as easily have made it determined not to expand beyond the limited wall space where it found itself.

It was possible this obstinate hybrid hadn't even bothered to populate the entire building, opting for small communities governed by what amounted to a zero-population-growth policy.

So Strain Two was a failure, that much he knew. And while discouraging, the information was useful. Even without knowing why Strain Two failed, simply knowing that it failed told Bob the combination of Masked Hunter/Wheel Bug traits were incompatible or at least inadequate to the task.

But what the hell caused the building to implode? Bob knew zip about structural engineering and besides, he couldn't afford to waste much time thinking about such things. He still had to install Strains Three and Four and then go back and check all the buildings. Bob walked slowly down Broadway and turned on Thirty-First, heading for Sixth Avenue. He stopped occasionally to poke at the rubble, only to find more roaches. Realizing there was nothing more to do there, he headed for the subway.

As he stepped onto Sixth Avenue, against the light, the tow truck pulling Ramon's rented Dodge nearly ran him over.

Klaus was satisfied that whoever the hell Bob was, he was no longer a problem. He was also pleased that he didn't have to do the deed himself. That, plus the money he had won, made Klaus happier than he'd been in quite a while, and as he descended to the street, he began to sing, "Start spreading the news..."

Ramon, meanwhile, stuffed a limp piece of buttered toast into his mouth along with some omelet. He chewed viciously as he looked across the street at his handiwork, a self-satisfied smile revealing bits of egg and bell pepper between his teeth.

However, when Bob walked past the Coffee Shop—right in front of Ramon—the South American assassin did a double take and blew wet bits of Spanish omelet all over the window.

Bob, still fazed, didn't notice.

But the waitress did. She hurried over and started smacking Ramon with her towel. "The hell's the matter with you, Poncho? Spitting omelet all over the goddamn window! Clean that shit up, you stupid spic!"

Ramon tried to push the waitress aside, but she was a tough old coot and she forced him back into the booth.

"Hey, Paco, you ain't goin' nowhere until you clean up that goddamn mess, you wetback son of a bitch."

He quickly wiped it up and started for the door, but the waitress tripped him and hopped on his back like a weasel in heat. "Umphfff!" Ramon wheezed as the stout waitress put the sum of her weight on his chest.

"Listen here, you stupid greaser, I frown on that dine and dash routine!"

As the waitress groped Ramon's pockets, he wiggled uselessly, rather like the larva of a Mexican Bean Beetle (*Epilachna varivestis*) emerging from its eggshell. She finally found a wad of bills.

"Whaddya say there, Carlos, you a big tipper?"

She helped herself to about $50 and let Ramon up. He nearly shattered the glass door on the way out, skidding comically to a stop on the sidewalk and almost knocking over a street vendor's pretzel stand.

Ramon looked up the sidewalk, but Bob was nowhere in sight. He had vanished. Dematerialized. Evaporated, just like that. And then, just as magically, Bob reappeared, emerging from behind two rolling racks of dubious-looking stretch lace calf-length gowns with faux pearl buttons which were making their way east from the Garment District. Bob was just past Thirty-Fourth Street, across from Macy's, when Ramon pulled a gun from his jacket and raced after his target. Klaus emerged onto Sixth Avenue just in time to be brushed by the fleet-footed Ramon charging up the street

"Hey, watch where you are going, friend," Klaus said, not realizing whom he was addressing. Then the disfigured face registered—it was Ramon with his gun pulled and a wild look in his eye. That could mean only that Bob had somehow survived the explosion and Ramon was trying to clean up his mess.

Klaus looked for Bob among the thick swarm of tough, damaged people who crowded the sidewalk. He couldn't spot him, so he followed Ramon, who, he assumed, knew where Bob was. As he raced up the sidewalk, Klaus wondered who the hell this Bob Dillon was and how on earth had he gotten out of that building alive?

Ahead, Ramon looked for an angle to shoot Bob, but the sidewalk was too crowded to get a clean shot. Frustrated, Ramon stepped into the street, leveled his gun, and got a bead on Bob. As Ramon was about to squeeze the trigger, he was hit by a frantic bike messenger peddling maniacally up the avenue trying to get an important contract to the offices of BBC Worldwide America.

Ramon's gun discharged when he hit the pavement.

BAM!

No one on the sidewalk batted an eye, but half a block ahead a pigeon shit white on the green head of Horace Greely's statue in the square that honored his name.

Bob shook his own head when he heard the shot but, like the rest of the natives, he kept moving since he knew he hadn't been hit.

Ramon struggled to his feet and ran to where he had parked his Dodge. Seeing it was gone, he began screaming obscenities and shaking his fist at the sky.

Klaus watched with amusement as the inept Bolivian struggled to regain some semblance of composure and make his next move. A cab dropped off a fare nearby and Ramon seized the moment. He yanked the driver from behind the wheel, hopped in, and floored it up the avenue.

It appeared that Ramon was simply going to run Bob down on the sidewalk ahead. Messy, but effective. He accelerated, swerving wildly to avoid the other cars.

A block or so north of Ramon, Bob strolled past Herald Square, oblivious to what was going on behind him. He was trying to decide whether to put his Strain Three hybrid in the SoHo building or the warehouse in Queens.

He stepped into the crosswalk to traverse Thirty-Fifth Street.

Ramon's cab picked up speed and hurtled recklessly across two lanes of traffic. He was bearing down on Bob when suddenly—out of nowhere—another cab cut him off, screeching to a halt halfway into the crosswalk.

Bob neatly dodged the second cab, and, in his best Ratso Rizzo imitation, pounded on the hood, yelling. "Hey, watch it, asshole! I'm walkin' here. You trying to kill me or something?"

Ramon cursed wildly at the cabbie that had cut him off. The cabbie responded with his own stream of scatological references and a colorful native hand gesture.

And that did it. In that instant, unable to endure any more of the madness that was indigenous to Manhattan, Ramon snapped. He pulled out his gun and fired at the cabbie. A shot rang out. He missed.

In one swift and natural movement, the cabbie pulled a .45 automatic from under his seat and fired back, nailing Ramon right between the eyes. The Bolivian assassin slumped onto the horn of his cab.

The fare sitting behind the gun-wielding cabbie never looked up from his *Spy* magazine. He just urged his driver on. "C'mon, pal, step on it. I've got an appointment." The cab drove off.

Klaus watched in awe as this fantastic sequence of events unfolded before him.

Intent on catching the Broadway local at Seventh, Bob continued west on Thirty-Fifth Street, still oblivious to what had transpired behind his back.

Klaus thought something was very wrong with this picture. Bob was like no killer he had ever seen. His movements were dangerously predictable, and even after someone had tried to blow him up in a building and shoot him on the streets, he never so much as flinched. He either had Freon in his veins or he was stupid and lucky beyond repair. Perhaps the puzzle was missing a piece—a piece the sloe-eyed man had failed to find—a piece Klaus would have to find himself.

As Bob descended to the subway, he muttered to himself, "God, I hate this city."

Klaus decided to return to his hotel and review Bob's file.

Just then, the first police arrived at the scene. Eventually, the street was choked with cop cars, the coroner's van, and murmuring bystanders.

A social critic on the scene commented to his friend, "Life's cheap in this town."

His friend agreed, "Yeah, and death's usually on sale too."

And he was right. According to NYPD figures, a contract killing could be had in Brooklyn for a mere $500. More often than not, though, people in New York were killed for free.

A plainclothes detective poked through Ramon's effects: two state-of-the-art handguns, a few detonator caps, three passports. Not exactly typical, even for New York.

The detective turned to his partner. "This guy's carryin' fake passports and enough weapons to be a flippin' arms dealer. And he's drivin' a boosted hack. Some weird shit if you ask me."

"Nobody's asking you," a patronizing voice replied.

A hand attached to the voice snatched the passports from the detective, the other hand flashed an ID. The hands, voice, and ID belonged to a man behind a pair of sunglasses. "Parker," he said, "CIA. We'll be taking over now."

Chapter Forty-one

The news of Ramon's failure and subsequent demise did not sit well with Miguel DeJesus-Riviera. "That bastard! That dog!" Miguel screeched as several of his men stood cringing nearby. "I will have his liver cut out, wrapped in bacon, and served to my soldiers!"

The men looked uneasily at each other, none of them really cared for liver.

"How is this possible?" Miguel continued. "Ramon was my best man! I will kill this son-of-a-bitch Exterminator yet!"

Miguel's tirade was punctuated with a buzz from his intercom. "They are here," said a disembodied voice.

"Good, send them in," Miguel said.

A door opened and four men as tough as goat's knees entered. They were heartless bastards from a world gone wrong. They had spent the last two years running death squads in Sao Paulo, hired by wealthy businessmen to kill the *meninos de rua*, the homeless street children, who they blamed for slow retail sales. Their hearts were harder than trying to open an oyster with a wet bus ticket.

Miguel looked them over and smiled.

An assistant handed the men copies of the now famous fax of Bob's photograph.

Miguel spoke. "This is the *cabron* who murdered my beloved brother." He spit on the photo for effect before continuing. "Kill this pig and I will pay you…" He paused as he did some mental calculations, "…one million dollars!"

The four murderers looked at each other with cold eyes. One of them finally spoke.

"Each?" he asked.

Miguel shook his head. "No, split."

The leader mulled that over for a moment. "Are you firm on that?"

Miguel nodded as the three assistants mentally began to spend their quarter of a million dollars.

"Very well, if that is your final offer I have no choice." The leader casually pulled a handgun from his waistband and shot one of his three assistants, dropping him like a bad transmission. "We accept."

Chapter Forty-two

There was a buzz in the CIA office that afternoon. The Exterminator's reputation had received quite a boost because of his recent kill. Two young agents stood by the water cooler discussing the incident in reverential tones.

"Nailed the sucker between the eyes," said the first. "One shot. Bang!" He slapped his hands to give the "bang" an effect.

"This guy's the best," said the second agent. "First he did that job in Istanbul, then he iced Madari and Pescadores. Then he 'accidents' Huweiler and takes out Riviera and Ramon, all within what, six months? And nobody knows where he came from?"

Mike Wolfe appeared, casually stirring a cup of tea. "Almost nobody," he said.

"You know him, sir?" asked one of the agents.

"Is he as dangerous as they say?" asked the other.

"Worse. Much worse," he said dramatically. "Either of you debutantes ever hear of Dan Mitrione?"

The historically challenged agents shook their heads no.

"Figures," Wolfe said disdainfully. "See, the problem with you techno-pups is you never bother to read books. You get more useful information from one good book than a hundred intercepted satellite transmissions. Mitrione worked for us, and believe me, he was no altar boy. But I tell you, this Dillon character makes him look like a pissy little Girl Scout."

"I hear he calls himself the Exterminator. I love that," said the first agent. "I think that'd make a great TV series."

"Or a movie," said the second.

"Yeah, well, you can bet your little green asses the screenplay's gonna be based on my book. And they damn sure better get Sean Connery to play my part."

Chapter Forty-three

Klaus was looking over the *Racing Form*. The knock on the door startled him as it would any assassin not expecting guests. He pulled a gun from under the pillow and went to the door.

"Yes?" Klaus said.

A man's voice replied. "Room service."

"I didn't order room service."

"Complimentary breakfast and newspaper, sir."

Klaus hid his gun behind his back and quickly threw open the door. From the corner of his eye he saw the glint of chrome and his instincts took over. He fired a lightning-quick side kick toward the gleaming object, sending his complimentary breakfast to the floor, the toast jelly-side down.

"Fuckinay!" the waiter said, his weapon a silver cream pourer. "You seem a little jumpy sir, let me get you some decaf."

Klaus apologized profusely and helped clean up. He tipped the waiter generously and asked for wheat toast next time.

Klaus returned to his room and skimmed the *Times* as he waited for his decaf. It was there, buried deep in the D section, that Klaus noticed a small headline:

"BOLIVIAN ASSASSIN GUNNED DOWN"

The text revealed that government sources had credited an American assassin known as the Exterminator. The government sources also denied any other knowledge of this assassin, except to insist that the U.S. government had never hired him or any other professional killers to do anything in this or any other country as that was illegal and not the sort of thing they did, or even thought about doing and anyone who said otherwise was lying.

Klaus lowered the newspaper slowly into his lap. Something was definitely wrong with this picture. He had to figure out exactly what the hell it was before he made the decision to kill.

Chapter Forty-four

Bob woke the next morning feeling especially hopeful. In his dreams he had been at the wheel of a gleaming new Dodge Ram full-size pickup with an exquisite fiberglass Termite (*Reticulitermes flavipes*) perched proudly on its roof, its wings flapping excitedly as the truck hurried Bob from one job to the next.

Bob was about to sign a multimillion-dollar Natural Pest Control contract with Sy Silverstein when his alarm went off.

Bob took the dream as a good omen. In his bones Bob felt certain that success was looming large and nearby, like a mugger in a dark alley.

Today Bob was installing his third strain of Assassin Bugs, bringing him one step closer to his dream. But the glow of his impending success dimmed at the thought of carrying his tool kit and boxes of bugs on the subway.

Screw it, he thought. Today he'd drive into the city.

After a weak cup of instant coffee, Bob mounted the old smoking Pinto and rode it down to the edge of SoHo near where he was going. He had the address on a scrap of paper, but had lost the damn thing. All he remembered was that he was looking for a failed restaurant that had been named for its location in North SoHo.

There were no parking meters in sight. For half an hour Bob cruised up Mercer, down Greene, and back up Wooster. He finally lucked into a nine a.m. to seven p.m. spot on Sullivan across from the Napoli Bar and Grill. He had no idea how far he was from where he'd be working, but an all-day parking space was a rare and wonderful commodity, so he seized it.

He grabbed his tools and his boxes marked "ASSASSINS, STRAIN THREE" and started looking for…what the hell was the name of the damn place? It had something to do with its location. That was it! NoSoHo—as in North SoHo—a flash-in-the-pan eatery which had been frequented by pointless people resembling characters in Tama Janowitz novels. And while the name—NoSoHo—was bad, the food (a mix of French Vietnamese, Cajun, and Tex-Mex) had been much worse, and the restaurant had failed. Somehow, bayou blackened snails in cilantro mole sauce had not caught on in the Big Apple.

Bob roamed the streets aimlessly for twenty minutes and was beginning to wonder if he should be roaming around SoSoHo instead of NoSoHo. He finally accepted the fact that he was lost and began looking for someone of whom he could ask directions.

Bob turned when he heard a noise approaching from the corner. The noise became a homeless man pushing a shopping cart. Like many people, Bob assumed anyone pushing a shopping cart down a sidewalk was homeless.

The cart rattled with cans and bottles and big plastic sacks stuffed with God-knows-what hung like saddlebags from the sides. The cart rolled ahead smooth and straight. Bob had long wondered why the carts at his supermarket always pulled to the left with the front wheels shuddering wildly. Now he knew—all the good ones had been converted into poor men's Winnebagos.

The man at the wheel had a long, Rasputin-like beard drizzling from his chin which ended up neatly tucked into the top of a dingy white mix-and-match costume, apparently assembled from thrift shops and trash bins. It looked like a uniform that might be required at a radioactive deconstruction sight after World War III. A white hardhat sat so low on his head that his jaundiced eyes were hardly visible. His ears were protected by a headset normally worn by people directing jets around a tarmac. A dirty white scarf around his neck assured that the only skin visible was his nose. His yellowing pants looked to be made of plastic and were rubber-banded tightly around the ankles. A pair of soiled white Converse high-tops completed the post-nuclear apocalypse ensemble.

Bob approached the man to ask directions. But just as he was about to speak, the man urgently held up a white-gloved finger. Bob stared at the finger in silence. The man's eyes opened wide and looked around at things Bob couldn't see. The man then took a step forward, farted loudly, and began laughing and shouting, "I stepped on a duck! I stepped on a duck!"

The man suddenly became quiet again and fixed a stare at Bob as if daring him to say something.

What the hell, Bob thought. "You wouldn't happen to know where the NoSoHo restaurant used to be, would you?" Bob asked.

The man began laughing again as he pushed his cart up the sidewalk past Bob, as if he hadn't heard the question.

Farther up Thompson Street he noticed a forlorn brick building across the street. A sign in its broken window read, "NoTSoHoT." Was that it? The placard said it was a Silverstein Enterprises building, but Bob didn't recognize the name. A moment later he realized some local artist had added the two T's as a postmortem restaurant review. This was the place.

Bob hauled his tools and his Strain Three Assassins into the NotSoHot building. The moment he entered, his nostrils were assaulted by the malignant stench of old ashtrays and tarry cigarette smoke. Sticky brown streams of residual nicotine sweated down the walls like rivulets of poison pancake syrup.

Bob struggled against his gag reflex. He thought that if the food hadn't killed this place, it would have gone under soon enough when its patrons died of various cancers. He tied a bandanna over his nose and mouth to filter out the carcinogenic reek and got busy installing his bugs.

Strain Three was the Western Corsair/Bee Assassin hybrid that, during experiments in the Bug Room had exhibited an uncanny resourcefulness in capturing large, winged insects such as the various types of cockroaches and the winged castes of termites. This hybrid also had an insatiable appetite for the egg capsules and the larvae of most household insects, so Bob saw them as both prevention and cure for infested dwellings. Bob was especially optimistic about Strain Three.

He prepared his drill and again went to work. He drilled hole after hole, feeding his mutant assassins through the dear plastic tubes into the infested wall spaces before patching the holes up again.

At the end of his long day of stooping and crawling and drilling, Bob was stiff and sore. His body resisted as he stood to stretch. His joints protested as he struggled to raise his hands above his head. Once outstretched, he arched his back and took a deep breath, getting a momentous whiff of himself. His eyes watered. He stunk like a sweaty brown onion and, what was worse, he really didn't care.

Bob hadn't showered in days; in fact, all his personal grooming habits, especially flossing, had gone down the toilet since Mary left. The fact that Bob wasn't now considering a bath indicated bad judgment, if not clinical depression.

He slowly packed his tools and departed, leaving the floor littered with empty Strain Three boxes.

Bob slouched toward the battered Pinto and saw the ticket on the window. It was 7:07 p.m. and the ticket was the city's way of reminding Bob that he had lost track of time. He snatched the citation and slid behind the wheel. "Damn," he wheezed. Another expense he couldn't afford.

Bob gripped the ignition weakly and went to turn the key, but he didn't have the strength. His hand dropped to his lap. Where the hell was he going, he wondered glumly. Home? There was nothing for him to go home to. No wife, no child, no love, just a room full of noisy, stinking bugs.

He slumped in the seat, defeated. He looked into the empty night with a glazed stare, his eyes fixed but unfocused the way they used to get while looking at the campfire when his father took him to Big Moose Lake. Only this time, no one was going to yell "fireflies" to snap him from his trance. He felt like crying.

For the first time in his life a crushing black depression pressed down on him. Hopelessness pulled his optimism down a dark alley and cut its throat. He had failed to provide for his family and they had left—and who could blame them? Pratt was right; Bob was a loser. How depressing. He was inadequate and worthless and wasn't kidding anyone but himself with this stupid bug plan. Bob deserved to be shit on and blamed for all the problems in the world. He had sinned against nature and-

"Whoa! Get a grip on yourself," he finally thought, "things aren't that bad." Bob seized control of his swarming thoughts and reflected on his life for a moment.

First of all, Mary was just upset; she'd be back. He knew Mary and Katy still loved him. Secondly, too many people whose opinions Bob valued had said his idea was worth pursuing. He certainly didn't deserve to be shit on and if anyone was a loser and had sinned against nature it was Dick Pratt, not Bob.

Heck, Bob was a dreamer; a visionary perhaps. Without people like Bob there wouldn't be light bulbs or fiber optics or any of the exciting Ronco products. Bob deserved a pat on the back for his persistence alone.

Fall seven times, stand up eight, as the proverb said. Be tenacious. Show resolve. Bob smiled. Things were going to be fine. He just had to keep at it and be patient and pray that success arrived before another dose of that depression.

Bob looked up and noticed the bar across the street. Why the hell not, he thought. He reached in his pocket—two bucks and some change. That might buy a beer, and no one deserved it more than Bob.

As he get out of his car, Bob was unaware of the man watching him from the dark sedan up the street. The man screwed a silencer into an H&K 9mm, holstered it, and followed Bob into the bar. It was an old neighborhood place filled with regulars and red Naugahyde. A television over the bar showed a Giants game.

As Bob approached the bar, a couple got up to leave. The woman wrinkled her nose as Bob's sweaty onion essence brushed past her. He grabbed the stool she left behind.

The man with the 9mm sauntered in a moment later and went directly to the empty stool next to Bob.

He sampled the air, wondering what had died behind the bar. Bob looked to his left to see what all the sniffing was about and found himself eye-to-eye with Klaus, an assassin on a fishing expedition.

Bob acknowledged the handsome stranger with a nod, then put his money on the bar and counted the change. The audit revealed two dollars and forty-eight cents. What if a beer cost two-fifty? It would be bad enough to stiff the bartender with no tip, but to be two cents short on the cost of the beer, well, it wouldn't be right. Maybe he would leave and go to the Pathmark, where beer money went a little further.

The bartender approached. Bob considered getting up. He didn't need the embarrassment. He stood just as the bartender arrived. "What can I get you?" the bartender asked.

Bob scraped his money together and jammed it into his pocket. "Uh, never mind, I just realized..." He was about to bail out with a lame excuse when the handsome stranger spoke.

"Buy you a drink, friend?"

Bob looked at the man. Maybe he was an eccentric who bought people drinks based on their smell. That would be weird, Bob thought, but screw it, New York's a weird place and a free beer's a free beer.

"Sure," Bob answered finally. "Why not? Thanks."

Klaus ordered a Bombay martini, up with a twist. Bob ordered a Bud. Klaus extended his hand. "My name is Kurt Schickling," he lied.

"I'm Bob Dillon." Bob waited for the joke, gesturing for Klaus to go ahead and get it out of his system, but Klaus had none of the usual reactions.

"Okay," Bob said finally, "so what do you wanna hear? 'Like a Rolling Stone'? No? How about 'Lay, lady, lay...'"

Klaus looked confused. "I do not understand," he said.

"Bob Dylan. That's my name, but I'm D-I-L-L-O-N instead of D-Y-L-A-N."

"I am sorry, I am not familiar with whomever it is you are speaking. I am not from your country."

"Dylan's the guy who...never mind."

The bartender brought their drinks.

"Thanks for the beer," Bob said.

"My pleasure." Klaus raised his martini. "*Salud.*"

Bob touched his bottle to Klaus' glass before they drank.

"So, your name, Schickling...that's what, German?"

"That's right," Klaus said. "My father was German. My mother was Greek."

There was a sudden excitement in the bar as everyone cheered a breakaway play in the Giant's game. Bob and Klaus watched.

Bob rooted for the home team. "C'mon Giants!"

"The Giants will never win without turnovers, but their turnover ratio has gone to hell since they lost Conrad and Harkins to free agency," said Klaus.

Bob looked surprised. "That's pretty good for someone not from this country."

Klaus shrugged it off until a loudmouth next to them slapped down a crisp hundred dollar bill and barked at Klaus. "Put your money where your mouth is, pal. Giants are number one."

Klaus calmly pulled some cash from his pocket and neatly laid eight Ben Franklins on the bar. "Let's at least make it interesting, friend."

The loudmouth eyed Klaus for a moment before putting his money back in his wallet. "Yeah, well, if they weren't down by 14 already I'd take you up on it."

Bob was impressed by Klaus' display. "Wow, you make Pete Rose and Michael Jordan look like a pair of Methodist ministers."

"Those two have a problem," Klaus scoffed. "I don't." He was deep in denial.

Bob stared at the cash as Klaus scooped it up. That was more money than Bob had seen in quite a while. "What do you do for a living?" he asked, wishing the money was his.

"I am a...corporate headhunter. And you?" Klaus' line was in the water, his fishing expedition under way.

When Bob blithely announced he was an exterminator, Klaus spewed a fine mist of gin across the bar. Bob patted Klaus on the back as he choked and sputtered.

"You alright?" Bob asked.

"Yes," Klaus said. "I just swallowed the wrong way." My god, Klaus thought, this guy is reckless. There was no telling what a loose cannon like this would do if he caught on to Klaus.

"Yeah, so anyway, I'm an exterminator and I'm starting my own business."

Klaus was wary, but he still had some bait on his hook, so he continued. Would this guy just come out and admit to a stranger that he was a hired gun? "So you're an independent contractor?"

"Yep," Bob said. "But right now I'm refining this special process I'm working on. It involves these insects from the order *Reduviidae*, that're called…"

"Wait," Klaus interrupted, "you kill…insects?" Klaus assumed this was a euphemism for victims.

"If it crawls, I'll kill it." Bob said proudly. "I'm starting with insects because of the naturally available predators. Someday I'd like to try the same with mammals, but I'm starting with bugs because they're easier to hybrid," he said, verbing the noun.

Klaus wasn't sure if Bob was simply having fun at his expense, speaking in extended metaphor, so he cast his line in again. "I understand that 'line of work' pays well." Klaus raised an eyebrow as if it would pry the truth from Bob.

"Truth is, I'm flat broke. I lost this one lousy job and now I'm tryin' to come up with some start-up money to get the business going, so things are pretty tight."

"Hard times, huh?" Klaus said sympathetically.

"You can say that again," Bob replied.

Klaus tried to interpret Bob's words in terms of professional murder, but that didn't work. He couldn't tell whether this guy was speaking literally or figuratively, so he tried a new lure. "So how is this 'business' coming? Have you had any… contracts?"

"Yes and no," Bob said. "I'm doing this one job that I'll get paid for if my idea works. If it doesn't, I'm screwed. I'm tellin' ya, I can't get no relief."

"Yes, I know that feeling," Klaus said warily.

"But you wouldn't believe some of the other stuff going on in my life lately. Some very weird shit, including this guy from France, I think his name was Marcel…"

"Marcel?!" Klaus thought he had a nibble. "Tell me about him."

"Yeah, well him and a guy from the CIA, well, he says he's with the CIA…they think I'm—" Bob looked around furtively before continuing, "—a hired killer."

"No," Klaus said. He was beginning to think what he had on the line was, in fact, a guy who killed insects for a living.

Bob laughed. "Yeah, what happened was I was out drinking one night when this buddy of mine talked me into answering this newspaper ad for an exterminator…"

As he spoke, Bob's napkin fell off his beer bottle. He lunged for it. Klaus reflexively went for his gun, but stopped himself when Bob whacked his head on the brass railing of the bar.

"Yowch!" Bob rubbed his head. "Anyway, can you believe that? Me a killer?"

"No, I can't." Suddenly it was all quite clear to Klaus. This guy was no more a killer than that odd American actor and film buff, Pee Wee Herman.

Outside, a black Cadillac lumbered slowly up the street. It came to a stop next to Bob's hapless Pinto. The doors opened spilling Miguel's three hardened killers onto the asphalt, their guns in hand. They looked the Pinto over, then scanned the street for Bob.

One of the killers barked something in Spanish causing the others to get back in the car. They drove slowly up the street.

Inside, Bob continued commiserating with his new friend. "The whole thing might even be funny if Mary and Katy hadn't sort of…left me."

"Who are they?" Klaus asked, unaware that he was growing fond of Bob after his second martini.

"My wife and daughter," Bob said. He pulled out his wallet and showed Klaus their picture. "How about you, Kurt, you married? Got any kids?"

Klaus hesitated before answering. "No. I have no one." He looked at his drink before continuing. "Your wife, why did she leave?"

"Well, I can't really blame her, I guess. Mary got kinda pissed off 'cause I didn't use poison."

"Poison?" Klaus was embarrassed that he perhaps had reached a premature conclusion. Now, plied with three beers, this man was beginning to talk about poisons. Maybe he was a killer after all.

"Yeah," Bob continued, "she wanted me to use poison on the French guy's job."

"A job for Marcel?" This was it, Klaus thought, Bob had slipped.

"No, no...Ahn-ree," Bob pronounced sarcastically. "I contracted to do his restaurant. I tried my first hybrid there instead of using poison like I promised Mary and, well, the place turned into a darn cockroach convention and Ahn-ree took his money back and Mary took Katy upstate to her mom's."

Nope, Klaus thought, he's back to the bug talk again.

Bob continued, "See, Mary's been edgy 'cause we've been broke so long. Since she lost her bank job, we've been two paychecks away from total disaster. So she was doing double shifts... she's a waitress..." Bob's voice trailed off as he lost interest in the story. He took another suck on his bottle.

"So life is a little hard right now?" Klaus asked.

"Yeah," Bob said, his optimism returning with every swallow. "But ya know, things may be turning around. I just got a big contract with this real estate guy; four buildings, well, there were four, there're only three now. One of them sort of, I don't know, it imploded. I don't know what the hell happened with that. Anyway, I got three more buildings and three more hybrid strains to try. If one of 'em works, I'll be set."

"Life is a lot of 'ifs,' isn't it?" Klaus took one last sip from his martini and stood, certain that Bob wasn't a threat to his career. "Well, my friend, it has been a long day. I must be going. I hope things go better for you."

They shook hands and their eyes met. There was some male bonding, but it wasn't too messy.

"Yeah, you too," Bob said just before he burped. "Listen, Kurt, thanks again. For the beers and for listening to all my yammering. I appreciate it."

Klaus wished Bob good luck, then left.

Bob drained his beer, then, noticing that Klaus hadn't finished his martini, he killed it too.

Between the male bonding and the alcohol, Bob felt giddy. As he stood to leave, Bob looked at the television and saw the Giants kick a game-winning field goal with 33seconds left on the clock. As the loudmouth grumbled something about missing his chance to make an easy $800, Bob rolled out to his car, probably blowing about a .2 on the breathalyzer. Lacking at the moment a friend who wouldn't let a friend drive drunk, Bob slid in behind the wheel of his potentially explosive Pinto and drove off not thinking about what would happen if he were hit from behind.

He had just turned onto Spring Street when the black Cadillac with Miguel's three killers pulled up next to him. Bob kept his eyes on the road until he heard the Cadillac's horn blowing. He saw the three swarthy killers, their guns leveled.

Assuming it was simply an attempted robbery, Bob signaled the men with the index finger of his right hand, indicating "Hang on half a second."

Steering with his left hand, Bob reached into his back pocket with his right, pulled out his wallet, and showed the men that it was empty. He shrugged his shoulders and mouthed "Sorry." He continued driving.

The killers looked at one another as Bob drove on, unshaken. A moment later, just past Broadway the Black Caddy screamed past Bob doing sixty. About 50 yards ahead of him the Cadillac did a 180-degree spin and stopped in the middle of the street, its high-beams nearly blinding him.

The only thing Bob could think of was carjacking, but he couldn't imagine why three guys in a nice Cadillac would want his old Pinto. After all these years, Bob figured he had to accept that almost anything could happen in this city. Still, he was surprised when the killers piled out of their car and leveled their guns at him as they approached. He was flat scared witless when he saw the brilliant muzzle flashes and felt the flying glass as his window shattered.

"Holy shit!" Bob yelled as he hit the brakes and dove for the floorboard. This didn't make any sense. Carjackers, Bob understood, tended to remove the driver before shooting. This seemed more like a direct, if mysterious, attempt on his life. He thought about praying, but where would he start?

"Uh, dear God, it looks like I'm just about toast here. If this car doesn't blow up first, I imagine one of these bullets is eventually going to hit me and could I make a reservation or do I need to contact St. Peter directly?"

That didn't seem very pious, so he crossed himself and said, "Mary, Katy...I love you."

Bob then heard three muffled pops in rapid succession, followed by silence.

For a moment, all Bob could hear was air hissing out of one of his tires and a man yelling from a second story window something about if they don't stop making all that goddamn noise down there, he was going to come down and show them a real gun.

Bob peeked up cautiously through what had once been his windshield. He saw no one, so he slowly got out of his car, surprised that it hadn't blown up in the hail of gunfire. Bob was too shaken to consider that what the killers had failed to do with their guns, they could have easily accomplished by rear-ending him in the Pinto.

Bob saw the gunmen lying in the street, dead and bleeding from similarly located holes in their foreheads. From the size of the wounds and the way the skin was peeled back, Bob knew he was looking at exit wounds, which meant they had been shot from behind.

Before he could examine the wounds further, the sound of leather on asphalt made him look up. Bob squinted and saw the figure of a man striding toward him, passing through steam from a sewer grate and backlit by the high beams of the Cadillac's headlights. The man carried a gun.

Bob didn't know whether to shit or go fishing so he froze, then fell to his knees, figuring he was about to die for reasons he did not understand.

"Please, please don't kill me," Bob pleaded. "I don't know what's going on, but please..." His supplication fizzled out.

Bob covered his head with his hands in the same futile gesture made by many who thought they were about to be killed. The man stopped directly in front of Bob.

"You really are just an exterminator, aren't you?"

Bob recognized the voice and peeked up through his hands. "Kurt? Is that you?"

Klaus helped Bob to his feet. "My name is Klaus. I am also an exterminator."

The full meaning of Klaus' words did not hit Bob right away. Klaus changed the subject too quickly, saying that they had to get out of there before the police arrived. Bob replied that there probably wouldn't be any police for at least half an hour, assuming anyone had even called in the disturbance in the first place.

Klaus insisted they flee the scene until Bob told him about the Kitty Genovese case where 38 people witnessed the slow and grisly murder of a woman involving three separate attacks over a 30-minute period. Despite her pleas for help, Bob explained to the bemused assassin, none of the 38 New Yorkers had done anything to stop the attack; in fact, none even bothered to pick up the phone to call the police.

Klaus wondered how Bob, or any decent human for that matter, could live in such a city. But instead of delving into that, Klaus took advantage of the situation and dealt with the messy details lying in the street. They changed Bob's flat and Klaus explained why he was in New York and why he had followed Bob into the bar. He also explained what had happened to the building that had imploded in front of Bob's eyes.

"Let me get this straight," Bob said as he tightened the last lug nut. "You came here to kill me because you thought I was going to put you out of the assassination business?"

Klaus nodded. Bob stopped and thought about that for a moment. "I'd like another drink."

"I think we should get out of Manhattan first."

Bob agreed. He started the bullet-riddled Pinto and led Klaus to the Queens-Midtown tunnel. They emerged on the other side of the East River and ended up at a mom-and-pop liquor store near the water on Kent Avenue. They ducked in to grab a bottle and found Mom and Pop behind the counter.

Though normally a martini man, Klaus refused to drink warm gin, so he ordered a bottle of Glenlivet. That suited Bob just fine. But as Pop reached for the whiskey, the door opened and two vicious punks with tattooed lips and cheap handguns slipped inside.

Punk one was heard to say, "Freeze or you're all fuckin' dead!" He said it with verve.

The second punk hurdled the counter and pistol-whipped Pop, exposing his cheekbone, and sending him face first into a stack of boxes. Mom went to his aid and got smacked by the first punk, drawing blood from the corner of her withered mouth. She tasted her blood, clinging to her beaten husband as one of the punks emptied the cash register.

By this point, Klaus had seen enough. He stepped up to the larger of the two shits.

"You shouldn't have done that," Klaus informed the lowlife. The scumbag looked at Klaus incredulously before putting his gun smack on Klaus' lips.

"Open wide for chunky, asshole!" The punk turned to his partner and laughed. And that was his mistake.

In that moment—a split second really—Klaus disarmed the little shit, grabbed his greasy hair, and fractured his skull on a cooler.

The other nitwit reacted with his gun, but not fast enough. Klaus drew his own gun and put two rounds through the middle of the punk's wrist. The witless cretin screamed hysterically and stared at his bloody arm.

"Oh, shit! Sonofabitch! Goddammit!" he yelped. "What'd you do that for? Oh, shit that hurts like a motherfucker!"

Klaus approached the bleeding punk and spoke softly. "You have a serious injury. You will need to remain calm until help arrives." With that, Klaus rocketed the butt of his hand into the punk's nose, knocking him out colder than a good martini. Klaus asked Mom and Pop if they were alright.

They were shaken but okay.

"Good, now about that whiskey."

Mom offered the scotch on the house, which Klaus graciously accepted. Then he had an afterthought. "Could I bother you for two lottery tickets?"

After calling 911, Bob and Klaus walked to a spot on the water across from East River Park and Manhattan's skyline. There they sat and drank in the warm whiskey and the gamy fragrance of the river.

It had been quite a night, even by a professional killer's standards, so Klaus tried to calm Bob by telling him harrowing tales of some of his near-death experiences.

There was the time Klaus found himself in Juarez, in the rain, pursuing a *chargé d'affaires* from the German embassy who had absconded with some computer disks of a sensitive nature. Naturally Klaus got his man, but not before having a close encounter with a small, fast-moving piece of lead. The bullet had peeled some skin from Klaus' head and revealed the sphenoid bone of his skull.

"Look," Klaus said, lifting the hair on that side of his head. "There is still a small scar." Bob saw the small white line of raised tissue and whistled. Wow.

Klaus dismissed the experience with a wave of his hand. He started telling Bob about a uniquely complex assignment he once undertook involving the execution of the head of a secret police force in the Philippines, when, suddenly, without warning, the conversation took a completely unexpected left turn.

Before either of them knew what had happened, they were knee-deep in bullshit—faulty memories leading the way—as they recounted imaginary punches thrown during the famous "Thrilla in Manilla," a discussion that soon gave way to the age-old argument of who was the best heavyweight ever.

"It was definitely Muhammad Ali. Float like a butterfly, sting like a bee," Bob said, as any good entomologist might.

Klaus begged to differ, "No. Iron Mike Tyson. In three."

"Three to five's more like it," Bob joked. "Besides, Ali had the reach, the speed. Ali in eight."

"Tyson," Klaus reminded Bob, "is also quick, and he has more power. The most savage punch in boxing history. I won a lot of money betting on Iron Mike."

"Yeah, but he had no defense."

"What? He had the best defense money could buy," Klaus said with a nod and a wink. "What was his name? Dershowitz? It's just that he had so little to work with."

"Good point," Bob said. "Now on the other hand, Marciano."

They looked at each other and laughed. Klaus remembered the lottery tickets and pulled them from his pocket. He handed one to Bob. Klaus scratched his ticket and blew away the soft grey matter that covered the prizes. "Damn," he said before casually tossing his ticket to the ground. Bob picked it up.

"Hey, bud, no littering. I might hate this city but I still gotta live here." Bob scratched his ticket. "Hey, I won two bucks! It's about time I won something."

Klaus shook his head and took a pull on the bottle. "You know, you are alright." Klaus handed the bottle to Bob. "I am glad I didn't kill you."

"Me too," Bob said.

Klaus was drunk for the first time in a long while and he felt warm inside. "You are a good person. You are genuine. I do not meet many people like that."

Bob looked at his new friend. "You're alright yourself, especially for a professional killer."

"You know," Klaus mused aloud, "this is the sort of thing I miss in my life. Sitting with a friend on a night like this, sharing a drink, just watching the river flow."

"Yeah, when it's the East River it's more like watching it ooze, but I know what you mean."

There was a pause as Bob pondered a question. "So, Klaus. Why didn't you kill those shits back at the store?"

Klaus answered quickly. "They did not deserve to die."

"Maybe," Bob countered, "but they're scum; they don't care about anybody else. Sooner or later they'll kill someone."

"Then they might deserve to die, but they did not earn it tonight." Klaus was resolute.

"You should have wasted them," Bob said. "This city's got assholes to spare."

Klaus looked at Bob. "I have rules about who I kill."

"Rules?" Bob asked.

Klaus outlined his philosophy, Klaus' Cliff Notes on Killing. Bob was impressed. He agreed that there was a long list of people who could do the world a great favor by being launched into eternity.

"You ever get scared?" Bob asked.

"I am always scared," Klaus said.

The confession surprised Bob. "C'mon, what about James Bond and laughing in the face of danger and stuff like that?"

"Bond was a spy, not an assassin," Klaus said as he looked out at the river. "Besides, this is not the movies."

Klaus turned to Bob. "You know, I envy you. You have a family. That is something I can never have." Klaus pulled out his wallet and showed Bob a photo of a woman and a young girl.

"I thought you said you didn't have a family," Bob said.

"No. This is the picture that came with the wallet. I just tell people they are my family. You see, I cannot have a real wife or children because they could be used against me. It would not be fair to them."

How sad, Bob thought. He felt sorry for Klaus.

For a long time they stared in silence across the river at the twinkling lights of Manhattan.

Finally, Klaus spoke. "It is quite beautiful at night."

"Imagine what it looks like to a dragonfly," Bob replied.

"Why would I do that?" Klaus asked.

"Their compound eyes have fifty thousand facets. It's probably like looking through kaleidoscopes while piloting a hang glider through a Fourth of July fireworks display on acid."

"I will take your word for it." Klaus looked at Bob for a moment before standing. "Well, my friend, I must go."

"Go where? What's going to happen now?" Bob asked.

"Most likely you'll go your way and I'll go mine. I must return home and settle an old account. And you have to get your family back and continue with your experiments."

Bob stood and wobbled a bit. "Uh, well, since you didn't, uh, eliminate me…is that going to cause you a problem?"

Klaus draped his arm over Bob's shoulder and spoke gravely, "No, but if I hear that you've 'assassinated' anyone else, I will have to come back and kill you."

Chapter Forty-five

Miguel DeJesus Riviera was enraged when he heard that his three killers had been gunned down in the street by this man who called himself The Exterminator. "Who is this son of a bitch?!" he screamed at no one in particular. He kicked a hole in the wall of his newly redecorated office as he planned his next move.

At first, putting out a contract on Bob was simply Miguel's plot to cover up the fact he had killed his own brother; a smoke screen to prevent disloyalty among his troops. But now it was becoming a vital professional consideration and a personal point of pride. No one would fear Miguel if he couldn't pull off a simple hit. And if no one feared him, he too would end up peeling the garlic.

Then again, maybe it wasn't such a simple hit after all. Perhaps this Exterminator, this man with the look of death in his eyes, was indeed a better killer than Klaus. That was a frequently repeated theory being discussed lately by those who discussed such things.

Miguel needed a guarantee that The Exterminator would die and, after considerable thought, he came up with what he felt was a good plan. The plan called for immediate dissemination of a certain piece of information throughout the world, so he did what everyone else did when they wanted to share their thoughts with the world—he called another press conference.

Hungry for good footage and sound bites, the press arrived at Riviera's palace that afternoon. Miguel stood at the podium behind a forest of microphones. He was excessively emotional as he played his part. Method acting, south of the border.

"And as my beloved brother lay dying in my arms, I swore that I would avenge his death!"

On this cue two men carried into the room a large poster rolled up on eight-foot-long poles. They unfurled the poster to reveal a greatly enlarged version of Bob's photo from the fax. Superimposed on the photo was a red circle with a slash through it. A moment later an electric forklift whirred into the room and burst through the paper partition like a high school football team taking the field at homecoming. Six heavily armed men trotted alongside the forklift, which carried a large pallet on which was stacked an immense pile of cash.

Ooooh, ahhhs, and polite applause echoed through the room.

Miguel conceived of these theatrics on the premise that better video had a better chance of making the news. The more who saw this, the more would respond.

Miguel pointed at the cash and pounded the podium. "Ten million American dollars! That is what I will pay whoever kills this Exterminator." Worked into a fever pitch, he screamed, "I will see blood on the tracks! My brother will be avenged!"

When it was over, the stringers for all the American, European, and Pacific Rim television networks did their stand-up wraparound routines and dutifully uplinked the footage to their employers. That night, just as Miguel had hoped, his presentation was broadcast throughout the global village. CNN broke the story. And within minutes of the broadcast, dangerous people from every continent were contacting their travel agents and making arrangements to get into the hunt.

Chapter Forty-six

Klaus was the only professional killer to miss the news. He had just flown in from the States and his in-flight news update had been taped earlier, leaving him in the dark regarding the ten million dollar contract on his new friend Bob.

The taxi driver dropped Klaus at his villa and pulled away quickly, as if he knew there was good reason not to stick around. At the front door Klaus paused to yawn. He was tired from the long flight and needed some rest.

Klaus opened the front door, and upon stepping into the foyer, was seized from behind by two strong men. Klaus reacted with an astounding back flip, landing suddenly behind them. They turned to catch him and he hammered a fist to a windpipe, an elbow to a jaw. They dropped. Klaus readied for more.

Shadow Man spoke from the living room. "Why so tense, Klaus? Perhaps you should consider switching to decaf."

Four guns instantly stared Klaus down.

"Do we have a communication problem?" Shadow Man asked.

"More of a cash flow problem," Klaus said.

"We have been most patient, I think you will agree, but we cannot afford to carry you much longer. It is time to pay your debts."

Klaus gestured to a painting on the wall. "Take my Gauguin. It will more than cover my debt."

Shadow Man took the painting from the wall and examined it. He moved to the hearth, pulled out a jeweled butane cigar lighter, and set the painting on fire, tossing it into the fireplace. "I'm afraid that its market value has just dropped."

"Well, sure, now it has," Klaus said.

"We are interested in money, not post-modern paintings."

"Gauguin was post-impressionist, " Klaus lectured. "Post-modernism was an architectural movement."

The Shadow Man detested being lectured. He gestured again and his thugs tightened their grips on Klaus. "You still owe us a substantial sum."

"Have I ever not paid you?" Klaus asked. He hoped that his exemplary credit record might save him some pain.

"Klaus, my friend, you have a simple problem to which there is an equally simple solution," the Shadow Man said.

Klaus asked what those simple things were, even though he had a good idea of what the Shadow Man was talking about. Klaus believed in buying time in these sorts of situations. That time in Pakistan was a perfect example.

A question came from the darkness, "You have heard of this man who calls himself The Exterminator?"

The image of Bob whacking his head on the brass railing at the bar in Soho flashed in Klaus' mind. "He is a myth," Klaus scoffed. "He is nothing more than a…"

"Perhaps," the Shadow Man interrupted. "But this 'myth' is now worth ten million dollars dead." The Shadow Man explained about Riviera's contract.

"That is ridiculous," Klaus remarked.

"I agree, the job is vastly overpriced," the Shadow Man said. "Those cocaine guys have far more money than good sense. Nevertheless, by killing this Exterminator you can settle your debt to us, restore your prestige, and most importantly, stay alive."

Lately Klaus had thought a great deal about whether he truly wanted to stay alive any longer. The debilitating bouts of depression were growing intolerable, and what used to pass as his reason for living was no longer justifiable. To make matters worse, the world he once had under his command was now completely out of control. Bob Dillon, a simple family man in Queens, New York, had inadvertently put Klaus out of business. And now some coked-up Bolivian was offering ten million dollars for his murder.

Klaus was torn. He liked Bob, but he didn't owe him anything. On the other hand, Bob didn't deserve to die.

Before Klaus could make sense of any of this, one of the thugs pressed a gun to Klaus' head and cocked the hammer.

Tiring of the game, Klaus rolled his eyes. "Oh, please," he said sarcastically, "as if you would just kill me. Dead men don't get much work, you know, and they rarely pay their debts."

"Of course, you are right," the Shadow Man agreed with a chuckle, "but only to a degree." He gestured for his man to put his gun away. "The business of extending credit can exist only if there is an adequate penalty for those who don't repay. Am I right?"

"Granted," Klaus said.

"So," the Shadow Man continued, "after we give you a few stern warnings, we have but two options. The first is that we can put a blotch on your credit record."

The Shadow Man's entourage chimed in with a facetious chorus of "Ewwwww."

"My second option," he said, "and the one I believe sends a more convincing message to others who might consider welshing on their debts, is to kill you."

"I cannot disagree with that," Klaus said. He turned to the Shadow Man's goons. "What about you fellows?"

The goons shook their heads in unison.

"Good," the Shadow Man said, "then we are in agreement. Now, should it become necessary to kill you, I'm sure you understand we cannot afford to do it…humanely."

"Not if you want to be taken seriously," Klaus said.

"Thank you. Now, if you don't mind, I shall demonstrate."

Another gesture from the shadows and one of the goons shot Klaus in the chest with a taser, sending him into electric spasms on the floor. After a moment he was practically paralyzed.

Two goons picked him up and set him in a chair. They produced a pair of pink knitting needles and two small wooden
mallets. As one goon held Klaus by his hair, two others put
the tips of the needles into Klaus' ears and poised to send the
mallets home.

"What is the expression?" the Shadow Man asked. "There
are some things worse than death? A man in your profession
should know this better than anyone. Now, Klaus, I have done
this before and it is not pleasant. Surprisingly, it does not kill
you right away. You suffer intensely for quite some time before
you die. That said, I trust you will listen."

"I'm all ears," Klaus said.

Finally, the Shadow Man stood and walked slowly out of the
darkness. Klaus found himself curious about this man's face. Was
he horribly disfigured? Had some hideous birth defect rendered
his countenance so grotesque that grown men shrank from him?

With each step the Shadow Man took toward the light, Klaus
grew increasingly apprehensive. When the light finally hit his
face, Klaus recoiled, flabbergasted that the Shadow Man was the
spitting image of Buddy Hackett.

"Kill this man," the Shadow Man said with a delicate lisp,
"your 'mythical' Exterminator, and get, at the very least, your
financial life back together, or I promise you will die in a way
even you cannot imagine."

Chapter Forty-seven

Without fear of exaggeration, Mary's scream could have been described as blood-curdling. It was the sort of scream one might expect from a woman confronted by a killer with a jagged and bloody knife. But, as it was, Mary had simply walked through some tall grass, upsetting a few Northern Katydids (*Pterophylla camellifolia*).

Lacking, as they do, sophisticated aviation skills, the large green insects had flown clumsily toward Mary's face, causing her to scream and flail about with her hands.

Katy finally stopped laughing when Mary fixed her with a steely gaze that said, "It's not funny."

"Sorry," Katy lied. "But they won't hurt you. They're just trying to get away."

"How am I supposed to know what they're doing?" Mary asked. "They flew right at me, for God's sake! I thought they were attacking me."

"Oh, right, Mom," Katy said with a roll of the eyes. "Evil, man-eating Katydids. Sure, we've all heard of those."

Her sarcasm notwithstanding, Katy was right. Katydids were plant eaters and were not known to attack humans. Katy was particularly familiar with these *Orthopterans* (from the Greek, meaning straight wings) because of a story Bob told her about how they got their common name.

Bob found the story in Hubbell's *Broadsides from the Other Orders—a Book of Bugs*, a repository of fascinating details and playful writing on insects and the people who study them.

Hubbell turned up a tale out of North Carolina involving a young woman named Katy who fell in love with a handsome young man. But the young man ignored Katy and instead married her prettier sister. Tragically, if predictably in stories like these, the newlyweds were murdered on their wedding night.

As the story goes, to this day these noisy, chirping insects continue debating whether Katy did or Katy didn't do the crime, with the majority opinion being Katydid.

"Do you want to know how they got their name?" Katy asked. "See, there was this beautiful, really smart girl named Katy, sort of like me, and she painted the most beautiful painting anybody had ever seen in the whole world. Then her sister, who was jealous because she was ugly and not as talented as Katy, told everybody she had painted it and that put everybody into a tizzy. So they finally asked the insects who painted it and they all said, 'Katydid! Katydid!' Isn't that a great story?"

Mary, as it turned out, had read Ms. Hubbell's book. She gave her daughter a reproving glance. "That's not the way I heard it."

"Oh," Katy said, "you heard the one about the murder, huh?"

Katy tromped ahead of her mother into the tranquil woods a few miles north of Mary's mother's house in Tarrytown.

"So what are we doing out here anyway?" Katy asked as she watched a Painted Lady (*Cynthia cardui*) flutter by.

It was a good question; the answer to which Mary wished she knew. Sure, she had a goal she hoped to achieve while in the woods, but what did it mean in the overall scheme of her life?

Why were they out there? What did it mean that Mary was about to do what she was about to do? Did it mean she was taking Bob back? Did she think Bob had learned his lesson? Did it mean anything?

"Well," Mary said. "I need your help with something."

"Cool," Katy said. "Like what?"

"Yeah, well, ummm…" Mary didn't want to admit that she had stomped Bob's little mascots into bug dust. Not only would that set a bad example, but Katy would give her endless shit about it and who needed that?

"Well, remember those bugs your dad had sitting on his computer?" Mary asked. "His little mascots?"

"You mean Jiminy, Ringo, and Slim?"

"Exactly," Mary said. "What were they, anyway?" Katy paused. "What do you mean…were?"

"Do me a favor, Katy. Don't worry about the tense of my verbs. Just answer my questions, okay? Now, what were they?"

"Well, let's see," Katy said as she counted them on her fingers. "Jiminy *was* a Northern Mole Cricket, Ringo *was* a European Ground Beetle, and Slim *was* a Northern Walkingstick."

"Thank you for that subtle response," Mary said.

"No sweat," Katy said with a grin.

"Now, where do we find some more?" Mary asked.

"Mo-om," Katy said, turning the one-syllable word into two. "It's not like a department store, like crickets and beetles are on aisle four and walkingsticks are over in Appliances."

"Just answer the question, please."

"But I wanna know what you want 'em for," Katy said.

"Alright, if it will speed the process, I'll tell you. We, uh, they, well, we need to replace your dad's bugs."

"Why?" Katy asked. "What happened to them?"

"That's not really important, honey."

Katy thought about that for a second. "I bet it would be important if I'd done whatever it is I bet you did." Katy's tone indicated she recognized a double standard when she saw one. "So what'd you do?"

"I told you, it's not important."

"I'm going to tell Daaaaad," Katy said.

"He already knows," Mary said. "So you can just abandon whatever little blackmail scheme you're cooking up. Right now we just need to find some more of those bugs."

"Well," Katy said as her hands lighted firmly on her hips, "technically speaking, none of them were bugs in the first place. See, true bugs are a special group of insects with itty-bitty sucking mouthparts, like Daddy's Assassin Bugs. In other words, not all insects are bugs. Beetles and crickets and…"

As Katy explained, with little relation to fact, her idea of the distinction between insects in general and true bugs in particular, Mary bit her tongue and listened, deciding this was her penance for taking Katy away from her father in such traumatic fashion. She also figured if Katy got to hear herself talk for long enough, she'd forget the original question and Mary would be off the hook.

Chapter Forty-eight

The reader board at JFK indicated the flight from Nigeria had arrived twenty minutes late. And now an extremely tall, well-dressed black man made his way through American Customs.

The Nigerian had been to New York only once before, and his knowledge of America as a whole was rather limited, consisting solely of what he had seen on television; including a documentary on American racism produced by the Center for the Study of Southern Culture, the entire *Roots* miniseries, several dozen episodes of *The Cosby Show,* and three *Oprahs*. So he had no idea what to expect in the country that enslaved his forebears yet revered Alex Haley and made Cosby and Oprah two of the wealthiest individuals in the country.

Despite the fact that he was currently ranked number two on the top ten list of assassins, the Nigerian was somewhat apprehensive.

After clearing Customs he collected his luggage and made for the door. But before he reached the cab stand, a group of noisy kids wearing "SHAQ ATTACK" T-shirts surrounded him, pleading for his autograph. Assuming he had been mistaken for someone else, and never guessing it was fellow countryman Hakeem Olajuwon, of whom he had never heard, he quickly signed several scraps of paper and a pair of Reeboks before jumping into a cab and directing the driver to take him away as quickly as possible.

Chapter Forty-nine

The four towering brick smokestacks of the old Schwartz Chemical Company reached into the sky and looked to Bob like the legs of a huge overturned table.

It was early morning and Bob was at Fifty-First Avenue and Second Street on the west edge of Queens, near where Newtown Creek branched off the East River and headed toward Calvary Cemetery. This once thriving industrial neighborhood was now in full decay, taunted nightly as it looked across a debris-choked lot over the river toward the lights of the city.

Weeds stood proud in the cracks of the neglected sidewalks, the eastern seaboard equivalent of tumbleweed in a ghost town. The gutters were littered with ragged old work gloves and rusting spigot handles apparently dropped from trucks as they left the defunct Keystone Iron & Wire Works Company across the street.

Bob walked down the sidewalk toward Sy's dilapidated warehouse. He looked at the deserted three-story red brick building to his right. All the windows were broken; those on the first floor were boarded up. A small bouquet of wilted pink flowers was nailed to the plywood covering the doorway, a pathetic memorial for…what? The building? Some poor schnook who overdosed there? Another gang killing?

Bob read recently in the *Times* that nearly 5,000 people were shot in New York each year. One in ten murders in the U.S. were committed here. How come ole Blue Eyes never sang about that?

Bob began reworking the lyrics to "New York, New York," to accommodate this reality as he continued down the sidewalk with his boxes marked "ASSASSINS, STRAIN FOUR."

This was the Thread-Legged/Bloodsucking Conenose cross, the most vicious and voracious of the hybrids. They unhesitatingly cannibalized their own kind when other food sources were unavailable. They were small sharks with elbowed antennae, rarely sleeping; they were perpetual-motion eating machines.

Their kills were savage, bloody frenzies involving unnecessary dismemberment of their prey before pumping in their digesting enzyme and draining them of their fluids. Bob had a good feeling about this strain and felt the industrial setting fit their killing style.

At Sy's old warehouse, Bob found Walter, the security guard, sitting in a folding chair reading the paper. They had met a week earlier when Bob dropped by to survey the place.

Walter was a wizened old coot of 88 years who had a bad palsy, a large handgun, and a hat that swallowed his head. He wore a hearing aid but was unaware that the batteries had run down, so you had to yell when you spoke to him.

Preoccupied with the task at hand, Bob forgot about Walter's hearing situation and was thus operating under the mistaken assumption that the guard had heard him coming. "Hey, Walter," he said.

Startled and confused, Walter dropped his paper and fumbled for his gun before he realized it was Bob. "Oh, Bruce, yeah, it's just you. You shouldn't sneak up on me like that, I've got an itchy trigger finger, you know. Why, back in World War One, or was it Two? I get them confused…" His voice trailed off for a moment as he tried to remember. "Anyway, how are ya?"

After an exchange of pleasantries, Walter returned to his paper and Bob moved on to do his work, drilling hole after hole, creating perfectly round portals for his Strain Four Assassins.

Hours later Bob watched with fatherly pride as the clear tube reached from the final bug box into the wall space. A stream of mutant bugs marched down the plastic gangway until the box was almost empty. Bob thumped the bottom of the box and one last bug scooted down the tube. He quickly patched the hole, then stood and brushed his hands, satisfied his job was complete.

Walter was on routine patrol when Bob came up on him from behind. "See ya, Walter," Bob said loudly.

Walter looked as if he might have a stroke, but the resilient old guard recovered from the surprise, rolled slowly through his mental Rolodex, and replied, "Alright, Bart, have a good night."

Bob was exhausted after his day crawling around on his knees, drilling and feeding and patching the walls, and yelling at Walter during their frequent conversations as the security guard patrolled the place. All Bob wanted at this moment was a place to sit as he rode the subway home.

Chapter Fifty

The lanky guy was tired of sitting, so the first thing he did when he set foot in the Port Authority Bus Terminal was to stretch his six–feet–four inches as if he'd spent the last two and a half days on a bus from Oklahoma. Which, in fact, was exactly what he had done.

He checked his cowboy hat to see that the rim was crisp and the fold was just so, then he snugged it back onto his greasy head. His shirt and belt were pure rodeo; somewhere between Dwight Yoakam and the Marlboro man. His belt buckle was in fact a hard-won rodeo trophy, a commemorative for having survived eight and a half distorted seconds of hell on a Brahman bull named Butt Pucker, a bull who had earned his name.

It hadn't taken the Cowboy long to realize that rodeo riding didn't pay well relative to the job, so he looked for other, better-paying work and soon found it as a hired killer.

The Cowboy had left home when he was fifteen, driven away by his parents' poverty and abuse, and had spent his youth riding herds on the fringe of the Black Kettle National Grasslands and the few remaining stretches of the Chisholm Trail. Most of the men who did that sort of work were antisocial types who had problems with authority figures. At any rate, it was there, with a friend from the dwindling Kiowa Apache tribe, that he learned to shoot straight and chew tobacco.

The few people who knew him called him the Cowboy, and they never crossed him because he was pure mean.

After quitting the rodeo circuit, the Cowboy's first job earned him $1,000 for killing a rancher in Montana who stubbornly refused to give up some mineral rights he owned. Soon after that a frustrated grad student at Oklahoma State approached him about killing his adviser, who had ferreted out some plagiarism in the student's thesis on animal husbandry. Eight hundred dollars later Oklahoma State was looking for a new professor who could explain the differences between a Brown Swiss and a Red Poll.

The Cowboy spent a few years in the bush leagues killing cheating husbands and over-insured wives before getting his big break. A friend of a friend knew a man willing to pay $10,000 for the murder of one Anthony "Artichoke Bottom" Puttanesca, a big wheel in Vegas who had crossed one too many lines.

Two days after he heard about it, the Cowboy went to Vegas, marched into Mr. Puttanesca's office, put a twelve-gauge sawed-off shotgun in his mouth, and repainted the walls with Mr. Puttanesca's brain.

Based largely on that contract, the Cowboy had hurtled up the charts and was now considered by many to be the sixth best killer for hire in the world. Most of the old pros figured him for a flash in the pan, a one-hit wonder. They felt he lacked the subtlety and sophistication necessary to go the long road.

But the Cowboy didn't pay attention to what other people thought. He felt he had found his calling. A few days ago, in fact, he had received a sign confirming just that.

He was drinking a beer in a honky-tonk in Anadarko, Oklahoma. The owner of the bar had just hooked up a satellite dish and was trying to tune in a *Three Stooges* marathon on TBS when he came across the CNN news bite of Miguel Riviera offering ten million dollars for the head of the Exterminator. The Cowboy knew a good deal when he saw one, so he bought a bus ticket and headed east.

He wandered into the Port Authority gift shop and bought a street map and a pouch of Red Man. On his way out, a blue

satin Mets jacket caught his eye. He liked the way it felt when
he rubbed it between his fingers, but when he saw the price tag,
he shook his head and moved on. He didn't have that kind of
money, not to spend on a jacket, at least not yet.

Despite the fact that nearly $200,000 of his hard-earned
pay was hidden in a cramped, insect-infested cave in Badlands
National Park, South Dakota, the Cowboy was still tighter than
a pair of size four panties on Rosanne.

He asked a passerby to show him, on his newly acquired
map, where he was and which way was north. Once he had
his bearings, the Cowboy thanked the stranger and exited onto
Forty-Second Street with grim determination in his eyes and a
wad of tobacco resting between his cheek and gums.

Unsure of how he was going to find his target in this big city,
the Cowboy figured he'd get a motel room and make a plan.

A little farther down Forty-Second Street toward Ninth
Avenue was the dingy gray three-story brick Elk Motel. The
Cowboy looked up to the third floor and saw a man leaning
out his window, buck naked and gazing nonchalantly down the
street. The Cowboy stared at the man, somewhat unnerved, as
the man's impressive penis swayed in the breeze. What the hell
kind of city was this? he wondered.

It was then that the Cowboy noticed he had become aroused
while staring at the naked man; the bulge in his jeans betraying
him. This upset the Cowboy a great deal and sent him hurrying back toward Eighth Avenue, looking for somewhere else to
spend the night.

About halfway between Eighty and Ninth Avenues, a couple
of predators spotted the Cowboy and stopped to engage him in
some conversation, intending to separate him from what they
figured was his vacation money. One of the punks was wearing a satin Mets jacket like the one the Cowboy had admired
moments earlier. The other punk spoke to the Cowboy like he
had just fallen off a turnip truck, kidding him in the way city
folks tended to kid visitors from the hinterlands.

The one thing the Cowboy hated more than anything else was being treated like he was stupid, so he smiled at the two and admired the jacket, playing the role he knew they had in mind.

"Listen, hoss," one of the toughs said, "I know where a good-looking bronco-buster like you can get some of that fine New York pussy you've no doubt heard about. Girls who'll do things to you you've never dreamed of."

"Isssat right?" the Cowboy asked.

"You bet," the tough said. "All you need is a little cash."

The Cowboy said that sounded like his kind of fun, so he followed the toughs down an alley where the door to this pleasure palace was supposed to be located. No one paid any attention to the screams or the muffled pops that came from the alley—after all, it was probably just some kids playing with a handgun, or perhaps a pro-life activist murdering another physician.

A minute later, the Cowboy emerged from the darkness wiping tobacco spittle onto the sleeve of his new satin Mets jacket.

Chapter Fifty-one

The Flushing local was squeezed tight with piggish business-men scuttling home after committing the grotesque hustle of commerce all day. Others, desperate to make their mortgage payments, ate speed and headed to grim night jobs. Those already defeated by the process stared blankly ahead, dreaming of TV and alcohol as they headed back to dismal apartments with the drained look that washed the faces of those pummeled stupid by the numbing effect of relentlessly dull work.

Bob shuffled through this cheery-looking subway crowd looking for a place to sit. Ahead he glimpsed an empty seat and a moment later he discovered why; the seat was next to the lunatic he had encountered before.

Bob named him Norman, as in Bates, and it appeared Norman rode the subway day and night, waiting for someone to try to rob him or to do anything that might, however unreasonably, justify his gunning them down. That way he would get his name in the paper and, more importantly, get his face on TV and that, he felt certain, would make his mother proud. After all, that damned Andy Warhol had promised everyone 15 minutes of fame and all Norman wanted was what was coming to him. And if fame wasn't going to find him, he was damn sure going to find fame.

Norman saw Bob coveting the empty seat. He eased his jacket back just enough to reveal the butt of a cheap pistol. Norman's chapped and crusty lips split painfully as they peeled back into a deranged grin.

After a peek into Norman's bloodshot eyes—pink windows to a demented soul—Bob decided standing would be a good character builder. He continued past Norman until he found an unused stanchion that he could call his own.

Not wanting to risk eye contact, Bob scanned the advertisements and public service messages overhead. There was one for treatment of acute depression that he considered briefly. Another touted a hotline for abused bi-sexual children of elderly alcoholics. A third offered a helping hand to co-dependent transsexual coke addicts, while a fourth tried to catch the eyes of asexual runaways with attention deficit disorder. Even while trying to lose himself in the dream world of advertising, Bob couldn't escape reminders of why he wanted out of New York.

Chapter Fifty-two

The stunning woman stepping from the cab on Park Avenue was pretty enough to make a priest stop thinking about altar boys. In fact, it had been said that Chantalle could make a bench of bishops piss on the ceiling of the Sistine Chapel.

Her close-cropped brown hair looked pampered and European and her mouth, while soft and erotic, looked capable of suck-starting a Harley. Her body appeared to be the result of a phenomenal gene pool or years of Olympian workouts or both. It was surprising then to see her beeline into the confectionery store.

She was unmoved by the sickeningly sweet smell of chocolates and toffees that burdened the air. She swept past the rows of marzipan and carob fudge as if they were digits sloughed off by multi-colored lepers. The rum candies and the Mexican orange drops begged for attention, but she ignored them.

Chantalle knew exactly what she wanted and she wasted no time in getting it. She stepped to the glass counter and gave close inspection to a tray of exquisite white chocolate truffles, only three of which passed muster.

She had the clerk place the three perfect confections into a small box padded with white tissues and she departed as deliberately as she had come. Chantalle wanted the ten million dollars more than anything except perhaps the notoriety of being the assassin who killed the man known as the Exterminator.

Chapter Fifty-three

The lights from the bugquariums lent their purplish glow to the room, comforting all present. Bob sat in his creaking swivel chair making detailed notes about the day's work.

The crickets were chirping again in the wall spaces, but Bob was too busy to care.

After hours of annotation, Bob closed the notebook and stretched, tilting backwards in his chair and extending his arms far enough to knock a bottle off one of the crowded shelves. It was one of a matching set of six Bob had bought at an estate sale—old-fashioned atomizers with elegant tubes leading to squeezy balloons covered in gold lamé, and once used to mist rare liquid fragrances onto the alabaster skin of pampered women.

Never one to be functionally fixated, Bob used the atomizers to store and dispense various insect pheromones in the course of his experiments. These rare chemical substances were quite expensive, and Bob found that the containers preserved them well. The bottles contained several cockroach secretions, a powerful defensive fluid obtained from the nasute caste of subterranean termites (*Reticulitermes hesperus*), and a sex attractant pheromone for ants which Bob periodically considered using in a nonspecific revenge plot against Dick Pratt.

Bob returned the upset atomizer to the shelf and paused to look into the large jar next to it. Climbing about on the leaves and twigs in the jar were a dozen African Leaf Beetles (*Polyclada bohemani*). These innocuous-looking, medium-sized beetles were tan with a balanced pattern of black dots on their elytron.

Like harvested pheromones, exotic insects did not come cheap. Purchased through an entomology mail-order catalogue (when Bob still had a full-time job), the beetles had cost ten dollars each. He had acquired them early on in his experiments because of something South African bushmen had discovered long ago, namely, when handled, these innocent-looking invertebrates secreted a remarkably powerful poison.

Like a savy coupon-clipper, the bushmen (always on the lookout for an edge when it came to getting dinner on the table), used minute amounts of this compound to tip their hunting arrows. Thusly armed, a hungry bushman could drop a 300-pound gazelle with nothing more than a graze shot. Then it was gazelle-ka-bobs for a month.

Bob initially hoped to cross-breed this awesome weapon into his assassin hybrids, but, alas, the species were genetically too different. Bob now kept the beetles around as conversation pieces, only occasionally considering them as part of his plot against Pratt.

Bob returned to the warmth of the swivel chair and picked up the framed photo of himself with Mary and Katy that stood nearby. He considered calling and telling Mary about his progress, but lately her mother had taken to saying she was busy and couldn't come to the phone.

God, he missed her. Hugging her, just being with her. He didn't just love Mary; he was crazy about her. She made him laugh and he longed to put his finger in her belly button and tickle her, even though she sometimes protested when he did.

Maybe writing would be better than calling. Bob always felt he was better able to express himself on paper because he could choose his words more carefully. He picked up a notepad, wrote "Dear Mary," then got stuck for his opening sentence. He chewed on his pencil for a minute before it came to him. He'd write a poem:

A young man named Bob loved his Mary,
On his sleeve his true love he did carry.
But devotion to bugs,
Led to getting no hugs,
So he wrote her to say he was sarry.

Okay, so it wasn't a poem, it was a limerick, and not a very good one at that, so he tried again:

Bob Dillon was an avid entomologist,
But his lie made his wife entomolo-pissed.
So she packed her suitcases,
And made off like the races,
And now he just wanted to apologist.

That one was a real stinker, so he tried again:

A buggy young man with a dream,
Lost his wife because of his scheme.
So he wrote her a poem,
Saying please come home,
I think we work best as a team.

They were getting worse, he thought. Maybe he was trying too hard. It was getting late and he was tired. Bob leaned back in the creaky old chair, put his feet up, and soon he was sound asleep with the photo held close to his heart.

Chapter Fifty-four

On the flight from Athens, Klaus looked for something to distract him from his troubles. The in-flight movie was a thriller about an assassin which had received "two thumbs down"—not what Klaus wanted to watch while on his way to kill someone he liked.

He ordered another martini and reflected on the irony that he, once the world's best killer, could be so vulnerable. But being a good killer didn't mean you were good at staying alive; they were different games and Klaus was expert only at the former. He gulped down the martini and ordered a third.

Klaus despised his position but there was truth in what the Shadow Man had said; if Klaus wanted to continue living in the style to which he had become accustomed—in fact if he wanted to continue living at all—he had to kill Bob, and that went against every principle Klaus had.

Wait. There was the answer.

Killing Bob would violate Klaus' most important rule. And that, it suddenly occurred to Klaus, just might be the ticket.

If he killed someone who didn't deserve to die, Klaus might be able to bring himself to suicide. His own death would be atonement for Bob's and it would bring his own miserable existence to an end. He would leave the ten million dollars to Mary and Katy and then launch himself into eternity with a clear conscience.

My God, he wondered, how had it come to this?

Klaus ordered another martini and spent the rest of the flight wondering how he would kill Bob.

Chapter Fifty-five

After tipping the bellboy generously, the man of diminutive stature closed and bolted the door behind him. A lurid grin spread across his tiny face as he stripped to his Lilliputian altogether and began an eccentric and suggestive dance that might have been stolen from the dream sequences in *Twin Peaks*. The gnomish gyrations made for a most unpleasant sight. When the freakish dance moved onto the bed, his runty parts wiggled and fidgeted in an up-and-down motion that seemed gratifying to this Tom Thumb cum Twyla Tharp.

He circled his suitcase several times in fastidious prance, a genuine excitement palpable in his nether region. His eyes rolled back in his head as orgasm approached unstoppably and suddenly he collapsed into a tiny pile and began massaging his rigid elfin part.

Upon completion of this peculiar gambol, the naked height-impaired man rolled over and, breathing heavily, threw open his suitcase revealing several dollish dresses, three pairs of frilly pink panties, a sawed-off shotgun, and a snub-nose .38.

This was no ordinary product of endocrine malfunction and dysfunctional family. This was a killer pygmy in a size one, a murdering titmouse, a dandiprat mercenary with a twelve-gauge.

His name was Reginald. He was ranked in the top five. And he was there to kill Bob.

Chapter Fifty-six

Bob savored the smell of the steaming hash browns as they mixed with ketchup on the plates passing by. He was on the Lower East Side at the coffee shop where Mary used to work. A palace of white linoleum flecked with blue and green specks and marred with the short brown trails left by unattended cigarettes. Bob cupped his hands around the coffee mug as he talked to a waitress.

"When did you talk to her?" he asked.

"She called and asked me to send her last paycheck. That's all she said, Bob."

"Did she say when she was coming back?" There was an urgent loneliness in his voice.

"Bob, honey, I'm not sure she's thinking about that, sorry. Listen, I gotta get back to work. You want some more coffee?"

"Decaf."

Two flights up the partially covered exterior stairwell of a building across the street, Klaus watched through his binoculars. He would wait until Bob left the coffee shop and isolated himself. Klaus wanted no one else to get hurt.

Bob stared absently out the window. He didn't notice the man who stopped at his booth, but Klaus did. Klaus knew Mike Wolfe well. They had done business together more than once. But why was Wolfe there? Had Bob snowed him? Was he in fact the Exterminator? Klaus wondered if he was slipping.

When Wolfe spoke, it startled Bob.

"Hey, Zimmerman."

Bob spilled hot coffee into his lap. "Yow! Oouch! Yayaya!" Bob jumped up, startling Wolfe, who held up his hands. "Whoa, big fella, it's just me."

"Oh, Christ," Bob said when he recognized the alleged federal employee.

"I guess you've earned the right to be jumpy after Riviera's little press conference. I hope that's decaf you're drinking. Mind if I sit?"

"What do you want?" Bob asked, not in the mood for this. Wolfe eased into the seat opposite Bob. "You mind if I ask what you're doing sitting by the window?"

Bob looked at the window, then at Wolfe. "Could you repeat that? Maybe I didn't understand the question."

"Ohhhh, wait a second," Wolfe said as he held a finger to his nose before pointing at Bob. "I get it. If you're so obvious, they can't see you. That's from *The Art of Camouflage* if I'm not mistaken. I should've known you read the classics."

"You don't happen to speak any plain English, do you?"

"Look, Bob," Wolfe said, ignoring the question, "I got a favor to ask."

"Wait a second," Bob said, "listen to me. I talked to Klaus. He explained everything."

"You talked to Klaus?" Wolfe was surprised.

"Yeah, now I know…"

"…about the ten million dollars on your head? I bet you do. What else did Klaus say? How's he doing, anyway? I haven't seen him since, well, I probably shouldn't say when."

"The ten million…what?" Bob asked, not sure he had heard Wolfe correctly.

"Ahhh. Just as I expected." Bob's denial confirmed that he knew exactly what was going on.

"Good," Wolfe said. "I just wanted to be sure. Oh, and do me a favor, would you? Try and keep the gunplay to a minimum if you can…Mr. Zimmerman." Wolfe winked at Bob.

"What are you talking about?" Bob asked. "Who is Zimmerman? And stop winking at me. It makes me nervous."

"C'mon…'Bob.'" Wolfe winked again.

"Is there something in your eye?"

"Look," Wolfe continued, "we figure that much money is going to bring out all the top mechanics."

"What is that," Bob asked, "some sort of obscure warning about a Mr. Goodwrench convention?"

Wolfe smiled. "Yeah, Mr. Goodwrench, that's good. You are one cool customer, if you don't mind my saying so."

Bob thought the man might go away if he just humored him. "Listen, I'll do what I can about the mechanics and the gunplay," he said. "Time for you to go now. Thanks for dropping by. Hi to the wife."

Wolfe stood to leave. "Thanks, Bob. And good luck."

"Hey, I don't need luck," Bob said, "I'm Zimmerman, remember?"

Wolfe turned and gave Bob a final wink before leaving.

Across the street Klaus considered the possibilities. He wasn't sure what to make of this meeting between his friend Bob, and his former CIA contact. Was Bob one of them? Had Wolfe tipped Bob on Klaus' money problems and the fact that he had reentered the country? Was it possible Bob was the killer everyone said he was? Could he afford to wait to find out? Maybe he had better kill Bob now instead of waiting.

Klaus opened the small suitcase at his side.

As Bob stared out the greasy window of the coffee shop, Klaus assembled the Steyr AUG .223 with the laser sight.

Bob was on the verge of making the biggest decision of his life. Would he lose his dream or would he dream alone? Which would be worse? Were those his only options?

As Bob thought about choices and the pursuit of happiness, Klaus thought about trajectory and crosswinds, though at this distance, those were of minimal concern. His weapon assembled, Klaus focused the sight and lined up a shot in the center of Bob's forehead.

The choice was obvious. Forced to choose between his dream and his family, Bob would abandon his dream. Mary was right. He was past that time in his life when he could indulge in the pursuit of something so frivolous. Maybe he would get another chance someday, and if not, he had no one to blame but himself.

The words from an old song popped into Bob's head, "Is a dream a lie if it don't come true, or is it something worse?" Who wrote that? Bob wondered. Oh yeah, Bruce Springsteen, the man once hailed as the new Bob Dylan.

"I'm sorry to do this Bob, but it will be painless." Klaus started to squeeze the trigger when a dark blob suddenly obscured his scope. A young man had stopped to check his hair in the window, directly in the line of fire.

"Damn," Klaus muttered.

Bob stood and headed for the pay phone. He was going to call Mary, tell her what he had decided, and ask her to come home. He'd get a job at Orkin and see about a teaching position somewhere.

When the self-centered pedestrian finally moved, Bob was no longer in Klaus' sight. "Shit!" Klaus said. He wanted to get this over with and he was beginning to feel unusually frustrated.

Bob dropped a quarter into the pay phone and dialed. He waited for an answer, half wanting to hang up and rethink his decision. Then a voice behind him said, "Entomolo-pissed?" Bob recognized not only the voice but also the word he had coined. He dropped the receiver and spun around.

It was Mary and Katy, all smiles and just in time to save Bob's dream. "Daddy!" Katy squealed as she leapt into his arms. Mary stood by, smiling at her nutty professor.

From his perch, Klaus looked like some goofus at an amusement park shooting gallery scanning back and forth with his rifle looking for ducks to shoot. He finally found his prey near the pay phone with Katy hugging his neck. He then saw Mary, smiling broadly. Klaus recognized them from the photo Bob had showed him.

Shit, maybe Bob really was just a guy whose wife left him after a little blowup. And if that were true, this touching scene had rapprochement written all over it.

"I don't need this," Klaus said as his trigger finger went limp. "It's a goddamn Hallmark card."

Katy finally let Mary have a turn. She and Bob regarded each other for a moment, then dove into a rib-bending hug.

"Hi, honey," Mary said. "Sorry I let you down."

"No. It was my fault," Bob confessed. "I lied. I'm the one who should apologize."

"You're right," Mary said. "You did lie."

"Let it go, Mom," Katy said.

"You're back, that's all I care about. You know, it's funny, I was just calling to tell you…"

Another lie suddenly forced its way into Bob's head. Why tell Mary he was ready to abandon his dream if she was already back? Telling the truth would only take away from the sacrifice Mary had made. It would be selfish for Bob to tell the truth just so he could play the martyr. Lying was the considerate thing to do.

"I was just calling to tell you I got all the hybrids installed and now all I've got to do is check them. I'm positive one of them is going to work." Bob paused for a moment before continuing. "God, I'm glad you're back!"

"Me too." Mary hugged Bob. Katy put her arms around her parents and they drew her in.

"Hey, Mom," Katy said as she pulled away from their huddle, "show Dad what we got him."

"Oh, I nearly forgot," Mary said. She unzipped her purse and removed a small jar with three airholes poked in the lid. In the bottom of the jar, four glistening examples of *Cotalpa lanigerae*, heavy and egg-shaped, clambered about.

"Goldsmith Beetles!" Bob exclaimed. "They're beautiful!"

Bob was right. The metallic sheen of their bright yellow exoskeleton made these scarabs look like jewelry. The soft white woolly hair that brushed out from their undersides looked like the winter fur of the ermine that trimmed the coronation robes of kings. It lent the bugs a sense of royalty as their distinctive clubbed antennae fanned out to take in the odors of the coffee shop.

Bob knew the Goldsmith Beetle from high school lit class. As his teacher was sleepwalking through an uninspired reading of Poe's "The Raven," Bob flipped back a few pages in the literature textbook and found an engaging short story entitled "The Gold Bug," which featured one of these very same insects in an important role.

He was touched that Mary had made the effort to find them.

"We got four of them," Katy said. She pointed at two of the beetles which were sidling up to one another. "These two spend a lot of time together, so I named them John and Paul. The one tapping his tarsus is Ringo, so that makes the other one George."

"To replace the ones I stepped on," Mary said by way of reminder.

"You stepped on them?" Katy asked incredulously.

"More like crushed under her boot heel," Bob said to Katy. "But there's no need to get into that."

"I can't believe you stepped on them!" Katy said.

"Why not?" Mary said a bit brusquely. "I mean, they're just bugs for God's sake!"

"Well," Bob said, "technically speaking, they're not true bugs."

"See?" Katy said.

Mary laughed. "Actually, I knew that. Katy explained about the sucking mouthparts. I just wanted to see if you were paying attention."

"C'mere," Bob said as he extended his arms, "I'll give you some attention." He took Mary and Katy into his arms again. "I love you guys."

As Klaus watched the Dillon family reunion through his rifle scope, the scene dissolved in his mind's eye into an image of a family of his own. A family that had never existed.

For a moment Klaus imagined happier days, days spent playing with a little girl laughing on white sandy beaches and making love with a wife on warm Mediterranean nights. These were days and nights Klaus had never allowed himself and never could.

With a blink, the scene of the Dillons returned. And Klaus knew he couldn't kill Bob. He discarded all the double-talk and went with his gut; Bob was just a guy with a family and a dream. He didn't deserve to die and Klaus wasn't going to kill him, no matter what the personal cost.

Klaus wanted Bob to have what he himself never did: the love of a family. The moment revealed Klaus as nothing more than a hopeless romantic with a high-powered, laser-scoped rifle.

As Klaus' scope wandered from Bob's head, it chanced upon a pair of nefarious-looking fellows standing by Bob's car. They appeared to be discussing a small package, vis-a-vis the hapless Pinto. Klaus watched one of the two slip underneath the car with the small package while the other produced a silenced handgun and slithered up the sidewalk toward the coffee shop. Klaus didn't recognize their faces, but he recognized their intentions.

It was an easy decision. After all, they say every man must need protection. Klaus aimed carefully and squeezed the trigger.

Fwap! A kneecap split in two. The guy under Bob's car screamed and smacked his head on the transmission, knocking himself out cold.

Klaus squeezed again. Fwap! Crack! The sound of lead shattering the second kneecap was sickening. The guy would have screamed again, but mercifully he had not regained consciousness. He lay under the Pinto with the package resting on his chest. Klaus, meanwhile, acquired his second target. The guy with the gun by the coffee shop window raised his weapon when Klaus squeezed again.

Fwap! Frontal cortex. A red mist of blood and tiny splinters from the frontal and parietal bones scattered in the breeze. All the impulses controlling involuntary activity were permanently interrupted. But before he buckled into a flaccid mound on the sidewalk, the shooter squeezed off one shot. Then he soiled himself.

The shot shattered the window and a ketchup bottle which exploded tomato-y shards of glass all over some nearby patrons.

Not sure and, for that matter, not caring whether it was a postal employee or a Mafia matter, Bob grabbed Katy, Mary, and the Goldsmith Beetles and joined the other patrons on the floor.

After several seconds of silence, Bob turned to Mary. "C'mon! The car's outside!"

"So is the shooting!" Mary said pragmatically.

"Good point," Bob said. "Let's wait here a minute."

As they waited for a break in the gunplay, they watched a female German Cockroach (*Blattella germanica*) scuttle past. The common name for this cockroach was the Croton Bug. The name derived from the fact that they first became household pests in 1890 when New York City began augmenting its municipal water supply with water from the Croton Reservoir. Bob knew by the way she scooted low to the ground, she was going to deposit her ootheca, a leathery egg capsule. In two days the eggs would hatch and thirty German nymphs would be welcomed to The Big Apple.

After two or three minutes without any more shots fired, many of the customers stood and began complaining about the interruption of service and the shards of glass in their food. With things returning to normal, Bob scooped Katy into his arms, took Mary by the hand, and hurried toward the door.

"Hey! What about the Beatles?" Katy asked.

"We'll leave them as a tip," Bob said.

As they left the coffee shop and headed up the sidewalk, Katy imagined the expression of the overjoyed waitress when she found her gratuity.

As they jaywalked toward the Pinto, Mary noticed the missing windsheild, the bullet holes, and the man with two bleeding kneecaps underneath.

"Bob, what the hell happened to the car and what's that guy with the kneecaps doing?"

Before Bob could answer, a large sedan screeched up, fishtailing, and cut them off. The driver reached across the seat and threw open the passenger door. He gestured with a large handgun and yelled, "Get in! We're not safe here!"

"We're from here," Mary said. "We know it's not safe."

"Get in!" he shouted.

"We've got a car, thanks," Mary explained.

Klaus raised his gun, "Now, Bob!"

"How does this guy know your name?" Mary asked.

"Just do what he says," Bob advised.

"Hurry!" Klaus screamed.

When they got in the car, Klaus gunned the powerful eight cylinder engine up the street. Behind them—KABOOOOM!— the Pinto blew sky high.

Katy spun and watched the rising fireball out the rear window. "Wow! Cool! Now can we finally get a new car?"

No one answered.

Klaus was driving like a bat-out-of-hell in a top-fuel funny car; everything spinning past them in an alarming blur.

"What the hell's going on?!" Mary asked as she held on tight. "What happened to our car? Who the hell are you?"

"Tell me where to go!" Klaus shrieked.

"This left then a quick right," said Bob.

"There are people trying to kill Bob. That was probably a plastic explosive. I'm Klaus." He reached over the seat and shook Mary's hand while simultaneously making a 90-degree turn at 60 miles per hour. Mary screamed.

"Yeeaaaaaaa!" Katy howled with delight.

"What the hell is he talking about, Bob? And where the hell did he learn to drive?"

"Take the next right!" Bob yelled. "Well, honey, there are a few things I haven't told you."

"Hey, let's go back and watch the car burn," Katy said. No one responded. She wished adults wouldn't always ignore her. She sat in the back seat and amused herself by making explosion and crash sound effects. "Kaboom!"

Bob continued yelling at Klaus. "Left at the light! I thought you'd gone home. What happened?"

Klaus made the left turn, nearly clipping the pedestrians in the crosswalk. He glanced in the rearview mirror as he said, "I did go home, but I came back when I found out Miguel put out a contract with your name on it."

"Miguel?" Mary asked. "A contract? You finally got a contract? Oh, honey!"

"You came back to protect me?" Bob was touched.

"No, I came back to kill you," Klaus said.

"You what?" Bob squawked.

"Don't worry, I changed my mind."

"Somebody back up and tell me what's going on," Mary said.

"Miguel Riviera killed his brother Ronaldo so he could take over their cartel," Klaus explained to Mary, "then he blamed Bob because of Wolfe's contract on Ronaldo."

"What cartel? Who the hell is Wolfe?" Mary inquired.

A light rain began to fall as Bob attempted an explanation. "Wolfe's CIA, or so he says. Take Fourth Street, Klaus! Ronaldo and Miguel are coke dealers, I think."

"Fourth? Are you sure?" Klaus asked.

"Positively! Fourth Street!" Bob repeated.

"Wolfe is definitely CIA," Klaus said as he fishtailed the sedan around the rain-slicked corner.

"Ka-boom!" Katy yelled from the back seat. "This is so cool!"

Chapter Fifty-seven

A somber Asian man moved down the crowded streets of Soho in the rain searching for a place to eat. He was looking for a place called Lee Ho Fooks. He wanted to get himself a big dish of beef chow mein. He was quite hungry, having worked up a hearty appetite on the first day of his hunt for the Exterminator.

As he stood on a corner waiting for the light to change, a bratty eight-year-old came out of nowhere and shoved an old *Teenage Mutant Ninja Turtle* doll into the hungry man's face.

In a flash the man flipped his wrist, and in a glimmer a razor-knife materialized in his hand. Fast as an impulse he surgically lopped off the Turtle's plastic head, spilling imaginary turtle blood on the sidewalk.

The child screamed horribly as he tried in vain to reattach the decapitated head. In another twinkling the blade disappeared, the light changed, and the Asian man smiled sadistically as he crossed the street in search of food.

Chapter Fifty-eight

Klaus was not driving as maniacally as he had been. He felt he had put sufficient distance between them and the smoldering pile of Ford that used to be Bob's Pinto.

"So, let me see if I got this straight," Mary said. "Wolfe knew *somebody* wanted Huweiler dead."

"Right," Klaus said, "probably Mrs. Huweiler, given how those things usually work."

"So, Mrs. Huweiler hired Marcel to hire someone else to kill her Mr. Huweiler. Then, for some reason, Marcel thought he had hired Bob to kill Huweiler."

"Because I answered that ad in the *Times*," Bob said.

"Okay, right, that night at Freddy's. Right. Then Huweiler died in a car accident and both Marcel and Wolfe concluded Bob had killed him and made it appear accidental."

"It's classic Wolfe-logic," Klaus pointed out. "*Post hoc, ergo propter hoc.*"

"Let me finish," Mary said. "Next, a cab driver killed Miguel's man, Ramon. That pissed Miguel off even more so he sent a trio of killers after Bob. And Klaus killed those three guys the night you two met."

"I think you've got it," Klaus said.

"Now, Miguel thinks Bob killed Ramon and his hit squad, which humiliates Miguel in the eyes of the international criminal community, so he put a ten million dollar bounty on Bob to make sure *someone* kills him. That's the part I don't get. Why do that if he knows Bob didn't kill his brother in the first place?"

"It was probably just part of a smokescreen at first, but when his hirelings failed, machismo took over and now he just wants to get it done to save face."

"Wow!" Katy exclaimed. "This is neat. Somebody's paying ten million dollars to kill dad?"

"I thought about doing it for free after you lied to me," Mary said, though she only half-way meant it. At this point she'd definitely take the money.

"Now that you know the story, you know we cannot stay here. We are in very serious danger." Klaus' tone was severe. "That bounty is going to bring out the best players. A few amateurs, like those two at the coffee shop, will also join in, but they should not prove any more troublesome than the ordinary citizens of this damned city. But the others…They will be well informed, well armed, and not so well-intentioned."

"By the best players, I assume you mean assassins?" Bob asked.

"Yes, most likely we will have to deal with the Nigerian," Klaus explained. "He is an expert marksman who uses cyanide-tipped bullets."

"Isn't a poison bullet redundant?" Mary asked.

"Not if he only grazes you. He leaves nothing to chance," Klaus said.

"Oh, that's good," Bob said, impressed.

"Another one likely to show up is the Cowboy, a ruthless killer. Money means everything to this man. He will kill for a dollar, so ten million will certainly motivate him. I have come up against him before. He is unyielding and crude and he usually gets what he is after. When he is done, he marks his victims with tobacco spittle."

"Oh, gross!" Katy said.

As she listened to Klaus, Mary looked to Bob and mouthed "Is this guy for real?" Bob nodded.

"Then there is Chantalle, from Marseilles," Klaus said wistfully. "I believe she is currently ranked fourth. She never stumbles. The law cannot touch her. She is like a leopard, exquisite and terrifying. I have seen her kill with lipstick."

"Wow, how cool!" Now Katy was impressed.

"She wears an Egyptian ring when she works and she leaves a white chocolate truffle in her victim's mouth. She once spent an entire week in Madrid looking for one perfect chocolate."

"How do you know that?" Bob asked.

"Someone told me," Klaus said flatly. Then, after a short pause, he yelled, "I was with her, for God's sake! It's obvious how I know. It's not as if any of this is original!"

"Sorry," Bob blushed.

"There is also Reginald, the dwarf," Klaus continued. "He is a cunning little executioner who likes to wear dresses. He sometimes disguises himself as a child—albeit an ugly one, to get close to his victims. He has never failed."

"What size dress does he wear?" Katy wanted to know. "Has he ever been on Oprah?" Still, the adults ignored her.

"Almost certainly we will have to deal with Ch'ing," Klaus continued. "He is an expert in barehanded killing techniques, though he prefers the use of edged weapons in his work. He may be the best—next to myself, of course."

"What's the deal with the trademarks?" Katy asked.

"It's a signature. It confirms who did the job. I never bothered with that sort of thing. To me, dead is dead." Klaus shrugged.

"That's a comforting thought, Klaus," Bob said before pointing out that the light had turned green.

"Can't we just tell these people Bob didn't do what they think he did?" Mary asked.

"Sure," said Bob. "And you can tell the nice folks at TRW that we always wanted to pay our bills on time…"

"He is right, they do not give a damn. They are only after the money. The point is, we are in terrible danger. We must leave the city immediately."

"Okay," Bob said. "I'll check the last three buildings, then we're outta here."

"No. You do not understand. We must leave now. Which is closer, La Guardia or JFK?" Klaus was insistent.

Mary was not pleased that the assassin was suddenly playing travel agent. "Airport? Where are we going? When are we coming back?" she asked.

"You are not coming back if you want to live," Klaus said.

"Well that's ridiculous," Mary said. "I've got to go home and get some things. You don't just go to the airport and hop on a plane without luggage. It just isn't done."

"You can buy new clothes," Klaus said.

"I'm not just talking about clothes, there's other stuff."

"It is out of the question," Klaus replied. "These people will find your house as easily as I did."

"How'd you find our house?" Bob asked.

"We're in the phone book, dad!" Katy said.

"Oh, yeah."

Mary looked to Bob, putting a hand to her throat and mouthing "My locket." Bob nodded.

"Yeah, Klaus, listen, we really would like to swing back by the old homestead real quick if you don't mind."

"You people are insane!" Klaus was losing his patience. "Didn't you hear the part about the assassins?" Suddenly, Klaus hit the brakes to avoid slamming into a cab. He looked around and saw they were stuck in gridlock. "Now we are sitting ducks."

"We have to go home," Mary insisted.

"Impossible," Klaus said. "You cannot go home. Whatever you want cannot be worth dying for."

"Listen," Mary said, "it won't take five minutes. See, Bob's grandfather gave me a locket on our wedding day. It was Bob's grandmother's and someday Katy will give it to her daughter, and yes, to me it's worth risking my life."

After a lifetime in New York, glib phrases about risking one's life had lost real meaning for Mary. She had no understanding of the danger they were in.

In the mirror, Klaus saw a tall black man unfolding from a cab half a block behind them. It was the Nigerian.

"Alright!" Klaus exclaimed.

"Really?" Mary said, surprised. "That's more like it."

"Bob, out of the car! Now!" Klaus turned urgently to Mary. "A landmark near the airport?"

"Which one?" Mary asked.

"Uh, JFK," Klaus said.

"Hmmm, well, there's Howard Beach," Mary said, "but you don't really want to go there."

"Aqueduct!" Klaus blurted. "Meet us there in four hours. Do not go home! Swear that you will not go home! I will get your damn locket later."

"Alright, alright," Mary said, "don't get so excited. We'll meet you at the track."

Mary clambered into the front seat as Bob and Klaus got out of the car.

The Nigerian, 50 yards away, drew his weapon. Klaus took Bob's arm and pulled him down an alley, away from the car. A block away, on First Avenue, they were still running. Bob looked over his shoulder. "Who are we running from?"

"Back there," Klaus said without looking back.

"I don't see any ..." Bob finally saw the enormous Nigerian and his gun. "Wait a second, black guy, about six foot eighteen? Carrying the gun? Him?"

Klaus nodded.

"Take a left here. I know a building we can cut through and shake him."

A few moments later, Bob and Klaus were at the front door of the abandoned apartment building in the Lower Bast Side, gasping for breath. Bob had the key in the lock, but the lock was rusty and he was having a hard time getting it open.

"This is where I'm trying my second strain of Assassin Bug," Bob said as he fumbled with the key. "It's a cross between an Ambush Bug and a Spined Assassin. I bet you didn't know there were Assassin Bugs, did you?"

"Hurry up," Klaus said as he looked around anxiously.

"It's true," Bob said. "There are about a dozen different species of them."

Klaus could wait no longer for Bob to get the door unlocked. In one sudden, powerful movement, Klaus kicked it open.

"Hey! Who's going to pay for that?" asked Bob as he fingered the splintered doorjamb.

Klaus shoved Bob inside, slammed the door, then peered out the window to see if the Nigerian had spotted them. The towering black assassin was nowhere to be seen.

Bob began inspecting the floor of the building. He noticed something and bent to pick it up. "Hey, look!"

Klaus spun, his gun drawn, only to find Bob holding up a dead roach by its antennae.

"Dammit," Klaus said. "Do not say things like that."

"I gotta check this out," Bob said, excited by the possibility of success.

"Are you mad?" Klaus asked. "Have you simply lost your mind? If the Nigerian saw us come in here, we have a serious problem. We will be dead."

"Just give me thirty seconds," Bob pleaded.

"We don't have thirty—" But it was too late, Bob ran up the stairway. Incredulous, Klaus followed.

In a large, windowed room on the second floor—a room that would probably rent for $3,500 a month when it was renovated—Bob stood on a crate trying to pry a ceiling panel loose.

Klaus watched nervously until he heard a noise behind him. Instinctually, he spun and fired two silenced shots. FWAP! FWAP! It was a rat. A dead rat now.

Bob looked down. "Nice shot. I bet you could get steady work doing that for the city." After another moment futzing with the ceiling panel, Bob got it loose and peeked inside. As he lifted the panel, several roaches and some hybrids spilled onto the floor below.

"Holy cow!" Bob had never in his life seen anything like this. "What the hell happened here?"

He could hardly believe his eyes. Writhing within the crawl space as far as he could see was a four-inch-thick black mat of roaches and hybrids slithering over one another in some sort of Caligulian orgy of insects. There appeared to be a third type of bug in the mix, but its phylum was at that moment unknown to Bob.

From what he could see, Bob figured that Strain Two, with its unrelenting sex drive, had been so busy mating that it had not taken the time to be an assassin. This resulted in a stunning and grotesque population explosion of both cockroaches and the Strain Two hybrid.

As that much became clear, Bob put it all together. The third insect must be a fourth-generation cross of the cockroaches and Strain Two—a hybrid whose DNA told the bug it was both a roach and a roach killer. An insect so full of self-loathing that it killed itself and became food for Strain Two.

"I'm such an idiot," Bob mumbled.

Accepting failure, Bob pushed the ceiling panel back into its original position. Suddenly, one of the windows exploded in a spray of glass and the Nigerian crashed into the room, knocking Klaus down and sending his gun spinning off to lodge against the dead rat. The Nigerian quickly rolled away toward the deceased rodent and retrieved Klaus' gun.

Bob was still on the crate, his hands up, holding the ceiling panel. The tall Nigerian smiled, one gun on Bob, the other on Klaus. He ordered Bob to keep his hands up. Then to Klaus, "My friend, you are getting soft."

"Not soft," Klaus said, "just tired. Very tired."

"Regardless," the Nigerian said, "I must kill you both." He sidestepped over to Bob and cocked both guns. "But first, I must ask why you are protecting this one?"

"It doesn't matter," Klaus said.

Even if it didn't matter, Bob wished Klaus had at least come up with some long-winded explanation to buy some time.

The Nigerian shrugged. "Very well." He turned to kill Bob.

"Wait a second," Bob pleaded. "It does matter, Klaus. I mean, since he brought it up, you may as well tell him."

The moment the Nigerian looked to Klaus, Bob dropped the ceiling panel spilling thousands of cockroaches, Strain Two hybrids, and the fourth-generation mutants onto the Nigerian.

The black assassin screamed and, in his panic, threw one of the guns out the window. He fired the other gun aimlessly as buckets of flat-bodied invertebrates swarmed over him. The Assassin Bugs inflicted their painful bites on the Nigerian's neck and face while the roaches scurried for the nearest darkness, finding their way into the Nigerian's shirt and up his pants leg. His skin crawled and tickled as the pointy legs and probing antennae searched for warmth. The Nigerian was so panicked and repulsed as thousands of tickling digits worked their way toward his crotch, that for a moment he considered suicide. But the thought of ten million dollars pulled him through his crisis.

As the tormented Nigerian pressed his hands hard against his clothes in an attempt to crush the filthy little bugs, he saw Klaus and Bob race out the back door and hit the street sprinting. A moment later the Nigerian raced after them, removing his pants on the run.

Down a nearby alley, Bob and Klaus huddled behind a large green dumpster, gasping for breath.

"That was brilliant!" Klaus exclaimed as he gasped for air. "I would not have bet that man could be distracted, but you did it."

"Oh yeah, real brilliant. Did you see all those bugs, for chrissakes?! I've only got two strains left! I'm never gonna get this right."

"If we live, you will have time to correct your errors. Let's worry about staying alive right now. He is on our tail and we are unarmed."

As Klaus peeked out to see if the pants-less Nigerian was coming, Bob thought about what Klaus had said. Unarmed? In New York?

Something floated around the periphery of Bob's consciousness, an idea that answered the question. Unarmed? A weapon? Synapses fired wildly and neurons sucked in neurotransmitters as Bob struggled to capture the thought. Finally an electro-chemical surge hit him like he had jammed a wet fork into a toaster and he captured the thought.

Klaus saw Bob suddenly steel, filled with a new determination.

"This is fantastic," Bob said in a tone that suggested great inner peace. "We're not unarmed, not at all." Bob's voice was growing more excited. "As a matter of fact we have the most dangerous goddamn weapon on the face of the planet at our fingertips!"

Klaus had the uneasy feeling that Bob was no longer plugged in correctly. "Bob, what are you talking about?" he asked gently.

Bob spread his arms wide as if to say, "Look around." Klaus looked, but he did not see.

"This city—New York—is an immense killing machine," Bob said with the assurance of one who knew the truth. "It's our weapon. It kills dozens each day without breaking a sweat. It's a loaded gun on a bedside table waiting to be fired by a curious toddler. All we have to do use it. C'mon!"

Bob darted from behind the dumpster and Klaus followed, sucked into the wake of Bob's tremendous conviction. They raced down Broome to Bowery and headed south.

Looking back they saw the Nigerian in hot pursuit, a hundred yards back, his gun in full view. Passersby moved casually aside as the assassin sprinted powerfully up the streets of Little Italy. The fact that he wore no pants struck no one as particularly unusual.

"What are we doing?" Klaus huffed as he ran. "He is going to kill us!"

"Trust me," Bob said, "I know what I'm doing."

Klaus followed Bob as he turned first onto Grand, then onto Mulberry Street and suddenly into Cafe Palermo. They raced passed the maitre d' without so much as a reservation and continued through the dining room, past a plate of *peperonata* and into the kitchen where the aroma from a simmering saucepan of *bagna cauda* called like a Siren, singing a sweet song of hot anchovy and garlic. But Bob and Klaus refused to listen and dashed out the back, never breaking stride.

A moment later the Nigerian sped through the bistro, his gun drawn. A woman spit an olive across the room when she saw the large, armed black man in his all-cotton briefs. Another patron screamed when the olive splashed into her minestrone.

Bob and Klaus raced down the alley behind the restaurant, emerging on Hester Street. Bob paused to scan the scene. "What the hell are we doing?" Klaus asked again.

"There!" Bob said, pointing across the street. "Follow me!"

Bob raced toward La Bella Ferrara. Klaus followed. The same thing happened; Bob and Klaus raced through the dining room, resisting the *trotelle alla savoia* and the *parmigiana di melanzane*, though the waiters had been recommending both all day.

The Nigerian was following, like an entree after antipasto.

Again, out the alley onto Mulberry Street, searching. And again, across the way, Bob led Klaus to yet another restaurant, this time Angelo's (since 1902).

Having worked up an appetite from all the running, Klaus thought he might like a bite to eat before he died—a last supper, as it were. As they streaked through Angelo's, thick with the perfume of braised veal with black olives, Klaus noticed the patrons there looked significantly tougher, like extras from Goodfellas.

"What are we doing?" Klaus gasped one last time. "He is going to catch us and we will die…hungry!"

"Trust me," Bob yelled confidently as he ran toward the back of the restaurant.

Racing through the kitchen, Klaus finally surrendered to his hunger and grabbed a slice of pizza, disappearing out the back door behind Bob.

The Nigerian entered Angelo's sweating and wheezing from the chase, his gun, and now his abundant manhood, in full view.

An alert wiseguy stood abruptly and pointed. "It's a hit!" he yelled.

Mafia dons were thrown to the ground. Button men pulled their guns. And before the Nigerian realized what had hit him, he was face down in a plate of *fegato alla veneziana*, his own liver stuffed with lead and as useless as the one on the plate.

In the alley Bob and Klaus heard the gunfire. Lots of it. They stopped and, after catching his breath, Bob took a bite from Klaus' slice of pizza.

"Mmmm, that's good," Bob said with his mouth full. "Is that cilantro? That's unusual, but I like it." He took another bite.

Inside, the gunmen calmly sat down and returned to their *fettuccine al burro* as if nothing had happened. The restaurant's owner snapped his fingers and waiters dragged the Nigerian away and prepared him for a slow sail to the bottom of the Hudson.

Klaus, still trying to catch his breath, shared the pizza with Bob as they walked down the alley and onto Baxter Street, out of danger for the moment. Bob picked at a bit of pepperoni lodged between his teeth.

"That was impressive," Klaus wheezed. "I assume you knew that would happen?"

Feeling cocky, Bob answered in his best Edward G. Robinson, "Listen, pal, everybody knows the joints where you can get lead poisoning around here." He hunched his shoulders the way he thought they did in old gangster movies.

Klaus smiled, then pointed at Bob. "Humphrey Bogart?"

"Close enough," Bob said with a smile.

Chapter Fifty-nine

Mike Wolfe was alone his office, worrying. Ever since he'd seen Bob in the coffee shop, something had been bothering him, something Bob had said. "Hi to the wife," wasn't it? Wolfe didn't have a wife, and if Bob was the thorough professional everyone said he was, he'd have known that.

One tape at a time, Wolfe absentmindedly sifted through the pile of cassettes stacked on his credenza. *Blonde on Blonde, John Wesley Harding, Highway 61 Revisited.* The titles brought back memories of counterintelligence operations the Agency had executed in cooperation with Hoover's Bureau during the sixties. Many had been named after various Bob Dylan albums.

In that period, Hoover had himself liked to be called "Quinn, the Eskimo" or "The Mighty Quinn" and had once summarily fired an agent he thought had called him "The Mighty Queen." Hoover would never stand for that sort of slander from his underlings, so for 15 of the most uncomfortable minutes in Bureau history a dozen embarrassed agents had listened to Hoover as he ranted about how all homosexuals were communists and wore dresses and did filthy things in dark places.

Hoover's eyes had bugged even farther out of his puffy red face as he gave an elaborate demonstration of how they lisped and swished and flopped their wrists. He also swore that if called before a Senate subcommittee he could produce photographs of himself "in action" with various women to prove his heterosexuality.

Then suddenly realizing he was, perhaps, protesting too much, Hoover deemed the entire harangue classified and offered to reassign all those present to the duties of their choice in hopes of buying their silence.

Those were the days, Wolfe thought. He randomly choose one of the tapes and popped it into the cassette player. He then returned to what he had been doing for the past several days; namely, sorting through the massive pile of documents that comprised the file on Bob Dillon.

He studied one document, then another, then he looked away, furrowing his brow. Something was wrong, but what? The cassette played and sang, "Yes, and how many times can a man turn his head and pretend that he just doesn't see?"

Wolfe looked again at Bob's banking records, his tax returns, his unpaid parking tickets. What was it? Had he missed something? What were his instincts telling him?

"...the answer, my friend...is blowin' in the wind..."

Chapter Sixty

Klaus looked over his shoulder for the hundredth time that afternoon, keeping a wary eye peeled as Bob led the way, east on West Houston, heading toward the NotSoHot restaurant.

"This is foolishness," Klaus said finally. "We must get Mary and Katy and go to the airport now. Forget your damn bugs and this absurd experiment. Do you not want to live?"

Bob turned on Klaus with an intense stare.

"Listen, Mr. Swivel-Headed-World-Famous-Assassin-Boy, you might not understand this since you're considered the best in the world at what you do, but see, I'm not even considered very good in my own goddamn neighborhood! I've worked damn hard all my life, but I've never been able to provide very well for my family. Hell, I've never had any real success doing anything.

"But right now, with every professional-goddamn-killer in the world after my hairy little butt, I may be close to a victory—maybe the only one I'll ever have. So if you want me to quit, you'll just have to shoot me yourself. I'm not gonna do it on my own. Understand?"

"Your family is your success," said Klaus.

"Yeah, maybe," Bob said, "and if that's the only thing I ever do, I suppose I should be happy. But I'm sick and tired of being broke and being called a crackpot or a loser. And I'm tired as hell of eating shit in this town. I just want to succeed with something of my own, just one goddamn time."

"Even if it means getting killed?" Klaus asked.

"Maybe. 'Cause I'll be damned if I'm going to quit before I find out whether or not my idea works. If nothing else, they can write 'At least he tried' on my headstone."

Moved by Bob's tone, if not the speech itself, Klaus followed Bob toward Thompson Street.

As soon as they rounded the corner onto Thompson, five men leveled their weapons and opened fire in their direction. Klaus was blinded almost immediately as the door frame to Bob's right exploded into splinters and the plate glass window to Klaus' left shattered.

Bob and Klaus knew they were good as dead and there was nothing either of them could do about it.

Then, from behind the five gunmen, a short black man sporting a goatee and an attitude began shouting angrily, "Cut! I said cut, goddammit!" And the shooting stopped as suddenly as it had begun.

Klaus shaded his eyes from the blinding glare of the klieg lights, regaining some of his sight. The dolly tracks and the cherry picker were oddities from a world he knew nothing of. The bystanders, steeped in indifference, milled about with arms folded. They seemed remarkably unfazed, even for New Yorkers who witnessed shootings with some regularity.

Bob, on the other hand, understood. He recovered from the shock of the ambush and pointed enthusiastically at the angry black man who was approaching them with a scowl. "Hey, Klaus, lookit. That's Spike Lee!"

"What?" Klaus said.

"The director," Bob said. "You know, *Crooklyn, She's Gotta Have It*, those old Nike commercials with Michael Jordan."

"Ohhhh yeah," Klaus said. "It's gotta be the shoes!"

After being escorted off the set, Bob and Klaus headed a few blocks farther down Thompson Street to the NotSoHot restaurant, which was currently occupied by Strain Three, the Bee Assassin/Western Corsair hybrid.

Klaus wrinkled his nose as they entered the building. The smell of tobacco, rotted lung, tumors, and phlegm filled the air. "Pheww!" he exhaled as he looked out the window, watching for anyone following them. Bob poked around in the wall spaces, making a hopeful inspection of his work.

As he scanned the street, Klaus wondered why the hell he was doing this. Why was he protecting an eccentric entomologist from a legion of highly motivated mercenaries? Maybe the theories were true, maybe he did have a death wish.

"How could I have been so stupid?" Bob said after a moment of inspection.

"What is it now?"

"Come see for yourself."

Bob gestured disgustedly at an ashtray containing several cigarette butts submerged in a putrid brown liquid. There were seven or eight peculiar looking insects lying feet-up in and around the ashtray. The bugs were black with a deep red ring around their abdomens and all their appendages were fringed with thin fuzzy hair.

"Those," Bob said flatly, "are my Strain Three hybrids."

"What's wrong with them?" Klaus asked.

"What's wrong is they're dead as the Kennedys!" Bob answered not so democratically. "The water in the ashtray extracted the nicotine from the tobacco and they drank it."

Klaus stared at Bob. "So why are they dead?" he asked.

Bob rolled his eyes like an exasperated science teacher. "Nicotine is a poisonous, water soluble alkaloid for chrissakes! In the aqueous solution of its sulfate, it's used as an insecticide! Any idiot knows that! Look…see that sticky brown stuff on the walls? It's nicotine! It's a highly addictive poison and this place is painted with it!"

"So why didn't it kill the roaches?"

Bob looked dumbfounded. "Haven't you heard a word I've said? Roaches have become immune to almost every chemical man has made. Look at this…"

To Klaus' surprise, Bob kicked a hole in the wall and several agitated Oriental Cockroaches (*Blatta orientalis*), black and scallop-shaped, scurried across the floor.

Bob snagged one. Because of its wing stubs, Bob knew it was a female. He brought her to the ashtray and she waved her antennae about excitedly before she calmed. Bob set the roach on the lip of the ashtray and she dipped her mouthparts into the brown liquid and drank. In a moment, the once excited bug was moving in a slow-motion, narcotic haze. Her once frantic antennae relaxed and dragged on the table top.

"See? Roaches love this stuff," Bob said. "Love it? Hell, what am I saying? They're addicted to it. But my hybrids had never been exposed to nicotine. I bet all 1,000 of my bugs were dead within two days."

"Well, you will have to worry about it on someone else's time," Klaus said. "Let's just get out of here."

"God, I'm such a bonehead!" Bob blurted. He paused. "Wait a second. I don't know if this strain worked or not. All I know is they can't handle nicotine."

"Can we go now?" Klaus asked.

"Yeah." Bob sounded hurt. "God, what a stupid waste of time. I should've seen this coming. "

The street appeared safe. The only people in sight were a small tribe of itchy homeless people—luckless throwbacks to our days as hunter/gatherers. Klaus stopped, watching with macabre interest as the doomed atavists harvested a row of dumpsters for spoiled food and recyclables. Periodically they stopped to scratch themselves.

"They've probably got Brill's disease," Bob said.

"And I suppose Brill has theirs," Klaus, being a longtime devotee of S.J. Perelman, quipped. "I'm sorry, I should not make sport of their misfortune. What is this Brill's disease?" Klaus asked.

"A relapsing form of louseborne typhus, usually comes with trench fever."

"You know some very strange things," Klaus said.

"It's transmitted when lice are crushed on the skin and contaminated blood comes in contact with a cut."

Klaus scratched his chest as he cast a sympathetic eye toward these unfortunate people. He followed Bob down the sidewalk, listening to the unsolicited lecture.

Bob scratched behind his ear.

"Head lice cement their eggs to human hair on the back of the neck. They make a new puncture each time they feed. That causes the itch. See, their mouthparts are designed for piercing and sucking." Bob used his fingers to mimic the mouthparts as he described them. "They've got these three stylets which retract within the head when not in use. It's a beautiful design really."

Bob scratched a little lower as they approached Spring Street.

"They've probably got Crab Lice too, uh, *Phthirus pubis.* They cement their eggs to pubic hairs or in armpits or the eyebrows."

Klaus looked over his shoulder while scratching discretely at his private parts. He had the feeling someone was following them. He wasn't sure, but he felt something.

As they rounded the corner onto Spring Street…BAM! Klaus ran smack into Bob, who had stopped without warning. Frozen in his steps. Mouth agape.

Klaus looked around frantically. Instead of an assassin, he saw a 1994 Chevy half-ton parked at the curb. It had a massive, grinning fiberglass bug on its top.

Awed by the sight, music swelled in Bob's head. A hallelujah chorus sung by a choir of thorax-heavy cherubim swept Bob across the sidewalk until he touched his Holy Grail.

Klaus watched as Bob examined the fiberglass insect, a composite. It appeared to be a sculptor's hybrid incorporating the body of the Oriental Rat Flea (*Xenopsylla cheopis*) with the head of a Mediterranean Fruit Fly (*Ceratitis capitata*) and the elegantly swept back antennae of the American Cockroach.

Klaus was embarrassed as Bob gently stroked the large bug's multifaceted eyes.

"It's…beautiful…" Bob was enthralled.

Klaus stared at Bob. "You know, I think you may have some sort of…problem."

"This is it," Bob said reverently. "This is what it's all about." Bob stroked the polished fender and looked like he might go to his knees to offer a prayer to the gods of pest management.

Klaus was so fascinated by Bob's reaction that he was distracted momentarily from the seriousness of their situation. He waited, his head bowed, in deferential silence, as Bob paid his respects.

Then suddenly, Bob's worship service was shattered by a gleaming steel throwing star that whizzed past his head and lodged into the Fruit Fly's compound eye.

"Shit," Bob said. Klaus quickly identifying the star as a lethal weapon of Far East origin.

Bob and Klaus quickly got to the other side of the bug truck, crouching close to one another.

"Who the hell threw that?" Bob asked the expert.

"Ch'ing, I imagine," Klaus said. "Though he used to have much better aim." Klaus looked for a way out, but there didn't appear to be many options. He gestured to a nearby subway entrance. "Should we take the underground?"

"Hell no," Bob said urgently. "You can get killed down there."

"Well, there must be some way out of here," said the assassin to the exterminator.

"Alright, let's make a run for the alley just beyond the stairs to the subway," Bob said.

Bob bolted from behind the truck, but Klaus grabbed him by the shirt and pulled him back. Bob whacked his head on the truck's side panel. "Owww!"

"Sorry," said Klaus. "When we go, do not run in a straight line, it will make you too easy a target."

"Good idea," Bob said, rubbing his forehead. "I don't think I can run straight now anyway."

On Klaus' command, they dashed from behind the truck like drunken sprinters coming out of the blocks. Bob led the way, running down the sidewalk in a zigzag pattern.

Ch'ing hurled another throwing star, but this one sailed wide right and stuck in a street vendor's wagon filled with meatball sandwiches. Bob and Klaus were almost past the stairs to the subway when a garbage truck lurched out of the alleyway in front of them, blocking their path and leaving the subway as their only option.

They charged down the stairs three at a time. Ch'ing was on their butts like a big nasty pimple.

They raced toward the platform. Bob groped in his pockets for change. As they hurtled over the turnstiles Bob flung the coins at the token booth. Nickels and pennies tinkled on the concrete just as—ZING!—another throwing star whizzed past. The doors of the Eighth Avenue local were closing as Bob and Klaus squeezed in.

But Ch'ing, a veteran subway rider after years spent in Japan, wedged himself in as well.

"Shit," Bob said as he led Klaus away from their pursuer.

"I thought this city was a weapon," Klaus said. "What do you propose we do now?"

"Alright, no reason to get excited," Bob said. "I'll figure something out. But if you think of something first, feel free to speak up."

Bob led Klaus to the next car. Ch'ing followed, his already dark mood growing nastier with each inconvenience.

Bob was running out of train and Ch'ing was long out of patience when the answer to Bob's prayer suddenly materialized. For there at the end of the car sat Bob's longtime friend, the demented, fidgeting, gun-toting Norman.

Bob glanced at the approaching assassin, then at Norman. He thought for a second, then leaned over and whispered something to Norman while gesturing with his head down the aisle at the approaching Asian. Bob apparently chose his words wisely, because Norman swiftly assumed a countenance of genuine agitation. His bloodshot eyes shifted madly to the approaching Ch'ing.

When Ch'ing was upon them, Norman reached into his coat, finally ready for his moment of fame. He stood, staring fiercely at the Asian assassin, and shouted, "You ain't going nowhere!"

As the train approached the West Fourth Street station, those waiting on the platform heard the familiar BAM! BAM! BAM! of a large-caliber handgun.

Moments later, the train eased to a stop and the passengers piled out, business as usual, casually stepping over the lifeless and well-ventilated body of the Ninja assassin.

On his way out, Norman kicked his victim in the side and screamed, "The name's Elston Gunn! Those were shots of love! Infidel!" Then he dashed up the stairs to the streets above.

"We must get a gun," Klaus said.

"I just killed a man with a subway ride," Bob said. "I don't think we need a gun." He then led Klaus down to the platform for the Sixth Avenue local for their trip to Queens.

Chapter Sixty-one

Mary steered Klaus' rental car in what Katy knew was the wrong direction. "Hey," Katy said, "I thought we were supposed to go straight to the racetrack."

"We'll get there soon enough," Mary said. "But first we're going home for a second."

"Mom," Katy said peevishly, "Klaus is a professional killer. I really think you ought to do what he says."

"Don't worry, we'll be careful."

"Oh boy," Katy said, "are you gonna get in trouble!"

Mary turned the corner and passed the neighborhood Waldbaum store where Katy's plump friend Ann and her portly mother, Lillian, the circus lover, were selling Girl Scout cookies.

Katy abruptly reached across the seat and honked the horn long and hard, startling Mary. Katy leaned out her window and yelled at her friend, "Hey, my mom's about to get us killed! Pretty cool, huh?"

Chapter Sixty-two

The intricately tiled wall indicated Bob and Klaus were getting off the Sixth Avenue local at the Twenty-Third Street–Ely Avenue platform. They took the stairs up to the street and were soon headed down Vernon Boulevard on the fringe of the gritty industrial neighborhood in Queens. Broken glass crunched under their feet as they walked past graffiti scarred walls.

"We are nowhere near Aqueduct," Klaus said accusingly. "I have played the ponies there. I know what I am talking about."

"Keep your pants on," Bob said. "We'll get to Aqueduct soon enough."

"Where are we going?" Klaus glanced over his shoulder nervously.

"I've just gotta check one last building, then we're done."

"What? You have almost gotten us killed twice!" Klaus stopped. "Are you even listening to me?"

"No," Bob said. "Not really." He continued up with sidewalk.

Klaus was unusually nervous; looking over his shoulder, around every corner, back, front, sideways, every conceivable direction from which someone might attack.

"Your head's going to unscrew if you keep doing that," Bob said.

They passed a burned out liquor store, a pawn shop, and a methadone clinic. When they came to a small store with a large "LOTTO" sign in the window, Klaus went in.

A moment later Klaus was scratching lottery tickets and tossing them away. Bob picked up the discarded tickets, annoyed. "Hey, what'd I say about the littering?"

"Oh. Sorry." Klaus handed Bob the last ticket.

"You know," Bob said, "I think you may have a serious gambling problem. You ever tried therapy?"

"You are not one to throw stones, my friend. You are a gambler too, you know. The difference is, you gamble with your family's future."

Bob stopped. "That's a cheap shot," he said.

"It's true, but I understand why you do not admit it."

"Well I never thought of it that way," Bob said.

"Anyway, we still need a gun," Klaus said.

"Alright, alright," Bob said. "We'll get you a gun." Bob went to a phone booth, a shroud of graffiti and urine. A discarded hypodermic lay on the floor by a rag. In the phone book they found a neighborhood gun dealer.

The sign outside said: HANSEN'S WORLD OF GUNS.

Inside Klaus handled the weapons expertly as he spoke the arcane language of weapons with the store owner. He was a large friendly man with a full mustache who seemed excited talking with someone who asked all the right questions.

While Klaus shopped, Bob wandered about the store. A few minutes later, Klaus called Bob over. He was perplexed. "I don't understand," Klaus said. "What is this...cooling off period?"

"Oh shit, I forgot all about that," Bob said. "It's so guys like us who might want to kill somebody on the spur of the moment can't just go out and buy a gun." Bob paused. "I used to think that was such a good idea."

"We absolutely must have a gun," Klaus insisted. "I thought you could buy anything on the streets of this town."

"Well, yeah, you can, but you have to go to some pretty rough neighborhoods. And we really don't—"

Klaus hailed a cab before Bob could finish his speech on the dangers of East New York.

Chapter Sixty-three

The Cowboy looked country-chic in his satin Mets jacket, blue jeans, and boots. He looked back and forth between the house numbers and the scrap of paper with Bob's address on it.

He couldn't seem to find the right house number. There was one house with an even number on the odd-numbered side of the street, a six where a nine was supposed to be. As the Cowboy looked around, he noticed a nosy neighbor watching from his porch, so he went over for a chat. The guy had a beer in one hand and a nasty little cigar in the other.

"Hey, son," the Cowboy drawled, "you know a fella name o' Bob Dillon? And I don't mean that old folk sanger."

Pratt sized up the Cowboy. "Listen, Hopalong, if you're looking for some money from that shithead, you can just get in line. I'm first. You got it?"

"Heck, friend," the Cowboy said as sweetly as he could to someone he already wanted to kill. "I got money to give him. Who're you?"

Pratt lit up like a chain smoker. "I'm his landlord. How much you got to give him?"

"You know," the Cowboy said, leaning in toward Pratt conspiratorially, "I haven't seen ole Bob in years and I'd really appreciate it if you could help me." The Cowboy looked around, drawing Pratt in close so he could whisper. "Listen slick, why don't you just let me in his place, so's I can surprise him when he gets home."

"Yo, I ain't lettin' no strangers into my properties," Pratt said. "Besides, like I said, he owes me money."

The Cowboy winked and reached for his wallet. "Ohhhh, I gotcha...Exactly how much does he owe ya?"

"Uhhhh, 600 bucks," Pratt said, not thinking fast enough to tell a $1,000 lie.

"How about if I give you three?" The Cowboy winked again.

"What am I, a friggin' car salesman?" Pratt thought for a moment. "Make it 320 and you got the key." The Cowboy handed the money to Pratt.

"He lives right there." Pratt pointed across the street. "I'll get the keys, oh, and hang on a second...I got a couple of packages for that deadbeat, you can take those with you."

Chapter Sixty-four

The gypsy cabdriver who had reluctantly agreed to take Bob and Klaus into East New York had fled his native Kurdistan two years earlier. The wretched living conditions, filth, disease, and poverty had been overwhelming. Roaming homeless in a craggy no-man's-land surrounded by spiteful Syrians and antagonistic Armenians wore on a man's spirit—and eventually crushed him. Yet after two years in New York behind the wheel of a cab, he had begun to miss his native land.

Bob and Klaus rode in silence for a while until Bob's curiosity got the better of him. "Mind if I ask you something?"

"Go ahead," Klaus said in a tired voice.

"Well, exactly how did you get into, uh"—Bob lowered his voice—"your line of work."

Klaus had expected Bob to ask this sooner or later. He looked out the window. "I've never told anyone this," he said. "But my father was a terrible man. He beat my mother to death on my 15th birthday. The next day, I killed him."

Klaus saw all the color drain from Bob's horrified face.

"Just kidding," Klaus said with a smile. "I was an orphan. I never knew my parents."

Bob was miffed at having his emotions manipulated. "I see," Bob said. "So you went into the assassin business after failing as a stand-up comic?"

"It was just a joke," Klaus said. "How is it you say, lighten up?"

"Forget I asked."

"No, you really want to know? I will tell you. From the time I was a little boy I wanted the world to be a better place than what it was. I read in the newspapers about the atrocities committed every day and I could never understand why so many people suffered so at the hands of evil and corrupt leaders."

"I felt that way as a kid," Bob said.

"Yes, but you didn't end up as an assassin."

"Depends on who you ask."

"As I grew older my idealism intensified. I just wanted to make the world a better place, but I did not know how. I spent time in the military service and found I was very good with weapons. Then I realized how I could make my life a useful one. My own government hired me for my first job. After that I was on my own. I was adept at killing, and I believed I was making a difference. You know, a lot of people complain about the despots of the world, but I actually do something about it."

"You know, Klaus," Bob said, "most people just contribute to Amnesty International."

Chapter Sixty-five

Wolfe flipped the Dylan tape over, hit play, then returned to the Dillon file. Something was bothering him, but he couldn't nail it down.

As he paused, a lyric caught his ear, "Do you take me for such a fool?..."

Maybe Bob Dillon was exactly what his file said, an exterminator with a lower-case e. But if that were true, how to explain that kill in Istanbul, and the Madari and Pescadores assassinations, and Riviera, and the ten-million-dollar bounty on Bob's head?

Wolfe absentmindedly fast-forwarded the tape and let it stop at random on another song. "He's not selling any alibis..." the troubadour sang in his nasal voice. "How does it feel?"

Why would Riviera offer ten million dollars for an exterminator with a lower-case e?"

"How does it feel?"

Just then, a ten-million-watt light bulb flashed above Wolfe's otherwise dim head.

"To be on your own?"

Wolfe grabbed the Dillon folder and headed down the hallway with great resolve.

"With no direction home?"

He heaved Bob's file through a shredder and took the stairs two at a time down to the basement.

"A complete unknown."

He blew into the Munitions Room, stepped up to the counter, flashed his ID, and checked out a sniper rifle.

"Like a rolling stone…"

Chapter Sixty-six

As the cab pulled to the curb on Putnam Avenue, deep in BedStuy, Klaus gave Bob the final word on the negotiation techniques for the acquisition of a murder weapon.

"Dicker," he said.

He handed Bob 200 dollars and urged him onto the sidewalk. Confessing that he didn't know a forty-five magnum from Magnum P.I., Bob asked Klaus if he wouldn't mind going.

"First of all," Klaus said as he leaned out the window of the cab, "I am not going any farther without a gun. Secondly, you seem better able to take care of yourself on the streets of this Godforsaken city than I do. Finally, my Kurdish friend and I are at a crucial point in our discussion of the atrocities committed by Abd al-Hamid II prior to his overthrow by the Young Turks."

"Fine," Bob said in a snit. "But don't blame me if I pay too much." Bob turned away from the car just as a loud noise erupted from around the corner. He rounded the block and saw a half dozen gangstas wearing wraparound sunglasses and faces that would have been at home in Attica. Bob watched one of them complete a transaction with someone in a car that quickly pulled away from the curb.

That's when they noticed Bob standing at the other end of the street, his lily-white face standing out like an intelligent comment on Rush Limbaugh's show. For a moment Bob considered running, but he forced himself to stay rooted to the ground. He had stumbled across exactly what he was looking for—a group of ambitious young men working outside the conventional framework of the free enterprise system.

Bob went to take a step forward but his shoe was stuck in something. He imagined a large pink wad of chewing gum, but looking down he saw the reddish-brown goop in which he was standing wasn't someone's Bubble Yum, rather it was a day-old pool of coagulated blood spilling across the head of a chalk outline of a human body.

Bob saw several Northern House Mosquitoes (*Culex pipiens*) supping at the edge of the pool, their abdominal segments marked with broad yellowish-white bands. Their apical bands identified them as female vectors of St. Louis *encephalitis*.

Bob's shoe made a sticky sucking sound as it pulled from the congealed glop and moved toward the booming urban symphony that played up ahead.

The gangstas passed a 40-ounce malt liquor as the sonic booms and inflammatory lyrics issued from their ghetto blaster. The vocalist—which stretched the term somewhat—labored to rhyme "no peace" with "po-lice" and "dis the mutha" with "beat my luvva."

Bob sidestepped a second pool of blood as he approached, then stopped a few feet away and made eye contact with the largest and most dangerous looking member of the gang. He attempted what he thought was a cool head gesture indicating he wanted to talk. It worked. The large gentleman descended the steps, got uncomfortably close to Bob's face, and amiably inquired of the nature of Bob's visit.

"Yo! What you doin' in my neighborhood, muthafucka?"

Given the afternoon's events, this guy wasn't terribly intimidating. Bob noticed that one of the man's front teeth had a shiny gold star imbedded in it. "Yo," Bob said, "nice piece of dental work, Jim."

The gang leader was taken aback by Bob's confidence. Anyone who wasn't scared at this point was either armed or had money and wanted to buy something. "Yeah, well fuck you, punk ass faggot! You want somethin' or what?"

Bob looked around and lowered his voice. "Uh, I'm lookin' to buy a couple of pieces, you know?"

"A coupla pieces o' what? Rock? You want some fuckin' rock, white boy?" The others hooted and laughed while Bob explained that he wanted a gun.

"Oh, you wanna get strapped, huh? Whatcho want, somthin' like a A-K or a TEC-9? That's some live shit, muthafucka. Are you down with that?"

"Yeah, whatever," Bob said feebly.

"You must be a cop! You look like a muthafuckin' cop to me. And you know what? We don't much like cops here in the 'hood!" The gold tooth turned to the gentleman at the controls of the high-fidelity system. "Yo, Easy-D! Let's have a oldie-goldie. Put on the Ice-T about how we do muthafuckin' cops!"

The music director complied with the request and put on "Cop Killer."

Bob tried to remain cool in light of the not so thinly veiled death threats. "A cop? Me? Heck no," Bob said. "If I was a cop, I'd already have a gun, wouldn't I?" Bob smiled a nervous smile. "No, the deal is, well, I got a bunch of assassins after me. It's a helluva mess and, well, I really do need a gun."

The gold star peeked out from the middle of a grin. "Yeah, alright, punk! I might have something. How much money you got?"

Bob was caught off guard. He hadn't expected it to be this easy. "Really? Uh, I've got 50 bucks. What can you do for me?"

"Oh, yeah? You got 50 bucks? Fuck you then! I ain't got nothin' for 50 muthafuckin' bucks, punkassmuthafucka!"

Bob laughed nervously and considered his next gambit. "What did I say, 50 bucks? No, I've got a hundred. What can you do for a hundred?"

"I'll tell you what I can do for you. I can kill yo skinny white ass for a hundred bucks, that's what!"

Bob wondered whether this was a bluff. A negotiating ploy? Or was he being sized up for a chalk outline? He considered

Klaus' admonition to dicker before he simply pulled out his entire wad of cash.

"Hell, would you look at this?" Bob said, trying to sound surprised. "I meant 200. That's what I meant. What did I say, a hundred? I meant two. But I really do need a decent gun."

"Yeah, Slick, dat's cool." The gold tooth snatched the money from Bob and stuffed it into his shirt pocket before reaching behind his back and pulling an old Beretta from his waistband.

Bob reached expectantly for his purchase, thinking he had done rather well.

But the man behind the star cocked the hammer and snuggled the business end onto the tip of Bob's nose.

"Now get outta my neighborhood, punkassmuthafucka."

Klaus and the cabbie were still discussing the geopolitical imbroglio of Kurdistan when Bob returned, his tail between his legs. "Well, what did you get?"

"Robbed," Bob replied.

BOOM! BOOM! BOOM! Tupac Shakur was extolling the virtues of random violence when Klaus arrived and approached the man Bob had described as the executive sales representative.

"I would like to buy a gun," Klaus said.

"Well shit, this is yo lucky day, muthafucka," the gangsta with the gold star said. "Today only we having a white sale for everybody what's coming into the 'hood. How much you got to pay for it? I needs to see some green, muthafucka."

"You already have my money. Now I would like my gun."

Sensing trouble, the gangsta reached for his waistband. But before he got there, Klaus' right knee shattered the gangsta's family jewels. Crunch! The head of sales went to his knees. A roundhouse kick broke a jaw and sent one approaching member of the sales force flying into another. A second later, a knife dropped from a hand now limply connected to a broken wrist.

The two remaining members of the sales staff considered their options and fled the scene.

The head gangsta was on his hands and knees trying to catch his breath, hoping that this kung fu guy would shoot him in the head and put him out of his pain. But Klaus didn't think he deserved to die, so he simply picked up the gun, deftly snapped it open, and examined it. He took the cash from the young man's pocket and tossed a few bills onto the ground. "The action is dirty on this one," Klaus said. "I can only give you fifty."

"Deal," the salesman wheezed.

Finally armed with more than the inherent dangers of New York, Klaus and Bob hurried back toward Queens.

Chapter Sixty-seven

The cabbie was cursing, gesticulating, and dodging other cars, making time as best he could while struggling across the Triborough Bridge. In the back seat, Chantalle opened her purse and surreptitiously screwed a silencer into a small automatic handgun of Swiss manufacture. Her purse was, in fact, a holster designed specifically for this gun, its silencer, and two extra clips. There was no loose change rattling around in a bottom covered with face powder, no old crumpled receipts, and no perfumed pieces of cinnamon-flavored sugarless gum in tattered wrappers. Chantalle carried her American Express platinum card in her pocket and that was it.

Once the silencer was attached, she snugged its tip into a round hollow in the bottom of the purse and closed it, as designed, so that the grip of the pistol acted as the handle of the purse. Not exactly Louis Vuitton, but killer nonetheless.

From the paper sack next to her, Chantalle retrieved the small box from the confectionery store which contained her three perfect truffles. She untied the simple bow of gold string that bound the package and neatly folded back the puffy layers of white tissue. The last ply of tissue would not yield.

Upon closer examination, Chantalle discovered that the chocolates had melted into a shapeless mass. She was miffed. "*Merde*," she mumbled. "Driver, find me a chocolate store."

The driver, a native of Staten Island, replied with a derisive snort and a quick glance into the mirror. "Oh yeah, sure. A 'chocolate store' in Astoria. Right."

He glanced in his rearview mirror again to see if his sarcasm had registered. That's when he noticed the gun in Chantalle's willowy hand. "Ohhh!" he quickly amended, "A chocolate store. No sweat. Just hang on, we'll get you some sugar, sugar."

Chapter Sixty-eight

It was late afternoon when the cab dropped Bob and Klaus at the abandoned warehouse in Queens. As Bob paused to look at the decaying building which housed his Strain Four hybrids, he suddenly felt scared, not because his life was in danger, but rather because his dream was. This was it. His last chance. Do or die. His heart beat faster.

Klaus turned to look over his shoulder and noticed the anxiety on Bob's face. "What is wrong?" he asked.

"This is it, Monty. Door number three. Carol Merrill ain't bringing no boxes down the aisle and Jay's nowhere in sight. I gotta admit it, I'm scared."

The *Let's Make A Deal* references soared over Klaus' head, but Bob's resoluteness did not.

"You are the most determined man I have ever met," Klaus said. "You are also the craziest."

"You may be right," Bob replied absently.

After hearing Bob talk with such affection about his bugs, Klaus had become fascinated with the hybrids and Bob's experiment. Klaus was surprised to discover the strong emotional attachment he had in it. For a moment he completely forgot about the other assassins. He was focused on Bob and his dream.

"Which bugs are in here?" Klaus asked.

"Number four, the Thread-Legged Bug/Bloodsucking Cone-nose hybrid," Bob said. His hands were growing clammy.

"These are the ones I am betting on," he said. "Are you giving odds?"

Bob smiled. He sensed Klaus' interest was heartfelt.

With his heart pounding and his blood pressure moving into a dangerous neighborhood, Bob led Klaus into the vast warehouse.

Bob removed a pack of matches from his pocket as he crossed the vast warehouse floor, which was dotted with old shipping crates and failed, inefficient machinery from America's golden age of manufacturing. Sweat formed on Bob's forehead. He stooped and picked up a short steel rod from the floor as he approached the far wall.

"What are you going to do?" Klaus asked.

"You'll see," Bob said as he sat on the floor by one of his patched holes. His intestines tied themselves into a horrible knot as he used the steel rod to break through the plaster patching material. He lit one of the matches and laid down on his side, one eye closed and the other ready to inspect. He held the lit match to the hole in the wall and peered in.

Klaus looked on, sharing Bob's anxiety, completely caught up in Bob's dream. "Well, how does it look?" he asked.

"I can't really tell. I don't see anything." Bob gripped the side of the hole with his free hand and pulled out some of the drywall, then continued to peer into the hole for a moment, looking left and right. "Ouch!" Bob burned his finger with the spent match.

"Hurry up," Klaus said.

"Would you give me a minute?" Bob's heart was pounding. His blood pressure was 210 over 120. Hypertension and stroke lurked uncomfortably close as he lit another match. If Strain Four had failed, Bob thought, so had he.

He looked to the left but saw no evidence, so he looked to the right. Finally, he saw something. "Shit," Bob said. "Shit, shit, shit."

"What's wrong?"

"Goddammit!"

"What's wrong? What is it?" Klaus assumed this meant Strain Four had failed and he worried how Bob would react. He thought he'd better say something to cheer Bob up. "Listen, it is not the end of the world and…I tell you what, if we get out of New York alive, I will help you find some more buildings for your experiments."

Bob stuffed his left arm deep into the hole and made grunting noises as he groped blindly inside the space.

Klaus grew uneasy as Bob made guttural sounds, his face pressed hard against the wall, distorting his nose and lips into a Picasso.

Finally Bob extracted his cupped hand from the wall, stood, and walked over to an apprehensive Klaus. "Look at this!"

"What is it?" Klaus asked, backing away a few steps.

"What does it look like?" Bob thrust his open palm toward Klaus revealing the shriveled, dehydrated, and dismembered corpses of dozens of dead bugs. Klaus recoiled.

"It looks like shriveled, dehydrated, and dismembered corpses of dozens of dead bugs," Klaus said. "I thought that's what you expected from this strain."

"Do these look like cockroaches to you? Huh? No! These are my hybrids, goddammit!"

"What happened to them?"

"Who the hell knows? Maybe they scared all the roaches into hiding. If that happened, then they probably started fighting over the limited food supply and cannibalized each other." Bob looked forlornly at the handful of legless bodies. "Sons-uh -bitches probably self-destructed. Just like me."

Klaus feared the disappointment might be too much for his friend.

"I'm screwed," Bob said as the crumbling carcasses slipped through his fingers. His optimism had finally been defeated. It was the moment Bob had hoped would never come. In one aching instant, it flashed through his mind: all his work, and maybe his life, had been wasted. He had chased a dream he would never catch. He was a pathetic dreamer who let his family down. Pratt was right—what a loser.

"Are you alright?" Klaus asked gently.

"Yeah, I guess. It's just so damn frustrating," Bob sighed, "but it's not the end of the world."

Klaus was relieved Bob was taking this so well.

Suddenly Bob grabbed the gun from Klaus and jammed the barrel into his own mouth. "Woggamib! Ba gream bust bibbered ub ad habits lillyl glegs whipped wum iss fwobby."

"I'm sorry, I can't understand a word you're saying," Klaus said.

Bob pulled the gun out of his mouth and put it to his head. "I said, 'goddammit! My dream just withered up and had its little segmented legs ripped from its body.'"

"That's better," Klaus said. "Now I can understand you."

"Mary and Katy don't deserve to be stuck with a loser."

Klaus looked into Bob's eyes. "Mary would not have come back if she felt that way." He held out his hand to Bob. "Now give me the gun."

Bob held fast to the weapon. "No!" Bob paused for a moment and looked sideways at the gun as it pressed to his temple. "Where's the safety on this thing? Is it on?"

Klaus shook his head. "No it's not. If you pull the trigger now, you will probably die. If not, you will certainly be a vegetable for the rest of your life."

The thought repulsed Bob. "No! No life-support systems. You tell them I don't want to be hooked up to a bunch of machines, alright?"

"Listen, you may have a point," Klaus said. "Maybe you are a loser, but you can't kill yourself if you really care about Katy and Mary."

"I can't?" Bob queried.

"No. If you really want to cash in on this situation, give me back the gun and I'll tell you how we can double our money."

Bob lowered the gun and handed it to Klaus, who considered eating a bullet himself and ending his own miserable life. But the thought passed quickly. For some reason he felt obliged to help Bob get through this mess alive.

"Alright, assassin boy," Bob said, "what's your brilliant plan?"

"It is simple. We buy you a five million dollar life insurance policy with a double indemnity clause. Then I kill you, notify the media, collect the ten million from Riviera, and Mary gets the insurance money."

"Hey, I like that," Bob said with morbid enthusiasm. "That's good!"

"Thank you. I got the idea from a Barbara Stanwyck movie." Klaus had no intention of going through with the plan, but at least he had taken the gun from Bob.

"Only one problem, smart guy. I don't have a goddamn dime to my name. Where the hell am I going to get the money to pay for a five- million dollar insurance policy? I know you don't have it, since we spent the last of your money on that gun."

"Hmmmm, you are right. That does pose a problem. Well, we can think about it."

A thought suddenly seized Bob. He jerked backwards like he had caught his dick in his zipper. "Holy shit! Wait a minute!"

"What? What is it?"

"Marcel," Bob said, "the French guy."

"What about him?" Klaus asked.

"He thinks I killed, uh, what's his name? Huweiler, right? And Wolfe thinks I did the Bolivian guy, right?"

"Yes, but what is your point?"

"Well, my question to you, Mr. Professional Killer been-there-done-that-and-got-paid-plenty-for-it, is…where is my money?" Bob's tone was accusatory.

"That is a good question," Klaus admitted.

"Damn right it is! Somebody owes me some scratch! How much do I have coming to me? What do they do, send the payments to a numbered account in Switzerland? How's this shit work?"

Klaus was disappointed. This was rather obvious. "It depends," Klaus said. "Did you negotiate?"

"What negotiate?" Bob blurted. "I didn't know what was going on!"

"I turned down 250 for the Huweiller job," Klaus said. "And I believe Wolfe was willing to go as high as a million for Riviera, though, thanks to you, the job was never offered to me."

"Judas H. Jones! That's 1.25 million! So where the hell's my money?"

"Well," said Klaus, "if you do not make other arrangements, the payments are usually delivered in cash or certified check."

"Pratt!" Bob blurted.

"Pardon me?"

"My landlord. He said he had a UPS package for me. That's gotta be it."

"Then you are a wealthy man and we can finally get out of here," Klaus said.

"I'm not wealthy as long as Pratt has the money, am I?" Bob asked.

"Alright, we will get Mary and Katy, collect the packages, then get out of here. Where is this Pratt?"

"He lives across the street from me. Oh, man, this is fantastic!" Bob was musing on his bright and heavily taxed future when—KAPWINNGG!—a shot ricocheted near their heads. The acoustics of the massive space prevented Klaus from pinpointing the location of the shooter.

Bob and Klaus hit the floor. It was only then that Bob noticed the bullet had nicked him in the arm. A small drop of blood trickled from the wound.

"I'm hit!" Bob screamed.

Klaus looked at the scratched arm. "Relax, you won't lose it."

BAM! BAM! BAM! Flashes of light in the corner betrayed the gunman's position. They saw a small shadowy figure moving irregularly in the distance.

Bob turned to Klaus. "The Dwarf?"

"It looks that way," Klaus said. "I will circle over there and try to take him out. But remember, he is a cunning little bastard, so stay alert."

Klaus fired a few rounds for cover, then dashed around some crates.

BAM! BAM! Then click… click… click… came from behind a nearby crate.

"I think he's out of ammo," Bob yelled to Klaus.

"I know he's out of ammo," Klaus replied calmly. "You can come out now."

Bob emerged from behind the crate, one hand covering his wounded arm. He retraced Klaus' steps and found him holding Walter, the wizened old security guard, by his collar. He squirmed like a 72-pound tuna.

"Hiya, Bruce," Walter said.

"Hi, Walter."

"Listen, I'm sorry I shot at ya. The ole eyesight's not what it used to be. You okay?"

"I'm fine." Bob turned to Klaus. "You can put him down."

"Thanks, Bruce," Walter said.

The situation under control, Klaus regained focus. "Alright, we have eliminated the two by the coffee shop, the Nigerian, and Ch'ing. Aside from any amateurs who may be involved, that leaves us with Reginald, Chantalle, and the Cowboy." Klaus checked his watch. "We must get out of this city."

"And the money," Bob reminded him, "don't forget the money."

"Yes, you are right. The money too," Klaus agreed.

As they headed out of the warehouse, Bob began thinking out loud. "You know, it's a good thing none of the strains worked. If they had, I'd have to split the profits with Silverstein. Now I can finance myself. You know, I bet if I cross the Strain Two and Strain Four hybrids and get some more buildings—I can buy my own now, you know—I can make this work."

As they approached the cab, Klaus put the gray cloud inside Bob's silver lining. "Of course, on the other hand, you may be dead before sundown."

"Well, yeah," Bob said, "there is that."

Speeding toward Aqueduct, Bob listened as Klaus and the cabdriver debated an obscure point of the 1918 Treaty of Brest-Litovsk. Klaus considered the terms unnecessarily humiliating for the Russians while the driver felt the mere recognition of independence for the Balkan states and the Ukraine was not enough; the Russians needed to be thoroughly disgraced.

Before they reached unilateral agreement on the point, they reached the parking lot at Aqueduct, which, save a lonely sweeper doing rounds, was empty.

"Where are they?" Klaus asked.

Bob looked at his watch. "Well, we're late. Mary does this to me sometimes. She'll wait a couple of minutes but then she's outta there, thinks it's going to teach me a lesson about being considerate of other people's time. Of course, with Mary it's possible she didn't even come here in the first place."

"You mean she may have gone for that damn locket!" Klaus said. He blurted a sound of disgust and frustration. "This is just like a woman! Does she always do the opposite of what she is told?"

"Well, not always," Bob said. "But she's not known for letting things get in her way. She's pretty headstrong. I think that's where Katy gets it."

"For God's sake, she and Katy could get killed!" Klaus banged on the partition separating the front seat from the back. "Astoria! And step on it!"

As the cab screeched away from the track, the debate resumed on the Syrian Ba'ath Party's treatment of the Kurdish minority.

Chapter Sixty-nine

Reginald's sources had knocked him back an embarrassingly large sum in return for Bob's address. If he ever discovered they'd gotten it from the phone book, he would certainly kill them.

He was in the Long Island City section of Queens, a neighborhood adjacent to Astoria. He was looking for a disguise, preferably something indigenous, before approaching Bob's house. And moments ago, as he pulled into the Waldbaum parking lot, Reginald had seen exactly what he wanted.

Katy's young friend Ann and her chubby mother, Lillian, were seated behind a table outside the store. They were peddling boxes of the baked goods for which Girl Scouts were famous.

Ann looked hopefully at Reginald, the diminutive man who was approaching them hungrily. She had no idea he was wearing frilly pink panties under his trousers; all she knew was that she wanted to sell him some cookies.

Reginald eyed Ann from a distance. He wondered how was he would get what he needed. He didn't want to have to hurt the little girl, much less kill her, but he would if it became necessary. Reginald then noticed Ann's full-buttocked mother eyeing him lustily, and realized he could get exactly what he wanted.

"Good afternoon, ladies," Reginald said in his best House of Commons accent. "Selling some tasty little biscuits, are we?"

Lillian, as it turned out, loved men with English accents. She furtively unbuttoned the top button on her blouse, revealing tantalizing bits of her soft, fleshy bosoms.

A subtle look of acknowledgment crossed Reginald's face. He knew he was going to get what he needed.

As fate would have it, Lillian had come from a rather cold, unaffectionate family and her fondest memories of childhood were of the circus. She especially loved the "little people," as they were called. They were so cuddly-looking, and cuddling is what Lillian wanted the most as a child.

It was on one of her many trips to the big top as a young girl that Lillian discovered something new and exciting. With a large sack of salty peanuts held between her legs, she watched as a bevy of tiny clowns performed some thrilling acrobatic stunts which caused her to tingle with delight. Reaching between her legs, she had put her hand into the bag and was groping for a peanut when she felt something she had never felt before. It was a feeling she wanted to have again and again, so every time she reached into the bag she pressed harder and soon her hand began to linger.

The tiny acrobatic performance became more frenzied and soon her hand remained in the bag as she pressed the course shells of the nuts hard against herself, squeezing her legs tightly around the salty bag of delight. Her eyes closed dreamily as she humped the fibrous goobers, unaware that soon she would be overcome with a new sensation.

Since that day, Lillian had been perfecting an intricate sexual fantasy involving a sack of peanuts, some sawdust, and a dwarfed adult who, oddly, sounded like John Cleese. And now, here she was—a single mother of 39 whose urges were not being satisfied—and she was face-to-face with an exceptionally short British man with a devilish glint in his eye.

"You're a pretty one, aren't you?" Reginald said as he patted Ann on the head. "And I see you share your good looks with your…older sister?" he said with a nod and a wink.

"That's not my sister, that's my mother," Ann said delightedly.

Lillian leaned down and put her hands on the table so the Englishman could get an eyeful of her massive breasts.

"Do you see anything you like?" she asked.

"Oh my," he said. "Yes, I think I shall have to buy all the mint cookies you have."

"Yeah!" said Ann as Reginald handed over a crisp fifty.

"But how on earth shall I carry all this?" he asked. "I'm going to need a box or something, won't I?"

The mother grabbed her purse. "Ann, honey, you stay here. I'm going to go home and get a box for the nice man."

"Would you like it if I came along?" Reginald asked, feigning innocence.

"Well, yes. Would you? That would be awfully nice," Lillian answered as if the thought had never crossed her mind.

The apartment was only two blocks away and they were there in minutes. Lillian bolted the door and led Reginald quickly into her bedroom, never saying a word, not needing to. She worked feverishly to undress as Reginald lay on the bed slowly removing his trousers and revealing first the pink panties he was wearing, then his turgid little organ whose proportion surprised the delighted circus goer.

Lillian opened the drawer of the bedside table and removed a large sack of salted peanuts, a baggie of sawdust, and a strap-on clown's nose.

Reginald didn't know what to make of that, but he didn't care. He strapped on the nose and beckoned for her to join him. As if performing an ancient ritual, Lillian emptied the sawdust onto the bedspread and slid in next to Reginald, longing to have his glistening tumescence in her. After ten minutes the bag of nuts split open beneath the voluptuous clown-lover.

Lillian was left panting and sweating amid the smell of sawdust and wet, salted peanuts. And, as Reginald found his way to where Ann kept her clothes, Lillian drifted off to sleep.

Chapter Seventy

The cab stopped a few blocks from Bob's house. Bob and Klaus bid their Kurdish friend *adieu* and walked quickly up the sidewalk. As they crept through the neighborhood Klaus tried to prepare Bob for some of the unpleasant possibilities.

The most likely scenario—if one of the assassins had already located Bob's house and if Mary had been foolish enough to return for the locket—was that Mary and Katy would be used as hostages to get at Bob. Bob would, of course, surrender himself in exchange for their freedom, and then they would all be killed. That's just how these things worked.

However, since it seemed unlikely any of the killers knew Klaus was with Bob, they at least had that advantage. They'd have to play everything by ear and hope for the best.

They looked for Klaus' car.

"There it is!" Bob said.

They found Katy in the driver's seat, pretending to drive, the radio blaring something by Hootie and the Blowfish.

"Katy!" Bob shouted over the din of *Only Wanna Be with You.* "Where's your mom?" he asked.

Katy turned the radio down. "Where have you two been?"

"Never mind that," Bob said. "Where is she?"

"Where do you think? She went to the house."

Bob did a slow burn.

"Hey, I tried to talk her out of it, but she wouldn't listen. You know Mom. Said she'd be back in five minutes."

"When was that?" Klaus asked.

"Uh, 'bout an hour ago."

Klaus took the keys, went to the trunk, and removed a small canvas duffle bag. It appeared to be heavy.

"Bob, come with me," said Klaus. "Katy, you stay here."

"Okay, Klaus." Katy turned the radio back up and pretended she was driving back to see the Pinto burning in the streets of lower Manhattan.

Bob and Klaus were soon crouching behind Dick Pratt's old blue Cadillac with its rusting tail fins. Across the street the lights were on inside Bob's house and they saw the silhouette of a tall guy with a ten-gallon hat pacing the living room floor.

"It's the Cowboy," Klaus said flatly.

Bob was enraged; he felt violated. "Just give me the gun. I'll kill that redneck son of a bitch! If he's done anything to Mary..."

"Relax. He won't do anything to her until you're dead," Klaus said indelicately. "Just let me do my job and she should be fine."

"Should be?" Bob asked.

"There are no guarantees."

Klaus unzipped the canvas bag and removed an exquisitely crafted piece of killing machinery. It was the new fifty-magnum Desert Eagle, an elite weapon manufactured by Israel Military Industries, the same people who brought the world the Uzi.

Now the only thing Klaus needed was a ruse. Somehow he had to get face-to-face with the Cowboy.

Chapter Seventy-one

"It's the best I can do in this neighborhood, lady," the cabdriver said as he pulled up to the small market. He hoped the beautiful woman wouldn't shoot him because it wasn't a chocolate store.

Chantalle glared at the cabbie as she reached across the front seat and snatched the keys from the ignition. She got out of the cab and disappeared into the store.

She passed the rack with the beer nuts, the beef jerky, and the bright orange cheese-flavored crackers with peanut butter filling. She needed truffles and she needed them now.

She cruised up and down the aisles, her exquisite eyes scanning the shelves. She passed antiseptics and ointments, then lighter fluid, then an impressive array of paper products, pausing briefly to check the price on the light-day panty shields. The next aisle was dog food, kitty litter, and birdseed. Finally she charged the man behind the counter and demanded what she wanted.

"Truffles!"

The bewildered man thought for a moment and shook his head. He cringed when she yelled again. Finally he pointed tentatively at the rack of chips behind the madwoman. Chantalle turned to look, then, vexed, she screamed even more loudly, "I said truffles, you idiot! Not Ruffles!"

The man looked like a lost child as he shook his head and continued pointing at the potato chips with the ridges.

"Alright," she said, calming, "Swiss bonbons?"

The head continued shaking.

"Austrian cream chocolate?"

Still shaking.

Chantalle paused. She knew others would be looking for the ten-million-dollar man. The clock was ticking and she knew there wasn't time to return to the city in search of the perfect confection, so she scanned the candy rack, picked up a Kit Kat bar, and left in the mood to kill.

Chapter Seventy-two

Mary was on the sofa watching the television news, her hands bound and resting in her lap. She still hadn't noticed the two UPS packages the Cowboy had brought from Pratt's house even though they were sitting on the coffee table in front of her.

The local news was doing a story about some blond guy killed up in the West 140s. The Action News Team had learned that the victim was in fact, a known Swedish assassin who had wandered into Harlem and been killed. FBI and the CIA sources denied any knowledge of the man's reasons for being in the city.

Suddenly, one of the beautiful news readers put his hand to his earpiece and turned to the camera with a look of sincere urgency they must teach at electronic journalism school. "Right now," he intoned gravely, "we're going up to Roger in the Eyewitness Action-Copter, who is covering a breaking and related story. Roger?"

From the helicopter, the camera showed a lynch mob of young Italian-American men wielding bats and chains as they chased what would turn out to be a professional killer from Trinidad.

Roger took over, "Thanks, Bill. We're just above Bensonhurst, and as you can see…"

Chapter Seventy-three

"There's A&E, USA, Bravo, HBO..." Bob paused as he tried to think of more.

"I know, I know, and ESPN and CNN and fifty others," Klaus said in an agitated tone. "I have cable."

"Sorry," Bob said. "I just want to make sure. I mean that's my wife in there, you know."

"I know," Klaus said, trying to reassure his friend. "You are just going to have to trust me."

Convinced the ruse would bring him face-to-face with the Cowboy, Klaus started across the street with his canvas bag. He climbed the stairs to the front door of Bob's house, the Desert Eagle perched behind his back.

The Cowboy was stuffing a new wad of tobacco into his mouth when he heard the footsteps on the porch. He grabbed Mary and jerked her to her feet. He pulled his pearl-handled revolver from his belt and put it to the back of Mary's head. With Mary as his shield, the Cowboy walked to the door.

A knock came and the Cowboy nudged Mary to answer. "Who is it?" she asked nervously.

The voice from outside answered, "Queens Cablevision."

"We already got it, pardner," the Cowboy replied.

"We're offering a free month of HBO," Klaus said, not missing a beat.

"We ain't interested!" the Cowboy yelled at the pesky salesman. "Now git!"

"How about if I throw in a second hookup at no charge? Think of the money you'll save."

"Piss off, buddy! I said we ain't interested, goddammit!"

Klaus could tell from the Cowboy's tone that the plan was working. He readied his weapon.

"Would you like a free Discovery Channel T-shirt?"

"No I wouldn't, you stupid little shit, now git off my front porch 'fore I turn my dog loose on ya!"

"How about a Beavis and Butthead poster for the kids?"

Frustrated, the Cowboy shoved Mary face first onto the living room floor. He whipped open the door and yelled, "Look, you dumb sumbitch, I told you—"

Those were the Cowboy's last words before the Desert Eagle flapped its big wings and blew a large hole through the Cowboy's small brain. He should have taken the T-shirt.

As the corpse collapsed in a heap in the front hall, Klaus signalled for Bob, who raced from his hiding place. Klaus laid the Desert Eagle on the table, kicked the bloody cowboy hat out of the way, and quickly closed the door behind them.

Chapter Seventy-four

"Goddamit, what the hell was that?" Dick Pratt blurted when he heard the shot across the street. He shuffled across the dirty pea-green shag carpet and ripped the curtains back to see what all the noise was.

"What's that asshole doin' over there? I've just about had it with that lousy douche bag! First it's a roomful of goddamn bugs and now this shit," He turned to yell to the back of the house. "I'm tellin' you, Doris, I'm gonna evict that deadbeat sonofabitch! You hear me talkin' to you, Doris?"

Doris could hear her husband fine, but right now she couldn't see him too well. She had an ice pack over her recently blackened eye, and the other eye rendered only blurry images because of her tears.

"You better listen when I talk to you, Doris."

Pratt looked out the window again, but didn't see anything, so he shuffled back to the kitchen for another beer.

Chapter Seventy-five

After a long, sweet, loving embrace, Bob looked deep into Mary's eyes. "You scared the shit out of me, honey," he said. "What the hell were you thinking?"

Mary sheepishly pulled the locket from her pocket. "Sorry, but I couldn't leave without this. I got a little fixated."

"Excuse me," Klaus said, "but as our cowboy friend here might say, we need to skedaddle."

"Where's Katy?" Mary asked.

"She's fine," Bob said. "She's still in the car."

Bob saw the two UPS packages on the table. He grabbed them and handed them to Mary.

"What's this?" she asked as she ripped them open.

"Good news, honey," Bob said. "We're rich!"

When she got the package open Mary found the note from Marcel along with $100,000 in cash. Mary stared for a moment, unable to believe her eyes.

"Holy cow!" she said finally. "Look at all this!"

"Let us hope you live long enough to spend some of it," Klaus said as he propped the Cowboy's body up in the tattered BarcaLounger.

Bob told Mary to go back to the car and wait with Katy. He had to grab a few things but he and Klaus would catch up with them and they'd finally get out of New York.

Mary kissed Bob and, clutching her locket and the valuable UPS packages, she ran out the back door.

Klaus dropped the canvas bag into the Cowboy's lap. "Hold this for me, would you?" he asked the corpse.

Bob went to the Bug Room and lit a few burlap rags and stuffed them into the bee smoker. As the rags began to burn, he stacked up three bugquariums containing Bloodsucking Conenoses, Wheel Bugs, and Jagged Ambush Bugs. He took them to the front hall, then went back for another load. Klaus didn't notice what Bob was up to. He was busy watching out the window for other assassins.

Not yet used to the fact that he was now a wealthy man, Bob returned to the Bug Room intent on collecting his matching set of atomizers, his jar of African Leaf Beetles, and the queen from the killer bee hive, all of which he felt were too valuable to leave behind. He pulled the white bee hive from the window and put it on the workbench. He gently slid back the top of the hive, exposing several hundred agitated killer bees. He took the bee smoker, which by now was issuing a thick, white, calming burlap cloud. He poured the smoke expertly over the hive, soothing the bees, allowing him to kidnap the queen along with a bit of royal jelly for her to munch on.

Bob slid the queen into his shirt pocket, then grabbed the atomizers and the jar of African Leaf Beetles. When he reached the front hall Klaus was looking at the bugquariums. "What are you doing?" Klaus asked.

"Grabbing my stuff. What's it look like?"

"You cannot take any of this. You have to travel light—" The doorbell rang, cutting Klaus off mid-sentence. On reflex, Bob looked out the peephole.

Klaus whispered urgently, "Do not open the door!"

Bob pulled back from the peephole, reaching for the knob. "It's just a Girl Scout, for Pete's sake. Not everyone in the world is out to kill us."

Bob opened the door and an ugly, rather stocky Girl Scout stepped up, holding out a box of mint cookies. "Would you like to buy a box?" she asked. The girl's voice was surprisingly deep and quite British.

"I'm sorry," Bob apologized, "right now's not a good time. Could you come back later?"

"No bloody need for that, you wanker," the Girl Scout said as she dropped the cookies and drew her blue-steel .38. Merit badges notwithstanding, Klaus knew Reginald was no Girl Scout. But Klaus' gun was on the table in the front hall, right next to Reginald, so there was nothing he could do about it.

Reginald gestured at the bugquariums. "What's all this, then?" he asked, sounding much like John Cleese in Silverado.

"Insects," Bob said.

"I rather hate insects," Reginald replied.

Unarmed and unable to control the situation, Klaus' words betrayed his frustration. "Why don't you just shoot us and get it over with, Thumbelina?"

Reginald turned the gun on Klaus. "Right! All mouth and bollix, that's what you are, Klaus. Don't try and get my monkey up, you tosser. You've got yourself caught in a dog's dinner and you'll not bowl a googly over me to get out of it."

Bob hadn't the vaguest idea what that meant, and at the moment he didn't care. An idea had popped into his head. He caught Klaus' eye and winked, conveying confidence.

Reginald turned back to Bob, "Here now, what's that you're doing?"

Bob was groping around in his shirt pocket. "I want to show you something." He pulled the queen bee from his pocket and held it in the palm of his hand. She was mired in royal jelly. Her wings stuck to her abdomen, she was unable to fly.

"That's an ugly little customer," Reginald said.

"You are one to talk," Klaus replied, trying to participate in Bob's plan, despite not knowing what was.

When Reginald turned to Klaus to respond, Bob tossed the queen bee at him. "Here, take a closer look!" Bob said.

Reginald turned just in time to see the jelly-coated queen land on his shirt and slip down behind his sash of merit badges. He swatted at his chest, trying to brush it off, but the queen had landed in a torn seam in the sash and wasn't going anywhere.

Reginald kept his gun trained more or less on Bob as he swatted at himself with his free hand, all the while panicking the queen and causing her to send out enormous quantities of her alarm pheromone.

"I think you killed it," Bob said calmly. "What do you think, Klaus?"

"Yes, that would be my guess," he said, shrugging.

"I bloody well hope so, you spotty fuck!" Reginald said. "You rather dropped a brick on that gammon, old chap. Now, if you don't mind, I think I'll kill you both."

That's when Reginald heard an ominous, angry buzzing sound. "What's that noise?"

Reginald had never seen, or imagined, anything like it—a dense gold-and-black cloud flying at him so fast he couldn't get out of the way. He started to scream and, as the first barbed stinger found its mark, Reginald fired a shot straight at Bob.

Chapter Seventy-six

Pratt nearly dropped his beer as he ran back to the front window. "Goddammit, Doris," he bellowed, "there they go again! What the hell's going on over there? Sounds like the goddamn Fourth of July! I'm tellin' ya, if that deadbeat son of a bitch and his cowboy friend are settin' off fireworks, I'm gonna get the cops on their asses! I swear, I've had it with that asshole. Are you listening to me, Doris? You better be listening, you big cow, or I'll hit you so hard you'll wake up in Jackson Heights!"

Pratt pressed his greasy forehead against the window and squinted for a better look. "Goddammit Doris, you should see the shit goin' on over there! Some sort of goddamn party with a bunch of his drunk exterminator friends! Looks like one of 'em's doing Saint Vitus' dance in the front hall."

Pratt noticed something else. "And what's this shit? Looks like some woman's over in the friggin' bushes! I'm tellin' you, if they mess up that landscaping, I'm gonna have his ass! I'm callin' the cops in a minute. You just wait and see, Doris. This time I'm gonna do it! I don't have to put up with this kinda shit and you know it!"

Chapter Seventy-seven

Reginald finally stopped his spastic quivering and attempted one last scream, but 40 or 50 of the killer bees had flown down his throat and stung his vocal cords. His hypersensitivity to the proteins in the bee venom had led him deep into the pit of anaphylactic shock. Of course, it helped that Reginald was a little person; the Phospholipase-A component of the venom, which normally took several seconds to interfere with the neurons of an adult human, had arrested his miniaturized nervous system instantly causing his shot to miss Bob by a good meter.

Klaus and Bob swatted at the few bees which came at them, but since the pheromonic message was coming from Reginald's sash, most of the 500 or so members of the hive were on, or in, the diminutive assassin, some having flown down his throat and into his tiny stomach.

"What should we do?" Klaus asked as he thrashed at one particularly persevering worker bee. "Won't they kill us next?"

"Don't worry, they can't." Bob explained that a bee eviscerates itself when it uses its stinger. "That's why they don't just up and sting things for the fun of it," he said. "It's a suicide mission, a last resort used only to protect the hive or the queen."

And with one final gasp, it was over. Reginald's welt-covered body swelled dramatically, threatening to burst the seams of the Girl Scout uniform, the bodies of the disemboweled bees, either dead or twitching, modestly covering any skin that might be revealed if the uniform gave way.

Two down, Klaus thought, but how many to go? "Can we get out of here now?" he asked, exasperated.

"Not just yet, *mon cheri*," a voice said from the shadows of the front porch. A striking figure stepped into the house, legs first, so to speak. It was Chantalle, her gun trained on Klaus. She closed the door behind her.

Bob was incredulous. "Oh, I don't believe this! Why don't we just get a turnstile and sell tickets?"

Klaus smiled as he raised his hands. "Ahhh, Chantalle, *beaux yeux mais arriver comme un cheveu sur la soupe.*"

"*Merci,*" she said.

"Klaus, what did you just say?" Bob asked.

Klaus looked to Chantalle for permission to translate; she gave it with her eyes.

"I said she is, uh, how would you say, she is beautiful of face but she has arrived like a hair in the soup."

Bob's blank look encouraged Klaus to explain further. "It is an idiom roughly equivalent to your phrase 'turning up like a bad penny.' Frankly, I have never understood that one."

"Me either," Bob admitted. "I think it's the same as 'welcome as a turd in a punch bowl.'"

"Yes, that is the sense of it," said Chantalle. "Now, do you mind if we get on with this?" She glanced at her watch. "I would like to kill you both and catch an eight o'clock flight if at all possible."

Suddenly Bob lunged for Klaus' gun, which was still on the table. But Chantalle grabbed it first, so Bob snatched the next nearest item, which turned out to be one of the atomizers. It was labeled "*Blattodea*" and it contained a non-species-specific essence of cockroach. Desperate, Bob trained the spray bottle on Chantalle like a forty-five-caliber bottle of Chanel No. 5.

Chantalled looked down her perfect nose at Bob, in the French way. "What are you proposing, death by cologne?"

Lacking any options, Bob spritzed her several times with eau de cockroach, prompting Chantalle to laugh and turn her weapon on him. "You are a very silly little man," she said.

No one noticed, but the moment Bob sprayed Chantalle, the 600 or so Assassin Bugs in the bugquariums had flown instantly to the screens covering their cages. Bob hadn't fed them in three days. To these hungry assassins, Chantalle was a five-foot-seven, two-legged cockroach with nice breasts and no antennae.

Chantalle looked Bob up and down. "I find it hard to believe this is the famous Exterminator," she said. "He does not look so dangerous to me." And then, in the annoyingly snotty way French people say so many things, she uttered, "*Ecrasez l'infame!*"

"What the hell does that mean?" Bob asked.

"It means 'crush the infamous thing,'" Klaus said. He turned to Chantalle. "He is not one of us, Chantalle. Let him live."

Chantalle turned to Bob. "Is this true?"

"Would I lie to you?" Bob asked.

She dismissed the question with a wave of her hand. "*C'est la vie,*" she said, tossing Bob the Kit Kat bar. "Now, would you prefer to die first or second?"

"Well, that's a pretty big decision. Can I think about it for a second?" Bob unwrapped the candy bar and took a bite.

The bugs in the terrariums were in a frenzy, attempting to bite through the screens with their powerful mouthparts. Minute traces of insect saliva moistened their razor-sharp mandibles as they drooled for a chance to get at the giant French cockroach standing just four feet away.

"You are getting soft, Chantalle," said Klaus.

"Compassionate? *Moi?*" She spit the words out. "*C'est plus qu'un crime, c'est une faute.*" Chantalle drew a bead on Bob's forehead to make her point. "*A bientot, monsieur* Exterminator."

"Wait!" Bob shouted, spitting crumbs of the Kit Kat bar on the floor. "If you're going to kill me, uh, at least tell me what you just said. You owe me that much."

Again Klaus translated. "She said compassion is worse than a crime, it is a blunder."

"Oh. Thanks," Bob said. "You know, my parents made me take Latin in high school, said it would help with the Romance languages, but it never really did. Unless you count learning all the classifications of insects, phylum, species, all that." Bob was operating under the mistaken impression that he would live as long as he talked. "For example," he continued, "bees and wasps are in the order *hymenoptera*, which means membrane wing."

Bored with Bob's delay tactic, Chantalle started to squeeze the trigger. The hammer reared like a cobra about to strike. Certain he was about to be knocking on heaven's door, Bob stood frozen and helpless. The next thing he heard was not a gunshot, but rather a squeaking sound coming from the bugquariums. He looked down and immediately realized he had one chance to get out of this mess, so he shouted, "Wait!"

"Now what is it?" Chantalle asked, bristling like a Thistle-down Velvet Ant (*Dasymutilla gloriosa*). Her arm was tiring from holding the gun on Bob for so long.

"I want to ask one last question," Bob said.

"Oh, for the love of…go ahead!" Chantalle said, *ne savoir a quel saint se vouer*, which means "not knowing which saint to pray to," which is the French equivalent of "being at the end of one's rope," which is where Chantalle was at the moment. As she waited for Bob to ask his question, Chantalle rested her tired arm at her side.

"How do you think you'd react if I did this?" Bob pushed all three of the bugquariums onto their sides, shattering the glass and freeing the 600 or so starving assassins.

Chantalle's mistake was in keeping her eyes on Bob and Klaus. And normally that would have been the right thing for a person in her position to do, as diversions are usually no more than just that. But, if you happen to smell like a cockroach and 600 Assassin Bugs are scurrying your way, as was the case here, it's a big mistake.

As Chantalle alternated her aim between Bob and Klaus, the Jagged Ambush Bugs, Wheel Bugs, and Bloodsucking Cone-noses were touching antennae in rapid communication. They were getting their bearings and preparing to assault their huge prey.

"Did you really expect I would lose my concentration and let you escape?" Chantalle asked. "*Homme moyen sensual!*" Bob turned to Klaus.

"Did she say I was very sensual?"

"Not exactly," he replied. "She said—"

And then, quite suddenly, the insects attacked in what appeared to be an organized assault.

The Wheel Bugs—stout grayish-black brutes and powerful jumpers—sprang onto Chantalle's face. Taking special interest in the soft tissues of her eyes, they used their cutting beaks to puncture the sclera and choroid layers. They quickly injected their noxious saliva and began sucking out the vitreous humor, rendering Chantalle blind almost instantly.

As the Wheel Bugs chewed through her corneas, the Bloodsucking Conenoses, with their sharp, hypodermic beaks found the soft flesh of her neck and her fat, pulsing jugular and began the richest blood meal of their short lives.

The Jagged Ambush Bugs—forelegs swollen with muscle—latched onto the only other accessible flesh on Chantalle's body. The painful stabs of their piercing mouthparts preceded the flood of digestive enzymes which liquefied the surface muscles and nerve endings under the skin of her hands and forearms and prevented her from squeezing the trigger.

Unaware that Chantalle was already immobilized, Bob and Klaus took refuge behind the furniture in the living room in case she started shooting. Blind and paralyzed, all Chantalle could do was scream, allowing several dozen Wheel Bugs into her mouth.

By this point the insects had found their way under her clothes. Six hundred mouthparts had punctured her skin and other membranes and were sucking the life, not to mention the bodily fluids, from the French beauty. The deluge of enzymes and proteins from the hundreds of bugs stiffened her body. She stood rigid in the front hall.

Then, almost mercifully, as Chantalle began to wither in front of Bob's and Klaus' eyes, a half-jacketed Teflon-tipped

AP projectile hurtled through the picture window at 2,900 feet per second.

Everyone but Chantalle heard the splintering of glass and the dull thud a bullet makes when it enters a French woman's head from the side. What was left of Chantalle's *beaux yeux* bugged out of her once beautiful, but now tortured, face—resulting in an impromptu Marty Feldman impression.

The force from the shot rippled down through her body, knocking the gun from her shriveling hand. She wobbled slightly, but remained upright, dead on her feet like a bug-covered statue.

Chapter Seventy-eight

Pratt stood at the refrigerator gnawing on a cold pork chop when he heard the shot. "Goddammit!" he muttered.

As he wobbled back toward the living room he yelled, "Didja hear that, Doris?! Can you friggin' believe it? Sounds they they're shooting a gun or something over there!"

In the living room he peeled the curtains back and glared out the window. "I'm tellin' ya, I'm gonna call the cops. And you know what else?" He paused to finish off his ninth beer of the night, then he waved the pork chop as he bellowed. "If the cops won't do anything, I swear I'm goin' over there and stuff all those goddamn bugs up his ass! Are you listening to me, Doris? I'm talkin' to you! I've had it! I'm not messin' around anymore!"

Chapter Seventy-nine

Bob popped his head up and looked at the bizarre mess in the front hall. His mind was racing. How had he gotten into such a deranged situation? Who had put the bullet in Chantalle's head? And how the hell was he going to get all his Assassin Bugs back in the bugquariums?

"Get down!" Klaus yelled, snapping Bob back from his contemplative mood. Klaus crawled to where Bob was and gestured toward Chantalle. "That was brilliant…somewhat gruesome, but brilliant."

"You think she's dead?" Bob asked.

Klaus snorted. "As the French would say, Chantalle *casser votre pipe*."

"Klaus, enough with the French already."

"It means she 'broke her pipe.' It is the French equivalent to your phrase 'to kick the bucket.'"

Crouching by Bob's side, Klaus too wondered who had fired the shot. Clearly it was someone with a high-powered rifle, but at what distance? Was the shooter going to try to take them out from three hundred yards, or would he (or she, as the case might be) be so bold as to come into the house after already announcing his or her presence? He gestured toward the gun at Chantalle's feet. "We've got to get the gun before—"

Suddenly the door blew open, hitting Chantalle and knocking her stiff corpse onto the floor with a thud, crushing some of the assassins and frightening others back into their bugquariums.

A horrible moment passed as Bob and Klaus—unarmed and defenseless—readied to die.

Then, abruptly and quite dramatically, Mike Wolfe bounded into the foyer, all blood and thunder. He slammed the door, spinning around with weapon at the ready. Bob and Klaus watched from the floor, mesmerized, as Wolfe carried on with strike-force histrionics, crouching, spinning to cover his back, and rising and ducking like some sort of a machine-gun-toting bird.

"It's alright, you can come out now," Wolfe said as if he were the Good Witch of the West.

Bob stood up, delighted to see his friend from the CIA. Klaus followed suit.

"Thank God you're alive," Wolfe said heroically.

"I never thought I'd say it," Bob said, "but I'm actually glad to see you."

"Klaus," Wolfe said, greeting his longtime colleague. "How the hell are you? It's been a while."

"Yes, since that night in Benghazi, I believe." Klaus smiled. "So tell me, did she go back to your hotel?"

"You bet your ass she did!" Wolfe said proudly. "It was one helluva night too, my friend." He shook his head. "Boy, seems like that was a lifetime ago." Wolfe chuckled at his enhanced memories. "Tell you the truth, I don't think I'd be up to that kind of a night nowadays. Getting too old I guess."

"Yes, I know the feeling," Klaus said. "Lately I have been thinking about retirement myself."

"Funny you should mention retirement, Klaus. That's more or less what brought me here."

Klaus didn't like the look in Wolfe's eye so he started for the front hall to get his gun.

Wolfe turned his FN-FAL .308, a slick Belgian-made assault rifle, on Klaus and suggested he stay put for the time being.

"You know, Bob," Wolfe said, standing again, "you had me going with all the double-talk about the pest-control business. Then I did some digging, followed my instincts, you know, my gut, and I figured out you really are just an exterminator."

"That's what I was saying all along," Bob said.

"Right, I'll give you that," Wolfe admitted, his rifle still at the ready. "So now I get over here half expecting to find you taking a dirt nap, but instead I see you've iced some of the world's best talent. I must say, I'm quite impressed, a little confused still, but impressed nonetheless." Wolfe smiled and winked at Bob. "I suppose you might say we're seeing the other side of Bob Dillon, huh?"

"Listen, Mike," Bob said. "I can explain all of this."

"Doesn't matter, Bob. Really doesn't," Wolfe said. "What does matter is ten million dollars. Right, Klaus?"

"What do you mean?" Bob asked. "Can't you guys protect us somehow? New names and identities and all that witness protection stuff?"

"Not something you'll have to worry about," Wolfe said as he coolly leveled his sniper rifle at Bob. "I'm here to take care of you and all your problems."

"Uh, Mike, listen, I wish you wouldn't point that thing at me," Bob said nervously. "What are we going to do?"

"Well, Bob, ten million bucks is a shit load more than I'd get from my lousy federal pension, so I can damn sure tell you what *I'm* going to do…retire to a quaint coastal village in a country without an extradition treaty, a house on the beach, a little rum, and live happily ever after."

"But what about me?" Bob asked. "What about my family?"

"Would you get a clue?" Klaus snapped. "You'll be dead."

"Give the man a cigar," Wolfe said.

"What?" Bob finally figured it out. "Oh, man, and I trusted you. I thought you were on my side."

"Oops," Wolfe said with another wink. He looked at the Cowboy slumped in the BarcaLounger, then at the bodies in the front hall: Reginald, swollen and discolored, like a large pink sausage about to burst from its casing. And Chantalle, her fluids drained, corky and brittle.

"So what the hell happened here?" Wolfe bent over for a closer look at Chantalle, causing the Jagged Ambush Bugs to dig their claws deeper into the skin of her arms. Their large orange eyes rotated chameleon-like and fixed Wolfe with an unsettling, murderous stare.

"That's a helluva bug," Wolfe said. What's it called?"

"It's a Jagged Ambush Bug," Bob said.

"You know, I've always liked insects," Wolfe said, "spiders especially."

"Spiders aren't insects," Bob said flatly, "they're arachnids."

"Really, what's the difference? I mean, I better ask now since you won't be able to answer after I kill you, right?"

An idea began taking form in Bob's head. "Arachnids have eight legs and two main body parts; insects have six legs and three body parts. Plus, most insects have wings and antennae."

"Damn. Never too old to learn, I guess," Wolfe said.

"Here, you want to see a good example of the tri-segmented body?" Bob eased toward the front hall.

"Sure, why not?" Wolfe said. He kept the rifle on Bob and a wary eye on Klaus.

Bob picked up the jar and held it up for Wolfe to see. "Whoa, those are some beauts! What are they?"

"African Leaf Beetles." Bob pointed at the segments as he spoke. "There's the head, the thorax, and the abdomen, and see the legs? If it has six, it's an insect. Wanna hold one? But I gotta warn you, they bite a little sometimes."

"Ooooo, I'm scared," Wolfe said, rising to the challenge. "Listen, Bob, I've been with the CIA for 40 goddamn years and seen some pretty creepy stuff. You think I'm scared of a fucking bug bite?"

"Sorry, I didn't mean anything by that." Bob unscrewed the top and tipped the jar toward Wolfe's waiting hand.

The African Leaf Beetles tumbled into Wolfe's palm and began "smelling" it with their feathery antennae. "Sort of tickles," Wolfe said as he inspected the bugs. Then, "Ouch! You're not kidding they bite. Ouch! Ouch! Son of a bitch!" Wolfe slung the biting beetles off his hand. "Goddamn, that hurts."

"Sorry," Bob lied.

The human nervous system is divided into two parts, the central and the peripheral. The peripheral consists of cranial, spinal, and autonomic nerves. When a neurotoxin, such as the one secreted by African Leaf Beetles, interferes with the autonomic nervous system, the glands, lungs, and, most importantly, the heart can stop functioning.

And that's what happened to Mike Wolfe, very suddenly. Wham! His heart seized up like an engine without any oil. His body jolted from the shock and he dropped the Belgian assault rifle like a hot waffle. When it hit the floor it discharged. BAM!

Chapter Eighty

Pratt was slouched on his sofa, untroubled in his beer-induced stupor, watching a rerun of *Married... With Children*. He was thinking how much he wanted to grab the breasts of the various actresses when he heard the shot.

"Judas Priest!" He stood as quickly as he could, but the blood rushed out of his head and he crumpled to the floor in a pile. "Goddammit," he muttered.

He struggled back to his feet and scurried over to the window.

"That's it! I don't know what the hell's going on over there, but I'm callin' the friggin' cops this time! I don't need this kinda shit all night long, bunch of drunk goddamn pest-control sonsuhbitches."

He picked up the phone and dialed 912. Then he hung up and tried again, this time managing 911.

Chapter Eighty-one

His garlic peeled, his pipe broken, and his bucket kicked, Mike Wolfe lay dead on the floor between Chantalle and Reginald. Bob looked at Klaus. "You about ready to go?"

"Yes, it's time," Klaus said. "Grab your things."

Bob watched as Klaus lowered himself onto the sofa, morose and exhausted, dark circles sagged under his tired eyes. He seemed defeated. A look of hopelessness washed over him.

"You alright?"

Klaus didn't answer. Instead, he reached over and grabbed his canvas bag from the Cowboy's lap. He unzipped it, reached in, and pulled out something that Bob guessed was a plastic explosive with a timer and detonator attached.

As Bob watched, his confusion turned to shock as Klaus armed the device and started the timer. It began counting down from 10:00…9:59…9:58…

"What the hell are you doing?" Bob asked urgently.

"It doesn't matter," Klaus said.

A chilling thought occurred to Bob. "I'll be goddamned," he said. "You bastard. You saved me for yourself! You waited until all the others were out of the way so they couldn't claim the money, and now you're going to cash me in."

"You are a bad judge of character, my friend," Klaus said in a disappointed tone. "Relax, I want you to go."

"You got a lot of nerve to say you are my friend," Bob said. But he looked at Klaus again and saw he was telling the truth.

Bob didn't understand what was going on. He looked at his friend's sad face. This wasn't the same man Bob met at the bar in SoHo that night, the man who gunned down Riviera's henchmen in the street, the man who had saved his life more than once. The assurance and poise were gone. He seemed utterly resigned.

"I don't get it," Bob said. "Aren't you coming with us?"

"I am too tired," Klaus said. "I cannot go on like this any longer. It has become more than I can bear," he said. "Every time I start my car, or turn a corner, or open a door…I know I may die a sudden and violent death." He took a deep breath. "After a while it gets to you."

8:01…8:00…7:59…The device ticked.

"Besides, I have nothing more to live for," Klaus said. "I did the last thing I wanted to do, which was to save you and your family."

"But…" Bob tried to interrupt.

"No buts," Klaus said. "Listen, my friend, if you cherish your family as you should, you will leave now."

"Klaus, do me a favor," Bob said calmly. "Just turn the bomb off and let's talk about this."

"It cannot be turned off," Klaus said.

"What the hell do you mean, it can't be turned off?" Bob asked.

"It would not be a very effective bomb if you could just turn it off, now would it?" Klaus said. "Once it is set, it is set. Any tampering will cause it to go off. Now," Klaus said as he pointed to the door, "unless you want to die, I suggest you get out of here. Time is running out."

"No," Bob said. "I'm not leaving without you."

5:10…5:09…5:08…it ticked.

"Bob, you have a family," Klaus said. "That is the most important thing and it is something I can never have."

"We'll share," Bob said. "Now come on, snap out of it."

Klaus shook his head. "Bob, I made one big mistake in my life. I thought I could change the world by eliminating evil. But for all my efforts, the world is no better than before I did my work. And that is the only reason I did what I did, I simply wanted the world to be a better place. I have wasted my life and now I want to end it."

"Hey, look, you gave it a shot," Bob said, trying to encourage Klaus. "That's more than a lot of people can say."

"But because of who I became, I could never have a family of my own," Klaus said.

"It's never too late, Klaus. I know dating is awkward at your age, but--"

"No. I cannot have a family because they could be used against me."

Bob could sense Klaus' resignation, like an athlete at the end of a career who finally realizes he can no longer compete. But he also detected a longing in Klaus, a spark that wasn't yet ready to be doused. Klaus' heart wasn't really in all this talk of suicide; he was looking for a reason to live.

Bob glanced at the timer-3:10...3:09...3:08...He surveyed the room, bodies littered the floor. Again something percolated in his subconscious. He eyed Klaus, the bomb, the family photo on the mantel, and at that moment it came to him.

Bob had an idea. A great idea. An idea that could solve all the problems at hand. This idea was better than all-natural pest control. So Bob turned and ran.

He raced down the hall to the Bug Room. When he returned, he had his EXTERMINATOR cap in his hand. He snugged the cap tightly onto the Cowboy's head, steady on top of a neck stiff from the coagulation of muscle proteins.

Bob gently pulled up a chair and sat down in front of his depressed friend.

"You know, Klaus," Bob said calmly. "You're right."

"Yes," Klaus said suspiciously. "Now go, time is short."

2:20...2:19...2:18...

"No, I see exactly what you mean about life as an assassin. My problem is not only that the whole world thinks I'm a professional killer, but there's also a big contract out on me. So every waking moment I'll be worried about being killed, or Katy and Mary being killed to get at me. As long as I'm alive they'll always be in danger."

Klaus nodded, not making the connection.

"I'm afraid we all have to die," Bob said.

"Bob, don't play games," Klaus said. "It is not your time."

"Sure it is, Klaus. Mine. Mary's. Katy's. And yours too."

"But there is no time to get Mary and Katy even if you wanted them to die," Klaus said.

"Let me worry about that," Bob said. "You say we can't turn that bomb off, right? So I guess we'll all have to go up in a big ball of fire." Bob paused. "There will be a big ball of fire, won't there? I mean, it is that kind of bomb, right?"

"Well," Klaus said thoughtfully, "plastic explosives result in rapid decomposition as opposed to combustion. Do you have natural gas appliances?"

"Got a gas water heater," Bob replied.

"Yes, then there will be a big ball of fire," Klaus said.

"That's great," Bob said. "Perfect."

Klaus knew Bob was scheming, but despite Bob's impressive show of resourcefulness in getting them through the city alive, and in using his bugs to dispatch Reginald, Chantalle, and Wolfe, Klaus still didn't hold out much hope for the ingenuity of the plan.

"Lemme ask you, Klaus," Bob said as he inched his chair closer. "How much of a gambler are you?"

Chapter Eighty-two

Pratt stood at the window, swaying in an inebriated haze. He was looking at Bob's house, waiting for the cops to arrive.

"I swear, Doris," he shouted, "I don't care if they're shooting firecrackers or not. I'm throwin' 'em out tomorrow!" He poured some more beer down his gullet. "I've had it with that deadbeat. I want him out! Didja hear me, Doris? I'm gettin' ridda those shitheels tomorrow and we're gonna raise the friggin' rent and get some decent tenants over there! I've made up my mind! You can count on it!"

Pratt smiled a ten-beer smile as he considered how high he could boost the rent with new tenants.

"Yessiree, things are just about to turn around for Dick Pratt." He returned to the curtain. "Goddamit, where are those stupid cops? They sure as hell got here fast that time you called about me hittin' you! I bet you'll never do that again, huh, Doris? I made sure of that!"

Pratt smiled at the thought of the lesson he had given Doris for that transgression.

"Well, screw 'em. Screw the cops! Who needs 'em?"

He went to the coffee table and took a cheap handgun from the drawer. "If they're not gonna do anything about all that commotion, I'm gonna go over there and take care of it myself!"

Pratt stepped outside and felt a sturdy night breeze. He'd had it with Bob Dillon and his bugs. The time had come for Dick Pratt to take care of business.

With a beer in one hand and a gun in the other, he crossed the street and climbed the stairs to Bob's front porch and banged on the door. "Goddammit, Dillon, I've had it with your shit! Open this goddamn door before I kick it in."

00:03...00:02...00:01...

Pratt reared back and kicked the door with all his might.

And KA-BOOOOOMMMM!!

Bob's house exploded in a massive ball of fire that looked like a special effect that had escaped from another over-budget Schwarzenegger movie. Huge chunks of flaming debris and tiny bits of exploded insects rained down on the streets of Astoria.

Chapter Eighty-three

Fire trucks, ambulances, police cars, bomb squaders, and three of the coroner's meat wagons clogged the street. The variously colored emergency lights danced on the smoke and steam that rose from what had been the Dillon home. The firemen were wetting down the embers at this point. What was left of the house after the explosion had burned to the ground, bugs and all.

Doris Pratt stood on the porch of her house smiling broadly as she spoke with the police. She had already identified the body in the street as that of her late husband. The hole in the back of his head was caused by his Parodi; like a pine needle forced through a telephone pole in a hurricane, the cigar had blown through the back of Pratt's head when the bomb exploded.

Two men approached the coroner as he wheeled a gurney toward his van. The men flashed their badges. "I'm Parker, this is Hawkins. CIA. We're looking for our boss, Mike Wolfe. You seen him?"

Parker thrust a photo of Wolfe at the coroner, who glanced first at the photo, then at the pompous young agents. He threw back the gurney's blanket, revealing what looked like a very large, very burnt chicken. He smirked. "This him?"

Parker and Hawkins gagged at the sight.

"Fellas, all I got is what looks like three adult males, one adult female, and one child. The only one we could ID was a neighbor from across the street. You wanna see the rest of 'em?"

Parker and Hawkins declined and moved quickly to their car. Parker figured it out first. "That old son of a bitch was smarter than I thought."

"You mean Wolfe?" Hawkins asked. "You don't think that was him heading for the meat wagon?"

"Hell no, junior," Parker said condescendingly. "Weren't you listening? Other than the neighbor, there were two men, a woman, and a child. Think about it. Wolfe killed Dillon plus the wife and the kid he uses for cover. Klaus shows up too late to do the job and Wolfe gets him too. Two men, a woman, and a child. Then he blows the house as a diversion and hops a flight to Bolivia to collect a nice fee from Riviera, probably using a ticket Klaus had bought under a third name."

He looked up at a jet flying into the night sky. "That's probably him right there."

Hawkins was impressed both by Wolfe's plan and Parker's deductive ability. "Wow. That's some day's work," Hawkins said admiringly.

"And a ten-million-dollar payday," Parker added as they got into their car.

"Sonofabitch." Parker slammed his fist on the steering wheel. "I wish I'd thought of it." He threw the car into drive and screeched off into the night.

Chapter Eighty-four

A UPS van arrived at the Beebe Avenue Mission with a delivery for Gertrude.

She asked the driver if he was sure he was delivering to the right place. The driver smiled and assured her they didn't make many mistakes at UPS.

Gertrude thanked the driver and went inside, where she removed the airbill from the clear plastic on top of the package. The "FROM" section was blank.

"Hmmmm."

She opened the package and found a cashier's check for $50,000 made out to the Beebe Avenue Mission. There was also a note:

> Dear Gertrude, I hope this helps you fix some of those broken dreams.
>
> Sincerely, your friend Bob.
>
> (P.S. I'm still trying to make the bug thing work. And Mary and Katy came back, just like you said. Thanks again and good luck.)

Gertrude smiled a big, satisfied smile and looked heavenward. "Lawdy, yes, we can fix plenty o' dreams with this."

Sunlight streamed between the boards of the rickety building and lit a pair of hands as they deftly attached a silencer to a handgun.

The gun quickly swiveled and fired. FWUMP!

An unusually large Pine Sawyer Beetle (*Ergates spiculatus*) disintegrated in a haze of smoke and bug juice.

"He shoots, he scores!" Klaus blurted.

A startled Bob turned to Klaus. "Hey! What're you doing!?"

"I thought it was, uh, a squash beetle," Klaus said sheepishly. "I didn't want it getting into the pumpkin patch."

"First of all, you know there aren't any squash beetles east of the Rockies. Second of all, what did I say about the gun?"

"I know," Klaus said. "Rats only."

"That's right."

Chastised, Klaus locked his gun away in a steel box on the shelf.

"Thank you," Bob said.

"Sorry boss, old habits, you know."

Bob slapped Klaus on the back, then picked up two large boxes. "Now give me a hand with these will you? We need two more."

Klaus picked up two more of the boxes and followed Bob out of the shed to a dirt driveway. In the bright morning sunlight the words on boxes became clear: "ASSASSIN BUGS, STRAIN FIVE."

With the snowcapped Cascade Mountain Range behind them, they approached a shiny new Chevy half-ton pickup. Perched on top of the truck was a big goofy-looking bug with comically geniculated antennae. On the side of the truck was a magnetic sign that said: "BOB AND KLAUS' ALL-NATURAL PEST CONTROL."

They put on their brand-new EXTERMINATOR caps and slammed the tailgate shut just as Mary came out of the beautiful old farmhouse carrying sack lunches. A moment later Katy came running around the side of the house, giggling and squealing as young girls do.

She ran up to Klaus with her hands behind her back. "I've got a surprise for you," she said.

"What is it?" Klaus asked.

"You have to guess!"

"Alright, is it a flower?"

"No, silly, it's a Tumblebug." She held out her hand and showed him the greenish-black beetle.

"It's beautiful, Katy. Thank you." Klaus smiled and gave her a hug. "Would you put it in the terrarium for me?"

"Sure, but first I've got to find some cow shit for it to play on!"

"Katy!" her mother shouted. "It's dung. Cow dung."

"Whatever." Katy scurried into the house.

Bob leaned out the driver's side window and kissed Mary.

"Don't work too late," Mary said. "Remember Klaus, you're going to that singles mixer tonight at the Y."

"I hate those things," Klaus said. "I would really rather just stick to the personal ads."

"Let's see," Bob said, "ex-assassin seeks bug-loving nature girl. Enjoys long walks in the woods looking for predacious insects."

"No," Klaus said, "we must leave out the part about insects; most women find that a turnoff, I believe."

"Well, just go to the thing tonight and see what happens," Mary said. "We can do the personal ad next if you don't meet anyone nice."

Klaus waved good-bye as Bob piloted the truck with the big fiberglass bug down the dusty driveway and onto the paved road, heading off to another job. It was their third this week and it was only Tuesday.

They were half a mile down the road when Bob turned on the local Classic Rock radio station and was greeted with "Rainy Day Women #12 & 35." Bob sang along, badly off key, until Klaus' taunting and laughter made him switch to the all-news station.

After updating the African Republic Civil War situation, the news reader segued to a story about what many South American honey producers called *Abejas bravas*.

The American media preferred calling them killer bees, the Afro-Brazilian hybrid that had been working its way to North America since Dr. Warwick Kerr's debacle in 1956.

It seemed the bees had killed again, this time in Los Angeles, and panic was beginning to spread. They had arrived in the lower United States several years ahead of schedule and there would be no stopping them now. The beekeeping and honey industries were near hysteria; they wanted some prompt action. The government was searching desperately for a way to manage these aggressive killers and didn't know where to turn.

Pesticides, flamethrowers, genetics?

A sound bite from a Dow Chemical spokesperson indicated their scientists were creating a deadly new compound at this very moment. But Bob knew that wasn't the answer.

He turned up the volume as they played another sound bite, this one from a confused member of the Agriculture Department.

"This thing could get out of hand real quick if somebody doesn't come up with a way to stop these bees," she said.

It struck Bob like a message from God. The radio may as well have been a burning bush.

And when he turned to Klaus he saw the biggest bug-eating grin he'd ever seen.

Afterword

In March of 1988, I moved to Los Angeles hoping to become a sitcom writer. Things didn't go as planned...

It all started to go wrong in May of 1991. A screenplay brainstorming session with a former writing partner led to the germ of the idea that would lead to a screenplay called *Pest Control*. We finished a draft in September of 1991. A producer optioned the script for $4,000 in November of that year but the project went nowhere.

Two years later I decided to try writing *Pest Control* as a comic novel. Don't ask me why. In my entire life I had never thought about writing a novel.

I started doing research in June 1993. When I had the first 100 pages under my belt, I took a "Novels In Progress" class at UCLA Extension. I finished a draft in the fall of 1994 and started sending query letters. After rejections from 124 agents, I got a call from Jimmy Vines who loved it and signed me as a client. On the first list of submissions, all the major publishing houses passed. But Jimmy told me not to worry, told me to start writing another book because he was going to sell *Pest Control*.

In July 1995, Jimmy Vines sent the manuscript to the New York offices of Spring Creek Productions, a film company headed by producer Paula Weinstein. The New York book scouts loved it and sent it to their Los Angeles offices on the lot at Warner Brothers Studios.

On August 3, 1995, Spring Creek Productions bought the film rights to *Pest Control* for $500,000 against $1 million (i.e., half now, the other half if/when they make it).

So, four years and 125 agents later, I was a novelist and an overnight success. Over the next few months, we sold the publishing rights in the U.S., Canada, the U.K., Japan, Germany, and Italy.

May 1996, *Pest Control* was published in the U.K. The *Times of London* called it "one of the funniest, most off-beat thrillers to hit the bookstalls in years…Fitzhugh does for New York what Carl Hiaasen did for Miami." Not a bad start.

1997, *Pest Control* is published in the U.S., Canada, Germany, and Japan.

The Italians decided to wait for the film. Like me, they're still waiting.

Many screenplay drafts are written and several directors are considered, but none Warner Brothers likes enough to make the movie.

For the next ten years, Jimmy Vines urges me to write a sequel to *Pest Control* but I explain that while I have the characters, I don't have a good enough story. So I wrote six other books instead.

In early 2005, I finally figure out a story for the sequel and begin writing *The Exterminators*. Later that year, Jimmy Vines suddenly retires.

Then, out of the blue, ten years after *Pest Control* was published, a German Radio Production company buys the rights to produce it as a radio show. Go figure.

And a couple of months after that, and from even further out of the blue, I received an email from an attorney in New York who represented a theatrical producer who wanted to turn *Pest Control* into a musical.

Seriously? Yes, seriously.

July 2007, Canum Entertainment buys the STAGE MUSICAL RIGHTS for *Pest Control*.

Seriously. A musical with assassins and cockroaches.

August 2007, the German Radio version of *Pest Control* airs for the first time.

November 2007, a Romanian publisher buys the rights for *Pest Control*. Really? Ten years after the book is published someone wants to buy the publishing rights… in Romania?

April 2008, *"Pest Control* The Musical" hits the stage in Los Angeles to excellent reviews and sold out houses. It goes on to win the Los Angeles Ovation Award for Best Costume. Seriously, the best cockroach costumes you've ever seen.

June 2008, a Spanish publisher buys rights to *Pest Control*. Huh? It's been available for eleven years, but okay…Keep in mind that there is no agent trying to sell these foreign rights; somehow (I'm guessing the German radio broadcasts are behind it) foreign publishers just keep showing up.

September 2009. I'm talking to Reed Farrell Coleman who is saying great things about his publisher, Busted Flush Press.

October 2009, I contact David Thompson, who (and I quote) "craps his pants" when asked if he's interested in publishing *The Exterminators*.

In February 2010, David offers to publish *The Exterminators* as well as a reissue of *Pest Control* (the rights to which had just reverted to me). I accept his offer and we anticipate a publication date in the Spring of 2011.

In September 2010, David Thompson dies suddenly. A huge loss to the book world.

In April 2011, McKenna Jordon (David's wife) decides to cancel publication of the books pending at Busted Flush Press.

In March 2011, at Left Coast Crime in Santa Fe, a chance conversation with Barbara Peters leads to a publishing deal for *The Exterminators* with Poisoned Pen Press.

In early 2012, nearly 21 years after the original idea for the original *Pest Control* screenplay, the sequel to the story is finally published.

They say good things come to those who wait. It's true. If you enjoyed *Pest Control*, you'll love *The Exterminators*. The wait is finally over.

Bill Fitzhugh
Los Angeles, California
July 14, 2011

To receive a free catalog of Poisoned Pen Press titles, please contact us in one of the following ways:

Phone: 1-800-421-3976
Facsimile: 1-480-949-1707
Email: info@poisonedpenpress.com
Website: www.poisonedpenpress.com

Poisoned Pen Press
6962 E. First Ave. Ste 103
Scottsdale, AZ 85251